At Risk

At Risk

STELLA RIMINGTON

ALFRED A. KNOPF
New York 2005

THIS IS A BORZOI BOOK
PUBLISHED BY ALFRED A. KNOPF

Copyright © 2004 by Stella Rimington

www.aaknopf.com

Originally published in Great Britain by Hutchinson,
the Random Group Limited, London, in 2004.

Knopf, Borzoi Books, and the colophon are registered
trademarks of Random House, Inc.

Library of Congress Cataloging-in-Publication Data
Rimington, Stella.
At risk / Stella Rimington.
p.   cm.
ISBN 1-4000-4370-0
1. Terrorism—Prevention—Fiction.   2. Intelligence officers—Fiction.
3. Women spies—Fiction.   4. England—Fiction.   I. Title.
PR6118.I44A93 2005
823'.92—dc22
2004048965

Manufactured in the United States of America
First American Edition

To my granddaughter Charlotte

At Risk

1

With quiet finality, the tube train drew to a stop. A long hydraulic gasp, and then silence.

For several moments no one in the crowded carriage moved. And then, as the stillness and the silence deepened, eyes began to flicker. Standing passengers peered worriedly through the windows into the blackness, as if hoping for some explanatory vision or revelation.

They were halfway between Mornington Crescent and Euston, Liz Carlyle calculated. It was five past eight, it was Monday, and she was almost certainly going to be late for work. Around her pressed the smell of other people's damp clothes. A wet briefcase, not her own, rested in her lap.

At Risk

Nestling her chin into her velvet scarf, Liz leaned back into her seat and cautiously extended her feet in front of her. She shouldn't have worn the pointed plum-coloured shoes. She'd bought them a couple of weeks earlier on a light-hearted and extravagant shopping trip, but now the toes were beginning to curl up from the soaking they'd received on the way to the station. From experience she knew that the rain would leave nasty indelible marks on the leather. Equally infuriatingly, the kitten heels had turned out to be just the right size to get wedged in the cracks between paving stones.

After ten years of employment at Thames House, Liz had never satisfactorily resolved the clothes issue. The accepted look, which most people seemed gradually to fall into, lay somewhere between sombre and invisible. Dark trouser suits, neat skirts and jackets, sensible shoes—the sort of stuff you found in John Lewis or Marks and Spencer.

While some of her colleagues took this to extremes, cultivating an almost Soviet drabness, Liz instinctively subverted it. She often spent Saturday afternoons combing the antique clothing stalls in Camden Market for quixotically stylish bargains which, while they infringed no Service rules, certainly raised a few eyebrows. It was a bit like school, and Liz smiled as she remembered the grey pleated skirts which could be dragged down to regulation length in the classroom and then hiked to a bum-freezing six inches above the knee for the bus-ride home. A little fey to be fighting the same wars at thirty-four, perhaps, but something inside her still resisted being submerged by the gravity and secrecy of work at Thames House.

Intercepting her smile, a strap-hanging commuter looked her up and down. Avoiding his appreciative gaze, Liz ran a visual check on him in return, a process which was now second nature to her. He was dressed smartly, but with a subtly conservative fussiness which was not quite of the City. The upper slopes of academia, perhaps? No, the suit was handmade. Medicine? The well-kept hands supported that idea, as did the benign but unmistakable arrogance of his appraisal. A consultant with a few years' private practice and a dozen pliant nurses behind him, Liz decided, headed for one of the larger teaching hospitals. And next to him a goth-girl. Purple hair extensions, Sisters of Mercy T-shirt under the bondage jacket, pierced everything. A bit early in the day, though, for one of her tribe to be up and about. Probably works in a clothes shop or music store or . . . no, got you. The faint shiny ridge on the thumb where the scissors pressed. She was a hairdresser, spending her days transforming nice girls from the suburbs into Hammer Horror vampires.

Inclining her head, Liz once again touched her cheek to the silky scarlet nap of her scarf, enveloping herself in a faint scented miasma which brought Mark's physical presence—his eyes and his mouth and his hair—rushing home to her. He had bought her the scent from Guerlain on the Champs Elysées (wildly unsuitable, needless to say) and the scarf from Dior on the Avenue Montaigne. He had paid cash, he later told her, so that there would be no paper trail. He had always had an unerring instinct for the tradecraft of adultery.

She remembered every detail of the evening. On the way back from Paris, where he had been interviewing an actress, he had arrived without warning at Liz's basement flat in Kentish Town. She'd been in the bath, listening to *La Bohème* and trying half heartedly to make sense of an article in *The Economist,* and suddenly there he was, and the floor was strewn with expensive white tissue paper and the place was reeking—gorgeously and poignantly—of Vol de Nuit.

Afterwards they had opened a bottle of duty-free Moët and climbed back into the bath together. "Isn't Shauna expecting you?" Liz had asked guiltily.

"She's probably asleep," Mark answered cheerfully. "She's had her sister's kids all weekend."

"And you, meanwhile . . ."

"I know. It's a cruel world, isn't it?"

The thing that had baffled Liz at first was why he had married Shauna in the first place. From his descriptions of her, they seemed to have nothing in common whatever. Mark Callendar was feckless and pleasure-loving and possessed of an almost feline perceptiveness—a quality which made him one of the most sought-after profilists in print journalism—while his wife was an unbendingly earnest feminist aca-demic. She was forever hounding him for his unreliability; he was for-ever evading her humourless wrath. There seemed no purpose to any of it.

But Shauna was not Liz's problem. Mark was Liz's problem. The relationship was complete madness and, if she didn't do something about it soon, could well cost her her job. She didn't love Mark and she dreaded to think of what would happen if the whole thing was forced out into the open. For a long time it had looked as if he was going to leave Shauna, but he hadn't, and Liz now doubted that he ever would. Shauna, she had gradually come to understand, was the negative to his positive charge, the AC to his DC, the Wise to his Morecambe; between them they made up a fully functioning unit.

And sitting there in the halted train it occurred to her that what really excited Mark was the business of transformation. Descending on Liz, ruffling her feathers, laughing at her seriousness, magicking her into a bird of paradise. If she had lived in an airy modern flat overlook-ing one of the London parks, with wardrobes full of exquisite designer clothes, then she would have held no interest for him at all.

She really had to end it. She hadn't told her mother about him, needless to say, and in consequence, whenever she stayed the weekend with her in Wiltshire, she had to endure a well-intentioned homily about Meeting Someone Nice.

"I know it's difficult when you can't talk about your job," her mother had begun the night before, lifting her head from the photo album that she was sorting out, "but I read in the paper the other day that over two thousand people work in that building with you, and that there are all sorts of social activities you can do. Why don't you take up amateur dramatics or Latin American dancing or something?"

"Mum, please!" She imagined a group of Northern Ireland desk officers and A4 surveillance men descending on her with eyes blazing, maracas shaking, and coloured ruffles pinned to their shirts.

"Just a suggestion," said her mother mildly, and turned back to the album. A minute or two later she lifted out one of Liz's old class photos.

"Do you remember Robert Dewey?"

"Yes," said Liz cautiously. "Lived in Tisbury. Peed in his pants at the Stonehenge picnic."

"He's just opened a new restaurant in Salisbury. Round the corner from the Playhouse."

"Really?" murmured Liz. "Fancy that." This was a flanking attack, and what it was really about was her coming home. She had grown up in the small octagonal gatehouse of which her mother was now the sole tenant, and the unspoken hope was that she should return to the country and "settle down," before spinsterhood and the City of Dreadful Night claimed her for ever. Not necessarily with Rob Dewey—he of the sodden shorts—but with someone similar. Someone with whom, at intervals, she could enjoy "French cuisine" and "the theatre" and all the other metropolitan amenities to which she had no doubt grown accustomed.

Extricating herself from the maternal web last night had meant that Liz hadn't got on to the motorway until 10 p.m., and hadn't reached the Kentish Town flat until midnight. When she let herself in she found that the washing that she'd put on on Saturday morning was lying in six inches of cloudy water in the machine, which had stopped mid-cycle. It was now far too late to start it again without annoying the neighbours, so she rooted through the dry-cleaning pile for her least crumpled work outfit, hung it over the bath, and took a shower in the hope that the steam would restore a little of its élan. When she finally made it to bed it was almost 1 a.m. She had managed about five and a half hours' sleep and felt puffy-eyed, adrift on a tide of fatigue.

With a gasp and a long, flatulent shudder, the tube train restarted. She was definitely going to be late.

2

Thames House, the headquarters of MI5, is on Millbank. A vast and imposing edifice of Portland stone, eight storeys in height, it crouches like a great pale ghost a few hundred yards south of the Palace of Westminster.

That morning, as always, Millbank smelt of diesel fumes and the river. Clutching her coat around her against the rain-charged wind, watching for the sodden plane-tree leaves on which it was all too easy to turn an ankle, Liz hurried up the entrance steps. Bag swinging, she pushed open one of the doors into the lobby, raised a quick hand in greeting to the security guards at the desk, and slotted her smart pass into the barrier. The front of one of the security capsules opened, she stepped inside, and was briefly enclosed. Then, as if she'd travelled light years in an instant, the rear door slid open, and she stepped out into another dimension. Thames House was a hive, a city of steel and frosted glass, and Liz felt a subtle shift inside herself as she crossed its security threshold and was borne noiselessly upwards to the fifth floor.

The lift doors opened and she turned left and moved at speed towards 5/AX, the agent-runners' section. This was a large open-plan office lit by strip lights and lent a faintly seedy character by the clothes stands that stood by each desk. These were hung with the agent-runners' work clothes—in Liz's case a worn pair of jeans, a black Karrimor fleece, and a zip-up leather jacket. Her desk was spare—a grey terminal, a touch-tone phone, an FBI mug—and flanked to one side by a combination-locked cupboard from which she took a dark blue folder.

"And, coming into the home straight . . ." murmured Dave Armstrong from the next desk, his eyes locked to his computer screen.

"Courtesy of the bloody Northern Line," gasped Liz, spinning the cupboard lock. "The train just . . . *stopped*. For at least ten minutes. In the middle of nowhere."

"Well, the driver could hardly sit and smoke a joint in the station, could he?" asked Armstrong reasonably.

But Liz, folder in hand and minus coat and scarf, was already halfway to the exit. En route to Room 6/40, one flight up, she hurried into a washroom to check her appearance. The mirror returned an image of unexpected composure. Her fine, mid-brown hair fell more or less evenly about the pale oval of her face. The sage-green eyes were a little bruised by fatigue, perhaps, but the overall result would serve. Encouraged, she pressed on upwards.

The Joint Counter-Terrorist group, of which she had been a member for the best part of a year, met at 8:30 a.m. every Monday morning. The meetings' purpose was to coordinate operations relating to terror networks and to set weekly intelligence targets. The group was run by Liz's forty-five-year-old head of section, Charles Wetherby, and made up of MI5 investigators and agent-runners and liaison officers from MI6, GCHQ and Metropolitan Police Special Branch, with Home Office and

Foreign Office attending as required. It had been created immediately after the World Trade Center atrocity, following the Prime Minister's insistence that there must be no question of terror-related intelligence being compromised by lack of communication or turf wars of any kind. This was not a point that anyone had been in a mood to argue with. In her ten years with the Service, Liz could not remember such unflinching unanimity of purpose.

To her relief, Liz saw that although the doors to the conference room were open, no one had yet sat down. *Thank you, God!* She would not have to endure all those patient male glances as she took her place at the long oval hardwood table. Just inside the doors, a bullish duo from Special Branch were regaling one of Liz's colleagues with the inside track on the *Daily Mirror*'s cover story—a lurid tale involving a children's TV presenter, rent boys, and crack-fuelled orgies at a five-star Manchester hotel. The GCHQ representative, meanwhile, had stationed himself close enough to listen, but far enough away to pre-empt any suggestion of obvious prurience, while the man from the Home Office was reading his press cuttings.

Charles Wetherby had assumed an expectant attitude by the window, his pressed suit and polished Oxfords a mute reproach to Liz's clothes, on which the vaporous bathroom air had failed to work any significant magic. The ghost of a smile, however, touched his uneven features.

"We're waiting for Six," he murmured, glancing in the direction of Vauxhall Cross, half a mile upriver. "I suggest you catch your breath and adopt an attitude of saintly patience."

Liz attempted to do so. She looked out at the rain-slicked expanse of Lambeth Bridge. It was high tide, and the river was swollen and dark.

"Anything come up over the weekend?" she asked, placing the dark blue folder on the table.

"Nothing that's going to keep us here too long. How was your mama?"

"Annoyed that the weather isn't colder," said Liz. "She wants some frost to kill the vine weevils."

II

"Nothing like a good frost. I hate this running-together of the seasons." He ran large-jointed fingers through his greying hair. "Six are bringing over someone new, apparently—one of their Pakistan people."

"Anyone we know?"

"Mackay. Bruno Mackay."

"And what's the whisper on Mr. Mackay?"

"He's an old Harrovian."

"As in the story of the woman who walks into a room where there are three former public schoolboys. The Etonian asks her if she'd like to sit down, the Wykehamist pulls up a chair, and the Harrovian . . ."

". . . sits on it," said Wetherby with a pale smile. "Exactly."

Liz turned back to the river, grateful that she had a superior officer with whom she could enjoy such exchanges. On the far side of the Thames she could see the rain-darkened walls of Lambeth Palace. Did Wetherby know about Mark? Almost certainly. He knew pretty much everything else about her.

"I think we finally have a full house," he murmured, glancing over her shoulder.

MI6 were represented by Geoffrey Fane, their coordinator of counter-terrorist operations, and by the newcomer, Bruno Mackay. Hands were shaken and Wetherby moved smartly across the room to close the doors. A summary of weekend reports from overseas security services lay beside each place.

Mackay was welcomed to Thames House and introduced to the team. The MI6 officer had just returned from Islamabad, Wetherby informed them, where he had been a much-valued deputy head of station.

Mackay raised his hands in modest demurral. Tanned and grey-eyed, his flannel suit murmuring unmistakably of Savile Row, he cut a glamorous figure in this generally nondescript gathering. As he leaned forward to reply to Wetherby, Geoffrey Fane watched with chilly approval. He had obviously gone to some effort to manoeuvre the younger man on to the team.

To Liz, imbued as she was with the restrained, self-deprecatory culture of Thames House, Mackay appeared slightly preposterous. For a man of his age, and he couldn't have been more than thirty-two or -three, he was much too expensively got up. His good looks—the deep tan, the level grey gaze, the sculpted nose and mouth—were far too emphatic. This was an individual, and every ounce of her professional being rebelled against the idea, whom people would remember. For a moment, and without expression, her eyes met Wetherby's.

With the courtesies done, the group began to work their way through the overseas reports. Geoffrey Fane started the ball rolling. A tall, aquiline figure—like a heron in chalk-stripes, Liz had always thought—Fane had built his career on MI6's Middle Eastern desk, where he had acquired a reputation for unswerving ruthlessness. His subject was the ITS—the Islamic Terror Syndicate—the generic title for groups like Al Qaeda, Islamic Jihad, Hamas, and the myriad others like them.

When Fane had finished speaking he darted his patrician gaze leftwards at his younger colleague. Leaning forward, Bruno Mackay shot his cuffs and addressed his notes. "If I might return briefly to my old stomping ground," he began, "Pakistan liaison has reported a sighting of Dawood al Safa. Their report suggests that al Safa has visited a training camp near Takht-i-Suleiman in the tribal north-west of the country, and may have made contact with a group known as the Children of Heaven, who are suspected of involvement in the murder of a US embassy guard in Islamabad six months ago."

To Liz's acute irritation Mackay pronounced the Islamic names in such a way as to make it abundantly clear that he was an Arabic speaker. Just what was it with these people? she wondered. Why did they all think they were T. E. Lawrence, or Ralph Fiennes in *The English Patient*? A complicit flicker from Wetherby told her that he shared her sentiments on the matter.

"Our feeling at Vauxhall is that this activity is significant," continued Mackay urbanely. "Two reasons. One: al Safa's principal role is as a bag man, moving cash between Riyadh and the Asian terror groups. If he's on the move, then something nasty's in the pipeline. Two: the Children of Heaven are one of the few ITS groups thought to have included Caucasians in their ranks. A Pakistani Intelligence Service surveillance report from about six months ago indicated the presence in the camp of, and I quote, 'two, perhaps three individuals of identifiably Western appearance.' "

He extended spatulate, sun-browned fingers on the table in front of him. "Our concern—and we've communicated this over the weekend to all stations—is that the opposition may be about to deploy an invisible."

He let the remark hang for a moment. The calculated theatricality of his delivery did not lessen the impact of his statement. An "invisible" was CIA-speak for the ultimate intelligence nightmare: the terrorist who, because he or she is an ethnic native of the target country, can cross its borders unchecked, move around that country unquestioned, and infiltrate its institutions with ease. An invisible was the worst possible news.

"That being the case," Mackay continued smoothly, "we would suggest that Immigration be brought into the loop."

The Home Office man frowned. "What's your view on likely targets and the timing of all this? We should probably up the security status of all government buildings from black to red, but that causes administrative problems, and I don't want to move on it too soon."

Mackay glanced at his notes. "Pakistan is already checking all passenger lists out of the country, with particular reference to . . . let's see, non-business visitors under thirty-five whose stay has exceeded thirty days. So they're very much on to the case. No idea of targets yet, but we'll keep our ears very close to the ground." He looked across at Wetherby, and then at Liz. "And we need to stay in constant touch with our agents this end, too."

"That's already happening," said Wetherby. "If they hear about anything, so will we, but so far . . ." He glanced interrogatively at the GCHQ rep, who pursed his lips non-committally.

"We've had a bit more background noise than usual. No specific indicators though. Nothing approaching the traffic you'd associate with a major operation."

Liz looked covertly around the room. The Special Branch officers, as usual, had remained silent. Their habitual attitudes were those of busy men whose time was being wasted in a Whitehall talking-shop. But both were now sitting upright and alert.

Her eyes met Mackay's. He didn't smile or look away but stared straight back. She continued her scan of the room but knew that the MI6 officer was still watching her. Felt the slow, cold burn of his gaze.

Wetherby, in turn—his tired, forgettable features voided of all expression—was watching Mackay. The circuit held for a long, taut moment and then Fane cut in with a general question about MI5 agents in the UK's militant Islamic communities. "Just how close to the action are these people of yours?" he demanded. "Would they be amongst the need-to-knows if a major ITS operation was being mounted against this country?"

Wetherby let Liz field it. "In most cases probably not," she said, knowing from experience that optimism cut no ice with Fane. "But we've got people in the right orbits. Time will see them move closer to the centre."

"Time?"

"We're not in a position to accelerate the process."

She had decided not to mention Marzipan. The agent would have been a strong card to play but he had yet to prove his worth. Or, for that matter, his courage. At this early stage in his career as an agent she wasn't prepared to reveal him—certainly not to a circle as wide as this one.

Wetherby, inscrutable, was tapping his lips with a pencil, but Liz could tell from his posture that he considered her decision the correct one. She had not allowed Fane to bump her into a statement that could later be held against them.

And Mackay, she realised with a faint sinking sensation, was still watching her. Was she unknowingly transmitting some kind of bat-like sexual sonar? Or was Mackay one of those men who felt that he had to establish a complicity with every woman who crossed his path, so that afterwards he could tell himself that he could have had her if he'd wanted? Either way, she felt more irritated than flattered.

Above their heads one of the tube lights began to flicker. It seemed to signal the meeting's end.

3

In Trumper's in Jermyn Street, a mile to the northwest, Peregrine Lakeby settled himself into the well-stuffed comfort of his chair. With some satisfaction, he surveyed himself in the angled mirror. It was not easy to look elegant while a barber fussed around you with his towels and brushes, but despite his sixty-two summers Perry Lakeby congratulated himself that he managed it. Not for him the thread veins, pouchy eyes and multiple chins that rendered his contemporaries so physically unappealing. Lakeby's gaze was a clear sea-blue, his skin was taut, his hair a backswept gunmetal mane.

Why he should have escaped time's attrition when others had not,

Perry had no idea. He ate and drank, if not to excess, then certainly without moderation. The closest he got to exercise was the odd bout of adultery and, in season, a few days' shooting. If pressed, he would probably have attributed his well-preserved appearance to good breeding. The Lakebys, he was fond of informing people, descended from the Saxons.

"Good journey up to town, sir?"

Perry raised a dyspeptic eyebrow. "Not too bad, barring the mobile phone louts. People seem to think nothing of broadcasting the details of their ghastly lives to the world. And at balls-aching bloody length, too."

Mr. Park's scissors flickered. "I'm sorry to hear that, sir. Back to the country tonight, is it?"

" 'Fraid so, yes. My wife's got people coming over. The most boring couple in Norfolk, but there you go."

"Indeed, sir. Just tilt the head, if you would."

Perry took the train down to London once a month, on average, and usually went straight to Trumper's. Something about the dark panelling and the badger-bristle brushes and the sensible, soapy smell of the place—some reminder of school, perhaps—was immensely comforting to him. Perry valued continuity, and he had been going to Trumper's for several decades now. He could have gone to the barber-shop in Fakenham and achieved much the same result for a third of the price, but it would never have occurred to him to do so. His London trips were an escape—not least from the watchful eye of Anne, his spouse—and they had a ritual character that he had come to rely on.

"Chin up, sir, if you would."

Perry obeyed, and Mr. Park patted his customer's jowls with sharp-scented spirit.

"Will there be anything else, sir?"

Perry sat there in a pleasing miasma of talcum powder and Essence of Sicilian Limes. Not even the prospect of Ralph and Diane Munday hoovering up his gin could spoil the moment. "I don't think so, Mr. Park. Thank you."

He stood, and was assisted into the velvet-collared coat that he wore to town. Ascending the stairs to street level, he saw that although the wind was up, the rain had stopped, which was about as much as you could reasonably ask of a December morning.

Furled umbrella in hand, Perry sauntered westwards towards St. James's, past the bespoke shoe shops, the hosiers, the hatters, the perfumers, the bathroom suppliers, the cuff-link emporia, and the traditional shirtmakers with their windows piled high with bolts of striped cloth. All of these establishments further heartened Perry Lakeby, confirming as they did that there was still a world where the old order counted for something, and deference was still accorded to people such as himself. And if some of the old places had closed—had been replaced by mobile phone outlets or brashly egalitarian men's outfitters—he turned a blind eye to the fact. He wasn't going to let it spoil his day.

Outside New and Lingwood he considered treating himself to a tie. He had a particular affection for New and Lingwood—there had been one of their shops at Eton when he was there, and indeed there probably still was one. At the last moment, however, he turned away from the door. He could hardly arrive home wearing a new tie without a present for Anne, and he wasn't going to have the time to buy one. Or, in truth, the money. He had had to tighten his belt in recent months and if he occasionally indulged himself in certain areas he did so out of his own private funds. These funds were strictly limited, and—whatever the mitigating circumstances—not to be squandered on Liberty silk squares or presentation bottles of stephanotis bath oil from Floris.

Cigars, however, were something else. Kipling once wrote that a woman is only a woman, but a good cigar is a smoke, and it was with precisely this dictum in mind that Perry crossed the street to Davidoff, on the corner of St. James's. The shop's proprietor greeted him politely, and showed him into the humidor room. This was one of Perry's favourite places on earth, and for several long moments he simply breathed the Havana-scented air. The choice was, as always, exquisite, and Perry lingered indecisively over the Partagas, the Cohibas and the

Bolivars. In the end the proprietor intervened, drawing his attention to a fine old canary-wood humidor containing a couple of dozen El Rey Del Mundos in various sizes. Perry took three, a Gran Corona and a couple of Lonsdales, and handed over two large-denomination banknotes in return.

Crossing St. James's, avoiding the taxis which, these days, seemed to offer pedestrians no quarter at all, Perry made for the discreetly grand entrance of Brooks's Club. It was his goddaughter's birthday, and he was due to give her lunch there at noon.

Miranda Munday was the youngest offspring of Perry's Norfolk neighbours, and Perry was still not quite sure how he had come to be responsible for her spiritual well-being. On the basis of past form, however, he had a fair idea of what the next couple of hours would hold. The twenty-four-year-old would be resolutely unimpressed by her surroundings—by the club's vaulted ceilings, gilded mouldings, heavy burgundy draperies and forest-green leather armchairs. Instead she would comment disparagingly on the paucity of female members, frown humourlessly at the dining room menu, choose a vegetable starter instead of a main course, refuse the club claret in favour of mineral water, insist on camomile tea instead of a pudding, and regale Perry at length with the jaw-droppingly dull details of her job in advertising. Why, he wondered, were the young so deadly *serious*? What the hell had happened to fun?

Striding through the club's entrance, he greeted Jenkins, the hall porter, disposed of his coat, and placed his umbrella in the long mahogany stand. Eleven thirty. Half an hour to wait.

On impulse, instead of going straight upstairs, he turned right into the club's backgammon room, where two members were finishing a game.

"Morning, Roddy," said Perry. "Simon."

Roderick Fox-Harper MP and Simon Farmilow regarded him for a moment without recognition. "Lakeby, isn't it?" asked Farmilow, eventually.

"Peregrine Lakeby. Time for a board?"

Farmilow's eyebrows rose. He was a well-known tournament player, but if this pigeon was offering himself on the altar . . .

"Tenner a point?" suggested Perry, driven by the other man's silence to reckless bravado.

The game did not take long. Farmilow's first throw was a double six, which automatically doubled the stakes. A couple of minutes later, his position established, he turned the doubling dice from two to four. Rather than concede, and go down to the tune of £40, Perry accepted the raise with a faint smile—a smile which remained in place as, with faultless courtesy, Farmilow constructed a prime, closed Perry out, and gammoned him. A gammon, as both players knew, redoubled all existing stakes.

"Another?" asked Perry, his voice a little less steady than before.

"Why not?" agreed Farmilow.

This time things went a little better for Perry. A reasonable series of early throws encouraged him to double, but before long his opponent was bearing off his last counters.

"Call it a morning?" Farmilow suggested.

"I think I might," murmured Perry. Moving to a table at one end of the room, he wrote out an IOU to Farmilow for £100 and placed it in the slotted wooden box. He might as well have bought Anne that damned scarf. Still, accounts didn't have to be settled until the year's end. The day wasn't ruined.

Miranda Munday, her unremarkable figure enclosed in a beige suit, was waiting for him in the hall. As they climbed the winding staircase together Perry mused that at least she usually buggered off pretty quickly after lunch. With the help of a taxi he would easily be able to make his 2:30 appointment in Shepherd Market. At the thought of that appointment his hand tightened on the banister, the back of his neck prickled and his heart thumped like a regimental drum. Every man needs a secret life, he told himself.

4

On the other side of the river, a mile to the east, a Eurostar train from Paris was pulling in to the terminus at Waterloo station. Halfway along its length, a young woman stepped from the soporific warmth of a second-class carriage in to the bracing chill of the platform, and was borne on a hurrying crowd towards the terminus building. Electronic announcements echoed along the covered way, overlaying the rattle of baggage trolleys and the whirring of wheeled suitcases—sounds so familiar to the woman that she barely registered them. In the past couple of years she had made the journey to and from the Gare du Nord at least a dozen times.

She was wearing a parka jacket over jeans and Nike trainers. On her head, a brown corduroy Beatles cap from a stall on the Quai des Celestins, its peak pulled low over her face, and—despite the overcast day—a pair of aviator sunglasses. She looked somewhere in her early twenties, she was carrying a holdall and a large rucksack, and there was nothing to distinguish her from the other long-weekenders who spilled cheerfully from the train. A careful observer might have noted just how little of the woman was actually on display—the parka entirely disguised her figure, the cap completely covered her hair, the sunglasses obscured her eyes—and a very careful observer might have wondered at her unseasonally sunburnt hands, but on that Monday morning no one was paying a great deal of attention to the day's second consignment of passengers. The non-EU passport-holders were submitted to the customary examinations at the gate, but the vast majority of passengers were nodded through.

At the Avis rent-a-car counter, the woman joined a four-strong queue, and if she was conscious of the CCTV camera mounted on the wall above her she gave no sign of it. Instead, opening the morning's edition of the *International Herald Tribune,* she appeared to bury herself in a fashion article.

A sharp mobile phone beep from beneath the counter greeted her arrival at the front of the queue, and the assistant excused himself for a moment to read a text message. When he looked up again it was with an absent smile, as if he was trying to think up a snappy reply. He processed her with due courtesy, but he could tell from her cracked nails, poorly kept hands and choice of car—an economy hatchback— that she was not worthy of the full beam of his attention. Her driving licence and passport, in consequence, received no more than a glance; the photos appeared to tally—both were from the same photo-booth series and showed the usual blank, slightly startled features. In short, she was forgotten by the time she was out of sight.

Slinging her luggage on the passenger seat, the woman eased the black Vauxhall Astra into the stream of traffic crossing Waterloo Bridge. Accelerating into the underpass, she felt her heart race. Breathe, she told herself. Be cool.

Five minutes later, she pulled in to a parking bay. Taking the passport, driving licence and rental documents from her coat pocket, she zipped them into the holdall with her other passport, the one she had shown at the immigration desk. When she had done this she sat and waited for her hands to stop shaking from the delayed tension.

It was lunchtime, she realised. She should eat something. From the side pouch of the rucksack she took a baguette filled with Gruyère cheese, a bar of hazelnut chocolate, and a plastic bottle of mineral water. She forced herself to chew slowly.

Then, checking her mirror, she pulled out slowly into the traffic stream.

5

Reading through the Marzipan file at her desk in 5/AX, Liz Carlyle felt the familiar sick unease. As an agent-runner, anxiety was her constant companion, an ever-present shadow. The truth was grimly simple: if an agent was to be effective, then he or she had to be placed at risk.

But at just twenty, she asked herself, was Marzipan truly aware of the risks that he ran? Had he really taken on board the fact that, if blown, he might have a life expectancy of no more than a few hours?

Marzipan's name was Sohail Din, and he had been a walk-in. An exceptionally bright young man of Pakistani origin whose father was the comfortably-off proprietor of several Tottenham newsagents, he had been accepted to read law at Durham University. A devout Muslim, he had decided to spend his gap year working in a small Islamic book-shop in Haringey. The work was not well paid, but it was close to the family home, and Sohail had hoped that it would provide the opportunity for religious discussion with other serious-minded young men like himself.

It had rapidly become clear, however, that the tone of the place was rather less moderate than it had seemed. The version of Islam celebrated by those who came and went was a long way from the compassionate creed that Sohail had absorbed at home and at his local mosque. Extremist views were aired as a matter of course, young men openly discussed their intentions of training as mujahidin and taking up the sword of jihad against the West, and there was jubilation every time the press reported that an American or Israeli target had been hit by terrorists.

Unwilling to voice his dissent, but clear in his own mind that a world view which celebrated the murder of civilians was abhorrent before God, Sohail kept a low profile. Unlike his fellow employees, he saw no reason to hate the country of his birth, or to despise the legislature that he hoped one day to serve. The crunch came one late summer afternoon when three Arabic-speaking men had entered the shop from an elderly Mercedes. One of Sohail's colleagues had nudged him, indicating the oldest of them—a nondescript figure with thinning hair and a scruffy beard. This, Sohail learned when the three men had been taken to the rooms above the shop, was Rahman al Masri, an important fighter. Perhaps his arrival meant that Britain would at last taste some of the terror inflicted by its Satanic ally, the United States.

This was the point at which Sohail decided to act. At the day's end he had not caught his customary bus home but instead, after consulting an A to Z, had taken a main-line train half a dozen stops south to Cambridge Heath. Exiting the railway station, having satisfied himself that he had not been followed, he had pulled up the hood of his coat and made his way through the drizzle to Bethnal Green police station.

Special Branch had acted fast; Rahman al Masri was a known player. MI5 had been notified, an observation post had been set up near the bookshop, and when al Masri and his two minders left the following day, it was with a discreet surveillance escort. Intelligence allies had been informed, and with several countries working closely together, al Masri was allowed to run. He was eventually picked up at Dubai airport, and taken into custody by that country's secret police. After a week of what was officially described as "intensive questioning," al Masri admitted that he had visited London to deliver instructions to terrorist cells there. Attacks were to be unleashed against targets in the City.

Forewarned, the police were able to identify and arrest those involved. One of the prime objectives throughout the operation had been to preserve the original source of the information. When it was over, after extensive background checks on Sohail, it had been agreed between a senior Special Branch officer and Charles Wetherby that the young Asian might be suitable for development by Five as a long-term agent. Wetherby had handed the file to Liz, who drove up to Tottenham a couple of days later. Their first meeting took place in a disused classroom at the evening institute where Sohail took a weekly computer course.

She had been shocked by how young he was. Physically slight, self-effacing and neatly dressed in a jacket and tie, he still looked like a schoolboy. But there was a steeliness there too, and talking to him she was struck by the unswerving rigour of his moral code. Nothing justified murder, he told her, and if informing on his co-religionists helped to prevent it, and to protect the good name of Islam from those who sought the nihilist Apocalypse, then he was happy to do so. She had asked him if he was prepared to remain in place at the bookshop, and to meet her at intervals to hand over information, and he had told her that he was. He had guessed which organisation she represented without being told, and appeared unsurprised by their involvement.

Since then there had been three more meetings at the evening institute. Sohail kept a record of the comings and goings at the bookshop in an encrypted online file on his laptop, and as a Special Branch officer kept unobtrusive watch in the corridor outside, he read off his reports to

Liz. None of the information he had provided had been as momentous as the report of al Masri's presence, but it was clear that the bookshop was a key staging-post for, in Special Branch parlance, "the Bin-Men." If there was a big operation going down in the UK involving any of the ITS groups, the chances were that Sohail—Marzipan—would be aware of the advance ripples. Potentially, he was intelligence gold.

The last meeting had been a difficult one—for Liz at least. She had asked Sohail if he would consider putting off university for a further year in order to remain in place at the bookshop, and for the first time she saw the twenty-year-old flinch. He had been counting, Liz knew, on being free of the intense pressure of his double life by the following autumn. The sense of an end-date had probably made the whole business supportable. And now she was asking him to remain there for a further twelve months—twelve months in which, for all she knew, anything could happen. Pressure might be put on him to undergo training as an undercover fighter—several of the young men who had drunk mint tea and talked of jihad in the bookshop's upstairs room had made the journey to Pakistan and the camps. At the very least the delay would seriously threaten his dream of becoming a lawyer.

His distress had been almost invisible—a momentary shudder behind his eyes. And then, with a quiet smile, as if to reassure Liz that all would be well, he had agreed to continue.

His bravery had wrung Liz's heart. She prayed that she would never have to meet Sarfraz and Rukhsana Din, never have to tell them that their son had died for his faith and his country.

"Bad one?" asked Dave Armstrong from the next desk.

"You know how it is," said Liz, exiting the Marzipan file and kicking her chair back from the desk. "Sometimes this job can be really shitty."

"I know. And that supposed goulash I saw you tackling in the canteen can't have improved your mood either."

Liz laughed. "It was kind of a wild choice. What did you have?"

"A sort of chicken thing, glazed with Ronseal."

"And?"

"It did exactly what it said on the tin." His hands flickered briefly over his keyboard. "How was the meeting this morning? Legoland team fashionably late again, I hear."

"I think they were making a point," said Liz. "There was a new guy there. Ex-Harrovian. Rather pleased with himself."

"Don't tell me MI6 have started recruiting smug ex–public schoolboys," murmured Dave. "That I can't believe."

"He stared at me," continued Liz.

"With or without shame?"

"Without."

"You'll have to kill him. Kick him in the ankle with your pointy shoes, Rosa Klebb–style."

"OK . . . hang on a sec." Liz leaned forward towards her screen, where an icon had appeared. She clicked her mouse.

"Trouble?"

"Flash from German liaison. UK driving licence ordered from one of the fake documents guys in Bremerhaven. Four hundred marks paid. Name requested, Faraj Mansoor. Ring any bells?"

"No," said Armstrong. "Probably just some illegal migrant who wants to rent a car. Or some poor sod who's been banned from driving. You can't shout terrorist every time."

"Six reckons there could be an ITS invisible on the move."

"Where from?"

"One of the North West Frontier Province camps."

"Definitely?"

"No. Just smoke." She saved the message and scrabbled the mouse to check her messages.

The office door swung open and a hard-faced young man in an Aryan Resistance T-shirt strolled in.

"Yo, Barney!" said Dave. "How's the world of the Far Right? I take it from the haircut and the utility footwear that you've got a social engagement later on?"

"Yeah. In East Ham. A lecture on the European Pagan Tradition."

"Which is?"

"New Age Hitler-worship, basically."

"Excellent!"

"Isn't it just? I'm trying to look nasty enough to get alongside our man, but not so bloody horrible that I get my head kicked in by the Anti-Nazi League before I get there."

"I'd say you've struck pretty much the right note," said Liz.

"Thanks a lot." He grinned conspiratorially. "Can I show you guys something?"

"You sound like a flasher. Quickly—I've got a very full in-box here."

Barney reached beneath his desk, bringing out a limp rubber mask and a scrap of red felt. "It's for the Christmas party. I've found this place that makes them. I've had fifty done."

Liz stared incredulously at the mask. "It's not!"

"It is!"

"But that's brilliant! It's so like him."

"I know, but don't say anything. I want it to be a surprise for Wetherby. No one in this department can keep a secret for five minutes, so I'm not going to hand them out until the actual day."

Liz laughed out loud, the plight of Sohail Din temporarily but absolutely displaced by the thought of their section leader—customarily a late arrival at staff functions—faced with fifty beaming David Shaylers in Santa hats.

6

When Liz arrived back at her basement flat in Kentish Town, the place had a reproachful air about it. It wasn't so much untidy as neglected; most of her possessions still lay where she had left them at the beginning of the weekend. The CD dusty in the jutting maw of the player. The remote control in the centre of the carpet. The cafetière half full. The Saturday papers strewn about.

A faint funereal smell lingered; the armful of winter jasmine that her mother had given her, and that she had meant to put in water before going to bed the night before, was now a sad tangle of stalks on the table. Around it, and thick on the floor below, a constellation of dying five-pointed petals. On the answering machine, a tiny pulsing red light.

Why was the place so cold? She checked the central heating and found that the timer was two hours behind. Had there been some sort of power cut during the weekend? Possibly, but then as far as Liz was concerned, thermostats and the like had always seemed to wield some strange whimsical power that rendered them unaccountable. Moving the time forward to 19:30, she heard the boiler start up with a satisfactory *whoomf*.

For the next half-hour, as warmth permeated the small basement flat, she tidied up. When the place was well enough ordered for her to be able to relax, she took a cook-from-frozen lasagne from the stack in the freezer (had they defrosted and refrosted in the power cut, if indeed there had been a power cut? Was she about to poison herself?), pierced the protective foil with a series of neat incisions, slid the package into the oven, and poured herself a large vodka-tonic.

There were two messages on the answering machine. The first was from her mother: Liz had left a suede skirt and belt on the back of her bedroom door at Bowerbridge—would they keep until next time?

The second was from Mark. He had rung at 12:46 that afternoon from Nobu in Park Lane, where he was waiting to give an American actress an expense-account lunch. The actress was late, however, and Mark was hungry, and his thoughts had turned to the basement flat in Inkerman Road NW5, and the possibility of spending the night there with the flat's owner. Following a drink and a bite to eat, perhaps, at the Eagle in Farringdon Road.

Liz deleted both messages. The idea of meeting in the Eagle, a favourite hang-out of *Guardian* journalists, was insane. Had he told people at the paper about her? Was it common knowledge that he had that most chic of journalistic accessories—a pet spook? Even if he had said nothing to anyone it was clear that the game had moved beyond the realm of acceptable risk into crazy-land. He was playing with her, drawing her inch by inch towards self-destruction.

Taking a deep swallow of her drink, Liz called up his mobile. She was going to do it right now—finish the thing once and for all. It would hurt like hell and she would feel wretched beyond description, but she wanted her life back under her own control.

She got his voice mail, which probably meant that he was at home with Shauna. Where he bloody well should be, she mused sourly. Pacing around the flat, she was brought up short by the sight of the washing machine, and the inverted semi-circle of greyish water. Last week's washing had now been stewing there for two and a half days. Despairingly, she reached for the knob, and the machine lurched into life.

7

Anne Lakeby woke to see Perry standing in front of the open bedroom window, looking out over the garden towards the sea. The
day was a clear one, sharpened by the suggestion of a salt breeze, and
her husband looked almost priestly in his long Chinese dressing gown.
His hair was damp, and had been smoothed to a dull gleam by the twin
ivory-backed hairbrushes in the dressing room. He also appeared to
have shaved.

The old bugger certainly brushed up well, she thought, but it was
unlike him to take quite this much trouble so early in the day. Squinting
at the alarm clock she saw that it was barely 7 a.m. Perry might have

been a passionate admirer of Margaret Thatcher, but he had never shared her predilection for early rising.

As Perry pulled the window shut, Anne closed her eyes, feigning sleep. The door closed, and five minutes later her husband reappeared with two coffee cups and saucers on a tray. This was truly alarming. What on earth had he got up to in London the day before to prompt a gesture like this?

Placing the tray on the carpet with a faint rattle, Perry touched his wife's shoulder.

Anne mimed her own awakening. "This is a . . . nice surprise." She blinked drowsily, reaching for the glass of water on the bedside table. "To what do I owe . . ."

"Put it down to global warming," said Perry expansively. "I was expecting a titanic hangover after last night, but a benign deity has stayed his hand. The sun, moreover, is shining. It is a day for gratitude. And possibly for burning the last of the autumn leaves."

Anne pulled herself into a sitting position against the pillows and struggled to collect her thoughts. She was not sure that she quite believed in this considerate, coffee-making version of her spouse. He was definitely up to something. His bullish manner reminded her of the time when he had got her to buy those Corliss Defence Systems shares. The breezier his demeanour, in her experience, the closer to the wind he was sailing.

"They really are the bloody end though, aren't they?" Perry continued.

"Who? Dorgie and Diane?" Dorgie was Anne's nickname for Sir Ralph Munday, whose snouty features reminded her of one of the Queen's corgi-dachshund crosses. Inasmuch as the Lakebys and the Mundays owned the two largest and most consequential properties in Marsh Creake, they considered themselves "neighbours," although in reality their houses were a good half-mile apart.

"Who else? All that awful shooting talk. High cocks . . . full choke at fifty yards . . . he sounds as if he's learned the whole thing from a book. And she's worse, with her—"

"Where does he shoot?"

"Some pop-star syndicate near Houghton. One of the members, Dorgs was telling me, made his money out of internet porn."

"Well, you shoot with an arms dealer," said Anne mildly, stirring her coffee.

"True, but that's all very ethical these days. You can't just flog the stuff to African dictators off the back of a lorry."

"Johnny Fortescue paid for the restoration of the library ceiling at Holt by selling electronic riot batons to the Iraqi secret police. I know, because Sophie told me."

"Well, I'm sure it was all completely tickety-boo and DTI-approved at the time."

They drank their coffee in silence for a few moments.

"Tell me something," said Anne, her tone exploratory. "You know Ray?"

Perry looked at her. Ray Gunter was a fisherman who lived in the village and who kept a couple of boats and a tangle of lobster-nets on the two-hundred-yard stretch of private beach at the end of the Hall's grounds. "I ought to, after all these years. What about him?"

"Do we absolutely have to keep up this business of him coming and going through the grounds? To be perfectly honest, he rather gives me the creeps."

Perry frowned. "In what way?"

"He's just . . . *sinister.* You turn a corner and there he is. The dogs don't like him, either."

"The Gunters have had boats there since my grandfather's time, at least. Ray's father—"

"I know, but Ray's father is dead. And where Ben Gunter was the nicest old boy you could hope to meet, Ray is frankly . . ."

"Yobbish?"

"No, worse than that. He's sinister, like I said."

"I don't agree. He may not be the world's most sparkling conversationalist, and he probably niffs a bit, but that's fishing for you. I think we might get into all sorts of trouble if we tried to run him off the place. The local press would have a field day."

"At least let's find out what our legal position is."

"Why go to the expense?"

"Why not? Why are you so . . ." She placed her coffee cup on the bedside table, and reached for her glasses. "I'll tell you something else Sophie told me. You know the sister?"

"The Gunter sister? Kayleigh?"

"Yes, Kayleigh. Apparently the girl who does the Fortescues' garden was at school with her, and told Sophie that she—Kayleigh, that is—works a couple of nights a week in a club in King's Lynn as a stripper."

"Really?" Perry raised his eyebrows. "I didn't know King's Lynn offered such lurid temptations. Did she mention the name of the club?"

"Perry, stop it. The point I'm making is that the present generation of Gunters are not quite the simple fisherfolk their parents were."

Perry shrugged. *"Tempora mutantur, et nos mutamur in illis."*

"And what's that supposed to mean?"

He walked back to the window. Looked out over the shining expanse of Norfolk coastline to the east and west of them. "Times change," he murmured, "and we change with them. Ray Gunter's doing us no harm at all."

Anne removed her glasses and placed them on the side table with an exasperated snap. Perry could be wilfully obtuse when he wanted to be. She was worried, too. After thirty-five years of marriage she could tell when he was up to something—and he was up to something now.

8

Nu-Celeb Publications of Chelmsford, Essex, occupied a low modular building on the Writtle Industrial Estate to the southwest of the town. The premises were spare and utilitarian, but they were warm, even at nine in the morning. Melvin Eastman hated to be cold, and in his glass-walled office overlooking the shop floor the thermostat was set to 20° Centigrade. At his desk, still wearing the camel-hair overcoat in which he had arrived ten minutes earlier, Eastman was examining the front page of the *Sun* newspaper. A smallish man with neatly dressed hair of a slightly unnatural blackness, his features remained expressionless as he read. Finally, leaning forward, he reached for one of the telephones on the desk. His voice was quiet, but his enunciation precise.

"Ken, how many of those Mink Parfait calendars have we had printed up?"

On the floor below, his foreman looked up at him. " 'Bout forty thou, boss. Should be the big Christmas seller. Why?"

"Because, Ken, Mink Parfait are splitting up." Taking the newspaper, he held it up so that it was visible to the foreman.

"You sure it's kosher, boss? Not some publicity . . ."

Eastman laid the paper down on his desk. " 'Citing personal and musical differences,' " he read, " 'Foxy Deacon confirmed that the four-strong girl group would be going their separate ways. "We know that this'll come as a shock to the fans," says *FHM* cover girl Foxy, 22, "but we wanted to end things on a high." Insiders claim that tensions within the group date from . . .' etcetera. We're not going to be able to give those calendars away."

"I'm sorry, boss. I dunno what to say."

Eastman replaced the phone and admitted a frown to the pallid moonscape of his face. It was an unpromising start to the day. Nu-Celeb was not the only iron that he had in the fire—the celebrity calendar business had been created as cover for a raft of other, less legal activities that had made him a millionaire many times over. But it still irked him that he could take a bath to the tune of twenty large on the whim of a bunch of scrubbers like Mink Parfait. Half-caste scrubbers at that. Melvin Eastman did not subscribe to the dream of a multicultural Britain.

A key player in one of Eastman's other business activities, a narrow-featured man in a black bomber jacket and baseball cap named Frankie Ferris, was sitting against the wall. He had a mug of tea in one hand and was smoking, tapping the ash into the bin with nervous and unnecessary frequency.

Folding the newspaper and placing it carefully in the same bin, Eastman turned to Ferris. Noted the pallor of his lips and the faint shake of the cigarette between his fingers.

"So, Frankie," he said quietly. "How's it going?"

"I'm awright, Mr. Eastman."

"Returns coming in? Everyone paying their way?"

"Yeah. No problem."

"Any special requests?"

"Harlow and Basildon both want ketamines. Asked if we can do 'em a trial batch."

"No way. That stuff's like crack—strictly for coons and mentals. Go on."

"Acid."

"The same. Anything else?"

"Yeah, the Ecstasy. Everyone suddenly wants the butterflies."

"Not the doves?"

"Doves'll do but butterflies are best. The word is they're stronger."

"That's bollocks, Frankie. They're identical. As you know."

Frankie shrugged. "Just telling you."

Melvin Eastman nodded and turned away. From his desk drawer he took a plastic bank envelope, and handed it to Frankie.

Frankie frowned. Turned the envelope over incomprehendingly.

"I'm only giving you three fifty this week," said Eastman quietly, "because it's clear that I've been overpaying you. You did six fifty at the blackjack table in the Brentwood Sporting Club last Friday."

"I'm s-sorry, Mr. Eastman. I . . ."

"That kind of behaviour attracts attention, Frankie, and attention is very bad news indeed. I don't put a grand a week in your pocket for you to piss it away in public, understand?"

Eastman's tone and expression were unchanged, but the edge of threat was very close to the surface. The last man to seriously displease his employer, Frankie knew, had washed up on the mudflats off Foulness Island. The dogfish had had a go at his face and he'd had to be identified by his teeth.

"I understand, Mr. Eastman."

"You sure?"

"Yes, Mr. Eastman. I'm sure."

"Good. Then let's get to work."

Handing Frankie a Stanley knife from his desk, Eastman indicated four sealed cardboard boxes which were stacked against one wall. The boxes' stencilled sides indicated that they contained Korean-built document scanners.

Cutting across the seal, Frankie opened the first box, revealing the advertised hardware. With care he removed the scanner and its Styrofoam mould. Beneath were three tightly filled, sealed polythene bags.

"Do we need to check them?"

Eastman nodded.

Frankie cut a small incision in the first bag, drew out a wrap of paper, and passed it to Eastman. Unwrapping the paper, Eastman touched the tip of his tongue to the off-white crystal, nodded, and returned it to Frankie.

"I think we can take the jellies and the Es on trust. Just see if Amsterdam's sent us doves or butterflies."

"Looks like doves in this one," said Frankie nervously, peering at a bag of Ecstasy tablets. "Must be using up old stock."

The same operation was applied to the other three boxes. Carefully, Frankie packed a rucksack with the bags of Ecstasy, temazepam, and methamphetamine crystal, topping the load off with a T-shirt and a pair of dingy Y-fronts.

"The butterflies go to Basildon, Chelmsford, Brentwood, Romford and Southend," said Eastman. "The doves to Harlow, Braintree, Colchester—"

His phone rang, and he held up a hand, indicating that Frankie should wait. As the conversation progressed he glanced at him once or twice, but Frankie was staring out over the shop floor, apparently engrossed in the progress of a fork-lift truck.

Was he using? Eastman wondered. Or was it just the gambling? Should he offset the morning's stick with a bit of carrot—push a couple of fifties into his back pocket on the way out?

In the end he decided not to. The lesson had to be learned.

9

Faraj Mansoor," said Charles Wetherby, returning his tortoiseshell reading glasses to his top pocket. "Name mean anything to you?"

Liz nodded. "Yes—person of that name bought a fake UK driving licence last weekend in one of the northern ports . . . Bremerhaven, I think? German liaison flashed him to us yesterday."

"Any terrorist form?"

"I ran him through the database. There's a Faraj Mansoor who's on a long list logged by Pakistan liaison of all those spoken to or contacted by Dawood al Safa in the course of his visit to Peshawar earlier this year."

"Al Safa the ITS bagman? The one Mackay was telling us about yesterday?"

"Yes, that one. This Mansoor—and it's got to be quite a common name—is identified as one of half a dozen employees of an auto repair shop on the Kabul road. Apparently al Safa stopped there and looked at some second-hand vehicles. Pakistan liaison had a couple of guys on his tail and when al Safa moved on they dropped a man off to list the employees."

"And that's it?"

"That's it."

Wetherby nodded pensively. "The reason I'm asking is that for some reason I can't presently fathom, Geoffrey Fane's just called me with a request to be kept in the loop."

"About Mansoor?" asked Liz, surprised.

"About Mansoor. I had to tell him that, as things stood, there was no loop."

"And?"

"And that was it. He thanked me and hung up."

Liz allowed her eyes to wander round the bare walls. Wondered why Wetherby had called her to his office for a conversation which could easily have taken place over the phone.

"Before you go, Liz, is everything all right? I mean, are you . . . OK?"

She met his gaze. He was someone whose face, try as she might, she could never quite summon from memory. Sometimes she could recall the dead-leaf brown of the hair and eyes, sometimes the wry asymmetry of the nose and mouth, but the precise collision of his features evaded her. Even now, facing him, he seemed elusive. As always, a subtle irony seemed to pervade their professional relationship, as if they met at other times and on some different basis.

But they never had, and outside the context of their work Liz knew very little about him. There was a wife who was supposed to have some sort of chronic health problem, and there were a couple of boys at school. They lived somewhere on the river—Shepperton, perhaps, or was it Sunbury? One of those Ratty, Toad and Mole places out to the west.

But that was about the limit of her knowledge. As to his tastes, interests, or what car he drove, she had no idea.

"Do I look as if I'm not OK?"

"You look fine. But I know this Marzipan business hasn't been easy. He's very young, isn't he?"

"Yes. He is."

Wetherby nodded obliquely. "He's also one of our key assets—or promises to be—which is why I gave him to you. You debrief him, say nothing, and let me see the product—I don't want him declared for the time being."

Liz nodded. "I don't think he's registered on Fane's radar yet."

"Let's keep it that way. We have to play a long game with this young man, and that means no pressure from this end whatsoever. Just concentrate on getting him solidly dug in. If he's as good as you say he is, the product will follow."

"As long as you're prepared to wait."

"For as long as it takes. Does he still think he's going to university next year?"

"No. Whether he's told his parents or not I don't know."

Wetherby nodded sympathetically, stood up, and walked to the window. Stared out over the river for a moment before turning back to face her. "Tell me. What do you think you would be doing if you weren't working here?"

Liz looked at him. "It's funny you should ask that," she said eventually. Because I was asking myself more or less the same question only this morning."

"Why this morning in particular?"

"I got a letter."

He waited. There was a reflective, unforced quality to his silence, as if the two of them had all the time in the world.

Hesitantly at first, uncertain of how much he already knew, Liz began to sketch the outlines of her life. Her fluency surprised her; it was as if she was rehearsing a well-learned cover story. Plausible—verifiable even—but at the same time not quite real.

For more than thirty years her father had been manager of the Bowerbridge estate, in the valley of the river Nadder near Salisbury. He and Liz's mother had lived in the estate's gatehouse, and Liz had grown up there. Five years earlier, however, Jack Carlyle had died, and shortly afterwards Bowerbridge's owner had sold up. The woods and coppices which comprised the sporting estate had been sold to a local farmer, and the main house, with its topiary, greenhouses and walled garden, had been bought by the owner of a chain of garden centres.

The outgoing owner, a generous man, had made it a condition of the sale that his former manager's widow should occupy the gatehouse rent-free for the remainder of her days, and retain the right to buy it if she wished. With Liz working in London, her mother had lived in the octagonal lodge alone, and when the estate's new owner converted Bowerbridge House and its gardens into a specialist plantsman's nursery, she had taken on part-time work there.

Knowing and loving the estate as she did, the job could not have suited Susan Carlyle better. Within the year she was working full-time for the nursery and eighteen months later she was running it. When Liz came up to stay with her at weekends they would go for long walks along the stone-paved avenues and the grassy allées and her mother would explain her hopes and plans for the nursery. Passing the lilacs, rank after cream and purple rank of them, the air heavy with their scent, she would murmur their names like a litany—*Masséna, Decaisne, Belle de Nancy, Persica, Congo* . . . There were entire acres of white and red camellias, too, and rhododendrons—yellow, mauve, scarlet, pink—and orchards of waxily fragrant magnolia. In high summer, every corner turned was a new and dizzying revelation.

At other times, as the rain beat against the glass and the damp green plant odours rose about them, they would pace the iron walkways of the Edwardian greenhouses, and Susan would explain the various propagation techniques as the lines of cuttings and seedlings extended before them to perspective infinity.

Her hope, clearly, was that at some not-too-far-distant point Liz would decide to leave London and involve herself in the management of the nursery. Mother and daughter would then live in happy companionship in the gatehouse, and in the course of time "the right man"—a dimly imagined Sir Lancelot–like figure—would happen along.

Liz was by no means wholly resistant to this idea. The dream of returning home, of waking up in the bedroom in which she had slept as a child and of spending her days surrounded by the mellowed brick and greenery of Bowerbridge, was a seductive one. And she had no objection to handsome knights on white chargers. But in reality she knew that earning a living in the countryside was grindingly hard work, and involved a deliberate narrowing of horizons. As things stood her tastes and friends and opinions were all metropolitan, and she didn't think she had the metabolism to deal with the countryside on a full-time basis. All that rain, all those bossy women with their petty snobberies and their four-wheel drives, all those local newspapers full of non-news and advertisements for agricultural machinery. Much as she loved her mother, Liz knew, she just wouldn't have the patience for it all.

And then that morning the letter had arrived. To say that Susan Carlyle had decided to buy. That she was investing her savings, along with the money that she had earned from the nursery and the life insurance payout after her husband's death, in the Bowerbridge gatehouse.

"Do you think she's trying to draw you back there?" asked Wetherby quietly.

"At some level, yes," said Liz. "At the same time it's a very generous decision. I mean, she can live there for nothing for the rest of her life, so it's me she's thinking of. The trouble is, I think she's hoping for a . . ." she put her glass down and shrugged despairingly, "a corresponding gesture. And right now I just can't think in those terms."

"There's something about the place one grew up in," said Wetherby. "You can never quite return there. Not until you've changed, and can see the place through different eyes. And sometimes not even then."

A spasm of knocking seized the radiator behind his desk, and there was a faint smell of heated dust. Outside the windows the skyline was vague against the winter sky.

"I'm sorry," Liz said. "I didn't mean to burden you with my not very important troubles."

"It's anything but a burden." His gaze, touched with melancholy, played about her. "You're very much valued here."

She sat unmoving for a moment, conscious of things unsaid, and then rose briskly to her feet.

"A—you've been promoted," hazarded Dave Armstrong a couple of minutes later, as she arrived back at her desk. "B—you've been sacked. C—despite heavy-handed official disapproval you're publishing your memoirs. D—none of the above."

"Actually," said Liz, "I'm defecting to North Korea. Pyongyang's heaven at this time of year." She swivelled thoughtfully in her chair. "Have you ever talked to Wetherby about anything except work?"

"I don't think so," said Dave, stabbing pensively at his keyboard. "He once asked me if I knew the test match score, but I think that's as personal as it's ever got. Why?"

"No reason. But Wetherby's sort of a shadowy figure, even for this place, wouldn't you say?"

"You think perhaps he should appear on *Celebrity Big Brother*? As part of the new accountability?"

"You know what I mean."

"I guess." He frowned at his screen. "Do the words Miladun Nabi mean anything to you?"

"Yes, Miladun Nabi is the Prophet's birthday. Sometime at the end of May, I think."

"Cheers."

She turned her attention to the flashing message light on her landline. To her surprise, there was an invitation to lunch from Bruno Mackay.

"I know it's hideously short notice," came the languid voice, "and I'm sure you're already booked, but there's something I'd like to . . . *mull over* with you, if I may."

She shook her head in disbelief. That was so Six, the suggestion that the day—and the business of counter-terrorism—was really one long cocktail party. *Mull?* She never mulled. She anguished, and she did it alone.

But why not? At the very least it would be an opportunity to examine Mackay at close quarters. For all the supposed new spirit of cooperation, Five and Six would never be serene bedfellows. The better she knew her opposite number, the less likely he was to outmanoeuvre her.

She called the number he had left her and he picked up on the first ring.

"Liz!" he said, before she had opened her mouth. "Tell me you can come."

"All right."

"Fantastic! I'll come and pick you up."

"It's OK. I can easily—"

His words cut airily across her. "Can you be on Lambeth Bridge, your end, at twelve forty-five? I'll see you there."

"OK."

She hung up. This could be very interesting, but she was going to have to stay on her toes. Swivelling round to her computer screen, she turned her thoughts to Faraj Mansoor. Fane's anxiety, she supposed, sprung from his uncertainty as to whether the buyer of the fake driving licence in Bremerhaven was the same person as the al Safa contact in Peshawar. He'd probably have someone in Pakistan checking the auto repair shop right now. If they turned out to be different people, and there was still a Faraj Mansoor repairing jeeps on the Kabul Road, then the ball was fairly and squarely in Five's court.

Odds were that they *were* two different people, and that the Mansoor in Bremerhaven was an economic migrant who had paid for passage to Europe—probably some hellish odyssey in a container—and was now looking to make his way across the Channel. There was probably a cousin in one of the British cities keeping a minicab driver's position open for him. Odds were the whole thing was an Immigration issue, not an Intelligence one. She posted it to the back of her mind.

By 12:30 she was feeling a curious anticipation. As luck would have it—or maybe not—she was smartly dressed. With all her work clothes either damp from the washing machine or languishing in the dry-cleaning pile, she had been forced back to the Ronit Zilkha dress she had bought for a wedding. It had cost a fortune, even in the sale, and looked wildly inappropriate for a day's intelligence-gathering. To make matters more extreme, the only shoes that went with the dress were ribbed silk. Wetherby's reaction to her appearance had been a just-detectable widening of the eyes, but he had made no comment.

At twenty to the hour a call came to her desk which, she suspected, had already bounced several times around the building. A group of photographers describing themselves as plane-spotters had been intercepted by police in an area adjacent to the US base at Lakenheath, and USAF Security were insisting that they all be checked out before release. It took Liz a couple of minutes to pass the buck to the investigation section, but she managed it, and hurried out of the office with the Zilkha dress partly covered by her coat.

Lambeth Bridge, she discovered, was not an ideal rendezvous in December. After a fine morning the sky had darkened. A fretful east wind now whipped down the river, dragging at her hair and sending the litter dancing around her silk shoes. The bridge was, furthermore, a no-stopping zone.

She had been standing there for five minutes, her eyes streaming, when a silver BMW came to an abrupt stop at the kerb and the passenger door swung open. To the blaring of car horns she bustled herself into the seat, and Mackay, who was wearing sunglasses, pulled back out into the traffic stream. Inside the car a CD was playing, and the sounds of tabla, sitar and other instruments filled the BMW's high-specification interior.

"Fateh Nusrat Ali Khan," said Mackay, as they swung round the Millbank roundabout. "Huge star on the subcontinent. Know his stuff?"

Liz shook her head and tried to finger-comb her windblown hair into some sort of order. She smiled to herself. The man was just too good to be true—a perfect specimen of the Vauxhall Cross genus. They were crossing the bridge now, and the music was reaching a flurrying climax. As they slotted into the traffic-crawl on Albert Embankment the speakers finally fell silent. Mackay took off his sunglasses.

"So, Liz, how are you?"

"I'm . . . fine," she answered. "Thank you very much."

"Good."

She looked sideways at him. He was wearing a pale blue shirt, open at the neck and with the sleeves rolled halfway up so as to provide a generous expanse of tanned and muscled forearm. The watch, which looked as if it weighed at least half a kilo, was a Breitling Navitimer. And he sported a faded tattoo. A sea horse.

"So!" she said. "To what do I owe the honour . . ."

He shrugged. "We're opposite numbers, you and I. I thought we might have a bite of lunch and a glass or two of wine and compare notes."

"I'm afraid I don't drink at lunchtime," Liz rejoined, and immediately regretted her tone. She sounded shrewish and defensive, and there was no reason to suppose that Mackay was trying to be more than friendly.

"I'm sorry about the short notice," said Mackay, glancing at her.

"No problem. I'm not exactly a lady who lunches, unless you count a Thames House sandwich and a batch of surveillance reports at my desk."

"Don't take this the wrong way," said Mackay, glancing at her again, "but you do actually look quite like someone who lunches."

"I'll take that as a compliment. In fact, I'm dressed like this because I've got a meeting this afternoon."

"Ah. You're running an agent in Harvey Nichols?"

She smiled and looked away. The vast and intolerant bulk of the MI6 building rose above them, and then Mackay swung left-handed into the convolutions of Vauxhall's one-way system. Two minutes later they were turning into a narrow cul-de-sac off South Lambeth Road. Pulling into the forecourt of a small tyre and exhaust centre, Mackay parked the BMW, jumped out, and opened Liz's door for her.

"You can't just leave it here," protested Liz.

"I've got a little arrangement with them," said Mackay breezily, waving a greeting to a man in oil-streaked overalls. "Strictly cash, so I can't claim it as a business expense, but they do keep an eye on the car. Are you hungry?"

"I think I am," said Liz.

"Excellent." Taking an indigo tie and a dark blue jacket from the back seat, he rolled down his sleeves and put them on. Had he taken them off just for the drive? Liz wondered. Just so she didn't think him too much of a stiff?

He locked the car with a quick squawk of the remote. "Do you think those shoes will carry you a couple of hundred yards?" he asked.

"With a bit of luck."

They turned back towards the river, and after negotiating an under-pass came out at the foot of a new luxury development on the south side of Vauxhall Bridge. Greeting the security staff, Mackay led Liz through the atrium into a busy and attractive restaurant. The tablecloths were white linen, the silver and glassware shone, and the dark panorama of the Thames was framed by a curtained sweep of plate glass. Most of the tables were occupied. The muted buzz of conversation dipped for a moment as they entered. Leaving her coat at the desk, Liz followed Mackay to a table overlooking the river.

"This is all very nice and unexpected," she said sincerely. "Thank you for inviting me."

"Thank you for accepting."

"I'm assuming a fair few of these people are your lot?"

"One or two of them are, and when you walked across the room just then, you enhanced my standing by several hundred per cent. You will note that we're being discreetly observed."

She smiled. "I do note it. You should send your colleagues down-river for one of our surveillance courses."

They examined the menus. Leaning forward confidentially, Mackay told Liz that he could predict what she was going to order. Taking a pen from his pocket he handed it to her and told her to tick what she had chosen.

Taking care not to let him see, holding the menu beneath the table, Liz marked a salad of smoked duck breast. It was a starter, but she wrote the words "as main course" next to it.

"OK," continued Mackay. "Now fold the menu up. Put it in your pocket."

She did so. She was certain that he hadn't seen what she'd written.

When the waiter came Mackay ordered a venison steak and a glass of Italian Barolo. "And for my colleague," he added with a faint smile, nodding at Liz, "the duck breast salad. As a main course."

"Very clever," said Liz, frowning. "How did you do that?"

"Classified. Have some wine."

She would have liked some, but felt that she had to stick with her not-at-lunchtime statement. "I won't, thanks."

"Just a glass. Keep me company."

"OK, just one then. Tell me how you . . ."

"You don't have the security clearance."

Liz looked around her. No one could possibly have seen what she'd written. Nor were there any reflective surfaces in sight.

"Funny guy. Tell me."

"Like I said . . ."

"Just tell me," she said, overcome by irritation.

"OK, I will. We've developed contact lenses that enable us to see through documents. I'm wearing a pair now."

She narrowed her eyes at him. Despite her determination to remain objective, and to view the lunch as a kind of reconnaissance, she was beginning to feel distinctly angry.

"And you know something," he continued in a low murmur, "they work on fabric too."

Before Liz could respond, a shadow fell across the white tablecloth, and she looked up to see Geoffrey Fane standing over her.

"Elizabeth. What a pleasure to see you on our side of the river. I hope Bruno's looking after you properly?"

"Indeed," she said, and fell silent. There was something chilling about Fane's efforts to be friendly.

He gave a slight bow. "Please give my regards to Charles Wetherby. As you know, or should know, we hold your department in the highest esteem."

"Thank you," said Liz. "I will."

At that moment the food arrived. As Fane moved away Liz glanced at Mackay, and was in time to see a look of complicity—or the shadow of such a look—pass between the two men. What was that all about? Surely not just the fact that one of them was entertaining a female of the species to lunch. Was there an element of the put-up job about the occasion? Fane hadn't seemed very surprised to see her.

"Tell me," she said. "How is it, being back here?"

Mackay ran a hand through his sun-faded hair. "It's good," he said. "Islamabad was fascinating, but hard-core. I was undeclared there rather than part of the accredited diplomatic team, and while that meant I could get a lot more done in agent-running terms, it was also a lot more stressful."

"You lived off-base?"

"Yes, in one of the suburbs. Nominally I was employed by one of the banks, so I turned up every day in a suit and then did the social circuit in the evening. After that I'd usually be up all night either debriefing agents or encrypting and flashing reports back to London. So while it was fascinating being at the sharp end of the game, it was pretty knackering too."

"What drew you into the business in the first place?"

A smile touched the sculpted curve of his mouth. "Probably the same as you. The chance to practise the deceit that has always come naturally."

"Has it? Always come naturally, I mean?"

"I'm told that I lied very early. And I never went into exams at school without a crib. I'd write it all up the night before with a mapping pen on airmail paper, and then roll it up inside a biro tube."

"Is that how you got into Six?"

"No, sadly, it wasn't. I think they just took one look at me, decided I was a suitably devious piece of work, and dragged me in."

"What was the reason you gave for wanting to join?"

"Patriotism. It seemed the right line to take at the time."

"And is that the true reason?"

"Well, you know what they say. Last refuge of the scoundrel, and so on. Really, of course, it was the women. All those glamorous Foreign Office secretaries. I've always had a Moneypenny complex."

"I don't see many Moneypennys in here."

The grey eyes flickered amusedly around the room. "It does rather look as if I got it wrong, doesn't it? Still, easy come, easy go. How about you?"

"I never had a secret agent complex, I'm afraid. I was one of the first intake that answered that 'Waiting for Godot?' advert."

"Like the chatty Mr. Shayler."

"Exactly."

"Do you reckon you'll go the distance? Stay in till you're fifty-five or sixty or whatever the cut-off is for your lot? Or will you leave and join Lynx or Kroll or one of those private security consultancies? Or go off and have babies with a merchant banker?"

"Are those the alternatives? It's a grim list."

The waiter approached, and before Liz could protest Mackay had pointed at their glasses to indicate a refill. Liz took advantage of the brief hiatus to take stock of the situation. Bruno Mackay was an outrageous flirt but he was undeniably good company. She was having a much better day than she would have had if he hadn't rung her.

"I don't think I'd find it easy to leave the Service," she said carefully. "It's been my world for ten years now." And it had. She had answered the advertisement during her last term at university and had joined the next spring's intake. Her first three years, interrupted at intervals by training courses, had been spent on the Northern Ireland desk as a trainee. The work—sifting intelligence, making enquiries, preparing assessments—had been at times repetitive and at times stressful. Then she'd moved to counter-espionage and after three years—or had it been four?—there had been an unexpected secondment to Liverpool, to the Merseyside Police Force, followed by a transfer to the organised crime desk at Thames House. The work had been unremitting and her section leader, a dour ex–police officer named Donaldson, had made it abundantly clear that he disliked working with women. When the section finally had a breakthrough—a breakthrough for which Liz was largely responsible—things had started to look brighter. She was transferred to counter-terrorism, and discovered that Wetherby had been watching her progress for some time. "I'd quite understand if you'd had enough of it all," he had told her with a melancholy smile. "If you'd looked at the world outside, seen the rewards available to someone of your abilities and the freedom and sociability of it all . . ." But by then she was certain that she didn't want to do anything else. "I'm in for the duration," she told Mackay. "I couldn't go back."

His hand moved across the table and covered hers. "You know what I think?" he said. "I think we're all exiles from our own pasts."

Liz looked down at his hand, and the big Breitling watch on his wrist, and after a moment he released her. The gesture, like everything about him, was untroubled, and left no after-trace of awkwardness or doubt. Did his words actually mean anything? They had a well-worn ring about them. To how many other women had he said precisely the same thing, and in precisely the same tone?

"So what about you, then?" she asked. "Where are you in exile from?"

"Nowhere terribly special," he said. "My parents divorced when I was quite young, and I grew up shunting backwards and forwards between my father's house in the Test Valley and my mother's place in the South of France."

"Are they both still alive?"

"I'm afraid so. In rude good health."

"And did you join the Service straight out of university?"

"No. I read Arabic at Cambridge and went into the City as a Middle East analyst for one of the investment banks. Did a bit of territorial soldiering at the same time with the HAC."

"The what?"

"The Honourable Artillery Company. Running round letting off explosives on Salisbury Plain. Good fun. But banking lost its shine after a bit, so I sat the Foreign Office exam. Do you want some pud?"

"No, I don't want any pud, thanks, and I didn't really want that second glass of wine either. I should be thinking about getting back across the river."

"I'm sure our respective bosses won't object to a little . . . inter-Service liaison work," protested Mackay. "At least have some coffee."

She agreed, and he signalled to the waiter.

"So tell me," she said, when the coffee had been brought. "How *did* you see what I'd written on the menu?"

He laughed. "I didn't. But every woman I've eaten with here has ordered the same thing."

Liz stared at him. "We're that predictable, are we?"

"Actually, I've only been here once before, and that was with half a dozen people. Three of them were women and they all ordered what you ordered. End of story."

She looked at him levelly. Breathed deeply. "How old were you, again, when you started lying?"

"I can't win, can I?"

"Probably not," said Liz. She drank her thimbleful of espresso in a single swallow. "But then who you have lunch with is no business whatsoever of mine."

He looked at her with a knowing half-smile. "It could be."

"I have to go," she said.

"Have a brandy. Or a Calvados or something. It's cold outside."

"No thanks, I'm off."

He raised his hands in surrender and summoned the waiter.

Outside the sky was sheet steel. The wind dragged at their hair and clothes. "It's been fun," he said, taking her hands.

"Yes," she agreed, carefully retrieving them. "I'll see you on Monday."

He nodded, the half-smile still in place. To Liz's relief, someone was getting out of a taxi.

10

Dersthorpe Strand was a melancholy place at the best of times, and in December, it seemed to Diane Munday, it was the end of the world. Despite the goose-down skiing jacket, she shivered as she descended from the Cherokee four-wheel drive.

Diane did not live in Dersthorpe. A handsome woman in her early fifties with expensively streaked blonde hair and a Barbados tan, she lived with her husband Ralph in a Georgian manor house on the edge of Marsh Creake, three and a half miles to the east. There was a good golf links outside Marsh Creake, and a little sailing club and the Trafalgar. Carry on along the coast and you got to Brancaster and the yacht club proper, and three miles beyond that was Burnham Market, which in terms of desirability was pretty much Chelsea-on-Sea, with house prices to match.

There was evidence of none of these benefits in Dersthorpe. Dersthorpe had a Country and Western theme pub (the Lazy "W"), a coach park, a Londis mini-mart, and a wind-scoured council estate. In summer, an unlicenced burger van took up seasonal residence on the sea front.

Beyond Dersthorpe, vanishing westwards towards the Wash, was the desolate strip of coastline known to locals as the Strand. A mile or so along its length stood five 1950s-built bungalows. At some point in their recent history, presumably in an attempt to resist nature's relentless monotone, these had been painted in jaunty pinks and yellows and tangerines. The salt air, however, had long since leached the colour and curled the paint flakes from the weatherboards, returning them to faded homogeneity. None of them had a TV aerial or a telephone connection.

Diane Munday had bought the Strand bungalows a year earlier as an investment. She hadn't liked them—in truth, they gave her the creeps—but an examination of the previous owner's returns had convinced her that they would give a handsome cash profit in return for a minimum of expenditure and effort. The bungalows usually stood empty during the late autumn and winter, but even then the occasional birdwatcher or writer showed up. A surprising number of people, strange though it seemed to Diane, craved the near nothingness that the Strand offered. The unceasing slap of tide on shingle, the wind in the salt marshes, the empty junction of sea and sky—these seemed to be more than enough.

Hopefully they would satisfy the young woman now standing with her back to the westernmost of the bungalows. A postgraduate student apparently, completing a thesis. Dressed in a parka, jeans and walking boots, and holding the Tourist Board directory in which Diane advertised, she was staring expectantly towards the horizon as the wind blew her hair about her face and the sea dragged at the grey and white shingle in front of her.

Like the French Lieutenant's Woman, thought Diane, who had long harboured a *tendresse* for the actor Jeremy Irons, but younger, and not as pretty. How old was she? Twenty-two or three, perhaps? And could probably get herself looking quite presentable if she could be bothered to make the effort. The hair needed work—that dull walnut-brown bob was screaming for the attentions of a decent colourist—but the basic structure was there. Not that you could tell girls of that age anything; Diane had tried with Miranda and had her head bitten off for her pains.

"It's such a lovely spot, isn't it?" she said, assuming a proprietorial smile. "So peaceful."

The woman frowned absently. "How much for the week, including deposit?"

Diane hiked the price as high as she dared. The woman didn't look particularly wealthy—the parka, the mud-streaked Astra—but nor did she look as if she could be bothered to continue her search. Parental money, almost certainly.

"Can I pay cash?"

"Certainly you can," said Diane, and smiled. "That's settled then. I'm Diane Munday, as you know, and you're . . ."

"Lucy. Lucy Wharmby."

They shook hands, and Diane noticed that the other woman's grip was surprisingly hard. With the deal concluded, she drove off eastwards, towards Marsh Creake.

The woman who called herself Lucy Wharmby watched thoughtfully after her. When the Cherokee had finally disappeared into Dersthorpe, she took a pair of lightweight Nikon binoculars from beneath her coat and checked the coast road. On a clear day, she calculated, an approaching vehicle would be visible almost a mile away to east or west.

Opening the passenger door of the Astra, she reached for her holdall and rucksack and carried them through the front door of the bungalow into the white-emulsioned front room. On the table in front of the seaward window she placed her velcro-sealing wallet, her binoculars, her quartz diver's watch, a Pfleuger clasp knife, a small NATO survival compass, and her Nokia mobile phone. She switched on the Nokia, which she had recharged in her room in the Travel Lodge on the A11 the night before. It was almost 15:00 hours GMT. Seating herself cross-legged on a low divan against the wall, half closing her eyes against the thin light, she began the steady process of voiding her mind of all that was irrelevant to her task.

11

The call reached Liz's desk shortly after 3:30. It had come through the central switchboard, because the caller had dialled the publicly advertised MI5 number and asked for Liz by an alias she'd used a couple of years earlier when she was working in the organised crime section. The caller, who was in an Essex phone box, had been placed on hold while Liz was asked if she wanted to speak to him. He had identified himself as Zander.

As soon as Liz heard the code-name she asked for him to be put through, demanded his number, and called him back. It was a long time since she had heard from Frankie Ferris, and she was far from sure that she wanted to hear from him again. If he had sought her out after three years' silence, however, and defied all the standard agent protocols by ringing the switchboard, it was just possible that he had something useful to tell her.

She had first encountered Ferris when, as an agent-runner for the organised crime team, she had been part of a move against an Essex syndicate boss named Melvin Eastman who was suspected of—amongst other crimes—moving large quantities of heroin between Amsterdam and Harwich. Surveillance had identified Ferris as one of Eastman's drivers, and when gently pressured by Essex Special Branch he had agreed to provide information on the syndicate's activities. Essex Special Branch had passed him to MI5.

From her earliest days with the service Liz had had an instinctive understanding of the dynamics of agent-running. At one end of the scale there were agents like Marzipan who informed on their colleagues out of patriotism or moral conviction, and at the other end there were those who worked strictly out of self-interest, or for cash. Zander was halfway between the two. With him, the issue was essentially an emotional one. He wanted Liz's esteem. He wanted her to value him, to give him her undivided attention, to sit and listen to his catalogue of the world's unfairnesses.

Discerning this, Liz had made the necessary time, and gradually, like flowers laid at her feet, the information had come in. Some of this was of dubious value; like many agents avid for their handlers' approval, Ferris had a tendency to flannel Liz with half-remembered irrelevancies. But he managed to note and pass on the landline and mobile phone numbers of several of Eastman's associates, and to list the registration numbers of vehicles which visited the Romford works unit where Eastman then had his HQ.

This was useful, and added substantially to MI5's knowledge of Eastman's operations, but Ferris was never admitted to Eastman's inner circle, and had little or no access to hard intelligence. His days were spent as a glorified minicab driver, ferrying female croupiers from Eastman's casinos to and from lunch with Eastman's business associates, delivering smuggled tobacco to pubs, and distributing cases of bootleg CDs and DVDs around the markets.

In the end, it had proved impossible to build a satisfactory case against the highly security-conscious Eastman, and as a result he had grown stronger. And probably, thought Liz, moved into the sale of worse and more profitable commodities than dodgy CDs. He was certainly responsible for the regular distribution of Ecstasy to the many nightclub dealers in his area—a hugely profitable enterprise—and the Branch were certain that several of his legitimate businesses were covers for scams of one sort or another.

Essex Special Branch had remained on the case, and when Liz moved to Wetherby's counter-terrorism section, the running of Zander was taken over by one of their officers, a hard-bitten Ulsterman named Bob Morrison. It was Morrison rather than Liz that Ferris should have rung.

"Tell me, Frankie," Liz began.

"Big drop-off Friday, at the headland. Twenty, plus a special, from Germany." Ferris's voice was steady, but he was clearly nervous.

"You've got to tell Bob Morrison, Frankie. I don't know what this means, and I can't act on it."

"I'm not telling Morrison any fuckin' thing—this is for you."

"I don't know what any of it means, Frankie. I'm out of that game, and you shouldn't be ringing me."

"Friday, at the headland," repeated Frankie urgently. "Twenty plus a special. From Germany. Have you got that?"

"I've written it down. What's the source?"

"Eastman. Took a call when I was there a couple of days ago. He was furious—really done his bollocks."

"You still working for him?"

"Bits and pieces."

"Anything else?"

"No."

"You in a phone box?"

"Yeah."

"Make another call before you leave. Don't leave this as the last number dialled."

They hung up, and for several minutes Liz stared at the scraps of phrases on the notepad in front of her. Then she dialled the Essex Special Branch number and asked for Bob Morrison. Minutes later he called her back from a motorway payphone.

"Did Ferris say why he called you?" the Special Branch officer asked her, his voice echoing indistinctly in her earpiece.

"No, he didn't," said Liz. "But he was adamant he wasn't talking to you."

There was a brief silence. Reception was poor, and amongst the static Liz could hear the whine of car horns.

"As a source," said Morrison, "Frankie Ferris is a total write-off. Ninety per cent of the money Eastman pays him goes straight over the betting shop counter, and I wouldn't be surprised if he's using, too. He's probably made the whole thing up."

"That's possible," said Liz carefully.

There was a long moment of crackle.

". . . going to get anything useful while Eastman's putting money his way."

"And if he isn't any more?" asked Liz.

"If he isn't, I wouldn't give much for his . . ."

"You think Eastman would get rid of him?"

"I think he'd consider it. Frankie knows enough to bury him. But I don't think it would come to that. Melvin Eastman's a businessman. Easier to see him as a business overhead, throw a bit of cash . . ."

More car horns. "You're . . ."

". . . useful work out of him. They're joined at the waist, basically."

"OK. Do you want me to send you what Frankie told me?"

"Yeah, why not?"

They rang off. Liz had covered herself; as for the information being acted on, that was something else.

Once again she stared at the fragmentary phrases. A drop-off of what? Drugs? Weapons? People? A drop-off from Germany? Where would that have originated? If it was a sea landing, and the word "head-land" suggested that it was, then perhaps she should have a look at the northern ports.

Just to be on the safe side—and it could be hours before Morrison got back to his office—she decided to have a word with a contact in Customs and Excise. Where was the nearest UK landfall from the German ports? Had to be East Anglia, which was Eastman's patch. No small craft bringing dodgy cargo from the northeast was going to run the gauntlet of the Channel; they'd go for the hundred-odd miles of unguarded coastline between Felixstowe and the Wash.

12

The *Susanne Hanke* was a twenty-two-metre Krabbenkutter stern-trawler, and after more than thirty hours at sea Faraj Mansoor loathed every rust-streaked inch of her. He was a proud man, but he did not look like one as he crouched in the vomit-slicked fish-hold with his twenty fellow passengers. Most of these, like Faraj, were Afghans, but there were also Pakistanis, Iranians, a couple of Iraqi Kurds and a mute, suffering Somali.

All were identically dressed in used blue mechanics' overalls. In a warehouse near the Bremerhaven docks they had been stripped of the rancid garments in which they had travelled from their various countries of origin, permitted to shave and shower, and fitted out with second-hand jeans, sweaters and windcheaters from the city's charity shops. They were also handed the overalls, and by the time the twenty-one of them were gathered around the bonfire of their old clothing they looked, to the casual eye, like a team of guest workers. Before embarking on the sea crossing they had been given bread rolls, coffee, and individual servings of hot mutton stew in foil cartons—a meal which, over the course of the eighteen months that the Caravan had been up and running, had proved acceptable to the bulk of its clients.

The Caravan had been set up to provide what its organisers described as "Grade 1 covert trans-shipment" of economic migrants from Asia to Northern Europe and the United Kingdom. The passage was not luxurious, but a concerted attempt had been made to provide a humane and functional service. For twenty thousand US dollars, customers were promised safe travel, appropriate EU documentation (including passports), and twenty-four hours of hostel accommodation on arrival.

This was in marked contrast to previous people-smuggling endeavours. In the past, in return for hefty cash sums at the point of departure, migrants had been delivered filthy, traumatised and half starved to motorway lay-bys on the UK's south coast, and abandoned without currency or documents to fend for themselves. Many had died en route, usually of suffocation in sealed containers or trucks.

The organisers of the Caravan, however, knew that in an age of split-second communications their long-term interests were best served by a reputation for efficiency. Hence the overalls, whose grim purpose became clear the moment the *Susanne Hanke* cleared the port of Bremerhaven. The cutter's draught was shallow, perhaps a metre and a half, and while the vessel was equal in terms of stability to anything the North Sea might throw at it, it pitched and rolled like a pig in bad weather. And the weather, from the moment the *Susanne Hanke* made open sea, was very bad, blowing an unremitting December gale. On top of this the Caterpillar power plant, pushing out a steady 375 horsepower, swiftly filled the converted fish-hold with the queasy stink of diesel.

Neither of these factors worried the *Susanne Hanke*'s bearded German master or his two-man crew, as they held a steady westwards course in the heated wheelhouse. But they had a disastrous effect on the passengers. Cheerfully exchanged cigarettes and optimistic bursts of Hindi film song swiftly gave way to retching and misery. The men tried to remain seated on their benches, but the motion of the boat alternately pitched them backwards against the bulwarks or forwards into the ice-cold bilge at their feet. The overalls were soon streaked with bile and vomit—and, in a couple of cases, blood from cracked noses. Above their heads the men's suitcases and haversacks swung crazily in the netting carrier.

And the weather, as the hours passed, had got steadily worse. The seas, although invisible to the men crouched beneath the foredeck, were mountainous. The men clutched each other as the hull reared and fell, but were thrown, hour after hour, around the steel-ribbed hold. Their bodies battered and bruised, their feet frozen, their throats raw from heaving, they had given up any pretence of dignity.

Faraj Mansoor concentrated on survival. The cold he could deal with; he was a mountain man. With the exception of the Somali, who was groaning tearfully to his left, they could all deal with the cold. But this nausea was something else, and he worried that it would weaken him beyond the point where he could defend himself.

The migrants hadn't been prepared for the rigours of the four-hundred-mile voyage. The crossing of Iran in the stifling heat of the container had been uncomfortable, but from Turkey onwards—through Macedonia, Bosnia, Serbia and Hungary—their progress had been relatively painless. There had been fearful moments, but the Caravan drivers knew which were the most porous borders, and which the easiest-bribed border guards.

Most, but not all, of the border crossings had been effected at night. At Esztergom, in northwest Hungary, they had found a deserted playing field and an old football and enjoyed a kick-around and a smoke before trooping back into the truck for the Morava river crossing into the Slovak Republic. The final crossing, into Germany, had taken place at Liberec, fifty miles north of Prague, and a day later they were stretching their legs in Bremerhaven. There, they had dossed down amongst the warehouse's disused lathes and workbenches. The photographer had come, and twelve hours later they had received their passports, and in the case of Faraj, his UK driving licence. Along with his other documents, this was now zipped into the inside pocket of the windcheater which he was wearing beneath the filthy overalls.

Bracing himself in his seat, Faraj rode out the *Susanne Hanke*'s rise and fall. Was it his imagination, or were those hellish peaks and troughs finally beginning to subside? He pressed the Indiglo light button on his watch. It was a little past 2 a.m., UK time. In the watch's tiny glow he could see the pale, fearful faces of his fellow travellers, huddled like ghosts. To rally them, he suggested prayers.

At 2:30 a.m., Ray Gunter finally saw it. The light that the *Susanne Hanke* was showing was too muted to register to the naked eye, but through the image-intensifiers it showed up as a clear green bloom near the horizon.

"Gotcha," he muttered, flipping the butt of his cigarette to the shingle. His hands were frozen but tension, as always, kept the cold at bay.

"We on?" asked Kieran Mitchell.

"Yeah. Let's go."

Together they pushed the boats into the water, felt the spray at their faces and the icy water at their calves. As the more experienced seaman, Gunter took the lead vessel. Cracking a lightstick so that it glowed a fluorescent blue, he placed it in a holder on the stern; it was essential that the two boats did not get separated.

Yards apart, the two men began to row through the choppy offshore swell, correcting against the hard eastern blow. Both of them were wearing heavyweight waterproofs and lifejackets. A hundred yards out they shipped their oars and pull-started the Evinrude outboards. These burbled into life, their sound carried away on the wind. Locking into Gunter's wake, his eyes fixed on the lightstick, Mitchell followed the other man out to sea.

Ten minutes later they were alongside the *Susanne Hanke*. Clutching their meagre baggage items, and divested of the fouled overalls (which would be washed in preparation for the next consignment of illegals), the passengers exited the hold one by one, and were helped down a ladder to the boats. This was a slow and dangerous process to undertake in near darkness and high seas, but half an hour later all twenty-one of them were seated with their baggage stowed at their feet. All except one, that is. One of them, a courteous but determined figure, insisted on carrying his heavy rucksack on his back. And if you go over the side, mate, thought Mitchell, it's your bloody lookout.

Kieran Mitchell knew only one word of Urdu—*khamosh*, which means "silence." In the event, though, he had no need of it. The cargo, as usual, looked cowed, fearful and properly respectful. As a self-styled patriot Mitchell had no time for raghead illegals, and would have been much happier sending the whole bloody lot of them home. As a businessman, however—and a businessman in the full-time employ of Melvin Eastman—his hands were tied.

The return journey to shore was the part Mitchell dreaded. The old wooden fishing boats could only just manage a complement of twelve, and sat terrifyingly low in the water. Superior seamanship kept Gunter's people more or less dry, but Mitchell's were not so lucky. Waves broke almost continuously over their bows, drenching them. In the end it was a shivering and bedraggled group which helped him drag the boat up the beach and—as every consignment did—fell to its collective knees on the wet shingle to give thanks for its safe arrival. All except one, that is. All except the man with the black rucksack, who just stood there, looking around him.

Once the boats were in place Gunter and Mitchell removed their lifejackets and waterproofs. As Gunter unlocked a small wooden shed at the beach's edge and hung the gear inside, Mitchell lined the men up and led them in single file away from the sea.

The shingle gave way to a turf path, which in turn led up to an open ironwork gate, which Mitchell closed behind them. They marched upwards, and the shapes of trees appeared against the faint illumination of the false dawn. These gave way to formal hedges and the flat plane of a lawn before the path led them to the left. A high wall appeared in front of them, and a door. Gunter opened this with a key, and Mitchell pulled it shut behind the last man. They were now in a narrow side road bordered by the wall on one side and by trees on the other. Some fifty yards up the road, hard against the trees, was the dim outline of an articulated truck.

Unpadlocking the back entrance of the truck, Mitchell led the migrants inside. When they were all in position at the front of the container, Mitchell pulled an alloy barrier across which, draped as it was with ropes and sacking, effectively formed a false front to the container. Beyond it, the migrants were crammed into an area approximately three feet deep, with a ventilation fan in the ceiling. The arrangement was not foolproof, but to the casual observer—a policeman with a torch, for example, looking in from the back—the artic was empty.

Mitchell drove, and Gunter took the passenger seat next to him. To begin with, for a good five minutes, they crept along an uneven country lane without showing any lights. Once in sight of the main road, however, Mitchell turned on the headlights and accelerated.

"Force nine out there earlier," he said. "Bet they've been spewing their guts all the way."

"They did look a bit buggered," admitted Gunter, reaching into his pocket for his lighter and his cigarettes. He usually went home to bed at this stage of the game, but this morning he was taking a ride off Mitchell as far as King's Lynn, where his sister Kayleigh had a council flat. He'd rather have driven there in his own car, but that silly-bugger Munday woman had ploughed into the back of it with her four-wheel drive. The

Toyota was in Brancaster, getting a new tailgate, lights and exhaust system. The old exhaust was just knackered, nothing to do with the shunt, but the garage had been more than happy to quote for a new system and charge it to the insurance. Least said, soonest mended.

Twenty minutes later the artic pulled into the lorry park of a transport café on the A148 outside Fakenham. This was where, according to instructions, the "special" was to be let out.

As the lorry's hydraulics gassily exhaled, Gunter took a heavy fourteen-inch Maglite torch from the passenger-side locker and jumped down from the cab. Unlocking the rear doors he clambered inside, switched on the torch and opened the forward compartment a crack.

The man with the rucksack presented himself. He was of medium height, lightly built, with unruly black hair and a studious half-smile. The rucksack, expensive-looking but unbranded, hung heavily from his narrow shoulders. Victim written all over him, thought Gunter. No wonder these Pakis get pushed around. And yet somewhere he'd found twenty grand for his transit. His dad's life savings, that'd be, and probably half a dozen aunties chipping in too. And all so that the poor sod could spend his life shovelling curry or flogging newspapers in some dingy city like Bradford. Unbelievable. As he relocked the false wall, Gunter glanced at the young Asian—at the worn jeans, the cheap windcheater, and the narrow, fatigued features. Not for the first time in his life he gave sincere thanks that he'd been born white, and beneath the flag of St. George.

He watched as the special lowered himself to the ground, searched the unprepossessing nightscape, and hitched the heavy rucksack higher up his back. What did he have in there that had to be so carefully guarded? Gunter wondered. Something valuable, that was for sure. Maybe even gold—he wouldn't be the first illegal to carry in a slab of the shiny stuff.

Following Mansoor to the ground, Gunter locked up the truck. From the open cab window, up the front, came the drift of Mitchell's cigarette smoke.

Mansoor held out his hand. "Thank you," he said.

"Pleasure," said Gunter brusquely. His large callused hand dwarfed Mansoor's.

The Afghan nodded, his half-smile still in place. Rucksack on back, he began to walk the fifty-odd yards to the white-painted toilet block.

Gunter came to a snap decision, and when the door of the block had opened and closed, he followed in Mansoor's footsteps. Extinguishing the Maglite, he reversed it in his hand so that he was holding it by the knurled grip. Stepping into the toilet block he saw that one of the stalls was occupied, but that otherwise the place was empty. Genuflecting, he saw the base of Mansoor's rucksack through the gap beneath the door. It was shaking slightly, as if its contents were being repacked. I was right, Gunter thought, the sneaky bastard *has* got something in there. Shaking his head at the perfidy of Asians in general, he crossed to the urinal to wait.

When Mansoor stepped out of the stall a couple of minutes later with the rucksack hoisted over one shoulder, Gunter rushed him, swinging the big Maglite like a steel-jacketed nightstick. The improvised weapon smashed into Mansoor's upper arm, sending him staggering, and the rucksack sliding to the floor.

Gasping with pain, and furious with himself for having allowed fatigue to override caution, Mansoor made a desperate grab for the rucksack with his good arm, but the fisherman got there first, clubbing at Mansoor's head with the Maglite so that the Afghan had to throw himself backwards to avoid having his jaw or skull shattered.

Skidding the rucksack out of reach, Gunter kicked Mansoor hard in the guts and crotch. As his victim writhed and clawed for breath, he grabbed for his spoils. The rucksack's weight, however, slowed him down. The couple of seconds' hesitation as he swung it over his shoulder was long enough for Mansoor to reach agonisedly inside his windcheater. He would have shouted if he could have—attracted Gunter's attention to the silenced weapon, made the stupid English lout drop the rucksack before it was too late—but there wasn't the breath in his body.

And he couldn't lose sight of the rucksack; that would be the end of everything.

Faraj Mansoor's choices raced to the vanishing point.

The detonation was no louder than the snapping of a stick. It was the impact of the heavy calibre round that made the noise, such as it was.

13

Pruning shears in her gloved hand, Anne Lakeby moved purposefully along the bank of ornamental sedges and grasses at the foot of the front lawn, cutting back the dead stems. It was a fine morning, cold and clear, and her Wellington boots left crisp imprints in the frosted turf. The shoulder-high grasses prevented any sight of the beach below, but the brownish glitter of the sea showed beyond them.

In her youth, Anne had been described as "handsome." With age, however, her long features had contracted to a benign gauntness. Robust and unfussy—a pillar of local charities and good works—she was a popular figure in the community, and there were few events in and around Marsh Creake at which her loud neighing laugh was not to be heard. Like the Hall itself, she had become something of a landmark.

In thirty-five years of marriage Anne had never developed much of a fondness for the grey late-Victorian sprawl which her husband had inherited. The house had been built by Perry's great-grandfather, to replace a much finer building which had burnt down, and she had always found it severe and uninviting. The gardens, however, were her pride and joy. The weathered brickwork, the sweep of the lawn to the shore, the subtle interplay of textures and colours in the mature borders—all of these brought her deep and lasting pleasure. She worked hard to maintain them, and opened the grounds to the public several times a year. In the early spring, people came from far and wide to enjoy the display of snowdrops and aconites.

Perry had brought the house to their marriage, but it was all that he had brought. Born to a local landowning family, Anne had inherited on the grand scale when her parents had died, and had made it her business to keep her personal accounts separate from her husband's. Many couples would have found such a relationship unsustainable, but Anne and Perry managed to rub along together without too much friction. She was fond of him, she enjoyed his company, and within limits was prepared to indulge him in the little things which made him happy. But she liked to know what was going on in his life, and right now she didn't. Something was up.

A cold sea breeze rustled the sedges and agitated the feathery heads of the grasses. Pocketing the secateurs, Anne proceeded towards the path which led to the beach. This, like the lawn, was still frosted hard, but Anne noticed that it had recently been considerably churned up. That bloody man Gunter, she supposed. She didn't see him in person all that often, but she saw signs of his presence all the time—cigarette ends, heavy footprints—and it was beginning to annoy her profoundly. Given an inch, Ray Gunter was the type to take a mile. He knew that she had never liked him, and he didn't give a damn. Why Perry put up with him tramping backwards and forwards through their property, night and day, she would never know.

She turned back to the house. The bank of grasses and sedges marked the end of the garden proper. The lawn was bordered by frozen beds of closely pruned old roses. The whole was enclosed by a pair of brick walls, above which maples and other deciduous trees stood starkly against the winter sky. The sight gave Anne a moment's profound satisfaction before reminding her of the second reason for her irritation, which was that Diane Munday had decided to open her own garden to the public on precisely the same day that Anne herself had.

What had possessed the woman, God alone knew. She knew, or she damn well ought to have known, that the Hall always threw its gates open to the public on the last Saturday before Christmas. There wasn't a great deal to admire in the garden at that time of year, but it was a tradition: people paid a couple of pounds to wander round the gardens— all profits to the St. John Ambulance Brigade—and then, believers or no, went on to the carol service and mince pies at the church.

But there was no telling people like the Mundays. They had a decent house, granted. Several million pounds' worth of elegant Georgian manor house on the other side of the village, to be precise, all paid for out of the lavish salaries and bonuses that Sir Ralph Munday had seen fit to award himself in his final years in the City. And the gardens at Creake Manor were OK too—or had been before Diane had got her over-manicured hands on them. Now it was all Sheraton-style coach-lights and fancy trelliswork and horrid little fast-growing conifers. And that swimming pool, which seemed to think it was part of a Roman villa, and the pink pampas grass . . . One could go on pretty much indefinitely. When the Mundays opened their garden to the public the event had nothing in the world to do with horticulture, and everything to do with a crass display of wealth.

Which was fine, Anne supposed—not everyone had been born with one's social advantages. And one didn't want to appear boringly snotty and stuffy. But the silly woman could have troubled to check the date. Really, she could have bothered to do that, at the very least.

Her thoughts were interrupted by the crackling roar of fighter jets. She looked upwards as three US Air Force fighters drew cursive trails across the hard blue of the sky. Lakenheath, she supposed vaguely. Or Mildenhall. How many miles to the gallon did those things do? Pretty few, she supposed—rather like Diane's ridiculously oversized four-wheel drive. Which reminded her that police cars had been whizzing backwards and forwards in front of the house since well before breakfast. Extraordinary. The place was like Piccadilly Circus at times.

Anne walked down the path towards the sea. The Hall and its gardens occupied an elevated spit of land flanked to east and west by open mudflats. At high tide these were covered by the sea but at low tide they lay shining and exposed, the domain of cormorants, terns and oystercatchers. At the far point of the spit, beyond the garden, was the seventy-yard bank of shingle known as the Hall Beach. This was the only navigable landfall for a couple of miles in either direction, and as such afforded Anne and Perry Lakeby considerable privacy. Or would have done, mused Anne grumpily, had it not also been the place where Gunter kept his boats and nets.

The shingle crunched underfoot, and the brine was sharp in the air. There had been a bit of a blow the night before, Anne remembered, but the sea had settled. For a moment she gazed out towards the horizon, and surrendered herself to the ebb and wash of the tide. Then something caught her eye on the wet shingle at her feet. Bending, she lifted a tiny silver hand, a charm of some kind. Pretty, she thought absently, and slipped it into the pocket of her puffa jacket. She had taken several paces before she stopped dead in her tracks, wondering where in Heaven's name it had come from.

14

Liz arrived at her desk at 8:30 to discover a switchboard message to contact Zander as a matter of urgency. Glancing at the FBI mug, wondering whether there would be a queue for the kettle, she flicked on her computer and pulled down Frankie Ferris's encrypted file. The number he had left for her was that of a public call box in Chelmsford, and he had asked her to ring on the hour until he answered.

She rang at 9:00. He picked up on the first ring.

"Can you talk?" Liz asked, lining up a pencil and pad.

"For the moment, yeah. I'm in a multi-storey. But if I hang up, you'll . . . The thing of it is, someone got done on the pick-up."

"Someone got killed?"

"Yeah. Last night. I don't know where, and I don't know the details, but I think it was a shooting. Eastman's gone completely off his head, ranting on about raghead this and Paki that and all sorts . . ."

"Just keep to the point, Frankie. Start at the beginning. Is this something you've been told, or were you in Eastman's office, or what?"

"I went into the office first thing. It's on the Writtle estate, which—"

"Just tell me the story, Frankie."

"Yeah, well, I ran into Ken Purkiss, that's Eastman's storeman. He says not to go up, everything's come on top, the boss is like totally off his . . ."

"Because someone's been killed on a pick-up?"

"Yeah."

"Do you know what sort of pick-up?"

"No."

"Did he say where it happened?"

"No, but I'd guess that headland place, wherever that was. What he said, according to Ken, was that he'd told the Krauts they were overloading the network. Something about when their problems ended, his begun. And all the stuff about Pakis and that."

"So did you speak to Eastman yourself?"

"No, I took Ken's advice and slung it. I'm supposed to see him later."

"Why are you telling me all this, Frankie?" Liz asked, although she knew the answer. Frankie was covering his back. If Eastman was going down, as well he might if there was a murder hunt, Frankie didn't want to go down with him. He wanted to be in a position to make a deal while he still had a few cards in his hands, rather than from a police cell. If Eastman wriggled his way out of the charge, on the other hand, he still wanted to go on working for him.

"I want to help you," said Frankie, his tone injured.

"Have you spoken to Morrison?"

"I'm not speaking to that bastard. It's you and me or the deal's off."

"There's no deal on, Frankie," said Liz patiently. "If you have information relating to a murder you must inform the police."

"I don't know anything that'd stand up," protested Frankie. "Only what I told you, and that's all hearsay."

He paused.

Liz said nothing. Waited.

"I s'pose I could . . ."

"Go on."

"I could . . . see what I can find out. If you like."

Liz considered her options. She didn't want to step on Essex Special Branch's toes, but Frankie did seem adamant about not speaking to Morrison. And she would bounce the information straight back to them. "How do I contact you?" she asked eventually.

"Give me a number. I'll call you."

Liz did so, and the phone went dead. She stared at her scribbled notes. Germans. Arabs. Pakistanis. The network overloaded. Was this a drugs story? It certainly sounded like one. Drugs were Melvin Eastman's game. His stock-in-trade, so to speak. But then a lot of the drugs people had moved into people-smuggling. Economic migrants brought in from China, Pakistan, Afghanistan and the Middle East in return for fat wads of hard currency. Hard to resist when you'd got your border guards bribed and a good shipment line up and running.

But Eastman, as far as Liz was aware, had no Asian operation. He wasn't the type. He knew his limits, and competing with the Afghans and the Kosovars and the Chinese Snake-heads was a very long way out of his league. When all was said and done, Melvin Eastman was basically an East London wide-boy who imported Class A drugs from Amsterdam and distributed them in Essex and East Anglia. Bought wholesale and sold retail, with the Dutch taking the decisions about shipment and volume. It was a local operation—a franchise, effectively—and the Dutch were running at least half a dozen just like it up and down the UK.

So what business could Eastman have been doing with Germans and Arabs and Pakistanis? Who had been killed? And most vitally of all, was there a terror connection?

Still staring at her notes, Liz picked up her phone and rang the Essex Special Branch office in Chelmsford. Identifying herself by means of her counter-terrorism team code, she asked if any reports of a homicide had come in that morning.

There was a short silence, the faint clicking of a keyboard, and she was put through to the duty officer.

"Nothing," the officer said. "Nothing at all. We had a report of a firearm discharged outside a nightclub in Braintree last night, but . . . Hang on a minute, someone's trying to tell me something."

There was a short silence.

"Norfolk," he said a few seconds later. "Apparently Norfolk had a homicide early this morning, but we haven't got any details."

"Thanks." She punched out the number for Norfolk Special Branch.

"We've had a shooting," confirmed the duty officer in Norwich. "Fakenham. Discovered at six thirty this morning. The location's the toilet block of the Fairmile transport café and all-night lorry park, and the victim's a local fisherman named Ray Gunter. Crime are on the case but we've got a man down there because there was a query on the weapon used."

"What sort of query?"

"Ballistics identified the round as . . ." there was the sound of papers being shuffled, "7.62 millimetre armour-piercing."

"Thanks," said Liz, noting down the calibre. "What's the name of your bloke down there?"

"Steve Goss. Want his number?"

"Please."

He gave it to her and she broke the connection. For some minutes she stared at her notes. She was no expert, but she had been around firearms long enough to know that 7.62 calibre weapons were usually military or ex-military rifles. The Kalashnikov was a 7.62, as was the old British Army SLR. Perfect for the battlefield, but a pretty unwieldy choice for close-quarter murder. And an armour-piercing round? What was that all about?

She turned the facts around in her mind. Whichever way she combined them they looked bad. Dutifully, but with a sense of pointlessness, she rang Bob Morrison. Once again the Special Branch officer rang her back from a public phone, but this time the reception was better. He had heard about the killing at the transport café, he said, but not in any detail. He had never heard of the victim, Ray Gunter.

Liz repeated what Ferris had told her. Morrison's responses were curt, and she sensed his acute resentment that his source, however supposedly useless, had cut him out of the loop and was now reporting to her.

"Zander says that Eastman was livid," she told him. "Shouting about Pakis and ragheads and networks being overloaded."

"I'd be livid if I was Eastman. The last thing he wants is trouble on his patch."

"Is Norfolk on his patch?"

"It's on the edge of it, yeah."

"I'm sending you the details of Zander's call, OK?"

"Yeah, sure. Like I said, I don't believe a word the little toerag says, but do by all means nod the stuff over if you like."

"On its way," said Liz, and hung up.

Would he forward the conversation to the Norfolk Special Branch? she wondered. He certainly ought to. But he might just sit on it out of sheer bloody-mindedness. It would be a way of putting her—Liz—in her place, and if anyone asked questions afterwards he could claim that Zander was a compromised and unreliable source of intelligence.

The more Liz thought about it, the more certain she became that Morrison would say nothing. He was a jobsworth, a man whose entire life had become a bullying, nit-picking course of least resistance. The more valuable Frankie's product proved to be, the worse he'd look for having mishandled him. He'd probably just bury the whole thing, which was fine by Liz, because when all was said and done it meant that she had more pieces of the jigsaw than anyone else. Which was how she liked it.

Pencil in hand, she stared at her notepad and its headings. What did they tell her? What was it reasonable to surmise? Something or someone had been brought in by sea from Germany, and "dropped off" at "the headland." This activity related to Melvin Eastman's operations, but was not one of them—indeed she had the impression that Eastman might well be being squeezed, that things were out of his control. A fisherman, meanwhile—a boat owner, presumably—had been found shot dead in a lorry park near the Norfolk coast. Shot dead with a weapon which, as things stood, looked as if it might have been military.

Reaching for her keyboard she called up an Ordnance Survey map with Fakenham at its centre. The town was about ten miles due south of Wells-next-the-Sea, which was on Norfolk's long north coast. Wells was the biggest town for a good twenty miles along that northern coast—most of it seemed to be salt marshes and inlets, with a sprinkling of villages, wildfowl sanctuaries and large private estates. Lonely, sea-girt countryside, it looked. Probably a few coastguard stations and yacht clubs, but otherwise a perfect smuggler's coast. And less than three hundred miles from the German ports. Slip out of Cuxhaven or Bremerhaven when the light began to fade, and you could be lying off one of those creeks under cover of the early-morning darkness thirty-six hours later.

Bremerhaven again. The place where the fake UK driver's licence had been issued to Faraj Mansoor. Was there a connection? At the back of her mind, quiet but insistent, was Bruno Mackay's report that one of the terrorist organisations was about to run an invisible against the UK.

Could Faraj Mansoor be the invisible? Unlikely—it would almost certainly be an Anglo-Saxon type. So who was Faraj Mansoor, and what was he doing in Bremerhaven buying a forged driver's licence? Was he a UK citizen who'd been banned from driving and wanted a clean document? Bremerhaven was a known source of fake passports and other identity documents, and the fact that Mansoor wasn't after a passport suggested that he didn't need one, that he was already a UK citizen. Had anyone checked that?

Mansoor, she wrote, underlining the name. *UK citizen?*

Because if he wasn't a UK citizen, then two things were possible. That he was coming into the UK on a fake passport that he had acquired from some other source at some other time. Or, more seriously, that he was coming into the UK in such a way that he didn't need a passport. That he was someone whose entry had to remain unknown to the authorities. A senior ITS player, perhaps. A contact of Dawood al Safa, whose job in a Peshawar auto repair shop was a cover for terrorist activities. Someone who, whatever the state of his documentation, couldn't risk passing a customs point.

Every instinct that Liz possessed—every sensibility that she had fine-tuned in a decade of security intelligence work—whispered to her of threat. Pressed, she would have had difficulty in defining these feelings, which related to the way that particles of information combined and took shape in her subconscious. She had, however, learned to trust them. Learned that certain configurations—however fractured, however dimly seen—were invariably malign.

Beneath the words *Mansoor. UK citizen?* she wrote, *Still working at auto shop?*

A methodical search of the north Norfolk coastline yielded a number of possible headlands. The most westward of these, Garton Head, jutted several hundred yards into the sea from the Stiffkey Marshes, while an unnamed but similarly sized projection nosed into Holkham Bay a dozen miles to the west. Both looked like navigable landfalls. A third possibility was a tiny finger of land reaching out into Brancaster Bay. The property was on the edge of a village named Marsh Creake, a couple of miles east of Brancaster.

She examined the three headlands again, and tried to look at the map with a smuggler's eye. They were remarkably similar, in that each was a spit of land surrounded by mudflats. The Brancaster Bay headland, with its proximity to the village of Marsh Creake, was probably the least likely, as it appeared to have a large house on it. The sort of person who owned a property of that size was unlikely to allow it to be used for criminal activity. Unless, perhaps, the owner, or owners, were absentees. Impossible to tell by looking at a few inches of map on a flatscreen monitor. She'd have to check out the place on the ground.

Five minutes later she was sitting in Wetherby's office and Wetherby was smiling his uneven smile. If you didn't know him, she thought, you might think him a faintly donnish figure. A brogues and bicycle clips sort of man, more at home in some cloistered quadrangle than at the head of a high-tech counter-terrorism initiative. Facing him, but invisible to Liz, were two photographs in leather-look frames.

"What exactly do you think you would establish by going up there?" he asked her.

"At the very least I'd like to eliminate the possibility that there's a terrorism angle," said Liz. "The calibre of the weapon worries me, as it obviously does the Norfolk Special Branch, given that they've got a man sitting in on the investigation. My gut instinct, bearing in mind Zander's call, is that Eastman's had his organisation hijacked in some way."

Wetherby rolled a dark green pencil thoughtfully between his fingers.

"Do the Special Branch know about Zander's call?"

"I passed the information on to Bob Morrison in Essex—that's Zander's current handler—but there's a good chance he's going to sit on it."

Wetherby nodded. "From our point of view, that wouldn't necessarily be a bad thing," he said finally. "Not a bad thing at all. I think you should go up there, have a quiet word with the local Special Branch man—what's his name?"

"Goss."

"Have a quiet word with Goss, and see what's what. Give the impression that you're interested in the organised crime component, perhaps, and I'll wait on your word. If you're not happy I'll speak to Fane and we'll move on it straight away. If there isn't anything there for us, on the other hand . . . well, it'll give us something to talk about at the Monday morning meeting. You're sure Zander isn't just making the whole thing up?"

"No," said Liz truthfully. "I'm not sure. He's the attention-seeking type, and according to Bob Morrison is now gambling, so almost certainly has financial problems. He's an unreliable agent at every level. But that doesn't mean he isn't speaking the truth on this occasion." She hesitated. "It didn't sound made up to me. He sounded scared stiff."

"If that's your judgement," said Wetherby, returning the pencil to a stoneware jar that had once held Fortnum and Mason marmalade, "then I agree that you should go. Having said that, there's only that 7.62 rifle round to suggest that the killing wasn't the result of a falling-out between drug-dealers. Or a people-smuggling operation gone awry. Perhaps drug-smugglers have started carrying assault rifles. Perhaps Gunter was simply in the wrong place at the wrong time, and saw something he shouldn't have."

"I hope that's what happened," said Liz.

He nodded. "Keep me informed."

"Don't I always?"

He looked at her, smiled faintly, and turned away.

15

In the tiny bedroom at the east end of the bungalow, Faraj Mansoor slept in unmoving silence. Was this something he had learned to do? the woman wondered. Was even this aspect of his life subject to control and secrecy? Slung over the bedhead was the black rucksack that he had been carrying when she met him. Would he trust its contents to her? Would he be open with her, and treat her as a partner? Or would he expect her, as a woman, to walk behind him? To behave as his subordinate in all things?

In truth, she didn't care. The essential thing was that the task should be executed. The woman prided herself on her chameleon nature, her preparedness to be whatever she was required to be at any given moment, and was happy to assume whatever role was required of her. At Takht-i-Suleiman, to begin with at least, the instructors had barely acknowledged her existence, but she hadn't minded. She had listened, she had learned, and she had obeyed. When they had told her to cook, she had cooked. When they had told her to wash the other recruits' sweat-stinking combat fatigues, she had carried the baskets uncomplainingly to the *wadi*, squatted on her haunches, and scrubbed. And when they had tied her eyes with a scarf and told her to field-strip her assault weapon, she had done that too, her fingers dancing fast and fluent over the machined parts whose names she had only ever known in Arabic. She had become a cipher, a selfless instrument of vengeance, a Child of Heaven.

She smiled. Only those who had undergone the experience of initiation knew the fierce joy of self-nullification. Perhaps—*inshallah*—she would survive this task. Perhaps she would not. God was great.

And in the mean time there were things to do. When he woke Mansoor would want to wash—the smell in the car the night before had been of stale body-odour and vomit—and he would want to eat. The water was heated by a temperamental Ascot which seemed to gasp and die every five minutes—half a box of spent matches lay in the bathroom bin—and the Belling electric stove looked as if it was on its last legs too. The salt air, she guessed, probably shortened the lives of these kind of goods. The fridge whirred noisily but otherwise seemed to work, and after Diane's departure the day before she had driven into King's Lynn and stocked up with oven-ready meals from Tesco. Curries, for the most part.

Her name was not Lucy Wharmby, as she had told Diane Munday. But what she was called no longer mattered to her, any more than where she lived. Movement and change were in her blood now, and any kind of permanence was unimaginable.

It hadn't always been so. In the far beginning, in a past over which a kind of frozen unreality now shimmered, there had been a place called home. A place to which, with the simplicity of a child, she had thought she would always return. She could remember, in great detail, isolated moments from this time. Feeding stale bread to the greedy, snappish geese in the park. Lying in her paddling pool in the tiny south London garden, looking up at the apple tree and pressing her neck downwards on the rim of the pool so that the water rushed out through her hair.

But then the shadows had begun to fall. There was a move from the cosy London house to a cold block in a Midlands university town. Her father's new teaching job was a prestigious one, but for the book-ish seven-year-old it meant permanent separation from her London friends and a hellish new school in which bullying was rife, especially of outsiders.

She was desperately lonely, but said nothing to her parents, because by then she knew from the tense silences and the slammed doors that they had their own problems. Instead, she began to withdraw into herself. Her schoolwork, once sparkling, deteriorated. She developed mysterious stomach pains which kept her at home but which refused to yield to any kind of treatment—conventional or otherwise.

When she was eleven her parents separated. The separation would conclude with their divorce. On the surface the arrangement was amicable. Her parents walked around with fixed smiles on their faces—smiles which didn't quite reach their eyes—and made a point of telling her that nothing would change. Both, however, quickly took up with new partners.

Their daughter moved between the two households, but kept herself to herself. The mystery stomach pains persisted, further isolating her from her contemporaries. Her periods failed to materialise. One evening she punched her fist through a frosted glass door and had to be given ten stitches in her hand and wrist by a junior houseman at the Accident and Emergency department of the local hospital.

When she was thirteen, her parents took the decision to send her away to a progressive boarding school in the country which had a reputation for accommodating troubled children. Classroom attendance was optional and there was no organised sport. Instead, pupils were encouraged to undertake free-form art and theatre projects. In her second year her father's girlfriend sent her a book for her birthday. It sat on her bedside table for a fortnight; it was not the sort of thing which interested her, by and large. One night, however, unable to sleep, she had finally reached for it and begun to read.

16

Liz's mobile rang when she was on the North Circular, sandwiched between a school minibus and a petrol tanker. Her car, a dark blue Audi Quattro, had been bought second-hand with the modest sum of money left to her by her father. It needed cleaning, and the CD player was on the blink, but it ran smoothly and silently, even at her present crawl of ten miles an hour. As she scrabbled for the phone on the seat beside her, one of the boys in the back of the minibus extended his tongue at her like a lascivious dog. Twelve? she wondered. Fourteen? She couldn't tell children's ages any more. Had she ever been able to? She picked up.

"It's me. Where are you?"

She caught her breath. Other boys were at the minibus windows now, gesturing obscenely and laughing. She forced herself to look away. She hated taking calls in the car, and she had asked Mark never—under any circumstances—to call her during work hours.

"Not sure exactly. Why? What is it?"

"We have to talk."

The boys were in paroxysms now, their faces twisted like demons from a medieval painting. Rain suddenly lanced across the windscreen, blurring their outlines.

"What do you want?" she asked.

"What I've always wanted. You. Where are you going?"

"Away for a day or two. How's Shauna?"

"Fighting fit. I'm talking to her this weekend."

She switched on the windscreen wipers. The boys had disappeared. "Any particular subject? Or have you just pencilled in a general chat?"

"I'm talking about us, Liz. I'm telling her that I'm in love with you. That I'm leaving her."

Liz stared ahead of her, appalled, as her future cracked across like mirror glass. This, quite simply, must not happen. There would be a divorce, and she would be named in open court.

"Did you hear what I said?"

"Yes, I heard you." She swung on to the M11. Red brake lights were refracted through the rain.

"And?"

"And what?"

"What do you think?"

"I think it's just about the worst idea I've ever heard."

"I have to tell her, Liz. It's only fair."

Anger was racing through her now, darkening the stream of her thought. "If you tell her, Mark, I promise you, we're—"

"It'll be just us, Liz. Just us and the night."

An idea—the tiny splinter of an idea—flickered across the dark cloud of her fury.

"Say that again."

"Just us . . . and the night?"

The night. Silence.

"What is it?" he asked.

It was still there, pulsing just beyond her reach. And it was important. "I'll call you later," she said.

"Liz, this is . . . I'm talking about ending my marriage here. About leaving Shauna. About our future."

The night. Silence. *Damn.*

"I have to go. I'll call you."

"I love you, Liz, OK? But I can't—"

Two lanes were closed. Flashing arrows were bottlenecking the traffic. *Damn it.* She had to keep hold of this train of thought. Mark would try and ring back. She switched off her phone. It took ten minutes to stop and call Goss.

"Can I just check a couple of details with you?" she asked him. "Like, have you been able to establish an exact time of death?"

"The pathologist reckoned between four fifteen and four forty-five."

"Were there other people around?"

"A dozen or so drivers sleeping in their cabs."

"And the shot didn't wake any of them?"

"Not that we've spoken to, no."

"You saw the round?"

"Yes. Ballistics recovered it."

"And it was definitely 7.62 calibre?"

"So they say; 7.62 armour-piercing."

"Case of sledgehammers and walnuts at that range, surely?"

"Well, they'll certainly be regrouting the wall."

Liz fell silent, considering this information. The wind buffeted the car. She had no idea where she was.

"Thanks. Be with you in a couple of hours or so."

"OK. I'll be in the Memorial Hall at Marsh Creake. That's the village the dead man lived in. The DS is setting up an incident room there."

. . .

In the event it was almost three hours before she saw the first signpost to Marsh Creake. It stood at the junction of two narrow roads. To either side of her, windblown fields extended to the horizon; above, the wide skies were darkly charged with rain. Small villages, often no more than a handful of farmhouses, were strewn across the panorama, their flint-rendered walls and pantiled roofs visible for miles.

In late summer, Liz guessed, these fields would be a blaze of gold, and the drainage cuts which bisected them would reflect the clear blue of the sky. At this time of year, however, the landscape was a sullen brown; the corn stalks had long been ploughed into the wet soil, and the marsh reeds bristled secretively. You could walk for ever across this countryside and get nowhere.

As she drove into the village of Marsh Creake the fields became the outlying greens of a golf course. No one actually seemed to be playing but a few hardy souls were gathered outside a small clubhouse roofed in green-painted corrugated iron. She continued past rain-swept bunkers of pale sand on one side of the road and 1960s villas on the other, and found herself facing the sea. The tide was out, and beyond a low sea wall an uneven expanse of grey-green mudflat lay exposed. Narrow wind-ruffled channels snaked through this, their banks dimpled with worm casts. A hundred yards out a regiment of wading birds patrolled the incoming tide, stabbing delicately with their beaks.

Looking eastwards, Liz's curiosity was pricked by a wooded promontory and the roof of a grand-looking Georgian house. Was that the headland she had seen on the map? Surely that had been to the west of Marsh Creake. She decided to drive up there and make certain.

Two minutes later she came to a halt. To her right, the road was bordered by the outlying parts of the golf course. To her left, at the point opposite which the golf course became reeded marshland, a balconied and weatherboarded building announced itself as the Marsh Creake sailing club.

Like the golf clubhouse, this was on a miniature scale, and overlooked an inlet through the mudflats which provided anchorage for a dozen shallow-draughted craft. Liz listened to the faint clatter of the wind at their masts. It would be next to impossible to bring a cargo ashore here at night. Marker buoys lay at the end of muddy ropes at the side of the inlet to mark the channel at high tide, but without using torches or showing lights there would be a serious risk of grounding. This was not Eastman's headland.

Beyond the clubhouse was the Georgian building she had seen. Creake Manor, it called itself, and very imposing it looked. On the gravelled drive in front of it a blonde woman was sitting in the driver's seat of a metallic-green Cherokee jeep, talking on a mobile phone and, as far as Liz could see, thumbing through a magazine. The car's engine, meanwhile, was quietly turning over, blowing fumes into a hydrangea bush.

As Liz drew up outside the gates the woman looked over. Enquiringly, at first, and then with mild irritation. Returning her a vacant sightseer's smile, Liz drove away. The grounds, which were enclosed by a high wall, seemed to continue for some distance. Large trees—ilexes, oaks, a beech—rose above the rendered brickwork.

Creake Manor, Liz discovered, was the last house in the village, and neither it nor the sailing club looked remotely suited to any kind of smuggling. Returning to the T-junction on the sea front, Liz nosed the Audi into the main body of the village.

While this had a spare, old-fashioned charm, it didn't have the bijou look of a place which had expelled all its local inhabitants and replaced them with rich weekenders from London. Essentially, Marsh Creake consisted of a handful of houses strung unevenly along the coast road. There was a garage with three pumps and an oily-floored workshop, and next to it the Trafalgar pub, whose leaded lights and brick-and-beam exterior suggested that it had been built in the years immediately following the Second World War. Alongside the pub stood a gabled village hall through whose windows stacked chairs were visible. Continuing westwards along the sea front, Liz discovered the village stores and a ship's chandler and souvenir shop which appeared to have closed for the winter. Behind these were several streets of red-brick houses and a low council block.

A turn in the road and a stand of elderly pines masked the village's westernmost building. Headland Hall was a grey, rather charmless Victorian sprawl whose Gothic turrets and lancets suggested a hotel or town hall rather than a private home. On the seaward side of the house, dimly visible through the surrounding trees, a long walled garden reached out over the exposed salt marshes. The house was less elegant than Creake Manor, half a mile to the west, and the grounds less lavishly maintained. But there was a symmetry to the two establishments, enclosing the village like bookends as they did, and perhaps an implicit rivalry. Both unquestionably spoke of money and influence. Was Headland Hall where "twenty, plus a special" had been brought ashore? Liz wondered. It was certainly not impossible.

A three-point turn and a couple of minutes later she was back in the centre of the village. Parking the Audi on the sea front, she stepped out into a stiff east wind, causing a line of herring gulls to lift from the back of a concrete bench and wheel complainingly away.

The words *In Memoriam* were inscribed above the entrance to the village hall. Inside, it had the cold, slightly damp feel of a building that was not in regular use. Much of the space was taken up with stacked piles of canvas-backed chairs. At one end was a small stage, whose curtain hung half open to reveal a dusty upright piano. At the other a laptop computer and a printer had been set up on a trestle table. In front of the trestle table a female constable and a male plain-clothes officer were setting up a VCR and a monitor on an extension cable.

As Liz looked around, a wiry ginger-haired man in a waxed jacket stepped enquiringly towards her. "Can I help you?"

"I'm looking for Steve Goss."

"That's me. You must be . . ."

"Liz Carlyle. We spoke."

"We did indeed." He glanced at the rain-spattered window. "Welcome to Norfolk!"

They exchanged smiles and shook hands. He was about forty-five, Liz guessed.

"The DS is still winding things up at the transport café where the shooting took place, but the photographer's just e-mailed us the pictures. Why don't I take you through them, and then we can wander up to the pub for a sandwich and a chat and defrost a bit?"

"Suits me," said Liz. She nodded to the police personnel, who watched her warily and without expression. Stepping over a trail of electronic cables, she followed Goss to the trestle table. The Special Branch officer pulled up one of the canvas-backed chairs for her, sat himself in another, and flicked his fingers over the laptop's touchpad.

"OK, Gunter, Raymond . . . here we are."

Columns of thumbnail images flickered into view.

"I'll just give you the key shots," murmured Goss. "Or we'll be here all day."

Liz nodded. "That's fine. I can always check back if there's anything I need to see again."

The first image that Goss enlarged was a wide shot of the vehicle park. Along the far boundary of this muddied expanse the heavy goods vehicles crouched like sullen prehistoric beasts, their wet tarpaulins shining. To the left was a low prefabricated building with a sign reading *Fairmile Café*. Strip lights shone dimly inside it, and the coloured loops of Christmas decorations were visible. To the right stood a concrete toilet block, beyond which a line of policemen in fluorescent yellow foulweather jackets were conducting a ground search.

The shots which followed showed the interior of the café. This was probably a cheerful enough place when it was open for business and its tea urns were steaming. Empty, however, despite the paper chains and the inflatable Santas, it was decidedly mournful.

The third sequence showed the toilet block. First the exterior, with the pathology and forensics people milling around in their pale blue protective overalls, and looking glad of them as the rain sliced its way round the breeze blocks, and then the interior. This was empty—at least of the living. It was dressed in glazed white tiles, and contained a hand basin, two wall-mounted urinals and a toilet stall. A close-up shot showed that the lock on the stall door was broken. In place of a toilet roll, a Yellow Pages directory hung on a loop of baler twine.

The final sequence showed Ray Gunter. Dressed in an off-white sweater and a pair of dark blue Adidas track-pants, he was lying on the floor beneath a metre-wide starburst of dried blood and brain tissue. At the centre of this was a black hole where the bullet had passed through a ceramic tile. A long red-brown smear led downwards to the slumped body. The round had entered through the left eyebrow, leaving the face more or less intact. The back of the head, however, sagged formlessly away from the skull, and had voided its contents on to the concrete floor.

"Who found him?" asked Liz, narrowing her eyes against the photographs' bloody horror.

"An HGV driver. Just after six a.m."

"And the round?"

"We were lucky. It went right through the toilet block and lodged in the boundary wall."

"Any forensic from the gunman?"

"No, and we've been over every inch of the floor and walls. They'll be testing the victim's fingernail deposits too, but I'm not hopeful."

"Where was the killer standing when the shot was fired?" asked Liz.

"Hard to tell at this stage, but far enough away for there to be no obvious powder burns. Twelve feet, perhaps. Whoever did this knew exactly what he was doing."

"What makes you say that?"

"He went for the head shot. The chest shot would have been much easier, but our killer wanted his man down in one. Gunter would have been dead before his knees started to bend."

Liz nodded thoughtfully. "And no one heard anything?"

"No one will admit to hearing anything. But then there would have been lorries coming and going and all sorts of incidental noise."

"How many people were there around?"

"A good dozen drivers sleeping in their cabs. The café shut at midnight and opened at six a.m." He switched off the laptop and leaned back in his chair. "We'll know a lot more when the CCTV footage comes in, which'll probably be in about an hour. How about that drink?"

"The drink that started off life as a sandwich?"

"That's the one."

The warmth of the Trafalgar was welcome after the cheerless cold of the village hall. The saloon bar was panelled in oak and decorated with portraits of Nelson, knotted ropes, ships in bottles, and other naval paraphernalia. Above the service counter hung a framed Red Ensign flag. The place smelt of furniture polish and cigarette smoke. A handful of middle-aged customers were nodding and murmuring over ploughman's lunches, salads and half-pints of beer.

Goss ordered a pint of bitter for himself, a cup of coffee for Liz, and a plate of toasted sandwiches. Liz had no great hopes for the coffee, and didn't particularly feel like the sandwiches, but felt that she ought to eat. She had a tendency, she knew, to get caught up in the impetus of work and forget such things. Contributing to her lack of appetite—a quiet but insistent backbeat to the day's other issues—was Mark's phone call. If he meant what he said, then she would have to act. She would have to break things off; draw a once-and-for-all line beneath the affair.

Later, she thought. I'll deal with it later.

"So," she began, when they had settled themselves at a quiet corner table with their drinks, "this 7.62 round."

Goss nodded. "That's why I'm up here. It looks like a military-spec rifle was involved. An AK or an SLR."

"Have you ever come across a weapon like that used in an organised crime context?"

"Not in this country. Far too bulky. Your average UK gangster tends to go the handgun route—preferably tooling up with a status weapon like a nine-millimetre Beretta or a Glock. Professional hitmen prefer easy-carry revolvers like snub-nosed .38s, because they don't spray used cartridge cases around the place for forensics to pick up."

Liz stirred her coffee. "So what's your take on the whole thing? Unofficially?"

He shrugged. "My first thought, given that Gunter was a fisherman, was that he was involved in drugs- or people-smuggling and had a falling-out with someone. My second, which I'm still inclined towards, was that he stumbled into someone else's operation—some heavy-duty Eastern European mob's, perhaps—and had to be silenced."

"If that was the case, though, why do it ten miles inland at Fakenham, in a busy place like a transport café?"

"Well, that's the question, isn't it?" He looked at her assessingly. "Does your presence here mean that your people think there's a terrorist connection?"

"We don't know anything your people don't," said Liz.

Technically, given that she had reported Zander's call to Bob Morrison, this was true. Goss glanced over at her, but any suspicions that he might have been about to voice were silenced by the arrival of the toasted sandwiches.

"Has the murder caused a big stir?" she asked, when the barmaid had withdrawn.

"Yeah. Major chaos when the body was found. We had to clear the place, get all the HGV drivers out and behind the tape barriers. You can imagine how well that went down."

"Who actually found Gunter?"

"A driver called Dennis Atkins. He drove down from Glasgow last night and parked up at the Fairmile about midnight. He was due to make an eight thirty delivery of precision lathes to an industrial park outside Norwich. The café had just opened and he was going for a pre-breakfast wash."

"And all that checks out?"

Goss nodded. "It looks kosher enough. Atkins was pretty upset. And the CID have spoken to people both ends and confirmed that he is who he says he is."

"Much press interest?"

"The locals were there within the hour, and the nationals weren't long after."

"What did the DS tell them?"

Goss shrugged. "Man discovered dead as a result of a shooting. Statement as soon as we know more."

"Have they named Gunter?"

"They have now. They spent several hours trying to locate his only relative, a sister who lives in King's Lynn. Apparently she went out to work last night and has only just got home."

"What's the sister do?"

"Kayleigh? Not a lot. Takes her clothes off a couple of nights a week at a membership club called PJs."

"And that's what she was doing last night?"

"Yeah."

"And the dead man—do we know what he was doing last night? Apart from being shot?"

"Not yet."

"And none of the vehicles in the car park were his?"

"No—the police have identified all of them as driven there by other people."

"So we've got him ten miles from home in a transport café without any transport."

"That's about the shape and size of it, yes."

"Was Gunter known to the CID? Did he have any form?"

"Not really. He was involved in an affray after a pub lock-in in Dersthorpe a couple of years back, and there was talk of him having set light to a vehicle there at some point too, but no charges were brought. The car belonged to a small-time local drug-dealer."

"Was Gunter a dealer himself? Or a user?"

"Put it this way: if he was, it wasn't on a big enough scale to come to our attention."

"But a bit of a local bad boy?"

Goss shrugged. "According to the CID, not even that. Just a bit mouthy and free with his fists when he'd been drinking."

"I take it he was single," said Liz drily.

"Yes," said Goss, "but not gay, which was one of the first things that occurred to me when he was discovered in the toilets at the Fairmile."

"Is it a gay pick-up place, then, the café?"

"It's every kind of pick-up place. They get very frisky, these long-distance HGV boyos."

"Could Gunter have been there to pick up a woman?" Liz asked.

"He could have been, and there were certainly a few toms who worked the place, but that still leaves the question: how did he get there without a car? Who brought him? If we can answer that one I suspect we might get somewhere."

Liz nodded. "So what do we know about the shooting?"

"Not a lot, frankly. No one heard anything, no one saw anything. Unless we get a forensic break I'd say our best hope is the CCTV."

"Were the cameras definitely running last night?"

"The owner of the café says they were. It's a new system, apparently. There was a spate of thefts from rigs last year and the drivers threatened to boycott the place if he didn't install some decent security."

"Fingers crossed, then."

"Fingers crossed," agreed Goss.

They talked on, but soon found themselves retreading old ground. Liz remained studiedly neutral in these exchanges. The Special Branch were police, and information had been known to leak from police stations to journalists—usually in return for cash. Goss seemed like the better sort of Special Branch officer, just as Bob Morrison was without doubt the worse sort, but Liz was relieved when the local detective superintendent rang to say that the CCTV footage was back from Norwich.

"It's pretty rough, apparently," said Goss, returning his phone to his belt. "It's going to have to be enhanced if we're to get any useful information off it."

Liz looked down at the remains of her lunch. Half of the sandwiches were uneaten, languishing alongside an untouched mound of Branston's pickle. And she'd been right about the coffee. "I'll go up and pay," she said. "This one's on Thames House."

"That's very generous of them," said Goss drily.

"You know us. Sweetness and light."

As Liz got to her feet, a phone began to ring behind the bar. The barmaid picked up the receiver, and a few seconds later her mouth opened in a speechless gasp. She's just heard about the murder, Liz guessed. No, she already knew about the murder but has just found out that the victim was Gunter. She must have known him. But then everyone in a place this size would know each other.

Liz was beaten to the bar by a young man in a leather jacket and a lilac tie. Journalist, thought Liz. Almost certainly tabloid. That particular blend of the metropolitan and the downmarket was unmistakable.

"Another pint, love," he demanded, placing a glass and a ten-pound note on the bar. The barmaid nodded vaguely and turned away. A minute later, still visibly dazed, she delivered the drink and rang up the price on the till. As she handed over the change, Liz saw the man's eyes briefly widen.

"Excuse me," said Liz, addressing the barmaid. "I think you've made a mistake. He gave you a ten-pound note. You've given him change for a twenty."

The barmaid froze, the till still open in front of her. She was a heavy girl of about eighteen, with flustered gypsyish eyes.

"The fuck's it got to do with you?" asked the man in the leather jacket, turning to Liz.

"Give her a break," said Liz. "Her till's going to be out."

The man addressed his pint. "I think you're mistaking me for someone who gives a shit."

"Is there a problem?" asked Steve Goss, materialising at Liz's side.

"No problem," said Liz. "This guy accidentally pocketed some extra change, but he's about to give it back."

"Ah," said Goss sagely. "I see."

The man in the leather jacket took in the sober bulk of the Special Branch officer. Shaking his head and smiling as if in the presence of the mentally unhinged, he slapped a ten-pound note down on the bar and carried his drink away.

"Thanks," said the barmaid, as soon as the man was out of earshot. "I have to make it up out of my wages if I'm short."

"Local guy?" asked Liz.

"No. Never seen him before. When he came in he was asking me about the . . ."

"The murder?"

"Yeah. At the Fairmile. If I knew the dead man and that."

"Did you?" prompted Liz gently.

She shrugged. "Knew him to look at. He came in a few times. In the public bar." She flicked over the pages of her pad and handed Liz the bill. "That's seven pounds exactly."

"Thanks. Can you do me a receipt?"

The nervousness returned to the barmaid's eyes.

"On second thought," said Liz, "don't worry about it."

When they got outside, the wind was throwing down irregular spatters of rain.

"That was neatly handled," grinned Goss, forcing his hands into his overcoat pockets. "What would you have done if the guy had refused to give back the money?"

"Left him to your tender mercies," said Liz. "We're just an intelligence-gathering organisation, after all. We don't do violence."

"Thanks a lot!"

They turned back in to the village hall, where Don Whitten, the detective superintendent in charge of the case, had just arrived back from the Fairmile Café. A bulky, moustached figure, he shook Liz's hand briskly and apologised for the spartan conditions in which they found themselves.

"Can we sort out some heating for this place?" he demanded, looking exasperatedly around the bare walls. "It's brass bloody monkeys in here."

The constable, who was crouched in front of the VCR, got uncertainly to her feet. The DS turned to her. "Ring the station and ask someone to bring over one of those hot-air blowers. And a kettle, and some tea bags and biscuits and ashtrays and the rest of it. Jolly the place up a bit."

The constable nodded and thumbed a number on her mobile. A plainclothes officer held up a video cassette. "Norwich have identified the footage and run us off a copy of the Fairmile CCTV tape," he announced. "But the quality's terrible. The camera wasn't set right, and the tape's all ghosting and flare. They're working on an enhanced version, but we won't see it before tomorrow."

"I was afraid that might be the case," Goss murmured to Liz. He pointed her to one of the canvas-backed chairs, and took one for himself.

"Can we have a look at what we've got?" said Whitten, lowering himself into a third chair. He took out a packet of cigarettes and a lighter, and then remembering that there were no ashtrays, irritably returned them to his pocket.

The plainclothes officer nodded. As he had said, the CCTV footage was pretty much unwatchable. The time code, however, flickered strong and clear. "We've basically got two bursts of movement between four and five a.m.," he said. "The first is this."

Two shuddering white lines scribbled across the blackness as a vehicle arrived in the park, slowly reversed out of shot, and extinguished its lights, returning the screen to blackness.

"From the distance between the head- and taillights we reckon that's an HGV of some sort, probably quite a long one, and probably nothing to do with our case. As you can see, that sequence is time-coded 04:05. At 04:23 things get a bit more interesting. Watch this."

A second vehicle appeared to enter. This time, however, there was no reverse-parking manoeuvre. Instead, the vehicle, which was clearly shorter than the earlier one—a truck, almost certainly—performed a three-point turn, came to a halt, and extinguished its lights in the centre of the parking area. As before, the screen returned to blackness.

"Now we wait," said the officer.

They did so. After approximately three minutes a lower, smaller vehicle—a saloon car, Liz guessed—suddenly switched on its lights, reversed at speed from its position at the left-hand edge of the parking area, swung round the parked truck or van, and disappeared out of the front gates. More time passed—at least another five minutes, and then, rather more slowly, the truck followed it out.

"And that's it until five a.m. So given that the pathologist has given us four thirty as the time of death, give or take fifteen either way . . ."

"Can you show us again?" asked Whitten. "Speeding up the bits where nothing's happening."

They watched it again.

"Well, it's certainly not going to win any Oscars for best camera-work," said Whitten. He rubbed his eyes. "What's your reading of it, Steve?"

Goss frowned. "I'd say the first vehicle we saw is just a regular commercial rig. It's the second one I'd like to see more of. It doesn't park up, so is obviously expecting to be on the move pretty sharpish . . ."

Unobtrusively, Liz removed her laptop from its carrying case. There were a couple of queries that she had e-mailed to Investigations at Thames House, and with a bit of luck the answers might have come through. Logging on, she saw that there were two messages, with numbers in the place of sender names.

Liz recognised these as Investigations sender codes. The messages took a couple of minutes to decrypt, but they were short and to the point. They could only trace one UK citizen named Faraj Mansoor, and he was a sixty-five-year-old retired tobacconist living in Southampton. And Pakistan liaison had confirmed that Faraj Mansoor was no longer working at the Sher Babar auto repair shop on the Kabul road outside Peshawar. He had left six weeks earlier, leaving no forwarding address. His present whereabouts was unknown.

Switching off her laptop and replacing it in its case, Liz stared at a curling hand-lettered poster on the wall, advertising a production of *HMS Pinafore* by the Brancaster Players. As Whitten had said, the hall was bitterly cold, and it had the dour, institutional smell of all such buildings. Pulling her coat tightly around her, Liz allowed her mind to wander through the incoherent mass of loose ends that the case had so far thrown up. Before long, she began to meditate on the subject of 7.62mm armour-piercing ammunition.

17

Faraj Mansoor woke thinking that he was still at sea. He could hear the crash of waves, feel the sucking undertow as the *Susanne Hanke* reared up the side of the next peak to come crashing down into the trough. And then the noise and the sea seemed to recede, to recede beyond a window—a small wooden window framing a steel-grey sky—and he realised that the waves were some distance away, dragging at a beach of stones, and that he himself was lying fully clothed in a bed, unmoving.

With this realisation came the knowledge of where he was, and the surreal memory of the landing on the beach and the attack in the café toilet. He revisited the attack, ran it through his mind like a film, frame by frame, and concluded that the fault for the way things had turned was ultimately his own. He had played the role of the downtrodden migrant just a shade too effectively, and had failed to allow for the Briton's sheer venal stupidity. From the moment he had allowed him to approach, the outcome had been inevitable.

Faraj was not greatly troubled by the fact of having taken another man's life, and had examined Gunter's smashed skull with cold dispassion before deciding that a second shot was unnecessary and that it was time he was on his way. But the killing would attract attention to the area, and that was bad. The British police were not fools, they would calculate that the shooting was something out of the ordinary. And they would take the necessary steps.

Patting his trouser pocket, Faraj reassured himself that he had collected the spent cartridge case from the floor. For a moment he put it to his nose, and smelt the gunpowder residue. He had chosen his weapon with care. A target hit was a target down, flak jacket or no. When it came to the moment, he mused grimly, he might well need the few seconds this would buy him.

He swung his legs to the sea-grass flooring. He had said nothing to the girl about the killing of the boatman—he needed her to be calm, and the knowledge that a police murder hunt would soon be under way would have agitated her. For himself, he felt detached, a spectator of his own behaviour. How infinitely strange it was to find himself on this cold and lonely shore, in a land that he had never thought to visit, but in which—and he held out no illusions about this—he would almost certainly die. If it was to be, however, it was to be. The black rucksack hung where he had left it the night before—over the bedhead. The cheap windcheater they'd given him in Bremerhaven lay folded on a bedside chair. The gun was on the bed.

He could remember very little about the drive back to the coast from the service station. He had tried his best to stay awake, but fatigue and the after-effects of the adrenalin that had flooded his body during the fight had blurred his senses. The car, additionally, had been warm and smoothly sprung.

III

He had barely registered the girl. She had been described to him by one of the men who had trained her. She had been pushed hard at Takht-i-Suleiman, the man said, and she had not broken, as most soft city-dwelling women broke. She was intelligent, a prerequisite in the field of civilian warfare, and she had courage. Faraj, however, preferred to reserve his judgement. Anyone could be brave in the bullish, sloganeering atmosphere of a mujahidin training camp, where the worst you had to fear were bruises, blisters and the instructors' scorn. And frankly, anyone with half a brain could master the basic weapons and communications skills on offer. The important questions were answered only at the moment of action. The moment at which the fighter gazes into his or her soul and asks: What do I truly believe? Now that I have summoned death to my side—now that I can feel his cold breath on my cheek—can I do what has to be done?

He looked around him. Beside his bed was a chair, on which was folded a red towelling dressing gown. On the end of the bed was a towel. Accepting the invitation that these items seemed to offer, he stripped off his dirty clothes. The dressing gown seemed inordinately luxurious, given the situation. Feeling slightly foolish, he put it on.

Tentatively, weapon in hand, he pushed open the door to the main area of the bungalow and stepped through, barefoot. The girl was facing away from him, filling an electric kettle from the tap. She was wearing a dark blue sweater with its sleeves hitched halfway up her forearms, a heavy diver's watch, jeans and lace-up boots. Her hair hung straight and brown to her shoulders. When she turned round and saw him she jumped, sluicing water from the kettle's spout on to the floor. Her other hand went to her heart.

"I'm sorry, you gave me such a . . ." She shook her head apologetically and collected herself. *"Salaam aleikum."*

"Aleikum salaam," he returned gravely.

They stared at each other for a moment. Her eyes, he saw, were a hazel colour. Her features, while pleasant enough, were utterly unmemorable. She was someone you would pass in the street without noticing.

"Bathroom?" she hazarded.

He nodded. The stench of the *Susanne Hanke*'s hold—vomit, bilge and sweat—hung about him. The woman would certainly have noticed it in the car the night before. She preceded him through the door, handed him a zip-up sponge bag, and backed out. Laying the gun on the floor, he turned on the bath's hot tap. A roaring sound emanated from the wall-mounted heater, and an uneven thread of tea-coloured water wound into the enamel bath.

He unzipped the sponge bag. In addition to the usual washing equipment there was an extensive first aid kit, complete with sterile wound dressings and suture needles, a small oil-filled compass, and a diver's watch like her own. Nodding approvingly, Faraj set to work with the razor. The bath was clearly going to take some time to fill.

When he finally emerged, she had cooked. There were places set, covered dishes on the table and a smell of spiced chicken. In the tiny bedroom he dressed in the clothes she had bought for him in King's Lynn the afternoon before. These were of good quality: a pale blue twill shirt, a navy blue sweater, chinos, buckskin walking boots. A little hesitantly, he returned to the central room, where the woman was scanning the horizon with a pair of binoculars. Hearing him, she turned round, lowered the binoculars, and looked him up and down.

"You speak English, don't you?" she asked.

Faraj nodded, and pulled out one of the chairs at the table. "I went to an English-language school in Pakistan."

She looked at him, surprised.

"We have both travelled a long way," he said. "The important thing is not where we came from, but that we are here now."

She nodded and, suddenly galvanised, reached for a serving spoon. "I'm sorry," she said. "I hope this is OK, it's—"

"It looks excellent," he said. "Please. Let's eat."

She served him. "Are the clothes comfortable? I used the measurements they sent me."

"The fit is good, but the clothes seem . . . too fine? People will look at me."

"Let them look. They will see a respectable professional man taking his Christmas break. A lawyer, perhaps, or a doctor. Someone whose clothes say that he is one of them."

He nodded slowly. "The famous English caste system."

She shrugged. "It'll explain why you're here. This is a place where the middle classes come to play golf and sail and drink gin. England's full of well-off young Asians."

"And I look like such a person?"

"You will do when I've given you the right haircut."

His eyebrows rose for a moment, and then, seeing the seriousness of her expression, he nodded his acceptance. This was what she was here to do. To make these decisions. To render him invisible.

He took a knife and fork and began to eat. The rice had a flaccid, overboiled texture but the chicken was good. Taking a sip of water he slipped his hand into the pocket of his chinos, took out the tall cartridge case, and stood it upright on the table.

The woman noted it but said nothing.

Faraj ate in silence, chewing with the thoroughness of a man who is used to making a little go a long way. When he had finished he reached across the table for a Swan Vesta matchbox, split a match lengthways with his thumbnail, and began to pick his teeth. Finally he looked up at her and spoke. "I killed a man last night," he said.

18

So what do we know about Peregrine and Anne Lakeby?" asked Liz. "They sound rather exotic."

"I suppose they are, in their own way," said Whitten. "I've met them a few times, and she's much better value than he is. She's quite a laugh, actually. He's more your standard bow-your-head-and-tug-your-forelock aristocrat."

"Any form?" Liz asked hopefully.

Goss smiled. "That'd be too good to be true, wouldn't it?"

"So what's their connection with Gunter again?" asked Liz.

"He kept his fishing boats on their strip of waterfront," said Whitten. "That's as much as I know."

The three of them were standing beneath a vaulted stone porch out-side Headland Hall, and to Liz the place looked even more grimly insti-tutional than it had that morning. Its setting against the mudflats and the glitter of the sea spoke of Dickensian pitilessness, of vast sums of money made and hoarded at the expense of others.

"This certainly won't be the house I'll be buying when I win that ten million rollover," murmured Goss, eyeing the heavy oak front door. "What about you, Guv?"

"Nope. I'll trade in the wife for Foxy Deacon and buy a little place in the Seychelles," said Whitten.

"Who's Foxy Deacon?" asked Goss.

"The blonde one from Mink Parfait."

"They're splitting up," said Liz. "I heard it on the car radio this morning."

"There you are, then." Flipping his cigarette butt into the wet bushes, Whitten reached for the enamelled bell-push. There was a dis-tant ringing sound.

It was answered by a tall, thin-faced woman in a lovat tweed skirt and a quilted waistcoat that looked as if it had lost an argument with a rose-bush. On seeing the two of them, she exposed a mouthful of long teeth.

"Superintendent Whitten, isn't it?"

"Detective Superintendent, ma'am, yes. And this is Detective Sergeant Goss and a colleague from London."

The toothy smile switched directions. Behind the upper-class good manners a shrewd concern was apparent. She knows I'm not police, thought Liz. She knows our presence means trouble.

"You've come about this awful business with Ray Gunter."

"I'm afraid so," said Whitten. "We're speaking to everyone who knew him, and might have had an idea of his movements."

"Of course. Why don't you all come in and sit down?"

They followed her down a long corridor floored with patterned tiles. The walls were hung with foxes' masks, sporting prints and unpre-possessing ancestral portraits. Some of these were in near darkness, oth-ers were palely illuminated by the high Gothic-arched windows.

Peregrine Lakeby was reading the *Financial Times* before a log fire in a tall room furnished with books. Many of these, Liz saw, were bound editions of magazines—*Horse and Hound, The Field, The Shooting Times*—and there was an entire bookcase of Wisden's cricket almanacs. He stood as the others came into the room and were seated by his wife, and then, sitting down again, folded the newspaper with an air of courteous forbearance. "You're here, I assume, about poor Mr. Gunter?"

He was a good-looking man for his age, Liz thought, but unfortunately he was very much aware of the fact. There was a mocking, faintly supercilious quality to the grey-blue gaze. He probably considered himself a bit of a devil with the women.

Whitten, who was leafing through a notebook, fielded the question. "Yes, sir. We just have to make some routine enquiries. As I explained to Mrs. Lakeby, we're speaking to everyone who knew Gunter."

Anne Lakeby's brow knitted. "The truth is that we didn't actually *know* him terribly well. Not in the strict sense of the word. I mean, he came and went, and so on, and one saw him around, but . . ."

Her husband stood, moved to the fire, and stabbed at it languidly with an ancient steel bayonet. "Anne, why don't you go and make us all a nice pot of coffee. I'm sure we'd . . ." He turned to Whitten and Goss. "Or would you prefer tea?"

"That's quite all right, Mr. Lakeby," said Whitten. "I'll do without."

"Me too," said Goss.

"Miss . . ."

"Nothing for me, thanks, either."

In fact Liz would very much have liked a cup of strong coffee, but felt she should show solidarity with the others. She had noticed how Lakeby had avoided using the men's names—a subtle but unmistakable putting of them into their place. Or what Lakeby imagined to be their place.

"Just for me then," said Peregrine airily. "And if we've got some Jaffa Cakes, you might sling a few on to a plate."

Anne Lakeby's smile tightened for a moment, and then she left the room.

When she had gone, Peregrine leaned back in his chair. "So, tell me, what actually happened? I heard the poor bugger had been shot, of all things. Is that true?"

"It looks like it, sir, yes," said Whitten.

"Do you have any idea why?"

"That's what we're trying to ascertain right now. Can you tell me how you knew Mr. Gunter?"

"Well, basically, like his father and grandfather did before him, he kept a couple of boats on our beach. Paid us a peppercorn sum in return and offered us first refusal on his catches—not that they've amounted to a great deal in recent years."

"Were you in favour of this arrangement?"

"I saw no reason to discontinue it. Ben Gunter, Ray's father, was a very decent old boy."

"And Ray wasn't . . . so decent?"

"Ray was a rather rougher diamond. There were a couple of incidents relating to alcohol, which I'm sure you're aware of. That said, we never had any trouble with him. And I certainly can't imagine why anyone would want to go to the bother of killing him."

"Do you know when Gunter last went out fishing? Or out to sea for any other purpose?"

The languid smile remained in place but the grey-blue gaze sharpened. "What d'you mean, exactly? What other purpose could there be?"

Whitten smiled benignly. "I've no idea, sir. I'm not a boating man."

"The answer is no, I have no idea when he last went out to sea, or why. He had his own key to the grounds, and came and went as he pleased."

"Is there anyone who would know?"

"The fishmonger in Brancaster probably would. His name is . . . Anne'll know."

Whitten nodded and made a note in his book.

"When he went fishing, what time did he usually go out?"

Peregrine inflated his cheeks and exhaled thoughtfully. You're lying, thought Liz. You've been lying all along. Hiding something. Why?

"That depended on the tide, but usually at first light. Then he'd run the catch into Brancaster during the morning."

"Did you buy fish off him?"

"Occasionally. He had a permit for half a dozen lobster pots, and if we were having people for dinner we might take a couple of lobsters off him. Or bass, if he had any big enough—which in recent years wasn't often."

"So he was just a fisherman? That was the only way he made his money?"

"As far as I know. He inherited a house over by the church and I think he mortgaged it at some point, but he certainly didn't have any other job."

"So why do you think someone found it necessary to shoot him?"

Lakeby extended his arms proprietorially along the back of the sofa. "Do you want to know what I think? I think the whole thing was a horrible mistake. Ray Gunter was . . . well, he wasn't a very sophisticated chap. He probably had one too many at the Trafalgar or that ghastly place in Dersthorpe and . . . who knows? Picked a fight with the wrong man."

"Any idea why he might have been at the Fairmile Café in the early hours of the morning?"

"None whatsoever. I've always thought that place was an eyesore. On top of which, as you probably know, it's got a reputation as a queers' pick-up joint."

"Might that have been what Gunter was doing there? Looking for a male pick-up?"

Lakeby barked mirthlessly. "Well, I suppose it might have been. I must confess I'd never thought of him in that light. He was no Helen of Troy, as I expect you've observed . . . Anne, would you have said Ray Gunter was a bugger?"

With a faint rattle, his wife lowered the oriental-patterned tray to a table in front of the fire. "I wouldn't have said so, personally—especially since he's been seeing Cherisse Hogan."

"For God's sake—who on earth is Cherisse Hogan?"

"Elsie Hogan's daughter. You remember Elsie? Our cleaner? Left the house half an hour ago."

"I didn't know her name was Hogan. Or that she was married."

"She isn't married. She produced Cherisse when she was at school. That's how she got that council place in Dersthorpe."

"Was this a regular thing?" enquired Whitten. "This . . . 'seeing'?"

"Not as regular as Ray Gunter would have liked," said Anne. "Cherisse has quite a few admirers, and what one used to call a roving eye."

"So where might I find this young lady?"

"She's behind the bar at the Trafalgar most days."

Liz glanced surreptitiously at Goss, but the Special Branch man was impassive. Peregrine Lakeby, however, leaned forward in surprise. "The fat girl?" he asked.

Anne raised her eyebrows. "Peregrine! That's not very gallant."

"How long had she and Gunter been an item?" Whitten cut across her.

"Well," Anne replied, "it wasn't the untroubled romance he'd have liked it to be. According to Elsie, Cherisse had her sights fixed on bigger game."

"Namely?" enquired Goss.

"The publican. Mr. Badger."

Peregrine stared. "Clive Badger? He's treasurer of the golf club. He's got children at university and a heart condition."

"That's as may be, but according to Elsie there have been tender glances exchanged behind the pumps."

"You didn't tell me any of this," said Lakeby.

"You didn't ask," smiled Anne. "It's Gomorrah-on-Sea up here if you keep your ear to the ground. Much better than television."

Peregrine drained his coffee with an air of finality. "Well, all I can say is: I hope Badger's got life insurance." Replacing his cup and saucer on the tray he stretched and looked meaningfully at his watch. "Was there anything else? Because if not I might just . . . press on with various things."

"Nothing," said Whitten, remaining resolutely seated. "Thank you very much for your time." He turned to Anne. "I wonder if, before we go, I might perhaps just ask Mrs. Lakeby a few more questions?"

Anne Lakeby showed her teeth again. "Certainly. Go on, Perry, off you push."

Lakeby hesitated, rose to his feet, and, with the tight-lipped air of one unreasonably evicted, left the room. As his footsteps rang out on the tiled floor of the hall, Anne Lakeby drew a long white goose feather from her quilted waistcoat and turned it in her fingers.

"To be perfectly frank with you," she said, "I couldn't stand Ray Gunter, and I couldn't stand having him around. He'd rear up out of the mist like a ghost, smelling of old fish, and then disappear again, without a word. Just last week I told Perry that I wanted him off the estate for good, but . . ."

"But?"

"But Perry's got some incomprehensible attachment to him. Partly loyalty to old Ben Gunter, I suppose, even though he died years ago, and partly . . . Put it this way: if there was a court case, and we lost . . ."

"Things would have been much worse?"

"Quite. In every sense of the word. But that said, and whatever the legal ramifications, Ray Gunter was certainly up to something."

"Up to what, do you think?" asked Whitten.

"I don't know. I'd hear things in the night. Trucks, moving about on the side road. People talking."

"Surely that's what you'd expect to hear, given that he had a sack of fish to get into town."

"At three a.m.? Look, maybe I'm just being a batty old fool, and I certainly wouldn't have said anything if Ray was still around, but . . ." She shook her head and fell silent.

"Did your husband ever hear these noises?"

"Not once." She shrugged cheerfully. "Which of course makes me sound even more bonkers, senile, and generally ready for the scrap heap."

"I doubt that very much," said Whitten drily. "Tell me, could we possibly have a look at the garden and the place Gunter kept his boats?"

"Certainly you may. It's a bit blowy today, but if you don't mind that . . ."

The four of them proceeded through the house to the garden entrance. This was a stone-floored area housing a rack of Wellington boots and hung with gardening and shooting clothes. The garden itself, Liz saw, was much more attractive than the house's austere Victorian front suggested. A long rectangular lawn flanked by flower beds and trees unrolled towards a stand of tall grasses, and presumably some sort of descent to the sea. Through the trees to either side she could see the mudflats, now half submerged by the incoming tide.

"As you probably know, the thing about the Hall is that it's got the only halfway decent landing place for a couple of miles in either direction," Anne Lakeby explained. "Which is why, obviously, there have always been boats there. The sailing club's got a tidal inlet, but it's not much good for anything bigger or heavier than a Firefly."

"Is that a boat?" asked Whitten.

"Yes, one of those little yachty things that people learn to sail on. Come and have a look at the beach."

A couple of minutes later they were standing amongst the tall sedges and grasses, looking down at the shingle and the sea.

"It's really very private, isn't it?" said Liz.

"The trees and the walls are there as a windbreak as much as anything else," said Anne. "But yes, you're right. It is very private."

"Has anyone been on the beach today?"

"Only me. This morning."

"Did you notice anything out of the ordinary?"

Anne frowned. "Not that I can remember," she said.

"Which way did Gunter come and go?"

Anne pointed to a low door set into the garden's right-hand wall. "Through there. It leads out to the lane which runs up the side of the house. He had a key."

Whitten nodded. "I might get a couple of our blokes to give the place a quick look, if that's all right."

Anne nodded. "Mr. Whitten, do you think Ray Gunter was involved in anything illegal? I mean, drugs or anything?"

"It's too early to say," said Whitten. "It's not impossible."

Anne looked thoughtful. Worried, even.

It was her husband that she was worried about, thought Liz, not the late Ray Gunter. And she had every reason to worry, because Peregrine was undoubtedly lying.

Had Goss and Whitten realised that? Had they put the pieces together in the right order? If they hadn't, she wasn't in a position to help them.

19

As they left the Headland Hall driveway Liz glanced at her watch. It was 3 p.m. "I've got to get back to London," she told Whitten. "But before I go, could I see where Ray Gunter lived?"

"Sure. I'll get one of my people to walk you over there." He turned up his collar against the returning rain. "What did you think of the Lakebys?"

"I think I preferred her to him," said Liz. "You were right."

He nodded. "Never underestimate the upper classes. They can be much nicer—and much nastier—than you'd think possible."

"I'm sure," she smiled.

Ray Gunter, it turned out, had lived in a flint-walled cottage behind the garage. The front door had been taped off by the police, and the WPC from the village hall let Liz in with a key.

The outside of the cottage was attractive, but the interior was decidedly unprepossessing. The walls were grease-flecked, and the ceilings yellowed with cigarette smoke. In the kitchen the gas stove had not been cleaned for months, and a stack of washing-up languished in the stoneware sink. Liz's gaze moved from the discarded boots and waterproofs which lay heaped in one corner of the kitchen table, where a sliced white supermarket loaf spilled across a copy of the local paper. Beside it lay a tub of margarine, an open jar of marmalade, and an ashtray made from an unwashed Chinese takeaway carton.

She opened the large free-standing freezer. There was nothing inside except frozen fish, sealed inside plastic bags and painstakingly hand-labelled. Pollack, huss, rock salmon, codling, whiting . . . In this, if in no other department of his life, Ray Gunter had been assiduous.

At the bottom of the stairs was a small table with a telephone on it. Around the table, roughly inscribed on the wall in ballpoint and pencil, were a score of telephone numbers. Amongst these, Liz found the single name Hogan and a number, which she noted.

Upstairs, the cottage was no more appetising. Gunter had slept in an iron single bed, covered by a grime-shined duvet. A stale, mildewed smell hung in the cold air. There was a second room, not much more appetising. On its door a small plastic sign read "Kayleigh's Room."

The sister, thought Liz. Who'll presumably inherit the place now. And sell it—it would be worth a bit, cleaned up and restored. It would make the perfect weekend cottage, as Gunter must have known. Why had he hung on to it? Had he had some significant source of income beyond the fishing?

Returning downstairs, she searched the place for a local telephone directory, eventually locating one on the kitchen floor. Looking up the name Hogan she found and noted an address in Dersthorpe which corresponded to the telephone number written on the wall.

Outside, after returning the key to the WPC, she looked at the surrounding cottages. All bore the signs of gentrification, with neatly kept borders, ornaments in the windows, and antique knockers on the shiny front doors. Ray Gunter's passing would not be greatly mourned by his neighbours, she guessed. Kayleigh would have the place on the market by the spring, and by midsummer it would be identical to the others.

On the way back to her car, Liz looked in at the Trafalgar. The place was almost empty, and there was no sign of Cherisse behind the bar, only a middle-aged man in a cardigan whom she guessed to be Clive Badger. A strange object of desire for a girl like Cherisse, she mused, especially if he was the sort of employer who made her balance the till out of her own pocket.

A glance into the public bar told her that Cherisse wasn't there either. The busy times would be lunch and evening. She probably went home for the afternoon.

Dersthorpe was a couple of miles to the east of Marsh Creake. Liz slowed down as she drove past Headland Hall, but there was no sign of Peregrine or Anne Lakeby, just the dark trees bending before the sea wind.

It didn't take Liz long to find the council block where Cherisse Hogan lived. Outside it, in the rubbish-strewn car park, two youths were desultorily booting a punctured football around. Dersthorpe might have been just down the road from Marsh Creake, Liz reflected, but culturally it was another world. No one, surely, had ever bought a weekend cottage in Dersthorpe.

Cherisse lived on the third floor. She had changed from her work clothes into a crumpled black sweater and jeans. A tattoo of a baby devil was visible in the sweater's deep V-front.

"Yeah?" she asked, frowning, flicking her cigarette ash out of her front door.

"I was in the pub this morning," said Liz.

Cherisse nodded warily. "I remember."

"I want to talk about Ray Gunter. I'm working with the police."

"What's that mean, working with the police?"

Liz reached inside her coat and found her Civil Service identity card. "I report back to the Home Office."

Cherisse stared blankly at the card. Then she nodded, and took the door off the chain.

"Is this your place?" Liz asked, squeezing through the proffered gap.

"No. My mum's. She's out at work. My nan lives here too but she's gone into Hunstanton on the bus."

Liz looked around her. The air in the flat was close, but the place was comfortable. A three-bar electric fire blazed beneath a mantel-shelf decorated with glass ornaments and photographs of Cherisse. The wall held a framed print of waves breaking by moonlight. The TV was wide-screen.

Cherisse knew Gunter, she told Liz—she knew pretty much every-one in Marsh Creake—but denied that there had ever been anything between them. Having said that, she admitted, it was perfectly possible that Gunter had gone round telling people that there had been. In the public bar at the Trafalgar he liked to give the impression that she was his for the asking.

"Why?" asked Liz.

"He was that sort," said Cherisse blithely, stubbing her cigarette out in a tin ashtray. "When you're . . . busty, people think they can say what they like. That you're just there to make jokes about."

"Did you ever put the record straight about you and him?"

"I could have done. End of the day, though, he's a paying customer, and I'm not put behind that bar to make the customers feel like tossers, even if they are. Basically, Ray Gunter thought that if he wanted to impress someone all he had to do was start on me."

"So who was Ray Gunter wanting to impress?"

"Oh, various odds and sods. You know that house of his? There was always people trying to get him to sell to them. Like he was some sort of moron and didn't know the value of the place to the nearest penny. He'd take them down the Trafalgar and have them buying drinks for him all night."

"Anyone else?"

"There was one guy . . . Staffy, I used to call him, because he looked like a bull terrier."

"Do you know his real name?"

She nodded. "I'll remember in a minute. Cup of tea?"

"That'd be nice."

The kettle whistled. The electric heater seemed to shimmer in the radiated heat. Cherisse came back with two mugs.

"Thanks for this morning," she said hesitantly. "Helping me out."

"It was a pleasure," said Liz truthfully.

Cherisse grinned. "He didn't like the look of your friend, that's for sure."

"I thought it was me he was scared of," protested Liz.

"Well," said Cherisse, "perhaps it was."

There was a short silence, broken by the manic revving of an engine in the car park below. "Do you have any idea what Ray would have been doing at the Fairmile Café last night?" Liz asked.

"No idea."

"Do you know if he was into anything illegal? Anything to do with his boats?"

She shook her head again, her expression vague, and then brightened. "Mitch! That's what his name was. I knew I'd remember."

"Who was he?"

"I don't know. Like I said, he wasn't from round here. The reason I remember him is that when he came in Ray never sat at the bar like he usually did."

"Where did they sit?"

"Off in a corner. I asked Ray once who he was, because he'd been having, like, a good stare at me, and Ray said he was someone who bought from him. Lobsters and that."

"Did you believe that?"

Cherisse shrugged. "It wasn't a nice stare."

Liz nodded, and laid her empty mug on the table.

After the heat of the Hogans' flat, the sea front was bracingly cold. The phone box smelt of urine, and Liz was grateful when Wetherby picked up on the first ring.

"Tell me," he said.

"Things look bad," said Liz. "I'm coming back now."

"I'll be here," said Wetherby.

20

With each click of her scissors, another rat's-tail of black hair fell to the floor. Outside, the sky was dark with unshed rain. Faraj Mansoor was seated on a wooden chair in front of her, a white bath-towel around his shoulders. He didn't look like a murderer, but by his own account that was exactly what he had become—and within an hour of entering the United Kingdom for the first time.

That made her . . . what? A conspirator to murder? An accessory after the fact? It didn't matter. All that mattered was the operation and its security. All that was necessary was that they remain invisible.

There was much, of course, that she didn't know. It had to be this way—she wouldn't have had it any other. If she was taken, and subjected to whatever truth drugs and interrogation techniques the security services employed these days, it was essential that she had nothing to tell them.

She shivered, and almost cut him. If they were seen together or connected in any way, then this was her end-game. There would be, quite literally, nowhere to hide. She had been told enough about Faraj Mansoor, however, to know that he was a consummately professional operative. If he had shot and killed the boatman last night, then that would have been the best course of action at that particular moment. If it didn't worry him that he had ended the man's life, then it shouldn't worry her.

He was, she supposed, quite a good-looking man. She had preferred him as he had been when he'd woken up—still the wild-haired fighter. Now, beardless and neatly cropped, he looked like a successful website designer or advertising copywriter. Handing him the blued-steel scissors, she took the binoculars, stepped out on to the shingle, and scanned the horizon.

Nothing. No one.

The book that she had picked up shortly after her fifteenth birthday was a life of Saladin, the twelfth-century leader of the Saracens who had fought the Crusaders for possession of Jerusalem.

She had flicked through the first few pages, her mind on other things. She had never had much of a taste for history, and the events she was reading about had taken place in a past so distant, and in a culture so obscure, that they might as well have been science fiction.

Unexpectedly, however, she had found herself engaged by the book's subject. She pictured Saladin as a spare, hawk-faced figure, black-bearded and spike-helmeted. She learned how to write the name of his wife, Asimat, in Arabic script, and imagined her rather like herself. And when she read of the final surrender of Jerusalem to the Saracen prince in 1187, she was in no doubt that this was the outcome she would have wished.

The book represented the first step of what she would later describe as her orientalist phase. She read haphazardly and indiscriminately about the Mohammedan world, from swooning love stories set in Cairo, Lucknow and Samarkand to *The Arabian Nights*. In the hope of acquiring a Scheherezade-like mystique, she dyed her mouse-brown hair jet black, perfumed herself with rosewater, and took to painting the insides of her eyelids with kohl from the Pakistani corner shop. Her parents were bemused by this behaviour, but were pleased that she had found an interest and that she spent so much of her time reading.

Her early impressions of the Islamic world, refracted as they were through the prism of teenage escapism, would not have been recognised by many Muslims. Within a couple of years, however, the romantic novels had given way to dense volumes of Islamic doctrine and history, and she had begun to teach herself Arabic.

Essentially, she longed for transformation. For years now she had dreamed of leaving her unhappy and unremarkable background behind her, and of entering a new world where she would, for the first time, find total and joyous acceptance. Islam, it seemed, offered precisely the transformation she sought. It would fill the void inside her, the terrible vacuum in her heart.

She took to visiting the local Islamic centre, and, without telling her parents or teachers, receiving instruction in the Koran. Soon she was regularly visiting the mosque. She was accepted there, it seemed to her, as she had never been accepted before. Her eyes would meet those of other worshippers and she would see in them the same quiet certainty that she felt herself. That this was the right path, the only path. That the truths offered by Islam were absolute.

She told her teacher that she wanted to convert and he suggested that she speak to the imam at the mosque. She did so, and the imam considered her case. He was a cautious man, and something about this ardent, unsmiling girl worried him. She had done the necessary study, however, and he had no wish to turn her away. He visited her parents, who expressed themselves "totally cool" with the idea, and shortly after her eighteenth birthday he received her into the Islamic faith. Later that year she visited Pakistan with a local family who had relatives in Karachi. Soon, as well as speaking fluent Arabic, she was proficient in

Urdu. When she was twenty, after returning twice more to Pakistan, she was accepted as an undergraduate at the Department of Oriental Languages at the Sorbonne in Paris.

It was at the beginning of her second year at the university that the frustration began to bite. She was trapped, it seemed to her, within an utterly alien culture. Islam prohibited the belief in any god but Allah, and this prohibition included the false gods of money, status or commercial power. But everywhere she looked, amongst Muslims as well as unbelievers, she saw a crass materialism, and the worshipping of these very gods.

In response, she stripped her life to the bone, and sought out the mosques which preached the strictest and most austere forms of Islam. Here, the religious teachings were placed in a context of hard-line political theory. The imams preached the need to reject all that was not of Islam, and especially all that pertained to the great Satan—America. Her faith became her armour, and her abhorrence of the culture that she saw around her—a bloated and spiritless corporatism indifferent to anything except its own profit margins—grew to a silent, all-consuming, twenty-four-hours-a-day fury.

One day she was sitting on a Métro station bench, returning from the mosque, when she was joined by a young, leather-jacketed North African with a straggly beard. His face seemed vaguely familiar.

"Salaam aleikum," he murmured, glancing at her.

"Aleikum salaam."

"I have seen you at prayers." His Arabic was Algerian in inflexion.

She half closed her book, looked meaningfully at her watch, and said nothing.

"What are you reading?" he asked.

Expressionless, she angled the book so that he could see the title. It was the autobiography of Malcolm X.

"Our brother Malik Shabazz," he said, giving the civil rights activist his Islamic name. "Peace upon him."

"Just so."

The young man leaned forward over his knees. "Sheik Ruhallah is preaching at the mosque this afternoon."

"Indeed," she said.

"You must come."

She looked at him, surprised. Despite his unkempt appearance, there was a quiet authority about him.

"So what is it that this Sheik Ruhallah preaches?" she asked.

The young man frowned. "He preaches jihad," he said. "He preaches war."

21

On the drive back to London Liz thought about Mark. Her anger at his untimely call had faded, and she needed a break from the rigorous business of analysing the day's events. This would not, she knew, be time wasted. If she refocused her attention, her subconscious would continue to shuffle the pieces of the jigsaw. Continue to meditate on exposed headlands, terror networks, and armour-piercing ammunition. And perhaps come up with some answers.

How would it be if he left Shauna? At one reckless and wholly irresponsible level—the level to which Mark instinctively gravitated—it would be great. They would conspire, they would say unsayable things to each other, they would roll over in the night in the certain knowledge of the other's answering desire.

But at every realistic level it was impossible. Her career in the Service would not prosper, for a start. Nothing would be said to her face, but she would be regarded as unsound, and in the next reshuffle moved somewhere risk-free and unexciting—recruiting, perhaps, or protective security—until the powers that be saw how her private life worked out.

And how would it really be, living with Mark? Even if Shauna kept quiet and didn't make a fuss, life would change drastically. There would be new and only vaguely imaginable limitations on the freedoms that she currently took for granted. It would be impossible to behave as she had behaved today, for example—to simply get into her car and drive, not knowing when she would be back. Absences would have to be explained and negotiated with a partner who, not unreasonably, would want to know when she was going to be around. Like most men who hated to be tied down themselves, Mark was capable of being intensely possessive. Her life would be subject to a whole new dimension of stress.

And there were more fundamental questions to answer. If Mark left Shauna, would it be because the relationship between the two of them had been doomed from the start? If she—Liz—hadn't come along, would the marriage have imploded anyway? Or would things have been fine, give or take the odd hiccup? Was she an agent of destruction, a home-wrecker, a *femme fatale*? She had never seen herself in that role, but then perhaps one never did.

It couldn't happen. She would call him as soon as she got back to London. Where was she? Somewhere near Saffron Walden, it seemed, and she had just passed through the village of Audley End when she became aware of a familiar sensation. A prickling, as if soda bubbles were racing through her bloodstream. An expanding sense of urgency.

Russia. The memory struggling towards the light was something to do with Russia. And with Fort Monkton, the MI6 training school, where she had done a firearms course. As she drove she could hear the unemphatic Bristolian burr of Barry Holland, the Fort Monkton armourer, and smell the torn air of the underground firing range as she and her colleagues emptied the magazines of their 9mm Brownings into the Hun's-head targets.

She was almost at the M25 when the memory finally surfaced, and she realised why Ray Gunter had been shot with an armour-piercing round. The knowledge brought no sense of release.

She sat down opposite Wetherby shortly after eight. She had arrived at her desk to find a two-word telephone message: Marzipan Fivestar. This, Liz knew, meant that Sohail Din wanted to be rung at home as a matter of urgency. She had never received this message from him before, and it immediately concerned her, because a Fivestar request usually meant that an agent was fearful of discovery and, on either a temporary or permanent basis, wanted to cease contact. She prayed that this was not the case with Marzipan.

She dialled his number, and to her relief it was Sohail himself who picked up the phone. In the background she could hear canned laughter from a television.

"Is Dave there?" Liz asked.

"I'm sorry," said Sohail. "Wrong number."

"That's strange," said Liz. "Do you know Dave?"

"I know six or seven Daves," said Sohail, "and none of them lives here. Goodbye."

In six or seven minutes, then, he would call her back from a public phone. She had instructed him never to use the nearest one to his house. In the interim, she called up Barry Holland at Fort Monkton, and by the time Sohail called back, her laser printer was disgorging the relevant information.

Wetherby, she thought, looked tired. The shadows seemed to have deepened around his eyes, and his features had assumed a fatalistic cast which made her wish that she was the bearer of better news. Perhaps, though, it was just a matter of the time of day. His manner, as always, was fastidiously courteous, and as she spoke she was conscious of his absolute attention. She had never seen him take notes.

"I agree with you about Eastman," he said, and she noticed that the dark green pencil was once again between his fingers. "He's being used in some way, and it very much looks as if the situation's spiralled out of his control. It sounds certain that there's a German connection of some kind, and that the connection points east. More specifically there's the truck in the car park to consider, and the probability that some sort of handover was made at that point."

Liz nodded. "The police seem to be proceeding on the basis of the weapon in question being some sort of military assault rifle."

The faintest of smiles. "You clearly think otherwise."

"I remembered something we were told at Fort Monkton. How the KGB and the Russian Interior Ministry troops had phased out the old Stalin-era hand weapons in the early nineties because they kept coming up against ballistic body armour that the rounds couldn't penetrate."

"Go on."

"So they developed a new generation of handguns with massive payloads. Things like the Gyurza that weighed more than a kilo and fired tungsten-core and armour-piercing rounds. Barry Holland showed us a couple of them."

"Any of them 7.62 calibre?"

"Not that I remember. But there have been a lot of developments in the last ten years. The FBI have test-firing results on something that so far doesn't even have a name. It's just known as the PSS." She glanced at the print-out. *"Pistolet Samozaryadne Specialny."*

"Special Silenced Pistol," translated Wetherby.

"Exactly. It's an ugly-looking thing, but technically it's way out in front. It's got the lowest sound signature of any existing firearm. You could fire it through a coat pocket and the person standing next to you wouldn't hear a thing. At the same time it's got enough punch to take out a target wearing full body armour."

"I thought silencers reduced power."

"Conventional silencers do. The Russians rethought the issue, and what they came up with was silent ammunition."

Wetherby's left eyebrow rose a millimetre or two.

"It's called SP-4. The way it works is that the explosion is completely contained in the cartridge case in the main body of the gun. None of the gases escape, so there's no noise and no flash."

"And the calibre of this ammunition?"

"Seven point six two armour-piercing."

Wetherby didn't smile, but regarded her thoughtfully for a moment, lowered the sharpened point of the dark green pencil to the desk, and nodded. The fact that he didn't find it necessary to congratulate her afforded Liz a quiet pleasure, despite the topic's grimness.

"So why has our man gone to the trouble of acquiring a specialist weapon like this?"

"Because he is expecting to find himself up against armoured or flak-jacketed opposition. Police. Security guards. Special forces. He's going to need the technical edge that the PSS can give him."

"Any other conclusions we can draw?"

"That he, or more likely his organisation, has access to the best. This is a limited-edition weapon. You're not going to find one in an East End pub, any more than you're going to find one in a North West Frontier arms bazaar. So far they've only been issued to a handful of Russian Special Forces personnel, most of whom are currently engaged in undercover operations against Chechen militants in the Caucasus mountains. We're never going to get the facts and figures, but they will certainly have taken casualties, and it's reasonable to suppose that one or two of their personal weapons will have passed into rebel hands."

"And from there into the hands of the mujahidin armourers . . . Yes, I see where you're going." Wetherby glanced bleakly at the window. He seemed to be listening to the irregular beat of the rain. "Anything else?"

"I'm afraid it gets worse," said Liz. "When I came in this evening I returned a Fivestar call from Marzipan."

"Go on."

"There's some kind of online Arabic newsletter that his colleagues read. He thinks it's written by ITS militants in Saudi—possibly al Safa's crowd—who are in on the planning stages of anti-Western operations. Marzipan hasn't seen it himself—the letter's written in some sort of code—but those in the know seem to think that something's about to happen here in the UK. A symbolic event of some kind. No clue as to the what, when or where, but the reported wording is that 'a man has arrived whose name is Vengeance before God.' "

Wetherby sat unblinking for a moment. "We're definitely talking about an ITS operation here?" he asked carefully. "Not some flag-burning demonstration, or the arrival of a new imam?"

"Marzipan said that his colleagues didn't seem in much doubt about it. As far as they were concerned the letter signalled an imminent attack."

Wetherby narrowed his eyes a fraction. "And you think that the man they're talking about could be our silent gunman from Norfolk."

Liz said nothing, and returning his pencil to the Fortnum and Mason jar, Wetherby reached downwards to one of the lower drawers of his desk. Opening it, he took out a bottle of Laphroaig whisky and two tumblers, and poured a shot into each. Pushing one of the tumblers towards Liz, and raising a hand to indicate that she should stay where she was, he lifted the receiver of one of the telephones on his desk and dialled a number.

The call, Liz swiftly realised, was to his wife.

"How did it go today?" Wetherby murmured. "Was it awful?"

The answer seemed to take some time. Liz concentrated on the smoky taste of the whisky, on the beating of the rain at the window, on the knocking of the radiator—anything but the conversation taking place in front of her.

"I have to stay late," Wetherby was saying. "Yes, I'm afraid there's a bit of a crisis and . . . No, I wouldn't do this to you unless it was absolutely unavoidable, I know that you've had the most hellish day . . . I'll call as soon as I'm in the car. No, don't wait up."

Replacing the receiver, he took a long swallow of the whisky, and then reversed one of the photo frames on his desk so that Liz could see it. The photograph showed a woman in a striped navy blue and white T-shirt sitting at a café table, holding a coffee cup. She had dark hair and delicate, fine-boned features and was looking into the camera with an amused tilt of the head.

The thing that struck Liz most forcibly about the woman, however, was her complexion. Although she couldn't have been more than thirty-five years old, her skin was the colour of ivory, so pale and bloodless as to appear almost transparent. At first Liz thought this was the result of a photo-processing error, but a glance at the café's other customers told her that the colour balance was more or less correct.

"It's called red blood-cell aplasia," said Wetherby quietly. "It's a disorder of the bone marrow. She has to go into hospital for a blood transfusion every month."

"She went into hospital today?"

"This morning, yes."

"I'm sorry," said Liz. Her small triumph in identifying the PSS seemed almost childish now. She shrugged. "Sorry to be the bringer of news that keeps you here."

A minute shake of the head. "You've done exceptionally well." He swirled the Laphroaig and raised his tumbler with an oblique smile. "Apart from anything else, you've provided me with the wherewithal to ruin Geoffrey Fane's evening."

"Well, that's something."

For a minute or two, as they finished their drinks, they sat in complicit silence. Around them many of the offices were empty, and the distant sound of a Hoover told Liz that the cleaners had arrived.

"Go home," he told her. "I'll get started on telling everyone who needs to know."

"OK. First, though, I'm going back to my desk to run a few checks on Peregrine Lakeby."

"You're going back to Norfolk tomorrow?"

"I think I should."

Wetherby nodded. "Keep me informed, then."

Liz stood. A barge sounded a long mournful note out on the river.

22

After a wet night the day dawned clear, and as Liz drove northwards towards the M11 the roads hissed beneath the Audi's tyres. She had slept badly; in fact she was not certain that she had slept at all. The amorphous mass of worry that the investigation represented had taken on a crushing weight, and the more desperately she had sought oblivion between the crumpled sheets, the faster her heart had raced in her chest. People's lives were threatened, she knew that much, and the image of Ray Gunter's broken head endlessly replicated itself in her mind. At intervals the features of the dead fisherman became those of Sohail Din. "Why don't you take up amateur dramatics?" he seemed to be asking, until she realised that the voice in her head was her mother's. But she couldn't quite summon her mother to her side; instead, smiling know-ingly at her, was an ivory-pale figure in a striped navy blue and white T-shirt. Through her transparent skin, Liz could see the hesitant passage of the blood in the veins and arteries. "I'm telling her that I'm in love with you," Mark was shouting, somewhere at the edge of her con-sciousness. "I'm talking about our future!"

But she must have slept, because there was a point at which she quite definitely awoke, thirsty and sore-headed with the lingering smoke of Wetherby's Laphroaig in her mouth. She had aimed for an early start and a fast exit from London, but unfortunately a sizeable proportion of the city's inhabitants seemed to have had the same idea. By eleven o'clock she was still half a dozen miles from Marsh Creake, trapped on a narrow road behind a low-bed truck loaded with sugar beet. Its driver was in no hurry at all, and if he was aware that he was shedding a couple of beets with every rut and bump that he encountered, the fact didn't worry him. It worried Liz, though, and at times she had to swing wildly on to the verge in order to avoid the bouncing vegeta-bles, any one of which could have blasted through a headlight or found some other way of causing three figures' worth of damage to the Audi's bodywork.

Eventually, her shoulders aching with tension, she pulled up outside the Trafalgar, and on venturing inside found Cherisse Hogan polishing glasses in the empty lounge.

"You again!" said Cherisse, darting Liz a lazy-eyed smile. She was wearing a tight lavender sweater and looking, in her gypsyish way, rather spectacular. She had clearly recovered from any short-term dis-tress that Ray Gunter's death might have caused her.

"I was wondering if you had a room?" Liz enquired.

Cherisse's eyebrows rose, and she moved unhurriedly into the shad-owed fastness of the kitchen area—there presumably to consult her employer. Clive Badger should count himself lucky, thought Liz, if the rumours about the pair of them were true. And they almost certainly were true; women like Anne Lakeby had a knack for sorting the wheat from the chaff when it came to local intrigue.

Cherisse returned a couple of minutes later holding a key suspended from a miniature brass anchor, and led Liz up a narrow carpeted stair to a door bearing the legend "Temeraire." The three other rooms were "Swiftsure," "Ajax" and "Victory."

"Temeraire" was low-ceilinged and warm, with a plum carpet, a tiled fireplace and a divan with a candlewick bedspread. It took Liz no more than a couple of minutes to unpack her clothes. When she went downstairs again Cherisse was still alone in the lounge bar, and beckoned Liz over with an inclination of the head.

"You know I told you about that Mitch? The one that drunk with Ray?"

"The one who reminded you of a bull terrier?" asked Liz.

"Yeah. That one. Staffy. He was on the tobacco game."

"Importing and selling cigarettes for cash, you mean? Without paying the duty?"

"Yeah."

"How do you know? Did he offer you some?"

"No, Ray did. He said Mitch could get as many as I wanted. He said I could have them for cost and then mark them up and flog them on to the punters at bar prices."

"Hang on, Cherisse. You're saying that Ray told you this on Mitch's behalf?"

"Yeah—he obviously thought he was doing him a favour. But Mitch went completely off his head. Told Ray he didn't know what the fuck he was talking about—'scuse my French—and told him to button it or he'd drop him on the spot. Completely off his head."

"But you reckon that Ray was right? That Mitch was selling cut-price tobacco and cigarettes?"

Cherisse considered. "Well, it would be a strange thing to say if he wasn't, wouldn't it? And lots of people are into that. Working in a pub you're always being offered cheap booze and fags. Especially fags. Everyone's got a half-dozen cartons out in the van."

"And have you ever bought any?"

"Me? No! I'd lose my job."

"So Mr. Badger doesn't buy from them either?"

Cherisse shook her head and continued with her desultory processing of the glasses. "I thought I'd mention it, though," she said. "He's a nasty piece of work, that Mitch."

"He certainly sounds it," said Liz. "Thanks."

She stared out into the empty bar. Pale winter sunshine streamed through the leaded windows, illuminating the dust motes and gilding the accessories on the wood-panelled walls. If Mitch, whoever he was, was involved in the selling of cut-price tobacco, and had told Ray Gunter as much, why was he so angry when Gunter had mentioned it to Cherisse? Much of a tobacco-smuggler's life was taken up with persuading publicans and bar staff to take his goods off his hands.

The only reason that Liz could fathom was that Mitch had graduated from tobacco-smuggling to more dangerous games. Games in which loose talk could be fatal. Thanking Cherisse again, she changed a ten-pound note into coins, and called Frankie Ferris from the pay phone in the pub's entrance hall. The hall was overheated, and smelt of furniture polish and air freshener. Ferris, as usual, seemed to be in a state of advanced agitation.

"It's really come on top with this murder," he whispered. "Total, like . . . Eastman's been locked in his office since yesterday morning. Last night he was there till—"

"Was the dead man anything to do with Eastman?"

"I don't know, and I wouldn't ask. Right now I just want to keep my head down, and if the law comes knocking I want some serious . . ."

"Serious?"

"Like, protection, OK? I'm taking a major risk just making this call. What if someone—"

"Mitch," said Liz. "I need to know about a man called Mitch."

A short, charged silence.

"Braintree," said Ferris. "Eight o'clock this evening on the top level of the multistorey by the station. Come alone." The phone went dead.

He smells trouble, thought Liz, replacing the handset. He wants to keep on pocketing Eastman's money but he also wants to protect his back when it all blows up. He knows he'll get no change out of Bob Morrison, so he's come back to me.

She wondered briefly about going down to the village hall, re-establishing contact with Goss and Whitten, and finding out if they had moved the case forward. After a moment's thought, however, she decided to drive down to Headland Hall and speak to Peregrine Lakeby first. Once she had linked up with the others it would be harder to keep information to herself.

With a quiet popping of gravel, the Audi came to a halt outside Headland Hall. This time the doorbell was answered by Lakeby himself. He was wearing a long Chinese dressing gown and a cravat, and was surrounded by a faint odour of limes.

He looked surprised to see Liz, but swiftly recovered himself, and led her along the tiled corridor into the kitchen. Here, at a broad work table of scrubbed pine, a woman was drying wine glasses with an unhurried action which Liz immediately recognised. This must be Elsie Hogan, mother to Cherisse.

"Aga's smoking again, Mr. Lakeby," said the woman, glancing incuriously at Liz.

Peregrine frowned, pulled on an oven glove, and gingerly opened one of the Aga doors. Smoke whooshed out, and taking a log from a tall basket, he slung it in and slammed the door shut again.

"That should do it."

The woman looked at him doubtfully. "Those logs are a bit green, Mr. Lakeby. I think that's the problem. Did they come from the garage?"

Peregrine looked vague. "Quite possibly. Have a word with Anne about them. She'll be back from King's Lynn in an hour." He turned to Liz. "Coffee?"

"I'm fine, thanks," said Liz, reflecting ruefully that you couldn't say to a man what she was about to say to Peregrine Lakeby and be drinking his coffee at the same time. So she stood and watched as he boiled water, spooned ground arabica beans into a cafetière, mixed, plunged, and poured the steaming result into a Wedgwood bone-china cup.

"Now," said Peregrine, when they had quit the smoky realm of the kitchen and were once again comfortably disposed in the book-lined drawing room, "tell me how I can help you."

Liz met his enquiring, faintly amused gaze. "I'd like to know about the arrangement you had with Ray Gunter," she said quietly.

Peregrine's head tilted thoughtfully. His hair, Liz noticed, swept back into steel-grey wings over each ear. "Which arrangement was that, precisely? If you mean the arrangement by which he kept his boats on the beach, I was under the impression that we had discussed that in some detail last time you and your colleagues came here."

So, thought Liz, they haven't been back.

"No," she said. "I mean the arrangement by which Ray Gunter brought illicit consignments ashore by night, and you agreed to turn a blind eye and a deaf ear to any disturbance. How much was Gunter paying you to ignore his activities?"

Peregrine's smile tightened. The patrician mask showed minute signs of strain. "I don't know where you've got your information from, Miss . . . er, but the idea that I might have had a criminal relationship with a man like Ray Gunter is quite frankly preposterous. May I ask what—or who—led you to such a bizarre conclusion?"

Liz reached into her briefcase and removed two printed sheets. "May I tell you a story, Mr. Lakeby? A story about a woman known in certain circles as the Marquise, real name Dorcas Gibb?"

Peregrine said nothing. His expression remained unaltered, but the colour began to ebb from his face.

"For several years now, the Marquise has been the proprietor of a discreet establishment in Shepherd Market, W1, where she and her employees specialise in . . ." she consulted the printed sheets, "discipline, domination, and corporal punishment."

Again, Peregrine said nothing.

"Three years ago, the existence of this establishment was drawn to the attention of the Inland Revenue. Madame la Marquise, it seemed, had neglected to pay any income tax for a decade or so. It must have slipped her mind. So the Revenue asked the Vice Squad if they'd mind giving her a nudge, and the Vice Squad didn't mind in the least. They raided the place. And guess who—along with an eminent QC and a popular New Labour peer—they found strapped to a flogging-horse with a rubber gag in his mouth and his trousers round his ankles?"

Peregrine's gaze turned to ice. His mouth was a thin, taut-clamped line. "My private life, young lady, is my own business, and I will not, repeat *not*, be blackmailed in my own house." He rose from the sofa. "You will kindly leave, and leave now."

Liz didn't move. "I'm not blackmailing you, Mr. Lakeby, I'm just asking you for the precise details of your commercial relationship with Ray Gunter. We can do this the easy way, or we can do it the hard way. The easy way involves you giving me all of the facts in confidence; the hard way involves a police arrest on suspicion of involvement in organised crime. And given that, as we all know, there's a regular flow of information between the police and the tabloid newspapers . . ."

She shrugged, and Peregrine stared down at her, expressionless. She returned his gaze, steel for steel, and gradually the fight and the arrogance seemed to drain out of him. He sat down again in slow motion, his shoulders slumped. "But if you're working with the police . . ."

"I'm not quite working with the police, Mr. Lakeby. I'm working alongside them."

His eyes narrowed warily. "So . . ."

"I'm not suggesting you did anything worse than take Gunter's money," said Liz quietly. "But I have to tell you that there's an issue of national security at stake here, and I'm sure you wouldn't wish to endanger the security of the state." She paused. "What was the deal with Gunter?"

He stared bleakly out of the window. "As you surmised, the idea was that I turned a blind eye to his comings and goings at night."

"How much did they pay you?"

"Five hundred a month."

"Cash?"

"Yes."

"And what did those comings and goings consist of?"

Peregrine gave a strained smile. "The same as they've consisted of for hundreds of years. This is a smuggler's coastline. Always has been. Tea, brandy from France, tobacco from the Low Countries . . . When the Channel ports and the Kent marshes got too dangerous, the cargoes moved up here."

"And that's what they were landing, was it? Booze and tobacco?"

"That's what I was told."

"By who? By Gunter?"

"No. I didn't actually deal with Gunter. There was another man, whose name I never found out."

"Mitch? Something like Mitch?"

"I've no idea. Like I said . . ."

"How were you paid?"

"The money was left inside the locker on the beach. The place where Gunter kept his fishing gear. I had a key to the padlock."

"So apart from this second man, did you ever meet or see anyone else?"

"Never."

"Can you describe the second man?"

Peregrine considered. "He looked . . . violent. Pale face and a skinhead haircut. Like one of those dogs they're always having to shoot for biting children."

"How did you meet him?"

"It was about eighteen months ago. Anne was up in town for the day, and he and Ray Gunter came up to the house. He asked me outright if I wanted to be paid five hundred pounds on the first of every month for doing absolutely nothing."

"And you said?"

"I said I'd think about it. He hadn't asked me to do anything illegal. He rang me the next day, and I said yes, and on the first of the next month the money was in the locker, as he had said that it would be."

"And he specifically said that it was tobacco and alcohol they were bringing in?"

"No. His actual words to me were that they were continuing the local tradition of outwitting the Excise men."

"And you had no problem with that?"

He leaned back against the sofa. "No. To be absolutely frank with you, I didn't. VAT's the bane of your life when you've got a place of this size to run, and if Gunter and his chum were giving Customs and Excise a run for their money, bloody good luck to them."

"Is there anything else you can tell me? About their vehicles? About the vessels they picked up from?"

"Nothing, I'm afraid. I honoured my side of the bargain, and kept my eyes and my ears closed."

Honoured, thought Liz. There's a word.

"And your wife's never suspected anything?"

"Anne?" he asked, almost bullish again. "No, why on earth should she? She heard the odd bump in the night, but . . ."

Liz nodded. The second man had to be Mitch, whoever Mitch was. And the reason he had been so furious with Gunter for talking about tobacco-smuggling to Cherisse was that the two of them had something much more serious to hide. Gunter had clearly been an indiscreet and generally far from ideal co-conspirator. As the man who owned the boats and knew the local tides and sandbanks, however, he had equally clearly been a vital cog in the operation.

Would Frankie Ferris come up with anything on Mitch? His manner on the phone had suggested that he knew who Mitch was, which in turn suggested that Mitch was one of Eastman's people. But then that was Ferris all over—desperate to prove his usefulness, even if it meant stretching the truth.

She looked at Peregrine. The urbane façade was almost back in place. She had given him a brief scare, but no more. On the way out she passed Elsie Hogan, who was standing, arms folded, in the kitchen doorway. Peregrine didn't waste a glance on her but Liz did, and saw the calculated blankness of the older woman's expression. Had Elsie, she wondered, spent the last ten minutes engaged in the household servant's traditional pastime of listening at the door? Would there soon be lurid tales of bared bottoms and upper-class spanking orgies circulating in the local bus queues, post offices and supermarkets?

23

In the thirty-six hours since his arrival, Faraj Mansoor had spoken very little. He had described the circumstances surrounding the death of the fisherman and he had satisfied himself that there was no particular reason for the police to come knocking at the bungalow door, but otherwise he had kept his own counsel. From 8:30 to 10 p.m. on the evening of his arrival he had paced the beach in the dark. He had eaten the food that the woman had put in front of him, and smoked a couple of cigarettes after each meal. At the prescribed time he had prayed.

Now, however, he seemed disposed for conversation. He called the woman Lucy, since this was the name on her driving licence and other documents, and for the first time he seemed to look at her closely, to fully acknowledge her presence. The two of them were bent over the bungalow's dining table examining an Ordnance Survey map. As a security precaution they were using stalks of dried grass as pointers; both were aware that a bare finger leaves a fine but easily traceable grease trail on map paper.

Road by road, intersection by intersection, they planned their route. Where possible they selected minor roads. Not country lanes where every passing car was a memorable event, but roads too insignificant for speed cameras. Roads where the police were unlikely to be lying up waiting for boy-racers or drunk-drivers.

"I suggest we park here," she said, "and walk up the rest of the way."

He nodded. "Four miles?"

"Five, perhaps. If we push ourselves we should be able to do it in a couple of hours. There is a track for the first three miles, so we shouldn't look out of place."

"And this? What is this?"

"A flood relief channel. There are bridges, but that's one of the things we need to recce."

He nodded, and stared intently at the gently undulating countryside. "How good are the security people?"

"We would be foolish to assume that they are not very good."

"They'll be armed?"

"Yes. Heckler and Koch MP5s. Full body armour."

"What will they be looking out for?"

"Anything out of the ordinary. Anything or anyone that doesn't fit."

"Will we fit?"

She glanced sideways at him, tried to see him as others would. His light-skinned Afghan features marked him out as non-European in origin, but millions of British citizens were now non-European in origin. The conservative cut and idiosyncratic detailing of his clothing indicated someone who, at the very least, had been educated in Britain, and probably privately educated there. His English was flawless, and his accent was classic BBC World Service. Either he had attended a very smart school in Pakistan, or he had had some decidedly patrician friends over there.

"Yes." She nodded. "We'll fit."

"Good." He pulled on the dark blue New York Yankees baseball cap that she'd bought him in King's Lynn. "You know the location? They said that you knew it well."

"Yes. I haven't been there for several years, but it can't have changed much. This map is new, and it's exactly as I remember it."

"And you will have no hesitation in doing what has to be done? You have no doubts?"

"I will have no hesitation. I have no doubts."

He nodded again, and carefully folded up the map. "They spoke highly of you at Takht-i-Suleiman. They said that you never complained. Most importantly, they said that you knew when to be silent."

She shrugged. "There were plenty of others prepared to do the talking."

"There always are." He reached into his pocket. "I have something for you."

It was a gun. A miniature automatic, the size of her hand. Curious, she picked it up, ejected the five-round magazine, ratcheted back the slide, and tried the action. "Nine millimetre?"

He nodded. "It's Russian. A Malyah."

She hefted it in her hand, slapped back the magazine, and thumbed the safety catch on and off. Both of them knew that if she was forced to use it, the end would not be far away.

"They decided that I should be armed, then?"

"Yes."

Fetching her waterproof mountain jacket, she unzipped the collar section, pulled out the hood, and zipped it up again with the Malyah inside. The hood effectively hid the slight bulge.

Mansoor nodded approvingly.

"Can I ask you something?" she said tentatively.

"Ask."

"We seem to be taking our time. A recce today, a rest day tomorrow . . . What are we waiting for? Why don't we just . . . do it? Now that the boatman is dead, every day makes it more likely that . . ."

"That they'll find us?" He smiled.

"People don't get shot here every day," she persisted. "There will be detectives, there will be pathologists, forensics people, ballistics . . . What's that round of yours going to tell them, for example?"

"Nothing. It's a standard calibre."

"In Pakistan, perhaps, but not here. The security people here aren't stupid, Faraj. If they smell a rat they'll come looking. They'll send their best people. And you can forget any idea you might have about British fair play; if they have the faintest suspicion of what we are planning to do—and a search of this house would give them a pretty good idea—they will kill us outright, proof or no proof."

"You're angry," he said, amused. Both of them were conscious that it was the first time she had used his name.

She lowered her fists to the table. Closed her eyes. "I'm saying that we can accomplish nothing if we are dead. And that with every day that passes it becomes more likely that . . . that they will find and kill us."

He looked at her dispassionately. "There are things that you don't know," he said. "There are reasons for waiting."

She met his gaze for a moment—the gaze that at times made him look fifty, rather than a score of months short of thirty—and bowed her head in acceptance. "I ask only that you don't underestimate the people we are up against."

Faraj shook his head. "I don't underestimate them, believe me. I know the British, and I know just how lethal they can be."

She looked at him for a moment, and then, taking the binoculars, opened the door, stepped outside on to the shingle, and scanned the horizon to east and west.

"Anything?" he asked, when she returned.

"Nothing," she said.

He watched her. Watched as her eyes flickered to the jacket containing the concealed Malyah.

"What is it?" he asked.

She shook her head. Took an uncertain step back towards the front door, and then stopped.

"What is it?" he said again, more gently this time.

"They're looking for us," she replied. "I can feel it."

He nodded slowly. "So be it."

24

Pulling her coat tightly around her, Liz installed herself on the bench overlooking the sea. The mudflats were underwater now, and the incoming tide slapped fretfully at the sea wall in front of her. A seagull landed heavily beside the bench, saw that Liz had no food with her, and swung away again on to the wind. It was cold, and the sky was hardening to an ominous slate grey at the horizon, but for the time being the village of Marsh Creake remained washed in light.

The enhanced CCTV tape, according to Goss, was expected back from Norwich at noon. The Special Branch man had been surprised to see Liz back so soon, he had told her, given that Whitten's investigation had thrown up no clue as to Ray Gunter's killer. The detective superintendent had told Goss that he was "ninety-eight per cent certain" that the murder was connected with drug-smuggling. His theory was that Gunter had been in the wrong place at the wrong time, had seen a consignment brought to shore, and received a bullet in the head for his pains. Whitten wasn't particularly worried by the untypical calibre of the fatal round; British gangsters, he reckoned, used any firearms they could get their hands on.

Liz continued to turn over in her mind the facts that she had learned from Peregrine Lakeby and Cherisse Hogan. At another level, she came to a decision about Mark. As far as she was concerned, the affair was now over. There would be moments when she would long for his voice and his touch, but she would simply have to endure them. Quite quickly, she knew, such moments would become fleeting, and then they would cease altogether, and the physical memory of him would fade.

It would not be a painless process, but it would be one with which Liz was familiar. The first time had been the worst. A few years after joining the Service she had attended the private view of an exhibition of photographs by a woman she had known at university. She had not known the woman well, and several address books must have been trawled through when the guest list was made up. Amongst the others present was a handsome, scruffily dressed man of about her own age. His name was Ed, and like her he had only the faintest of connections to their host.

They escaped to a Soho pub. Ed, she discovered, was a freelance TV researcher, and was currently involved in putting together a film about the lifestyle of New Age travellers. He had just completed a fortnight's stint accompanying one such tribe as they moved from campsite to campsite in an old bus, and with his rough-edged, wind-burned good looks he might easily have been one of their number.

She proceeded with caution, but their mutual attraction had an air of inevitability about it, and she was soon spending nights in the converted warehouse in Bermondsey that he shared with a shifting cast of artists, writers and filmmakers. She told him that she worked in one of the personnel departments of the Home Office, that her job was fulfilling in an unspectacular sort of way, and that she couldn't be contacted at work. Ed, not on the surface the possessive type, appeared to have no problem with this. His researches took him away for days and sometimes weeks at a time, and she was careful never to press him for details of these absences, in case he should do the same thing to her. They lived lives which were physically separate for the most part, but which were lit by passionate points of contact. Ed was clever, he was entertaining, and he viewed the world from a fascinatingly oblique perspective. Most weekends there was a party, or something like one, at the Bermondsey flat, and after a grim week with the Organised Crime Group, the arty, kaleidoscopic world of which she had part-time membership provided a blissful escape.

One Sunday morning she was lying in bed in Bermondsey, the papers strewn about her, watching the slow progress of the barges and the Thames coalers on the river.

"Where exactly did you say you worked?" he asked, flicking through the pages of a colour supplement.

"Westminster," said Liz vaguely.

"Whereabouts in Westminster exactly?"

"Off Horseferry Road. Why?"

He reached for his coffee mug. "Just wondering."

"Please," she yawned, "I don't want to think about work. It's the weekend."

He drank, and returned the mug to the carpet. "Would that be Horseferry House in Dean Ryle Street, or Grenadier House in Horseferry Road?"

"Grenadier House," said Liz warily. "Why?"

"What number Horseferry Road is Grenadier House?"

She sat slowly upright and looked at him. "Ed, why are you asking me these questions?"

"What number? Tell me."

"Not until you tell me why you want to know."

He stared ahead of him. "Because I rang the main Home Office enquiries number at Queen Anne's Gate last week, trying to get a message to you. I said you worked in personnel and they gave me the number of Grenadier House. I rang it and asked to leave a message for you, and the person I spoke to had clearly never heard your name in her life. I had to spell it for her twice, and then she thought she had put me on hold but she hadn't, and I could hear her talking to someone else, and that someone else explaining that you never confirm or deny people, just get the caller to leave a name and number. So I left my name and number, and of course I never heard back from you, so I rang again, and this time someone else took my name and number but wouldn't say if you worked there or not, so I rang a third time, and this time I was passed on to a supervisor, who said my earlier calls were being processed, and no doubt the officer in question would get back to me in her own good time. So I'm wondering, what the hell is this all about? What have you not told me, Liz?"

She folded her arms tightly over her chest. She had made herself genuinely angry now. "Listen to me. The number of Grenadier House is 99 Horseferry Road. It is the headquarters of the personnel department of the Home Office, and it is the responsibility of that department, amongst other things, to make sure that Civil Service staff are properly protected. That means ensuring that people making decisions about immigration, say, or prison sentencing issues can't be harassed or threatened or pressured over the phone by any Tom, Dick or Harry who has picked up their name. Now as it happens I was away from my desk all last week, working at the Croydon office. I expect I'll find your messages first thing tomorrow. Satisfied?"

He had been, more or less. But it was a side of him that she had never seen before, and she was glad that, during training, they had role-played a question-and-answer session very similar to the one that had just taken place. She was under no illusions, though, that he would let the matter rest there.

"I'm sorry," he had said. "It's just that that side of your life is such an . . . area of darkness. I imagine things."

"What sort of things?"

"It doesn't matter."

She had smiled, and they had made breakfast, and later that day they had gone for a walk along the Grand Union Canal towpath, from Limehouse Basin up past King's Cross to Regent's Park. It had been a windy winter's day, much like this one, and the kite-flyers had been out in force in the park. It was the last time that she saw him. That evening she had written and posted a letter, saying that she had met someone else, and that they couldn't see each other any more.

The weeks that followed had been truly wretched. She had felt flayed, as if an entire layer of her life—all that gave it colour and excitement—had been ruthlessly stripped away. She had thrown herself into her work, but to begin with its painstaking slowness and multiple frustrations had just made her feel worse. Along with several colleagues, she had been trying to acquire intelligence about a recently formed association of southeastern crime families. The work—processing and analysing surveillance reports and phone taps—was grimly routine, and involved scores of targets.

It was Liz who finally spotted the minute chink in the syndicate's armour that had led to the breakthrough. A driver for a west London crime syndicate had agreed, in return for a guarantee of immunity from prosecution, to provide information to her. He was her first personally recruited agent, and when the Met had rolled up the entire Acton-based network, together with a cache of firearms and hundreds of thousands of pounds' worth of crack cocaine rocks, she had felt great satisfaction. Cutting away her relationship with Ed, agonising though it had been at the time, had been the only possible course of action.

It was at that point that she had finally realised the truth. That she was not, as she had sometimes thought, a square peg in a round hole. She was the right person in the right job. The Service's recruiters had known her better than she knew herself. They had recognised that her quiet sage-green gaze masked an unflinching determination. A hunger for the fierce, close-focused engagement of the chase.

It was for this reason, she supposed, that she chose men who, while attractive, were also ultimately disposable. Because when all was said and done—when the passion that had ignited the thing in the first place threatened to turn to something more demanding and complex—they would be disposed of. Each time—and there had been perhaps half a dozen such affairs, some longer-term, some shorter-term—it had promised to turn out differently, but each time, looking back on it, it had turned out the same. She had found herself unable to compromise her independence in order to accommodate the emotional needs of a lover.

That this cycle led to her denying her own emotional needs she was well aware. Each parting was an excision, a scalpel's downstroke, for which the only cure was immersion in work.

"Tape's here," said Goss, materialising at her side.

"Thanks." She snapped herself back to the present, to the wind and the high tide. "Tell me something, Steve. How obvious was it that there was a CCTV set-up at the Fairmile Café?"

"Not obvious at all. It was wired up in a tree. You wouldn't have seen it if you didn't know it was there."

"I thought the idea of those things was deterrence."

"It is, up to a point, but in this case it had got beyond that. There had been a number of thefts from rigs, and the café owners had a fair idea who was responsible. Basically, they wanted evidence they could use in court."

"So a general recce of the place wouldn't have told anyone that there were cameras there?"

"No. No way."

"A good place for an RV, then, or a drop-off."

"It would have looked like one if you weren't in the know, yes." He looked sombrely up at the darkening sky. "Let's hope that we've finally got something. We badly need to move this thing forward."

"Let's hope," said Liz.

In the village hall, a good fug had been got up. Ashtrays had been distributed, a kettle installed, and a hot-air blower roared quietly beneath the stage. As the female constable rewound the tape in the VCR, and Liz and Goss found themselves chairs, Whitten and three plainclothes officers milled purposefully in front of the monitor. There was a faint smell of conflicting aftershaves.

"Can you find the bit when Sharon Stone uncrosses her legs?" one of the plainclothes officers asked the constable, to sniggers from the others.

"Dream on, Fatboy," she retorted, and turned to Whitten. "We're cued up. Shall I run it?"

"Yeah, let's go."

"They've eliminated the first vehicle we saw on the tape yesterday," Goss murmured to Liz. "It was just some bloke parking up his rig for the night."

"OK."

As the police team retreated to their chairs, a frozen wide-shot of the vehicle park filled the screen. The enhanced version had a flaring, bleached-out look to it, and Liz found herself narrowing her eyes against the glare. The footage had been edited down, and the time code began to flicker at 04:22. It ran for a minute, and then the silvery image of a truck wobbled into the picture, its lights scribbling white trails. Unhurriedly, the truck negotiated a three-point turn in the centre of the puddled ground so that it was facing the exit. The headlights were then extinguished.

Stillness for several seconds, and then a bulky figure jumped down from the cab. Was that Gunter? wondered Liz, seeing a pale upper-body blur that might have been the fisherman's sweater. As the figure made for the truck's rear doors and disappeared, a light flared briefly in the cab, illuminating a second figure on the driver's side.

"Lighting a cigarette," murmured Goss.

Two shapes climbed from the back of the truck. One was the original figure from the cab, the other an anonymous blob, possibly carrying a coat or rucksack. The two seemed to drift together for a moment, and then separate. A pause, and then the darker figure began to walk in a straight line out of frame. Twenty-five seconds passed, and then the other followed.

The image cut to black, and then restarted. The time code now read

04:26. The truck was still in place, but no light showed inside the cab. After sixty seconds the darker of the two figures returned from the direction in which it had gone, and disappeared behind the truck. Forty seconds later a parked car switched on its headlights and reversed at speed out of its parking space. Inside the car, the pale figures of a driver and a passenger were briefly visible, but the vehicle itself was no more than a black and almost shapeless blur, and there was clearly no question of recovering its registration number. Swinging round the truck it drove at speed towards the road and exited the frame.

When it was over there was a long silence.

"Thoughts, anyone?" asked Whitten eventually.

25

The fenland village of West Ford, some thirty miles southeast of Marsh Creake and the coast, offered little in the way of entertainment. There was a panel-beating and exhaust repairs business, a small village store incorporating a sub post office, and a pub, the George and Dragon. But precious little, reflected Denzil Parrish, to engage the imagination of a sexually frustrated nineteen-year-old with time on his hands. And Denzil, over the next fortnight, would have quite a lot of time on his hands. The evening before, he had arrived home from Newcastle, where he was at university. He had considered staying in his Tyneside hall of residence until Christmas Eve; there were any amount of parties going on and a wild time had been prophesied by all. But he hadn't seen much of his mother in the last year—since her remarriage, in fact—and had felt that he should try and spend some time with her. So he had done what he considered the decent thing: packed a rucksack and crammed himself into a southbound train so crowded that the ticket collector had given up trying to push his way through—just as well, because Denzil had no ticket—and after several delays and missed connections had arrived at Downham Market station well after dark, and with no prospect of a bus to West Ford. He had walked over four miles through the rain, jerking out his thumb at every passing car, before an American airman from one of the bases had stopped for him. He had known the village of West Ford, and had joined Denzil for a beer at the George and Dragon before speeding on southwards to the USAF base at Lakenheath.

After he had gone Denzil had scanned the pub. Typically, there wasn't an unattached girl in the place, so there really wasn't a viable reason to go on drinking, although he would have liked to. But money was too tight to blow on solitary drinking—drinking that had no hope of yielding any kind of female acquaintanceship. With tuition fees and the rest of it he was already thousands of pounds into the red. He really should have stayed up north. Right now he could be at a party, drinking someone else's lager for free. And with a bit of luck locked on to some cheerful Geordie lass into the bargain. But it was not to be, and after the American's warm VW Passat had vanished into the wet darkness he had foot-slogged home, only to find the place empty except for a gormless creature who had identified herself as the night's babysitter. His mum, she had explained without taking her eyes off the TV, had gone to a function somewhere. A dinner-dance. And no, no one had said anything about anyone arriving from Newcastle. Denzil had dug out a frozen pizza and joined the babysitter in front of the TV. He was so dispirited he couldn't even bring himself to make a pass at her.

At least the sun was shining today. That was a plus. His mother had apologised for being out when he arrived home, given him a quick kiss and hurried off to mix up a new bottle of formula. What was the woman thinking of, wondered Denzil vaguely. Having a second baby at this time of her life. It was just undignified, surely? But what the hell. Her life. Her money.

Denzil had decided to get out his wetsuit and do some canoeing. He had had a vague project in mind for the last couple of years—since they had moved to West Ford, in fact—which involved the systematic exploration of the area's interconnecting grid of drainage channels. The Methwold Fen Relief Drain was only ten minutes' drive away, and promised many miles of deserted but navigable water. He might even take the fishing gear out, and see if he could pick up a pike. The single advantage of his mother's post-natal state was that she didn't use her car so much. He'd be able to borrow it for hours at a time. The knackered old Honda Accord wasn't exactly what you'd call a babe magnet, but then, mused Denzil pessimistically, rural Norfolk wasn't exactly troubled by a babe overload.

The problem, for all their geniality and likeability, was the Americans. There were hundreds of them, mostly single young men, and they had nowhere to go off-base in the evenings except to the local pubs. West Ford was several miles from the nearest base, but you still got a handful of them at the George most evenings, and while this was fine in itself it meant that a single, impoverished geology student didn't stand a great chance in the event of a halfway-decent-looking girl fronting up there.

Throwing his wetsuit into the back of the Accord, Denzil manoeuvred the glass-fibre kayak out of the garage and on to the car's roofrack, where he secured it with a couple of bungee cords. The kayak had belonged to the house's previous owners, or more precisely to their daughter, who had lost interest in it and left it behind when the family moved. It had been gathering dust and house-martin droppings in the garage rafters for several years when Denzil had decided to clean it up. Initially his idea had been to sell it, but he had taken it out for a trial run on the relief drain and enjoyed himself more than he had expected to. It wasn't something that he revealed about himself on first dates, but Denzil was a keen birdwatcher, and his silent glides between the rushy banks of the fenland cuts and channels had brought him into rewardingly close contact with bitterns, reed warblers, marsh harriers and other rare species.

On the way out of the village he was forced to brake the Honda behind a tractor and trailer which were blocking the road. The tractor's driver was attempting to back the trailer, which was loaded with fertiliser sacks, into a field. His inexperience, however, ensured that the trailer kept jacknifing into the gatepost. Realising that the operation was going to take some time, Denzil switched off the Honda's ignition and settled philosophically back in his seat. As he waited, he noticed a young couple in hiking clothes crossing the field towards him. They were covering the ground fast—much faster than tourists or sightseers usually did—and their step was purposeful. Or at least the woman's step was purposeful. The man, an Asian-looking guy, was more laid back. His arms swung loosely at his sides, and he appeared not so much to be walking over the damp, uneven ground, as floating over it. Denzil had only ever seen one person cover ground like that, and that had been the wiry old ex–Royal Marine sergeant who ran the Snowdonia climbing school he'd worked at in his gap year.

Absently, his thoughts touching briefly on the question of whether fancying a woman in a cagoule and mountain boots constituted sexually aberrant behaviour, Denzil watched the pair out of the car window. Neither was smiling, neither gave the impression of being on holiday. Perhaps they were a couple of those high achievers from the City that one heard about. People who could never fully unwind, and who, even away from work—even here, in soggy East Anglia—felt the need to submit themselves to rigorous and competitive activity.

Up close, he saw that the woman was quite attractive in a no-nonsense, no-make-up sort of way. All that was missing was a smile on her face. The answer to the perversion question, he guessed, was that you were perfectly safe up to the point when you actually had to dress women up in foul-weather clothing to fancy them. Thereafter you were in trouble.

The car behind him beeped, and Denzil saw that the tractor driver had finally managed to steer his load into the field and that the road ahead was clear. Engaging the Honda's ignition, he moved forward in a shudder of exhaust and non-specific erotic fantasy, and promptly forgot all about the couple in the hiking gear.

26

So tell me," said Liz, when she and Goss were established, once again, in the saloon bar of the Trafalgar.

Goss considered. "Going on the evidence of that tape, I'd say we were still in the dark. I think Ray Gunter was one of the two people in the cab of that truck, and I think he followed whoever was in the back to the toilet block, and got himself shot. The question is, who was in the back? Don Whitten, I know, thinks that we're looking at a people-smuggling operation, and that the person that Gunter let out was part of the cargo, but there isn't a shred of evidence to support that theory. All sorts of people travel in the backs of trucks, and most people-smugglers take their cargoes to one of the cities, they don't drop them off at rural transport cafés to be collected by people in saloon cars."

"Looked more like a hatchback to me," said Liz. She felt slightly guilty for keeping the Special Branch officer in the dark about "Mitch," Peregrine Lakeby, and the Zander calls, but until she had spoken to Frankie Ferris, as she was due to do this evening, she could see no sense in sharing what she had discovered. What had happened, she was now almost certain, was that a low-level Melvin Eastman people-smuggling operation had been hijacked in order to bring a specific individual into the UK unannounced. Someone who, for whatever reason, couldn't risk coming in with a false passport. Eastman's "Pakis and ragheads" rant suggested that the individual in question was probably Islamic, and assuming that this was the case, the use of the PSS pistol suggested a specially armed operative. Whichever way you looked at it, it was worrying.

"Two haddock and chips," said Cherisse Hogan breezily, depositing large oval plates in front of them and returning a minute later with a bowlful of sauce sachets.

"I hate these bloody things," said Goss, tearing at one of the sachets with his large fingers until it more or less exploded in his hand. Liz watched him without comment for a moment, and then, taking a pair of scissors from her bag, neatly decapitated a tartare sauce sachet and squeezed it on to the side of her plate.

"Don't say it," warned Goss, wiping his fingers. "No brain versus brawn gags."

"I wouldn't dream of any such thing," promised Liz, passing him the scissors.

They ate in companionable silence. "Beats the Norwich canteen," said Goss after a few minutes. "How's your fish?"

"Good," said Liz. "I'm just wondering if it was one of Ray Gunter's."

"It's had its revenge if it was," said a familiar voice.

She looked up. Bruno Mackay stood at her elbow, car keys in hand. He was wearing a tan leather jacket and carrying a laptop computer in a satchel over one shoulder.

"Liz," he said, extending his hand.

She took it, forcing a smile. Did his presence mean what she thought it meant? Belatedly, she glanced at Goss, frozen opposite her in an attitude of enquiry.

"Er . . . Bruno Mackay," she said, "this is Steve Goss. Norfolk Special Branch."

Goss nodded, lowered his fork and guardedly extended his hand.

Bruno shook it. "I've been asked to come up and share the strain," he explained with a broad smile. "Lend a helping hand."

Liz forced a smile of her own. "Well, as you can see, the strain's not too unbearable yet. Have you had anything to eat?"

"No. I'm ravenous. I might just go and have a quick word with Truly Scrumptious over there. Would you mind . . ." Dropping his keys proprietorially on the table, he marched off to the bar, where he was soon locked in intimate consultation with Cherisse.

"Something tells me you've been stitched up," murmured Goss.

Liz emptied her face of her feelings. "No, I've just had my phone switched off. I obviously missed the message that he was on his way."

"Get you anything?" Bruno called out cheerfully from the bar.

Liz and Goss both shook their heads. Cherisse's eyes were shining, Liz noted with irritation. Mackay, meanwhile, looked roguishly at home.

"Bit of a personality, then, your chum?" Goss remarked drily.

"Indeed," Liz confirmed.

The rest of the meal was distinctly unrelaxing. There were too many listeners-in at nearby tables for any discussion of the case to be possible. Instead, Mackay quizzed Goss about the area's competing attractions. Treating him, thought Liz, like a Norfolk Tourist Board representative.

"So, assuming that I was in the market for a weekend cottage, where would you advise me to buy one?" asked Mackay, pocketing the credit card with which he had just, with cavalier nonchalance, paid the bill for the three of them.

Goss regarded him levelly. "Perhaps Burnham Market?" he suggested. "That's very popular with the Range Rover set."

"Ouch!" Mackay displayed his preternaturally white teeth. "That's me well and truly put in my place." He stood up and reached for his keys. "Liz, might I just detach you from Steve here for an hour or two? Ask you to bring me up to speed?"

"I'm due back to Norwich at two o'clock," said Goss. "So I've got to make a move anyway." He gave Liz the ghost of a wink and raised a hand to Mackay. "Thanks for lunch. Next one's on me."

"Cheers," said Mackay.

"Will you just excuse me a minute?" Liz murmured to Mackay when Goss had left the bar. "I'll be right back."

She called Wetherby from the public phone outside on the sea front. He picked up on the second ring, and sounded tired.

"Please," she said.

"I'm sorry," he answered. "You have to have Mackay with you. I've no choice on this one."

"Fane?"

"Precisely. He wants his man there. In fact he insists on him being there, as indeed he has every right to insist."

"Full disclosure? Full data-sharing?"

The briefest of pauses. "That was the agreement between our respective sevices."

"I see."

"Make him work," suggested Wetherby. "Make him earn his keep."

"I certainly will. He's here for the duration?"

"For as long as it takes. He's reporting direct to Fane, just as you are to me."

"Understood. I have a meet with Zander tonight that I'm hopeful about. I'll call you afterwards."

"Do that. And take our mutual friend to the meet."

The phone went dead and Liz stared for a moment at the receiver in her hand. Conventionally, agent RVs were only ever conducted by one officer at a time. Shrugging, she returned the phone to its cradle. Strictly speaking, Zander was no longer her agent, but Special Branch's. And reading between the lines—interpreting the pauses rather than the words—she knew that Wetherby wanted her to continue playing her own game, whatever the notional ground rules. At the same time, however, she was under no illusions that Mackay would be sharing everything that he and his service knew with her. He would also be playing his own game. For that reason, it made sense to be the one who initiated the data-share.

"My room's called Victory," grinned Mackay, when she went back into the saloon bar. "I thought you might like to know that!"

"Fascinating. You've booked in already?"

"I have indeed. With Miss Scrumptious."

"I hope you're not teasing her," said Liz. "She's a potentially useful source on this one, and I'd like to keep her onside."

"Don't worry, I won't frighten her away. In fact I have the feeling I'd be very hard pressed to do so."

"Hooked already, is she?"

"I didn't mean that. I meant that she's not a girl who gives the impression of scaring easily."

"I see. Do you want to walk while I brief you, or sit upstairs? Sea breeze or gas fire, in other words?"

"Let's walk. I suspect that today's lunch wasn't the first outing for that chip oil. I could use some air."

They walked east to begin with, as far as Creake Manor, where Liz told him about her initial recce of the village and her calculations concerning the sailing club. After passing the Manor they turned, and strolled back to Headland Hall, which Mackay examined with interest.

Liz filled him in. Zander's calls. The conclusions she had drawn from the armour-piercing round. Her questioning of Cherisse Hogan and Lakeby. Her near certainty that the man in the front of the truck with Ray Gunter was "Mitch." Her hope that Mitch was an associate of Melvin Eastman, and that Zander would be able to help identify him.

"And if you do get an ID on this Mitch?" asked Mackay.

"Give him to the police to pick up," said Liz.

Mackay pursed his lips and slowly nodded. "You've done well," he said without condescension. "What's the score on Lakeby? Are you going to have him lifted too?"

"Not much point, I'd say—he's just one of the links to Mitch. Once we've got Mitch in the bag and talking, we won't need Peregrine Lakeby."

"Do you think he knew what was actually going on on that beach of his?"

"Not really. I think he preferred to take the money and not think about it. Hid behind the idea that they were honest smugglers bringing in a few cartons of booze and fags. He may be a snob and a bully, but I don't think he's any kind of traitor. I think he's just someone who found out that when you start taking the bad guys' money, the ratchet only ever turns one way."

"What kind of sweets do you like?" asked Mackay after they had taken another half-dozen paces.

"Sweets?"

Mackay grinned. "You can't walk along an English sea front without a paper bagful of something brightly coloured and sugary. Preferably poured into the bag with a plastic scoop."

"Is that official MI6 policy?"

"Absolutely. Let's go and see what the village store has to offer."

Inside the small shop a woman in a blue nylon overall was straightening copies of the *Sun* and the *Daily Express*. Elsewhere there were plastic toys, knitting patterns, and shelves of dusty sweet jars.

"Flying saucers!" Liz heard Mackay exclaim in reverent disbelief. "I haven't seen these since . . . And Love Hearts!"

"You're on your own," said Liz. "Those fish and chips were enough for me."

"Oh go on," said Mackay. "At least let me stand you a liquorice bootlace. They make your tongue go black."

Liz laughed. "You really know the way to a woman's heart, don't you?"

"Gobstopper?"

"No!"

In the end he left with a bag of flying saucers. "At school," he said, as the door chime rang behind them, "I used to empty the powder out of these and sell it for a fiver a line. No finer sight than a group of well-heeled public schoolboys snorting lemon sherbet and then trying to persuade themselves that they're completely off their heads." He passed the bag to Liz. "What do you think our man's here to do?"

"Our man?"

"Our shooter. Why do you think he's gone to so much trouble to get himself here in particular?"

She and Wetherby had discussed this the night before, but without reaching any particular conclusion. "Some sort of spectacular, perhaps?" she hazarded. "There are the USAF bases at Marwell, Mildenhall and Lakenheath, but they're on a very high state of alert, and would represent very difficult targets for a single individual or even a small team. There's the Sizewell nuclear plant, I suppose, and Ely Cathedral and various other public buildings but again, a very tall order. More likely, to my mind, is the assassination possibility: the Lord Chancellor's got a house in Aldeburgh, the Treasury Chief Secretary's got a place at Thorpeness, and the head of the DTI's up at Sheringham . . . Not the most high-profile of targets, internationally speaking, but you'd certainly make headlines if you managed to put a bullet through one of them."

"Have their people been warned?" asked Mackay.

"In general terms, yes, they've been told to step things up."

"And the Queen's at Sandringham for Christmas, I suppose."

"That's right, but again, you'd really be pushed to get anywhere near there with a weapon of any kind. Security's as tight as a drum."

Mackay placed a flying saucer into his mouth.

"I guess we'd better get back and see what the plods have uncovered. What time do you want to make a move for Braintree?"

"Not later than five?"

"OK. Let's go back to the Trafalgar, order up a pot of coffee from the lovely Cherisse, spread out a few Ordnance Survey maps, and try and think ourselves into this man's mind."

27

"This is a strange country," said Faraj Mansoor, ejecting the five-round magazine of the PSS into his hand and placing it carefully on the table. "It is very different from the place of my imagination."

The woman who had borrowed the name of Lucy Wharmby was peeling potatoes, stropping the blade in fast efficient sweeps so that the strips of peel curled damply over her left hand. "It's not all like this," she said. "It's not all so exposed and bleak . . ."

He waited for her to finish. Outside, the sun still cast its pale glaze over the sea, but the wind was whipping at the wave caps, lifting them into a fine spray.

"I think the country makes the people," he said eventually, checking the action of the PSS before slapping back the magazine. "And I think that I understand the British better for seeing their country."

"It's a cold country," she said. "My childhood was spent in a cold flat with thin walls, listening to my parents arguing."

Pocketing the handgun, he tightened his belt. "What were they arguing about?"

"I was never quite sure at the time. My father was a university lecturer at a place called Keele. It was a good job for him, and I think he wanted my mother to become more involved in the life of the university."

"And she didn't want to?"

"She had never wanted to move there from London. She didn't like the place and she didn't make any effort to get to know the people. She ended up having treatment for depression."

Faraj frowned. "What were her beliefs?"

"She believed in . . . books and films and holidays in Italy and having her friends round to dinner."

"And your father? What did he believe in?"

"He believed in himself. He believed in his career, and in the importance of his work, and in the approval of his colleagues." She reached for a kitchen knife, and began quartering the potatoes with short, angry strokes of the blade. "Later, when my mother's depression became serious, he believed that he had the right to sleep with his students."

Faraj looked up. "Did your mother know?"

"She found out soon enough. She wasn't stupid."

"And you? Did you know?"

"I guessed. They sent me away to school in Wales." She wiped her hair from her eyes with the back of her hand. "That's very different countryside from this. There are hills, and even one or two you might call mountains."

He looked at her, his head inclined. "You're smiling. That's the first time I've seen you smile."

The smile and the knife hand froze.

"You were happy there? At this school in the hills that were almost mountains?"

She shrugged. "I suppose I was. I've never thought about it . . . in those terms."

Unbidden, a memory rose before her, a memory she had not revisited for some years. It had been her friend Megan who had discovered the magic mushrooms growing in the pine woods behind the school. Hundreds of them, clustered on the rotted logs on the pine-needled forest floor. Megan—at fifteen already a formidable biochemist, particularly with reference to Class A narcotics—had recognised them immediately.

The following day, as the school permitted and indeed encouraged them to, the two friends had signed themselves out of classes in favour of a nature ramble. Armed with a tin sandwich box and a bottle of diluted orange squash, they had hurried to the woods, downed a half-dozen mushrooms each, spread out a groundsheet, and settled themselves down to wait for the psychotropic toxins in the mushrooms to take effect.

For at least half an hour nothing had happened, and then she had begun to feel simultaneously nauseous and fearful. Control of her reactions seemed to be sliding away from her; her limbs and her heaving stomach were no longer her own. And then suddenly the fear lifted and it was as if she was drowning in sensation. The sounds of the forest, previously a barely audible chorus of distant birdsong, shifting branches and insect twitterings, were amplified to levels of almost unbearable intensity. The muted pricking of the light through the pine branches, meanwhile, became a phalanx of rainbow spears. Her nose, throat and lungs seemed to fill with the sharp turpentine-scented resin of the pine. After a time—minutes perhaps, but maybe hours—these heightened sensations had begun to shape themselves into a kind of sublime architecture. She seemed to be wandering through a vast and constantly evolving vista of cloud-topped ziggurats, hanging gardens and dizzying colonnades. She seemed to be both inside and outside of herself, a spectator of her own progress through this strange, exotic realm. Afterwards, with the vision's slow dissolution, she had felt an intense melancholy, and when she had tried to discuss the experience with Megan that evening, she had been unable to find the right words.

Deep inside herself, however, she had known that the images she had seen were not accidental, but meant. They were a sign—a glimpse of the celestial. They had confirmed her in her path, and in her determination.

"Yes," she said, "I was happy there."

"So how did it end?" he asked. "Your parents' tale?"

"Divorce. The family smashed. Nothing unusual." Lifting the handle of the kitchen knife between two fingers, she dropped it so that its point stuck into the wet chopping board. "And your parents?"

Walking across the room Faraj picked up one of the cheap tumblers on the table, examined it absently, and replaced it. Then, as if shrugging off the Western culture that he had assumed with the clothes she had bought him, he sank to his haunches.

"My parents were Tajiks, from Dushanbe. My father was a fighter, a lieutenant of Ahmed Shah Massoud."

"The Lion of Panjshir."

"Just so. May he live for ever. As a young man my father had been a teacher. He spoke French and a little English, which he learned from the British and American soldiers who came to fight with the mujahidin. I went to a good school in Dushanbe and then, when I was fourteen, we moved to Afghanistan, following Massoud, and I went to one of the English-language schools in Kabul. My father hoped that I would not have to live the life that he had lived, my mother's family had a little money, and both saw education as the means of my betterment. Their dream was for me to become an administrator or government official."

"What happened?"

"In '96 the Taliban came. They had money from the United States and from Saudi Arabia, and they laid siege to Kabul. We managed to escape from the bombardment at night, and my father went north to rejoin Massoud. I wanted to go with him but he sent me south with my mother and my younger sister towards the border country. We had hoped to enter Pakistan from there, to escape the Taliban altogether, but many others had had the same idea, and after months of wandering we finally settled with other displaced Tajiks and Pathans opposed to the Taliban in a village named Daranj, east of Kandahar."

"What did you do there?"

"We dreamed of leaving. Of finding a better life in Pakistan."

Falling silent, he appeared to sink into a reverie. His eyes were open but his expression was blank. Finally he seemed to rouse himself. "In the end, it became clear that there was no way that we could legally cross the border. We could have found a way through—there were couriers who would take you over the mountains for a price—but we had no wish to be stateless refugees. We considered ourselves better than that.

"After several years of nonstop warfare my father returned. He had been wounded, and he could no longer fight. With him, though, was a man. A man whom my father had persuaded to take me with him, across the border to Pakistan. A man of influence, who would enroll me in one of the *madrassahs*—the Islamic colleges—in Peshawar."

"And this is what happened?"

"This is what happened. I bade goodbye to my parents and my sister, and together with this man I crossed the border at Chaman and journeyed north. A week later we were in Mardan, northeast of Peshawar, and I was taken to the *madrassah*. As at the border, I was admitted without question."

"So who was this man? This man of such influence?"

He smiled and shook his head. "So many questions, so little time. What would you have done with your life, had things been otherwise?"

"They were never otherwise," she replied. "For me, there was never any other path."

28

Liz insisted that she and Mackay travel in her car. The meeting with Zander was her operation and she wanted Mackay to realise that he was a passenger, there strictly on sufferance.

Mackay, sensing her determination, did not argue. Instead he made a point of deferring to her, even going so far as to check his appearance with her. This she okayed. It wasn't the clothes by themselves that would attract attention, although the tan leather jacket and chinos were visibly of better quality than most; it was the clothes in combination with the personality. In a crowded room, he was the sort of person you noticed straight away. He looked flash.

In Pakistan, Liz guessed, a European was a European. Different by definition. In Essex, however, there was an infinity of subtle distinctions in the way that people presented themselves. Liz had brought her work wardrobe with her, and had changed into the leather jacket and jeans. The jacket, in particular, was cheap-looking and unfashionable. Single mum doing the shopping. Dab of make-up, lank hair, sharp expression. Invisible in any high street.

Soon they were making their way southwards towards the town of Swaffham. Liz drove carefully, pointedly observing the speed limits.

"Tell me again why Zander should exert himself on our behalf," said Mackay, reaching back to adjust the Audi's headrest. "What's in it for him, apart from your approval?"

"You don't think that's enough?"

He grinned ruefully. "Well, I guess it's not so easily won; I could certainly do with a little of it myself. But yes, apart from that."

"I'm his insurance policy. He knows that if he comes across with good product then I'll stir myself on his behalf if the drugs squad or the CID march in and scoop him up on a charge. That's why he wouldn't talk to Bob Morrison. Morrison's the kind of hard-nosed Special Branch officer who despises the Zanders of this world on sight, and Zander knows it."

"Seems a bit short-sighted of Morrison."

"Well, I suppose it's a point of view. My suspicion is that sooner or later the police are going to pick up Melvin Eastman and make something stick, and when that happens they're going to need someone like Zander to go into the witness box and testify against him."

"From what you say, this guy Eastman wouldn't be too happy about that. He'd take out a contract on him, and Zander must know that."

"He does, I'm sure. But if he trusts me—and I've always played fair with him—then maybe I can still persuade him to give evidence."

They arrived in Braintree with forty minutes to spare, and followed the signs to the railway station.

"Can we just run through again how you want to play this?" asked Mackay.

"Sure. He's expecting me to arrive alone on the top level of the multistorey car park, so I'm going to drop you off a couple of minutes' walk away, outside. I'll drive up to the top storey and park; you follow on foot, install yourself near the staircase, and start logging incoming cars. As soon as I see Zander I'll call you and describe his car. As soon as you're sure that he wasn't followed in you call me back, and I'll approach him."

Mackay nodded. This was standard tradecraft. Frankie Ferris was a naturally cautious man, but it was just possible, given the events of the last couple of days, that Eastman might have put a tail on him.

Liz pulled up at the kerb outside the station, and they switched their phones to silent vibration and loaded in each other's numbers. Mackay then zipped up his jacket and slipped off into the shadows, while Liz drove up to the top floor of the car park.

In the course of the next half-hour, as she sat there, three cars left the top level. Several others entered the car park, but all occupied vacant bays on the half-empty lower levels. Finally, at five to eight, a silver Nissan Almeira climbed to the top level, and Liz recognised Frankie Ferris's pale features at the wheel. Quickly, she thumbed the speed-dial button on her phone.

"Give me a couple of minutes," came Mackay's voice, muted. Frankie parked in the corner furthest from her, and she saw him glance at his watch before turning off the Nissan's engine and lights.

At three minutes past eight her phone rang.

"He was followed," said Mackay.

"I'm aborting, then," said Liz immediately. "Meet me on the pavement outside in five minutes."

"No need. Go ahead with the meet."

"The meet's compromised. Get out of here."

"Zander's tail met with a problem. He's immobilised in the stairwell. Go ahead with the meet."

"What have you done?" hissed Liz.

"Secured the situation. Now go for it. You've got three minutes." Her phone went dead.

Liz looked around her. There was no sign of any movement. Deeply apprehensive, she climbed out of the Audi and crossed the concrete floor. As she approached the silver Almeira she saw the driver's window slide down. Inside the car's plush interior Frankie looked thin and scared.

"Take these," he said, his voice shaky. "And make like you're paying me." He handed her a small paper bag, and Liz reached into her pocket and pretended to pass him money.

"Mitch," she said urgently. "Tell me."

"Kieran Mitchell. Transport man, fixer, enforcer, whatever. He's got a big place outside Chelmsford on one of those gated estates."

"Works for Eastman?"

"With him. Got his own people."

"Do you know him?"

"Seen him. He drinks with Eastman. Nasty-looking bastard. White eyelashes like a pig."

"Anything else?"

"Yeah, he carries. Now get out of here, please."

Liz walked quickly back to the Audi and drove to the ramp. A level down, she picked up Mackay, who was leaning against a barrier. "What the hell is going on?" she asked angrily.

He jumped into the passenger seat. "Did you identify Mitch?"

"Yes, I did." She turned the steering wheel to full lock to negotiate the downward spiral ramp. "But what the bloody hell were you up to?"

"Zander was followed. Eastman obviously suspects something's up. The tail parked on this level. He arrived about a minute after your man went up to the top."

"How do you know he was a tail?"

"I followed him to the stairwell, and he went up, not down. So I zapped him."

She braked sharply, the Audi's tyres squealing on the ramp. "What do you mean, you zapped him?"

Reaching into his pocket, Mackay extracted a slim black plastic object resembling a mobile phone. "The Oregon Industries C6 stun-gun, aka the Little Friend. Delivers six hundred thousand volts straight into the central nervous system. Result: target incapacitated for a period of three to six minutes, depending on physical constitution. Ideal for cell clearance, resisted take-downs or the restraint of violent mental patients."

"And completely unlicensed for use in the United Kingdom," retorted Liz, furious.

"Undergoing trials with the Met as we speak, actually, but let's not get too anal about all that. The point is that zappers are established criminal accessories, which is why I relieved our man of his watch and wallet. My guess is he's going to keep quiet about the whole thing. He'd look pretty stupid admitting to Eastman that he failed to do his job because he was mugged in a stairwell."

"You hope."

"Look, Zander was blown," said Mackay. "The fact that there was a tail at all tells us that. The essential thing was to identify Mitch. We certainly wouldn't have had another chance. Right now I suggest that we get the hell out of here before our zappee finds his feet again."

Letting out the clutch with deliberate force, Liz spun the Audi forward. "If that was a member of the public you electrocuted . . ."

"If it was, he'll be fine," said Mackay. "These things do no last-ing damage whatsoever. They've tested them on the Los Angeles Po-lice Department—not the most highly evolved form of life, I grant you, but . . ."

"And what do you propose we do with that watch and wallet you've pocketed?"

"Run a check on the owner and see if they belong to one of East-man's people," said Mackay. "Then, if you like, we can post them back to him with an anonymous note saying we found them in the car park. How's that?"

She kept her eyes on the road.

"Look, Liz, I know that you're pissed off that I've come busting into your case, especially after you've done all the groundwork. I really understand that. But in the end we both want the same thing, which is to nail this bastard before he takes any more lives, agreed?"

She took a deep breath. "Let's get this straight," she said eventually. "If we're going to work together we fix the ground rules now, and the first of these is that we employ proper tradecraft. No freelancing, no cowboy weaponry. You risked the life of my agent back there, and with it the whole operation."

Mackay began to answer but she overrode him. "If this case ends up with an arrest, and we've broken the law, the defence lawyer'll have a field day. This is the UK we're in, not Islamabad, OK?"

He shrugged. "Zander's a dead man, and you know it." He turned to face her. "You think Bob Morrison's on the take from Eastman, don't you?"

"You worked that one out, then."

"I was wondering why you insisted on getting Zander to identify Mitch, when it would have been much easier just to go to Essex Special Branch. But you were worried that Morrison would slip Eastman the word, and Mitch would run."

"I thought there was an outside chance," admitted Liz. "A less than one per cent chance. I've got no proof of any kind against Morrison, nothing at all. It's purely instinct."

"In future, can we share your instincts?"

"Let's see how we go, shall we?" Taking a hand off the wheel, she reached into her pocket for the paper bag Frankie Ferris had given her, and handed it to Mackay. "Zander was very jumpy," she said. "He made me pretend that I was there for a drugs buy, so he must have suspected Eastman would have someone keeping an eye on him. Check these out."

"They're Smarties," said Mackay. "Excellent!"

29

By the time Kieran Mitchell reached the Brentwood Sporting Club, he knew that he was enjoying his last evening of freedom for a long time. His wife Debbie, frantic with worry and Stolichnaya vodka, had rung to say that the police had called at the house mob-handed, and voice-mail messages had piled in from contacts in at least half a dozen pubs and clubs. They were looking for him, methodically eliminating all his usual haunts. It was only a matter of time.

Looking around him at the familiar surroundings—the punters crowding the oxblood leather banquettes, the croupiers in their tight red dresses, the cigarette smoke hanging in the lights over the blackjack tables—he tried to impress its details on to his memory. He would need something to draw on in the months ahead. Wryly, he raised his glass of Johnnie Walker Black Label to his reflection in the mirror behind the bar. An ugly bastard, sure—he'd always been that—but a man who could hold things together when the situation called for it.

"You on your own, love?"

She was about forty, probably. Blonde streaks, glittery top, desperate eyes. You got them in every casino, the women who, having blown whatever they'd managed to scrape together that day, hung around the male punters like pilot fish. For a handful of chips, Mitchell knew, he could have taken her down to the car for ten minutes. Tonight, though, he just wasn't in the mood.

"I've got people coming," he said. "Sorry."

"Anyone nice?"

He laughed at that, and didn't answer, and finally she walked away. From the moment he'd walked into the toilet at the Fairmile and seen Ray Gunter's body lolling against the tiles, he'd known that the people-smuggling racket had been blown to the four winds. The police wouldn't have a choice; they'd have to go all the way with this one—follow as far as the trail led. And the short answer, of course, was that it led to him. He'd been seen with Gunter, he was a known confederate of Melvin Eastman . . . He took a deep slug of the Scotch and refilled the engraved tumbler from his private bottle. He was fucked, basically.

What the hell had Eastman been thinking of, getting into bed with those Krauts? Before they'd come calling he'd had a sweet little franchise running, bringing in illegals for the Caravan. Asians, Africans, working girls from Albania and Kosovo, all of them properly cowed and respectful. No trouble, no argument, and everyone going home happy.

The moment he'd clocked that Paki, though, he'd known he was going to be trouble. A rough crossing usually shook them down nicely, but not this one. This one was a psycho—a real hard nut. Mitchell shook his head. He should have drowned him while he had a chance. Nudged him overboard, rucksack and all—he'd heard that most Asians couldn't swim.

Ray Gunter, of course—idiot that he was—had spotted the rucksack and decided to take it off the Paki. He hadn't said anything about stealing it, but looking back it was blindingly obvious. And so the Paki—psycho nutcase that *he* was—had taken him out.

All of these events leading him, Kieran Mitchell, in his slate-grey silk suit and his midnight-blue Versace shirt, to this moment. To this glass of Scotch that could be his last for years. Conspiracy, immigration offences, terrorism, even. It didn't bear thinking about. Not for the first time, he considered cutting and running. But if he ran, and they found him—as they surely would find him—it would go worse for him. It would cancel out the one card that he held. The card that, if he played it properly . . .

In the mirror he saw what he had been expecting for the best part of an hour. Movement near the entrance. Purposeful men in inexpensive suits. The crowd parting. Downing his Scotch in three measured draughts, he felt in his trouser pocket for the coat-check disc. It was cold out, so he'd brought the dark blue cashmere.

30

Liz sensed the quiet excitement in the place as soon as she walked into Norwich police station. The Gunter murder investigation had been going nowhere fast and suddenly here was a solid lead in the shape of one of Melvin Eastman's senior associates. There had been some talk of taking Kieran Mitchell to Chelmsford, where all the Eastman files were held, but Don Whitten had insisted on Norwich. This was his murder hunt, and every aspect of the investigation would be carried out under his jurisdiction.

When Liz and Mackay walked into the station's operations room, the place was crowded with bullish-looking officers in their shirt sleeves taking it in turns to congratulate an uncomfortable-looking Steve Goss.

Amongst them, sent over as an observer by the Essex force, was the Special Branch officer Bob Morrison. Don Whitten, Styrofoam coffee cup in hand, presided over the mêlée.

Seeing Liz, Goss waved and extracted himself. "They think I lined up the arrest," he murmured, running a hand through his scrubby ginger hair. "I feel a total bloody fraud."

"Enjoy it," suggested Mackay.

"And let's pray it's not a dead end," agreed Liz.

She had called Goss with Kieran Mitchell's details as soon as she and Mackay were clear of Braintree. Then they had driven north to Norwich, stopping on the way to pick up a pizza and a bottle of Italian beer each. For the time being, perhaps as a way of acknowledging Liz's earlier fury, Mackay had shrugged off his romantic seducer's skin, and without it he proved a surprisingly entertaining companion. He had a near inexhaustible fund of stories, most of them concerning the extreme behaviour—or misbehaviour—of his service colleagues. At the same time, Liz noticed—and however much she tried to lead him on—he never actually fingered anyone directly. When names were named, they were never those of the actual perpetrators of the cowboy operations that he described. They were those of their friends, colleagues, or superiors. He gave the impression of extreme indiscretion, but actually gave away little that wasn't already reasonably common currency in the intelligence community.

He's on to me, thought Liz, enjoying the game. He's aware that I'm watching him, waiting for him to make a mistake. And he's playing up to my expectations of him as a reckless freelancer, because if he can convince me that that's what he is, then I'll stop taking him seriously. And the moment I stop taking him seriously he'll find some way of stitching me up. There was even a certain elegance to it all.

She had briefed Goss over the phone about the conversations with Cherisse Hogan and Peregrine Lakeby that had led her to Kieran Mitchell's name, and suggested that he set up the arrest. Impressed by her investigative work, and understanding her need to keep a low profile in the affair, he had agreed.

Liz had considered sharing her concerns about Bob Morrison with Goss, but had finally decided to let the matter lie. It was only her instinct that suggested that he might be in the pay of Eastman—she had no evidence of any kind beyond his dilatory attitude and a general impression of venality. Besides which, Eastman would know with or without Morrison that Kieran Mitchell had been arrested, and would make his arrangements accordingly. And if Mitchell came up with solid information and was prepared to go the distance in court, then Eastman would be out of the game anyway.

With the return from the custody suite of Mitchell's solicitor, a sense of order and restraint re-established itself. The solicitor, a silkily exquisite figure with an established reputation as a "gangster's brief," was named Honan. Thanking the custody officer who had accompanied him to and from the cells, he asked to speak in private to DS Whitten.

As Whitten and Honan took their places in one of the interview rooms, Goss ushered Liz and Mackay into the adjoining observation suite, where half a dozen plastic chairs faced a large rectangular panel of one-way glass. A moment later, with the faintest of nods, Bob Morrison joined them.

In the interview room, on the other side of the one-way glass, the overhead strip light cast a hard, bleaching glare. The off-white laminate surface of the table was pitted with cigarette burns. There were no windows.

"Could you repeat what you've just said to me," Whitten asked Honan. Amplified by the speakers in the observation suite, his voice sounded harsher and clearer than usual.

"Bottom line—and without prejudice—my client doesn't want to go down," said Honan. "In return for a guarantee of immunity from prosecution, however, he's prepared to go into the witness box and produce the wherewithal to put Melvin Eastman away for offences relating to narcotics, immoral earnings, and conspiracy to murder."

He hesitated in order to let this offer sink in. To her left, Liz was aware of Bob Morrison shaking his head in disbelief.

"My client also has information relating to the killing of Ray

Gunter which he is prepared to divulge, in full, to the appropriate parties. Understandably, however, he does not wish to incriminate himself in so doing."

Whitten nodded, bulky in his crumpled grey suit. A crease appeared in the bristled back of his neck. "May we ask what it is that he fears incriminating himself of, if he divulges the facts relating to the Ray Gunter case?"

Honan looked down at his hands. "As I said, I'm speaking entirely without prejudice here, but I am led to understand that the relevant area of criminal law might be that relating to immigration."

"People-smuggling, you mean?"

Honan pursed his lips. "As I said, my client doesn't want to go down. He feels—not unreasonably, in my view—that if he testifies against Melvin Eastman, and then goes to prison, he will be killed. Incarcerated or not, Eastman has a long reach. My client wants immunity from prosecution and a new identity—the full witness protection package. In return he will give you the wherewithal to roll up Melvin Eastman."

"That's the trouble with British criminals," Morrison murmured. "They all think they're in a Hollywood bloody Mafia movie."

On the other side of the glass, it was clear that Whitten's patience with Honan was wearing thin. At the same time, thought Liz, he badly needed any help that Mitchell might be able to give him. According to Goss, Whitten had managed to stall the press for the time being, but he was going to need to be able to report a solid lead in the Gunter case soon, or risk accusations of incompetence.

"Let me make a suggestion," he said. "That your client immediately and unconditionally tells us everything that he knows relating to the murder of Ray Gunter. *Everything*—as he is required to do by law. And that if we're completely happy with his level of cooperation, then we can . . ." he shrugged heavily, "we can make the necessary . . . representations."

"We can't do any such thing!" hissed Liz, looking from Goss to Mackay for support. "If I have to get on to the DPP and the Home

Office about this we'll be bogged down for days. We've got to get Mitchell to talk right now."

"Can you speak to Whitten?" Mackay asked Goss. "Tell him . . ."

"Don't worry," said Goss. "Don Whitten knows what he's doing. This whole immunity thing's just about the brief earning his fee. He's got to be able to go back to his client and say that he tried."

"Can I take that as a yes?" Honan was demanding. "An undertaking that you'll . . ."

Whitten leaned forward in his chair. His glance flickered to the interview suite's tape recorder and CCTV monitor. Both were switched off. When he spoke again it was so quietly that Liz had to crane towards the wall-mounted loudspeaker to hear him.

"Look, Mr. Honan, no one here present is in a position to offer Kieran Mitchell any kind of immunity deal. If he cooperates, I'll make sure that the relevant people are informed of the fact. If he holds out on us, on the other hand, bearing in mind that this is not only a murder hunt, but a matter affecting national security, I promise you that I'll do my level best to ensure that he never sees daylight again. And you can tell him that's my best offer."

There was a short pause, at the end of which Honan nodded, collected his briefcase, and left the room. Shortly afterwards Whitten appeared in the doorway of the observation suite. He was flushed. Sweat spots studded the pink expanse of his forehead.

"Nice one," said Bob Morrison.

Whitten shrugged. "They all try it on. They know it's a loss leader, we know it's a loss leader . . ."

"Is he right about his life being in danger?" asked Liz.

"Probably," said Whitten cheerfully. "I'll tell him that if he goes down we can recommend he's isolated from the worst of the nasties."

"In with the nonces?" grinned Morrison.

"Something like that."

When Honan returned to the interview suite five minutes later, he was accompanied by the duty sergeant and Kieran Mitchell. It was midnight.

31

Outside the bungalow, the woman sat in near darkness in the driver's seat of the Vauxhall Astra. Her head leaned comfortably against the head rest, and her face was faintly underlit by tiny pinpoints of blue and orange light from the car's hi-fi system. The local radio station's midnight news had just finished, and the only mention of the Gunter murder had been a recorded comment by one DS Whitten to the effect that enquiries were ongoing and that the police hoped to bring the person or persons responsible to justice as soon as possible. The on-the-hour news had segued into a medley of easy listening and cocktail tunes.

The police know nothing, she told herself, snapping off Frank and

Nancy Sinatra mid-croon. They have no coherent line of inquiry. As far as she could tell there had been no CCTV system at the Fairmile Café, and even if there had been they would have had trouble identifying the Astra. Black cars gave a notoriously poor signature at night, which was why the planners had told her to insist on one. But she was pretty sure that there hadn't been a CCTV system there anyway; it was one of the principal reasons, she guessed, that the place had been selected for the RV in the first place.

The only possible weak links in the chain were the spent PSS round and the truck driver involved in the pick-up from the German ship. And the truck driver's business surely depended on his absolute discretion; to betray his cargo would be to betray himself. On balance, she told herself, they were safe from the truck driver. It was the PSS round that worried her, as she was certain it would worry the police, and without doubt the anti-terrorism organisations too.

She had explained this to Faraj, but he had shrugged fatalistically and repeated that their task had to be performed on the appointed day. If the waiting increased the likelihood of failure, and of their own violent deaths at the hands of the SAS or a police firearms unit, then so be it. The task was immutable, its parameters unalterable. He had told her the bare minimum, she knew. Not out of mistrust, but in case she was taken.

Acceptance, she told herself. In acceptance lay strength. Remote-locking the Astra behind her with a muted electronic squawk, she walked quietly into the bungalow. The door to the bathroom was half open, and Faraj was standing stripped to the waist at the sink, washing.

For a moment she stood there in the centre of the room, staring at him. His body was narrow as a snake's, but corded with muscle, and a long pale scar ran diagonally from his left hip to his right shoulder blade. How had he acquired a disfigurement like that? Certainly not in the operating theatre; it looked more like a sabre slash. Without the smart British clothes that she had brought him, he looked like the Tajik that he was. The son of a warrior and perhaps the father of warriors.

Was he married? Was there, even now, some fierce-eyed mountain woman praying for his safe return?

He turned then, and stared back at her. Stared with that pale, incurious assassin's gaze. She felt naked for a moment, and self-conscious, and a little shameful. She had begun to realise that, more than anything else in the world, she wanted his respect. That she was not wholly indifferent to his regard. That if this was the last human relationship she was to enjoy on this earth, then she did not want it to be a thing of lowered glances and self-abnegating silences.

Raising her chin a millimetre or two, she returned his gaze. Returned it with something like anger. She was a fighter now, just as he was. She had the right to a fighter's recognition. She stood her ground.

Unhurriedly, he turned away. Dragged his wet hands through his cropped hair. Then walked towards her, still expressionless, and stopped with his face inches from hers, so that she could smell the soap that he had been using, and hear him breathing. Still she neither lowered her eyes nor moved.

"Tell me your Islamic name," he said in Urdu.

"Asimat," she answered, although she was sure that he already knew it.

He nodded. "Like the consort of Salah-ud-din."

She said nothing, just stared forwards, looking over his shoulder. In contrast with the weathered brown of his face, neck and hands, the skin of his torso was pale, the colour of bone.

Something in the sight froze her. We are already dead, she thought. We look at each other and we see the future. No gardens, no golden minarets, no desire. Just the darkness of the grave and the cold, pitiless winds of eternity.

His hand rose by his side, taking a hanging strand of her hair and looping it carefully behind her ear.

"It will be soon, Asimat," he promised her. "Now sleep."

32

"Tell us again about the Germans," said DS Don Whitten, smoothing down his moustache. This time Bob Morrison was sitting next to him in the interview suite. Both Whitten and Kieran Mitchell had chain-smoked their way steadily through the last hour's interrogation. A wavering blue-brown pall now hung in the strip-lit air over the interview table.

Mitchell glanced at his lawyer, who nodded. Mitchell's eyelids drooped, and against the dour backdrop of the interview room he looked cheap and gangsterish in his designer clothes. To Liz, watching through the one-way glass screen, it was clear that he was desperately trying to hold things together, to display a helpful patience rather than the snappish exhaustion that he felt.

"Like I said, I know nothing about the Germans. I only know that the organisation was called the Caravan. I think the cutter was crewed by Germans and I think that Germans organised the runners' transit from mainland Europe to the point when me and Gunter picked them up off the Norfolk coast."

"The runners being the migrants?" said Whitten, glancing at his Styrofoam coffee cup and finding it empty.

"The runners being the migrants," Mitchell confirmed.

"And the boat's point of origin?"

"I never asked. There were two boats, both converted fishing cutters. I think one was called *Albertina Q,* registered port Cuxhaven, and the other *Susanne* something, registered Bremen . . . Breminger . . ."

"Bremerhaven," murmured Liz. On the chair beside her in the observation suite, Steve Goss was opening a greaseproof-paper-wrapped clutch of double Gloucester cheese sandwiches. He nudged the packet in her direction and she took the smallest. She wasn't particularly hungry, but she sensed that Goss would feel self-conscious munching through all four sandwiches in front of Mackay. Was there a Mrs. Goss?

"To be honest," Mitchell was saying, "the name of the boat was the last thing on my mind. And it was Eastman who always called them the Germans, or the Krauts. If they'd been Dutch or Belgian I wouldn't have known the difference. But I do know that the organisation was known as the Caravan."

"And the Caravan paid Eastman?" asked Whitten.

"I assume so. He was responsible from the pick-up at sea to the delivery point in Ilford."

"The warehouse?"

"Yeah, the warehouse," said Mitchell tiredly. "I'd drive in, there would be a head count, and I'd sign them over. There'd be another crew waiting there with documents, and they'd take them on to . . . wherever."

"And there would be how many again in each consignment?"

Whitten was repeating earlier questions, checking the answers against his notes for inconsistencies. So far, Mitchell's answers seemed steady.

"If it was girls, it went up to twenty-eight. Ordinary runners twenty-five, tops. Gunter's boats couldn't take more than that, especially if there was a heavy sea."

"And Eastman paid you, and you paid Gunter?"

"Yeah."

"Tell me how much again."

Mitchell's head seemed to slump. "I got a grand per head for girls, one-five for runners, two for specials."

"So on a good night you might be pulling down forty grand?"

"Thereabouts."

"And how much did you pay Gunter?"

"Flat rate. Five grand per pick-up."

"And Lakeby?"

"Five hundred a month."

"Nice profit margin there!"

Mitchell shrugged and looked philosophically around him. "It was risky work. Can I take a piss?"

Whitten nodded, rose, spoke the time into the tape recorder, clicked it off, and called for the duty sergeant. When Mitchell had left the room, accompanied once again by Honan, there was a moment's silence.

"Do we believe him?" asked Mackay, rubbing his eyes and reaching into the pocket of his Barbour jacket for his mobile phone.

"Why would he lie to us?" asked Goss. "He'd just be defending the person who murdered his partner, wrote off a nice forty K–a–month earner, and basically got him nicked in the first place."

"Eastman could have asked him to feed us disinformation as part of a damage-limitation exercise," said Mackay, stabbing the message button and pressing the phone to his ear. "Mitchell wouldn't be the first career criminal to take the drop for his boss."

Liz pressed the intercom button connecting the two suites. "Could you take him through the Fairmile Café stuff again?"

"As soon as he gets back," said Whitten. He nodded at the Cona jug on the table. "Anyone want the last cup of coffee?"

Liz looked around at the others. It was 1:45 a.m., and in the indirect glow of the strip lights they looked grey-faced and drawn. The coffee, she could tell, was cold.

"Tell me about Gunter again," Whitten began, when Mitchell was once more sitting opposite them. "Why was he in the cab of the lorry with you?"

"His car had broken down, or was in the garage or something. I said I'd drop him off at King's Lynn. I think his sister lives there."

"Go on."

"So he got in, and we drove to the Fairmile Café, to drop off the special."

"Tell us about the special."

"Eastman told me he was some Asian fixer who was being brought in from Europe. He wasn't a migrant, like the others; he'd paid to be brought in and then, in a month's time, to be taken out again."

"A month's time?" interjected Mackay. "You're sure of that?"

"Yeah, that's what Eastman said. That he was due to go back to Germany with the cutter bringing January's runners."

"Had this happened before?" Whitten asked.

"No. The whole special idea was new on me."

"Go on," said Whitten.

"Ray and I picked up the runners at the headland—"

"Wait. Did the boats from Germany always drop off there? Or were there other places?"

"No. I think they considered other places, but in the end decided to stick with the headland."

"OK. Carry on."

"We picked the runners up, loaded them into the back of the truck, then I drove to the Fairmile Café, where the special was being dropped off. Ray let him out of the back—the special, that is—and followed him into the toilet."

"Do you know why Gunter followed him?" asked Whitten. "Had he said anything to you about needing to use the toilet?"

"No. But the Paki guy, the special, had a heavy rucksack. Small, but good quality, and whatever was in it was heavy. The guy wouldn't be separated from it."

"So you saw him close up, this Pakistani guy? The special?"

"Yeah. I mean, it was pretty dark on the beach and there were a lot of people there and quite a few of them looked, you know, the same. Pakistani and Middle Eastern types, thin faces, cheap clothes. They looked . . . they looked beaten."

"And the special was different?"

"Yeah. He carried himself differently. Like someone who'd been someone at one time and wasn't going to let anyone grind him down. Not a big guy, by any means, but hard. You could tell that about him."

"And what did he look like . . . physically? Did you see his face?"

"A couple of times, yeah. He was quite pale-skinned. Sharp features. Bit of a beard."

"So you'd recognise him again?"

"I reckon so, yeah. Although you've got to remember, like I said, it was dark, everyone was very jumpy, and there were a lot of these guys milling around . . . I wouldn't want to swear to anything, but if you showed me a photo I'd . . . I'd probably be able to say if it *wasn't* him, put it like that."

Behind the glass, Liz felt the steady drip feed of adrenalin. She felt weightless. Glancing at Goss and Mackay, she could see the same rapt attention, the same close focus.

"So why do you think Gunter followed him?" Whitten repeated.

"My guess is that he thought he had something valuable in the rucksack—the rich ones bring in gold, bullion, all sorts—and wanted to . . . well, take it off him, basically."

"So Gunter hadn't sussed him as a hard nut, then, like you had? He thought the Pakistani would be easy to rob?"

"I don't know what was in his mind. He'd probably seen less of the guy than I had. I was the one who brought him ashore."

"OK. So Gunter follows the guy into the toilets. You hear nothing. No shot . . ."

"No. Nothing at all. A few minutes later I saw the Paki walk across to a car, and get in. The car then drove off out of the car park."

"And you saw the car?"

"Yeah. It was a black Vauxhall Astra 1.4 LS. Couldn't see if it was a man or a woman at the wheel. I took its reg number, though."

"Which was?"

Consulting a scrap of crumpled paper handed to him by his lawyer, Mitchell told them.

"Why did you take the number?"

"Because I hadn't got any form of receipt for the guy. I hadn't signed him off, and in case there was any trouble later I wanted something to show that I'd brought him in. He was worth two grand to me, remember."

"Go on," said Whitten.

"Well, I waited ten minutes, and Ray didn't show. So I got out of the cab and walked over to the toilets and . . ."

"And?"

"And found Ray dead. Shot, with his brains all over the wall."

"What told you he'd been shot?"

"Well . . . the hole in his head, apart from anything else. Plus the hole in the toilet wall where his head had been."

"So what did you think?"

"I thought . . . it's illogical, because I'd seen the guy drive off, but I thought I was next. That the Paki had done Ray because he'd seen his face in the light and was going to do me too. I was crapping it, frankly. I just wanted to get out of there."

"So you drove away."

"Bloody right I did. Straight to Ilford, no stops, and dropped off the other runners."

"So when did you ring Eastman?"

"When I'd finished in Ilford."

"Why didn't you ring him straight away? As soon as you found the body?"

"Like I said, I just wanted to get out of there, to get clear of the whole business."

"What was Eastman's reaction when you rang?"

"He went totally spare, like I knew he would. I rang him in the office and he was like . . . he just went totally off his head."

"And since then? What have you been doing with yourself?"

"Waiting for you blokes, basically. Putting my house in order. I knew it was just a matter of time."

"Why didn't you come straight in? Give yourself up?"

Mitchell shrugged. "Things to do. People to see."

There was a pause, and Whitten nodded. As he walked to the door to call the custody sergeant, Honan touched Mitchell's elbow, and the pair got to their feet. Opposite them, Bob Morrison glanced at his watch. Frowning, he hurried from the room.

"Off to ring Eastman, do you think?" Mackay murmured, touching his forehead to the one-way glass.

Liz shrugged. "It's not impossible, is it?"

Don Whitten swung heavily through the door of the observation suite. "Well?" he asked. "Do we buy the story?"

Goss looked up from the notes he'd been studying. "It's logical, and it's certainly consistent with the facts we know."

"I'm the newcomer here," said Mackay. "But I'd have said the guy was telling the truth, and before the local uniform sit down with him tomorrow I'd like him to spend a few hours going through photographs of known ITS players. See if we can get a provisional make on the gunman."

"I agree," said Liz. "And I'd say that we need to get on to that black Astra as a matter of urgency—details to all forces, national security priority, et cetera."

"Agreed, but what do we tell people?" asked Whitten. "Do we link the search for the car to the Fairmile murder?"

"Yes. Put out a nationwide alert that the car has to be found and placed under observation, but that under no circumstances are the driver or passengers to be approached. Instead, Norfolk police should be contacted immediately." She raised an eyebrow at Steve Goss, who nodded, and turned back to Whitten. "Do you know where Bob Morrison went?"

Whitten shook his head uninterestedly. Yawning, he shoved his hands deep into his suit pockets. "My guess is that our shooter's still on our doorstep. Otherwise why did he have himself dropped off outside that transport café rather than going on to London with the others."

"The car could have taken him anywhere," said Goss. "Perhaps he was heading north."

Mackay leaned forward. "More than anything else, we need details of this Caravan organisation. These Germans that Mitchell told us about. Is there any reason why we can't just haul Eastman in right now and sweat him for twenty-four hours?"

"He'd laugh at us," said Liz. "I've got to know Mr. Eastman pretty well over the years, and legally speaking he's very switched on indeed. The only way we're going to get him to talk—as with Mitchell—is to deal from a position of strength. Once we've got enough information to put him away we can bring him in and break him, really give him a bad time, but until then . . ."

Mackay looked at her speculatively. "I love it when you talk dirty," he murmured.

Whitten sniggered, and Goss stared at Mackay disbelievingly.

"Thank you," said Liz, forcing a smile. "A suitable note to end up on, I think."

She kept the smile going until she and Mackay were in the Audi. Then, as they pulled their seat belts over their shoulders, she rounded on him, pale with fury.

"If you ever—*ever*—undermine my authority in that way again, I will have you off this case, and I don't care if I have to move heaven and earth to do it. You're the learner here, Mackay. On sufferance—*my* sufferance, and don't you forget it."

He stretched his legs in front of him, unperturbed. "Liz, relax. It's been a long night, and I was making a joke. Not a very good joke, I admit, but . . ."

Gunning the throttle and snapping her foot off the clutch so that he was thrown backwards against his seat, she swung out of the police station car park. "But *nothing*, Mackay. This is my operation, and you take your lead from me, understand?"

"As a matter of fact," he said mildly, "that's not strictly true. This is a joint service operation with joint service sanction, and with all due respect to your achievements to date, it's actually the case that I outrank you. So can we please loosen things up a notch? You're not going to catch these people single-handed, and even if you did, you'd have to share the credit with me."

"Is that really what you think this is about? Who gets the credit?"

"If it isn't about that, what is it about? And that was a red light, by the way."

"It was still yellow. And I don't give a toss about your rank. The point I'm making is that if we're going to have one tenth of a chance of catching our shooter, then we're going to need to keep the local uniform and the Special Branch a hundred per cent onside. That involves getting and keeping their respect, which in its turn involves your not treating me like some bimbo."

He raised his hands in surrender. "Like I said, Liz, I'm sorry, OK? It was meant to be a joke."

Without warning, the Audi screeched hard leftwards off the road, jolted over two puddle craters, and came to an abrupt halt.

"Bloody hell!" gasped Mackay, straining against the taut lock of his seat belt. "What are you doing?"

"I'm sorry," Liz said breezily. "It was meant to be a joke. Actually, I'm pulling into this layby to make a couple of calls. I want to find out who hired that black Astra."

33

A little over seventy minutes later, a dark green Rover pulled up outside a small terraced house in Bethnal Green, east London. The car
doors opened, and two nondescript men in their mid-thirties made their
way down the short flight of steps to the basement, where the taller of
the two rang three long, insistent blasts on the bell. It was a cold night,
and a pale edge of frost showed on the area steps. After a short pause
the front door was unlocked by a blinking, worried-looking young man
with a beach towel round his waist. A step or two behind him hovered a
woman, perhaps a few years older, in a lemon-yellow kimono.

"Claude Legendre?" asked the taller of the two men at the door.

"*Oui?* Yes?"

"We have a problem at the Avis office in Waterloo. We need you to bring the keys and accompany us there now."

Legendre stared beyond the men at the pinkish glow of the night sky, clutched at the knot of his towel, and started to shiver. "But . . . who are you? What do you mean, a problem? What sort of problem?"

The tall man, who was wearing a denim jacket over a heavy black sweater, held out a plastic-laminated identity card. "Police, sir. Special Branch."

"Let me see that," said the woman, reaching past Legendre to snatch the card from the taller man's hand. "You don't look like police. I don't—"

"I've just explained the situation to your London area manager, sir," the shorter man interrupted her. "Mr. Adrian Pocock. Would you like me to call him now?"

"Er, yes please."

Patiently, the shorter man took a phone from the pocket of his olive-green Husky jacket, dialled a number, and handed it to Legendre. Several minutes of conversation ensued, in the course of which the woman fetched a blanket from inside the house and draped it over Legendre's narrow shoulders.

Finally the young Frenchman nodded, snapped the phone shut, and returned it to the shorter of the two men.

"What's happening, Claude?" asked the woman, her voice shrill with concern. "Who are these people?"

"A security problem, *chérie. J'expliquerai plus tard.*" He addressed the two men standing outside. "OK. Two minutes. I come."

Liz's phone woke her at 7:45. She rolled over unwillingly, her mouth dry with the previous night's cigarette smoke and her hair smelling of it, and pressed the answer button.

After a drive conducted largely in silence, she and Mackay had arrived back at Marsh Creake shortly after 3:30 a.m., and as she was preparing to go to bed in Temeraire one of the Investigation team had

rung to say that they had identified the manager of the Avis car-hire out-
let at Waterloo Eurostar station and were on their way there to go
through the customer and CCTV records.

"We've got a fix on the Astra," he told her now. "It was hired by an
English-speaking woman, last Monday, and she paid cash in advance.
She also showed a British driving licence. The manager, who's French,
like most of his customers, handled the transaction himself and vaguely
remembers her, because she insisted on a black car and did not use a
credit card. The cash was put in the safe on the Monday night, banked
midday Tuesday, and is now effectively untraceable."

"Tell me about the driving licence," said Liz, reaching for the pen
and notebook on her bedside table.

"Name of Lucy Wharmby, age twenty-three, born in the United
Kingdom, address 17A Avisford Road, Yapton, West Sussex. Photograph shows brown-haired Caucasian woman, oval features, no distin-
guishing marks."

"Go on," said Liz fatalistically, certain of what was to follow.

"The driving licence, along with credit cards, cash, a passport and
other documents, was reported stolen to the British consulate in
Karachi, Pakistan, in August. Lucy Wharmby is a student at the West
Sussex College of Art and Design in Worthing, and was provided with a
replacement licence shortly after the beginning of the last academic
term, and this replacement licence is currently in her possession."

"You contacted her?"

"I rang her. She was at home in Yapton where she lives with her parents. Their telephone number's in the directory. She claims never to have
visited the county of Norfolk in her life."

"And the Avis CCTV?" asked Liz.

"Well, it took us a bit of time, but we found the right person eventually. The customer's a woman, about the right age as far as I can see,
and definitely dressed to beat the cameras. She's got sunglasses on and a
peaked cap pulled down over her face, so you can't see her features, and
she's wearing a long parka-style coat, so you can't see her figure. She's
also got a small rucksack and a valise-type case with her. All I can say

for sure is that she's white and somewhere between five seven and five nine in height."

"The invisible," murmured Liz.

"I beg your pardon?"

"Nothing . . . Just thinking aloud. We need to keep a whole team on this—can you clear that with Wetherby?"

"Sure. Go on."

"I want you to get the passenger list for that Monday morning's Eurostar arrival—the one immediately preceding the woman's visit to the Avis counter. Check if the name Lucy Wharmby's on the list, and if not, find out what name she came in on. My guess is that the person we're looking for is a UK citizen and passport holder aged between seventeen and thirty and will have used her own passport for the journey. So in the first instance go for English names, female, seventeen to thirty. This is still going to leave you with a pretty long list—the train was probably full of people coming home for Christmas—but every single one has to be checked and accounted for. Hit the phones, and if necessary get local uniform out checking. Where were these women on Monday night? What have they been doing since? Where are they now?"

"Got you."

"Call me the moment you hit an anomaly. Anyone who looks or sounds wrong. Anyone who, for whatever reason, hasn't been where they ought to have been. Anyone who hasn't got a rock-solid alibi for that night."

"It'll take a bit of time."

"I know. Get everyone you can on to it straight away."

"Understood. I'll keep you posted."

"Do that."

She fell back against the pillows, fighting the fatigue that was dragging at her. A session beneath Temeraire's unreliable-looking shower, a couple of cups of coffee downstairs, and things might seem a little clearer. The pursuit was taking shape now. There was the shooter and there was the invisible—the man and the woman—and both of them had been seen in the flesh. There was the car, the black Astra, clearly chosen for its indeterminate signature on CCTV film, just as the woman's clothing had been chosen for its concealing qualities.

Reaching out to the bedside table, she found her pen and notebook. Opening it, she wrote the words: *What, who, when, where, why?*

The five essential questions.

She could answer none of them.

34

Less than half a mile from the cell in which Kieran Mitchell had spent the night, a black Vauxhall Astra pulled in to a parking bay in Bishopsgate, Norwich. Climbing from the passenger seat, Faraj Mansoor glanced around him at the ranks of cars, the Georgian rooftops and the cathedral spire, and took a handwritten shopping list from the inside pocket of his coat. Remote-locking the Astra, the driver patted her pockets for change and sauntered across to the pay-and-display ticket machine.

At Faraj's side a man in a green and yellow Norwich City scarf was extracting a small child from a battered Volvo estate car and harnessing her into a Maclaren buggy. "Saturday mornings," he grinned, nodding at Faraj's shopping list. "Don't you hate them?"

Faraj forced a smile, not understanding.

"The weekend shopping," explained the man, slamming the Volvo's door and releasing the buggy's brake with his toe. "Still, it's the Villa game this afternoon, so . . ."

"Absolutely," said Faraj, conscious of the dead weight of the PSS in his left armpit. "Tell me," he added. "Do you know where there's a good toy shop here?"

The other frowned. "Depends what you want. There's a good one in St. Benedict's Street, about five minutes' walk away." He gave elaborate directions, pointing westwards.

Returning, the woman slipped her arm through Faraj's, took the shopping list from him, and listened to the tail end of the directions. "That's very helpful." She smiled at the man in the scarf, dipping down to pick up the mouse doll that the little girl in the buggy had dropped.

"She's called Angelina Ballerina," said the girl.

"Is she? Goodness me!"

"And I've got the video of *Barbie and the Nutcracker.*"

"Well!"

A little later, still arm in arm, the two of them arrived outside a shop window in which a sparkly Santa with a cotton-wool beard rode a fairy-lit sleigh piled high with games consoles, Star Wars light-sabres and the latest Harry Potter merchandise.

"What's the matter?" asked Faraj.

"Nothing," said the woman. "Why?"

"You are very silent. Is there a problem? I need to know."

"I'm fine."

"No problem, then?"

"I'm fine, OK?"

In the shop, which was small, hot and crowded, they had to wait almost a quarter of an hour to be served.

"Silly Putty, please," the woman said eventually.

The young male assistant, who was wearing a red plastic nose and a Santa hat, reached behind the counter and handed her a small plastic container.

"I, er, I actually need twenty," she said.

"Ah, the dreaded party bag! We actually sell party bags pre-filled, if you're interested. Green slime, orcs' eggs . . ."

"They've . . . they really just want the Silly Putty."

"Not a problem. Twenty Putty of the Silly variety coming up. *Uno, dos, tres . . .*"

As she followed Faraj out of the shop, bag in hand, the assistant called after her. "Excuse me, you've left your . . ."

Her heart lurched. He was waving the shopping list.

Apologetically pushing her way back to the counter, she took it from him. On it were visible the words *clear gelatin, isopropol, candles, pipe cleaners;* his fingers covered up the rest.

Outside, as she clutched the list and the carrier bag, Faraj looked at her with controlled anger from beneath the brim of his Yankees baseball cap.

"I'm sorry," she said, her eyes watering in the sudden cold. "I don't think they'll remember us. They're very busy."

Her chest, though, was still pounding. The list looked harmless enough, but to anyone with a certain sort of military experience it would send an unmistakable message. That said, of course, such a person was hardly likely . . .

"Remember who you are," he told her quietly, speaking in Urdu. "Remember why we're here."

"I know who I am," she snapped in the same language. "And I remember all that I have to remember."

She looked in front of her. At the end of an alleyway between two houses she could see the cold sweep of the river. "Superdrug," she said briskly, glancing down at the shopping list. "Or Boots. We need to find a chemist."

35

Liz stared despairingly at the image on her laptop. Lifted from the Avis car-hire CCTV at Waterloo, it showed the woman who had hired the Astra. Hair, eyes, body shape, all were obscured. Even the wrists and ankles, which might have given a clue as to physical type, were covered by clothing. The only clue lay in the lower planes of the face, which were tautly defined, with none of the puffiness which might have accompanied a larger body.

She'll be fit, guessed Liz. Someone who can move fast if need be. And she looks medium height—perhaps a little taller. Other than that, though—nothing. The image was too blurred to give up any useful information about the clothes, except that the parka buttoned on the right and had a small dark green rectangle on one faded shoulder.

From a military surplus wholesaler in the Mile End Road, which they had visited shortly before 9 a.m., the Investigations team had learned that this was almost certainly where a sewn-on German flag had been removed. The parka was ex-Bundeswehr, they were told, of a type sold in street markets and government surplus shops all over Europe. The hiking boots they had been less sure about, and staff from Timberland and several other footwear companies had been approached. The boots would turn out to be some worldwide brand, Liz was sure. Their target was a professional, and she wasn't going to make anything easy.

She glanced at her watch—ten to eleven—and snapped the laptop shut. It was cold outside the hotel, and a wet wind had been rattling Temeraire's leaded windows all morning, but she needed to walk. For the moment, there was nothing that she could do. The description and registration number of the Astra had gone out to all forces nationwide that morning, and Whitten's team was checking with all garages within fifty miles of Marsh Creake. Did anyone remember the car? Had anyone taken a substantial cash payment in the twenty-four-hour period preceding the shooting of Ray Gunter?

Liz herself had rung Investigations a couple of times to check on the Eurostar passenger-list search. The Investigations team was being led by Judith Spratt, who had been in the same intake as Liz a decade before.

"It's going to take time," Judith had told her. "That incoming train was at least half full, and two hundred and three of the passengers were women."

Liz had absorbed this piece of information. "How many of them are British?" she asked.

"About half, I'd say."

"OK. Claude Legendre specifically remembered an English woman in her early twenties, and Lucy Wharmby, the woman whose stolen driving licence our target used, is twenty-three and British. So we're right to focus first on female passengers between seventeen and thirty who hold British passports."

"Sure. That brings the number down to, let's see . . . fifty-one, which is a bit more manageable."

"And can you also get on to Lucy Wharmby and have her e-mail you half a dozen recent photographs; there's a good chance that she looks quite like our target."

"You think the driving licence was stolen to order in Pakistan?" Judith asked.

"I'd say so."

When the photographs came in an hour later, Investigations forwarded Liz a set. They confirmed the evidence of the driving licence, and showed an attractive but not especially memorable-looking young woman. Her face was oval, and her eyes and her shoulder-length hair were brown. She was five foot eight tall.

The team wasted no time. Of the fifty-one female passengers to be checked, thirty had addresses in the area served by the Metropolitan Police; the rest were spread countrywide. To help the police eliminate those who were clearly not their target—black or Asian women, for example, or the very tall, short or obese—the Avis CCTV stills were e-mailed to all the relevant forces.

The police responded to the investigation's urgency by drafting in as many officers as it took to man the phones and make up the door-knock teams. The process, however, was still a slow one. Every woman's story had to be confirmed and every alibi checked. Waiting was an inevitable part of any investigation, but Liz had always found it deeply frustrating. Taut-wired, and with her metabolism geared up for action, she paced the windy sea front, waiting for news.

Mackay, meanwhile, was in the village hall with Steve Goss and the police team, making personal calls to the heads of all the major civilian and military establishments in East Anglia that might possibly constitute Islamic Terror Syndicate targets. There were a huge number of these, from police dog–handling schools and local Territorial Army halls to full-scale regimental HQs and American air bases. In the case of the latter, Mackay suggested, perimeter patrols were to be doubled and vulnerable approach roads closed off from use by the public. Elsewhere, the Home Office was upgrading the security status of all government establishments.

At midday Judith Spratt rang her to request a call-back, and Liz returned to the shelter of the public phone box on the sea front, with whose every scratched obscenity and faded graffiti-scrawl she was now wearily familiar.

Out of the fifty-one women on the police check-list, she learned, twenty-eight had been interviewed and cleared as having verifiable alibis for the night of the murder, five were black, and so clearly not the target, and seven were "of a body size not compatible with existing subject-data."

That left eleven of the women uninterviewed, of whom five lived alone, and six lived in multi-person households. Nine had been out all morning, and were uncontactable by mobile phone, one had not returned from a party in Runcorn twelve hours earlier, and one was on the way to a hospital visit in Chertsey.

"The Runcorn one," said Liz.

"Stephanie Patch, nineteen. Catering apprentice employed by the Crown and Thistle Hotel, Warrington. Lives at home, again in Warrington. We've spoken to the mother, who says that she was working at the hotel on the night of the murder and returned home before midnight."

"What was Stephanie doing in Paris?"

"Pop concert," said Judith. "The Foo Fighters. She went with a friend from work."

"Does that check out?"

"The Foo Fighters were playing at the Palais de Bercy on the night in question, yes."

"Has anyone spoken to the friend?"

"She apparently went to the same party in Runcorn and hasn't come home either. Stephanie's mother thinks they've stayed away because one or both of them has gone out and got a tattoo, which they were apparently threatening to do. She told the police that her daughter has a total of fourteen ear-piercings. And can't drive."

"Which rather rules her out. What about the hospital one?"

"Lavinia Phelps, twenty-nine. Picture-frame restorer employed by the National Trust, lives at Stockbridge in Hampshire. Visiting her married sister who lives in Surrey and gave birth last night."

"Have the police spoken to her?"

"No, they've spoken to Mr. Phelps, who owns an antique shop in Stockbridge. Lavinia's taken the car, a VW Passat estate, but her phone's switched off. Surrey police are waiting for her at the hospital in Chertsey."

"That'll be a nice surprise for her. Any of the others look even faintly possible?"

"There's an art student from Bath. Sally Madden, twenty-six, single. Lives in a studio flat in a multi-occupancy building in the South Stoke area. Holds a driving licence, but according to her downstairs neighbour doesn't own a car."

"What was she doing in Paris?"

"We don't know. She's been out all morning."

"She sounds like a possible."

"I agree. Somerset police have their tactical firearms group standing by."

"Any word on the rest?"

"Five of them announced to other household members that they were going Christmas shopping. That's all we have at the moment."

"Thanks, Jude. Call me when you have more."

"Will do."

At 12:30, following a call from Steve Goss, Liz made her way to the village hall, where an air of unhurried urgency prevailed. More chairs and tables had been set up, and a half-dozen computer screens cast their pale glow over the intent faces of officers that Liz didn't recognise. There was muted but dense phone chatter as Goss, in shirt sleeves, beckoned her over.

"Small garage outside a place called Hawfield, north of King's Lynn."

"Go on."

"Just after six p.m. on the evening before the shooting at the Fair-mile Café, a young woman pays with two fifty-pound notes for a full tank of unleaded fuel, plus several litres which she takes away in a plastic screw-top container. The assistant particularly remembers her spilling fuel on her hands and coat—he remembers a green skiing or hiking-type jacket—presumably while filling the container. He makes some friendly remark to her about this but she blanks him and hands him the notes as if she hasn't heard him and he wonders if perhaps she's deaf. She also buys—get this—an A to Z of Norfolk."

"That's her. It's *got* to be her. Any CCTV?"

"No, which is presumably why she chose the place. But the guy has good recall of her appearance. Early twenties, wide-set eyes, mid-brown hair held in some sort of elastic band. Quite attractive, he says, and with what he describes as a 'mid-posh accent.' "

"Has the garage still got the fifty-pound notes?"

"No. Banked them a couple of days ago. But Whitten's got an Identi-fit artist on the case. He and the garage guy are putting a portrait together right now."

"When can we see it?"

"We'll have it on our screens within the hour."

"She's right under our noses, Steve. I can practically smell her."

"Yeah, me too, petrol and all. That A to Z suggests that whatever the hell she's up to—it's right here. Has London come up with anything?"

"They're down to a dozen or so possibles. No sighting of the Astra, I assume?"

"No, and I wouldn't hold your breath on that either. We've circulated the details and hopefully the reg number's taped to every squad car dashboard in the country, but . . . well, you need a hell of a lot of luck with cars. We usually only find them once they're dumped."

"Can we recirculate to the Norfolk force? So that every single policeman or -woman in the county is looking for that black Astra as a matter of absolute priority?"

"Sure."

"And have spotters in unmarked cars lying up on the approach roads to the American air bases."

"Mr. Mackay's already suggested that, and Whitten's on to it."

Liz looked around her. "Where is Mackay?"

"He told Whitten he was driving down to Lakenheath, to liaise with the station commander there."

"OK," said Liz. Good of him to keep me in the picture, she thought.

"I've heard they do a very nice hamburger down at those bases," said Goss.

Liz glanced at her watch. "Would you settle for a ploughman's at the Trafalgar?"

"Reckon so," he nodded.

36

They saw two police cars on the way back from Norwich. They were waiting in line at the intersection of the A1067 and the ring road when an unmarked red Rover with a tall antenna swept past southbound at close to the speed limit. The intent features of the driver and front-seat passenger and the closely controlled driving style had the unmistakable smack of officialdom about them, and she felt a sick thump of fear.

"Go!" said Faraj, who she guessed had not recognised the Rover for what it was. "What is it?"

The road ahead of her was clear, but traffic was now approaching from the right. She had to wait. In her mirror she could see the impatient face of the driver behind her, and when the road was finally clear she let out the clutch with a jerk.

"From now on," said Faraj tersely, "you drive smoothly, OK? When the time comes we will be carrying highly unstable material. Understand?"

"Understand," she said, breathing deeply in an attempt to control the residue of her fear.

"The next time you can stop, we change places, OK?"

She nodded. She supposed that it was important that he was familiar with the car. If she was taken out . . .

If she was taken out . . .

She faced the truth, and to her surprise the weight of the fear lifted a little. She could be killed, she told herself. It was that simple. If it came to a firefight she would be facing the best. A Counter-Terrorist Squad tactical firearms unit or an SAS Sabre team. That said, she had learned in the hardest of hard schools that she was good herself. That weapons obeyed her, and moved fluently in her hands. That close-quarter battle was her talent, her late-discovered skill.

If she was taken out . . .

She drove in silence for fifteen minutes and pulled up at a bus-stop in the village of Bawdeswell. As they changed places, and she buckled her seat belt, she saw the distant blue light of a patrol car at the roundabout a quarter of a mile ahead of them. Briefly engaging its siren, the police vehicle took a westbound exit lane and disappeared.

"I think it's time to get rid of this hire car," she said. "It was in the car park when you killed the thief. Someone could have made a connection."

He thought for a moment and nodded. She knew he had seen and heard the police car. "We'll need another."

"That was allowed for," she said. "I hire it in my own name."

"So what do we do with this one?"

"Disappear it."

"Where?"

"I know a place."

He nodded and pulled away from the bus stop, controlling the Astra with smooth, disdainful competence. There were no more police vehicles.

At the bungalow, when they had eaten, and she had spent several minutes searching the coastline to east and west of them with the binoculars, he laid the morning's purchases on the kitchen table. In silence, they rolled up their sleeves. She knew the routine well—the urban warfare cadre had been made to memorise it at Takht-i-Suleiman. It was curious, though, seeing it done here.

Taking a pyrex bowl, Faraj brought water to the boil. Adding two packets of clear gelatin, he carefully mixed it in with a stainless-steel dessert spoon. Pulling on the oven gloves that Diane Munday had provided, and which were striped blue and white like a chef's apron, he then removed the mixture from the heat. Handing the woman the gloves, he allowed the mixture to cool for a couple of minutes, added a half-cup of cooking oil, and stirred. As they watched, a thin surface crust of solids began to form. Ready with the spoon, she skimmed these off and placed them in a small Tupperware box, which she then put in the freezer compartment of the refrigerator. Both of them worked in silence. The atmosphere was almost domestic.

Pouring away the residue, and washing the pyrex bowl, Faraj then began to empty out the Silly Putty containers. When he had a large ball of the material, he dropped it into the bowl, pulled on the yellow Marigold gloves that were hanging over the sink, and began to work in the other ingredients. After a few minutes, leaving the greasy rubber gloves hanging over the side of the bowl, he went to the rucksack in his room.

The electronic hydrometer which he took out was still in its factory packaging. The printed instructions, which he briefly glanced at, were in Russian. A second bag held a selection of cellular batteries wrapped in a twist of greaseproof paper. Locking a single battery into the hydrometer, he tested the density of the grey-pink mixture in the bowl, and then, unsatisfied, returned to blending it. First by hand, and then with the spoon.

It was tiresome and messy work, but finally the mixture assumed the requisite melted-fudge consistency and the hydrometer showed the correct reading. Both of them knew that the next stage, in which the two highly unstable mixtures had to be folded together, was the most dangerous. Expressionless, Faraj laid the hydrometer on the table.

"I'll finish it," she said quietly, laying a hand on his wrist.

He stared down at her hand.

"Take the weapons, the documents and the money," she continued, "and drive a few hundred yards up the road. If . . . if it goes wrong, get out fast. Fight on without me."

He looked up from her hand to her eyes.

"You must live," she said. She tightened her hold on his wrist, which somehow required more courage than anything that had yet been required of her.

"You know . . ."

"I know," she said. "Go. As soon as I've finished you'll see me walk down to the sea."

Briskly, he moved away. It took him no more than a minute to assemble all that he needed. At the front door, he hesitated and turned back to her. "Asimat?"

She met his flat, expressionless gaze.

"They chose well at Takht-i-Suleiman."

"Go," she said.

She waited until she could no longer hear the popping of the gravel beneath the Astra's tyres, and moved to the fridge. Lifting the chilled Tupperware box carefully from the freezer, she added the fragile crusts to the mixture in the bowl. Gently but surely, murmuring a prayer to steady her hands, she worked the two compounds together until they had assumed the consistency of clotted cream.

C4, she murmured to herself. The north, south, east and west winds of jihad. Composition Four explosive.

Taking one of Diane Munday's cheap supermarket knives from the cutlery drawer, continuing her prayer, she cut the creamy paste into three equal-sized lumps. With the help of a teaspoon, she smoothed each lump into a sphere the size of a tennis ball. Spherical charges, they had told her, guaranteed the highest detonation velocity.

As she melted a couple of candles in the scratched Teflon saucepan, she allowed herself to draw breath. The worst was over, but one more test remained. "Too hot the wax," she remembered the instructor telling them at Takht-i-Suleiman, his eyes merry, "and *poo-o-o-o-f!*" He had shaken his head at the sheer hilarity of the idea.

Too cool the wax, though, and it wouldn't coat the explosive properly. Wouldn't seal it effectively from moisture, or sudden extremes of temperature or barometric pressure. Taking the saucepan off the flame, and waiting until a pale film had formed over the wax, she laid the three balls of compound in the pan with the teaspoon, and gently rolled them around. When they were evenly coated with the wax she nudged them with the teaspoon so that they fused together in a three-tiered line. Gradually the wax hardened, became opaque. The charges now looked like giant white chocolates, perhaps Belgian, like the ones that her mother . . .

Don't go there, she told herself. That life is dead.

But it wasn't quite dead, and the prayer that she was murmuring had somehow mutated into the Queen song "Bohemian Rhapsody," which, before the split-up, her parents had liked to play in the car. And there they were, their hazy figures drifting casually through the bungalow kitchen, laughing together and calling her by her old name, the name that they had given her. Furious, she stepped back from the table, closed her eyes hard for a second or two and slapped her pocket so that her hand stung as it met the loaded Malyah.

"Asimat. My name is Asimat. *My name is Asimat.*"

The intense pleasure that had accompanied Faraj's approval had evaporated. Instead, the self-doubt which periodically banked up like a stormcloud at the edge of her consciousness was threatening to inundate her. She felt a pain behind her breastbone, and the hard, bitter pounding of her heart.

Taking herself grimly in hand, she turned her attention back to the explosive. Taking three pipe cleaners, she pushed them through the cooling wax of the central sphere and out the other side—she was praying out loud now—and twisted the ends together for connection to the detonator hook-ups. Standing back, she cast a cold eye on the result. It looked as she wanted it to look, and the seamed, mirthful face of the Takht-i-Suleiman instructor seemed to nod in approval. The triple-cascade C4 detonation had always been favoured by the Children of Heaven. It was, you might say, their signature, and she, the fighter Asimat, was signing off.

Feeling more balanced now, and with the stormclouds in check, she carried the little pipe-cleaner-limbed fetish over to the fridge. It was very light, most of the weight was in the wax, and she laid it reverently on the top shelf. That done, she walked out of the back door and down the shingle to the sea's edge, where she stood expressionless and unmoving with her arms by her sides and the wind lashing her hair about her face.

37

Tell me," said Liz, pulling her coat around her as the wind shuddered the phone box door. It was the seventh reverse-charge call she'd made to Judith Spratt.

"As things stand, we've drawn a blank."

"The Bath woman?"

"Sally Madden? She spent the evening and night of the murder in the town of Frome with a friend whose dog was sick."

"Does that check out?"

"The friend corroborates and the Frome vet remembers the two of them bringing the dog to his surgery at five-ish. And according to your phone call earlier, the person we're after was buying petrol at a Norfolk garage by six."

"Damn. *Damn*. And none of the others . . . the ones who live alone, for example, what about them? And the Christmas shoppers?"

"They can all be accounted for at some point on that evening or night. Or were met off the Eurostar on the earlier date by someone who can vouch for the fact that they didn't hire a car. Or both."

"OK. Before you go through the same process with the French women and the non-EUs, I want you to do something for me. Have you got a copy of the passenger list there?"

"Yes."

"Right. Cross off all the passengers in the right age group that have been cleared."

"I've done that."

"How many women left?"

"Of the seventeen to thirties, about twenty non-EU—Americans, Aussies et cetera—and fifty-odd French."

"How do you know the French are French?"

"How do you mean?"

"How did you separate out the French from the Brits, when you first went through the passenger list?"

"By name, basically."

"Not by passport?"

"No, both British and French are just down as EU."

"OK. Go through the French names, and see if you can find a Christian name that's not specifically French. That could be English. Can you do that now?"

"OK, I'll do that right now. Here we go . . . I've got a Michelle Altaraz . . . Claire Dazat . . . Adrienne Fantoni-Brizeart . . . Michelle Gilabert . . . Michelle Gravat—that's three Michelles—Sophie Lecoq . . . Sophie Lemasson . . . Olivia Limousin . . . Lucy Reynaud . . . Rita Sauvajon . . . and, um, Anne Matthieu. That's it."

"Damn. They all sound very French. No possibility of a mistake there, or of any of that lot being English?"

"None of them sounds very English."

Liz was silent. The thought of having to ask the police, via Investigations, to check another fifty or so names, possibly with interpreters present, filled her with something close to despair. "The non-EUs," she said eventually. "What females have we got in the right age group?"

"Nine Australian, seven American, five Japanese, two South African, two Colombian, and one Indian."

"Forget the Japanese, but get your team on to locating and ringing the rest. All of them should have submitted details of where they're staying at the immigration desk at Waterloo. We're looking for an English accent, OK? A 'mid-posh' English accent, like I told you. Any that answer that description—get them checked out by the police as quickly as possible. And could you do something else? Encrypt and e-mail me the whole passenger list, divided by age, gender, and nationality. And have a team standing by to work tonight."

"Sure."

Ten minutes later, in her room at the Trafalgar, she was scrolling through the list on her laptop. It was just 2:30 p.m.

What have we missed? she asked herself, staring at the screen. *What have we missed?* Somewhere on that neat black and white list was the invisible's name.

Think. *Analyse.* Why did she come into the country under her own name?

Because whoever she was working for—whichever cell of whichever network—would have insisted on it. They would never have risked using false documentation and compromising their operation if they didn't absolutely have to. Because transparency was an essential element of invisibility.

Why use a stolen licence to hire the car?

Because once she was past Immigration and in the country there was nothing to connect her to the transaction. It was a cut-out. Even if the car was spotted its hirer would be untraceable, leaving the woman free to use her own identification as and when she chose. But for Ray Gunter, the plan would have been perfect. Gunter, however, had got himself killed, and from then onwards things had started to unravel.

But not quite fast enough. Whatever the terror cell were intending might still happen. Was Mackay right? Were they planning an assault on one of the American air bases, on Marwell, Lakenheath or Mildenhall? On the face of it, as symbols of the hated US–UK military partnership, they were the obvious local targets. But she had seen plans of the bases and they were vast. You couldn't get near them for security, both military and police, especially now that the status had been upgraded to red. What kind of attack could two people mount? Shoot a couple of guards at long range with a sniper's rifle? Loose off a rocket-propelled grenade at a gatehouse? Only with enormous difficulty, she suspected. You'd never live to tell the tale, and the press wouldn't be allowed within a mile of the story, so the impact of the attack would be minimised.

A bomb, perhaps? But how delivered? Every incoming consignment of baseballs, auto parts or hamburger buns was being X-rayed or hand-searched. No vehicle venturing outside a base was now left unattended or out in the open so that a device could be attached. All such scenarios had been played through in exhaustive detail by the RAF, the Military Police and the USAF security planners.

No, Liz told herself. Her best bet was to go at the problem from the other end. Find the woman. Catch her. *Stop her.*

Glancing at the laptop screen, a thought occurred to her. Had Claude Legendre been wrong? Was the woman in fact French, but fluent in English?

Instinct said no. Legendre dealt with English and French customers day after day, month after month, year after year, and would have subconsciously interiorised every tiny nuance of difference between the two nationalities. Accent, inflexion, posture, style . . . If his memory said that the woman was English, then Liz was prepared to trust that memory.

And if the same woman had been identified as "mid-posh" by a Norfolk garage assistant . . .

The woman looked English. You couldn't see the details on the blurry Avis CCTV footage, but in a strange sort of way you could see the person. Something in the diffident carriage of the upper body and shoulders spoke to Liz of a particularly English coupling of intellectual arrogance and muted physical awkwardness.

The clothes, she guessed, served as a disguise on several levels. They were ordinary, so people ignored her, and they were shapeless, so she escaped being identified by her physique. They were security-conscious clothes. But they were also the clothes, to Liz's eye, of a woman who wanted to pre-empt criticism. You will never be able to accuse me of failing to be attractive, these clothes said, because I will never attempt to be attractive. I despise such stratagems.

And yet according to Steve Goss the man in the garage had volunteered the information that she was attractive. Did he mean that she was pretty in the conventional sense, Liz wondered, or something else? Some men were subconsciously attracted to women in whom they detected low self-esteem, or fear. So was this woman afraid? Did she sense Liz's faint but insistent step behind her? From the moment she learned of Gunter's death she must have known that the operation was compromised.

No, Liz decided, she wasn't truly afraid yet. The arrogance was still curtaining off the fear. Arrogance and a trust in the controllers to whom, psychically or actually, she remained leashed. But the strain must be telling. The strain of remaining inside the hermetic cocoon that she had created for herself—the cocoon within which any mayhem appeared justifiable. Reality and the outside world must be beginning to bear on her now. England must be bleeding through.

By 5 p.m. the light had faded and afternoon had become evening. After the initial promise of the encounter at the garage at Hawfield, the Identifit portrait had proved disappointingly generic and unrevealing. The woman was wearing a blue-black baseball cap and olive-coloured aviator sunglasses and looked vaguely like Lucy Wharmby, although the eyes were a little wider-set.

The portrait was quickly e-mailed to Investigations, and to all the police forces involved. In response Judith Spratt requested a call-back, and, when Liz had once again made her way to the phone box that had practically become her second home, told her that the police had drawn a blank on all the non-EU seventeen to thirties.

Eighty-odd women checked. And none of them the target.

"So what do you want me to do?" asked Judith. "The area police chiefs want to know whether to have relief teams standing by for this evening. Do you want me to go with the French women?"

"I think we're going to have to."

"You sound unsure."

"I just don't believe she's French. Instinctively, I *know* she's English. Still, I guess it's got to be done."

"Go for it, then?"

"Yup. Go for it."

When Liz got back to the Trafalgar, Mackay had returned, and was holding a Scotch up to the light in the bar.

"Liz. What can I get you?"

"Same as you."

"I'm having a malt. Talisker."

"Sounds good." And maybe it'll help nudge the answer into place about our phantom Eurostar passenger, she thought tiredly. It wasn't Cherisse behind the bar, but a girl with a bleached crewcut, barely eighteen. Between her and Mackay a faint but detectable tension hung in the air.

"So what kind of day have you had?" he asked, when they were installed at a quiet corner table.

"Mostly, a bad one. Wasting the time of half a dozen police forces and running up the Service's phone bill amongst other activities. And failing to identify our invisible. On the credit side, I had a nice toasted sandwich with Steve Goss at lunchtime."

He smiled. "Are you trying to make me jealous?"

She tilted her chin at him. "It's no contest. Steve's a considerate guy. He's not arrogant. He keeps me in the picture."

"Ah, so *that's* the trouble." He sipped his whisky. "I thought I left a message."

"Yeah, and the cheque's in the post. Ring me, Bruno, OK. Keep me in the loop. Don't just bugger off."

He looked at her steadily, which she guessed was the nearest thing she was going to get to an apology.

"Let me fill you in now," he said. "I've had a quiet word with our friends at Lakenheath, all of whom seem very together and switched-on and generally *prepared* . . . and I've stressed the need for them to continue to be so. End of story, really, and I tell you, when you see those places—the sheer size of them—you do begin to wonder what a single bloke and a girl could achieve in the way of damage. Have you ever eaten a twenty-ounce steak?"

"Not to my knowledge. Steve Goss thought the USAF would feed you hamburgers."

"A fair guess. Hamburgers were indeed on the menu. But this Lakenheath steak . . . Unbelievable. I've had girlfriends with less meat on them. And frankly, a couple of chancers like our two, well, they'd be very hard pushed to get near enough to fire a Stinger or anything like that and have any hope of hitting an aircraft. I mean, I guess they might just about take out a couple of the guys at the gate, but even that would be pretty difficult."

"I've seen those bases, and I was thinking much the same thing. My instinct says that they're after a softer target."

"Like?"

"Like I don't know. Something." She shook her head. *"Damn it!"*

"Relax, Liz."

"I can't, for the moment, because I know there's something I've missed. When we've finished these drinks I want you to have a look at that passenger list, see if anything suggests itself."

"I'd be glad to. We're assuming that up to the point when Gunter was killed, our girl had no reason to disguise her actions in any way, right?"

"Right. All she had to do was make sure she wasn't picked up by the police for a driving offence. As long as she kept clean in that respect, she was fine: her only vulnerability was that stolen driving licence. So she's got to be on that list somewhere. But they've drawn a blank on every British woman between seventeen and thirty on that list. *Every one.*"

"So it's a French woman. A French woman who sounds English. Plenty of those."

"I guess you're right," shrugged Liz, unconvinced.

"Look, for the moment there's nothing we can do. Why don't we see what sort of a dinner Bethany can rustle up for us, order a decent bottle of wine . . ."

"I thought you were full of T-bone steak. And who on earth's Bethany? That sullen-looking adolescent behind the bar?"

"She's twenty-three, in fact. And the memory of lunch is fading fast."

Why not? thought Liz. He was right; until the French women had been checked there really was nothing they could do. And she really ought to try and unwind a few notches.

"OK, then," she smiled. "Let's see what Mr. Badger and his catering team can do."

"You're on. And until then, let's retire to your boudoir and examine this passenger list."

"Perhaps you should let your little friend Bethany know that we're eating here."

"Oh, she knows," murmured Mackay, throwing back the last finger of Talisker. "I told her when I got in."

A sudden paroxysm seemed to seize the windows. Outside, as the wind got up, the rain streaked against the leaded panes, blurring the yellow streetlights. Beneath these, Liz could see a white hatchback with police markings crawling along the sea front, checking the parked cars.

38

Twenty minutes later the white hatchback came to a stop in the car park below the Dersthorpe council flat where Elsie and Cherisse Hogan lived. Zipping up his dripping police waterproofs, Sergeant Brian Mudie reached under his seat for the heavy Maglite torch.

"Looks like they're mostly lock-ups," said PC Wendy Clissold, peering along the rain-hatched beam of the headlights. "I wouldn't leave a car out in the open in a dump like this. You'd come back and it'd be sitting on bricks."

Mudie considered staying in the car, and just shining the torch out of the window as Wendy Clissold cruised round the place. Don Whitten's instructions to them, however, had been to get out, to look through garage windows and behind walls—generally poke around and make nuisances of themselves. And so once again he pulled on his wet cap. The cap's elasticated rain cover was in the glove compartment, but Mudie left it there because he thought it looked daft, like a woman's shower cap.

Wriggling his toes experimentally in his sodden Doc Martens, he stepped out into the wet. The wind was coming in hard off the sea and he had to hold his cap on with the hand that wasn't holding the torch and nudge the car door shut with his knee. Inside the car he saw a brief flare as Wendy Clissold lit up. God, but she was a beautiful woman.

It took him five minutes to check the estate car park and a further eight to run the torch along the line of vehicles outside the Lazy "W," ensure that neither of the clapped-out hulks outside the Londis mini-mart was a nearly new Vauxhall Astra, and seriously alarm two young men who were smoking skunk in a Ford Capri on the sea front.

He got back to find that Clissold had switched the heater on. The patrol car smelt of hot dust and the peppermint scent of her breath-freshening spray.

"Any good?" she asked, as he bundled his wet kit over into the back seat.

"Course not. Give us one of those smokes."

As he lit up Wendy Clissold steered the car slowly out of Dersthorpe and back towards Marsh Creake. Halfway between the two, she pulled into a layby and switched off the engine and the lights, leaving only the faint hiss of the police intercom. On the seaward side of the road they could see the silent leap of the spray.

They sat in silence as he finished his cigarette.

"Are you sure your wife doesn't suspect?" asked Clissold eventually.

"Doreen? No, she's too busy with her soap operas and her lottery cards. Tell you the truth, I wouldn't care if she did."

"What about Noelle?" asked Clissold gently. "You said she'd just started at that new school."

"She's going to find out sooner or later, isn't she?" said Mudie with finality. Opening his window an inch and flipping out his cigarette butt, he reached for Clissold.

A minute or two later she drew her head back from his.

Mudie blinked. "What is it, love?"

"Those holiday cottages on the Strand? There was a light in one of them."

"Brancaster, Marsh Creake and Dersthorpe, Whitten said. Nothing about the Strand."

"I still think we should look."

"When they pay us the extra money, we'll go the extra mile. Until then, bollocks to 'em."

She hesitated. Rain beat at the windows. Dead air rasped from the intercom.

"Besides," he said, his hand squeezing the warm flesh above the waistband of her uniform trousers, "we're due back in Fakenham at half past. That gives us, what, fifteen minutes?"

She shifted doubtfully but pleasurably in her seat. "You're a bad man, Sergeant Mudie, and you're setting me a bad example."

"What are you going to do about it, PC Clissold?" he murmured, his face in her hair. "Arrest me?"

39

How's your fish?" asked Bruno Mackay.

"Long on bones and short on taste," said Liz. "A bit like picking cotton wool out of a hairbrush. This wine, on the other hand, is seriously fabulous."

"These out-of-the-way places sometimes do have good things in their cellars," said Mackay. "No one ever orders them so they lie there for years."

"Just waiting for a discriminating chap like yourself?" said Liz archly.

"Basically, yes," said Mackay. "Ah, here's Bethany with the tartare sauce."

"Who, like the wine, has been quietly maturing downstairs . . ."

"You know something," said Mackay. "You're a very judgemental woman."

Liz was searching for a reply when her phone sounded. It was Goss.

"Just calling to say that we might have a name for our shooter. Mitchell's been looking at photographs all day, and he's made a provisional identification. Would you like me to e-mail you the data?"

"Definitely."

"What's your address?"

"Hang on a sec."

She handed the phone to Mackay. "Tell Steve Goss your e-mail address. We've got an ident on the shooter."

He nodded, and she placed her knife and fork in the six o'clock position to indicate that she was giving up on the fish.

It was ten minutes before the pictures came through. They were sitting in Victory, Mackay's room. He had saved the wine and their glasses, but the pervasive smell of cheap air freshener put Liz off drinking any more.

"Makes the gorge rise," Mackay agreed, as the attachment downloaded. "It's a pity Ray Gunter couldn't have been offed on the beach in Aldeburgh—there are some wonderful hotels and restaurants there."

She nodded at the computer on the dressing table. "You know who this is going to be, don't you?"

He frowned. "No, do you?"

"I've got a pretty good idea," she said, as a dust-coloured portrait of a man in a mujahidin cap materialised on the screen.

"Faraj Mansoor," he read. "So who the hell's Faraj Mansoor?"

"Former garage worker from Peshawar. Known contact of Dawood al Safa and holder of a forged UK driving licence made in Bremerhaven."

He stared at the image on the screen. "How do you know? What haven't you been telling me?"

"What hasn't Geoffrey Fane been telling you? He's the one who picked up on this guy after German liaison flashed us about the driving licence. Are you really telling me you don't know anything about this man? You're Mr. Pakistan, after all."

"That's exactly what I'm telling you. Who is he?"

She told him the little she knew.

"So ultimately all we've got is a name and a face," said Mackay. "Nothing else. No known contacts, no—"

"Nothing else that I know about, no."

"Damn!" He sank down to the bed, which was covered with a faded green candlewick bedspread. *"Damn!"*

"At least we know what he looks like," said Liz, looking at the slight, sharp-featured figure. "Quite handsome, I'd say. I wonder what's going on between him and the girl?"

"I wonder," said Mackay drily. "The police are getting posters out, I assume."

"I guess so. It's a start."

He nodded. "There can't be too many people looking like that in East Anglia."

"I'm not so sure. He's very pale-skinned. Shave him, give him a fashionable haircut, dress him in jeans and a down-filled jacket, and he could walk unnoticed down any high street in Britain. My instinct is still to *cherchez la femme*. If we can identify her, and put her life under the microscope, I reckon we can find the pair of them. Did you get any inspiration—anything at all—from that Eurostar passenger list?"

"Only a confirmation of life's unfairness."

"What on earth do you mean?"

"Can you imagine the start in life it would give you to have a name like Adrienne Fantoni-Brizeart or Jean D'Alvéydre?" asked Mackay. "Every introduction would be a declaration of love."

"Were those two names on the list?" asked Liz. *Something, some urgent thread of an idea . . .*

"As far as I can remember, yes?"

"Just say it again," said Liz flatly. "Say those names again."

"Well, there was a woman called Adrienne Fantoni-Brizeart, I think, and a man called Jean D'Alvéydre, or something very like it. Why?"

"I don't know. Something . . ." She squeezed her eyes shut. *Damn.* "No. Lost it."

"I know that feeling," Bruno said sympathetically. "Best to file and forget. The memory'll throw it up when it's ready."

She nodded. "I know you went to Lakenheath today; did you go to either of the others, Mildenhall or Marwell?"

"No. I'd hoped to take in Mildenhall but the station commander was away. I'm due there tomorrow morning. Want to come?"

"No, I think I'll stay here. Sooner or later someone's going to spot that hire car. Whitten's had people looking for it all over the—"

There was a muted bleep, and she snatched the phone from her belt without checking the caller. "Jude?"

"No, it's not Jude, whoever she is, or he is, it's me. Mark. Listen, you know I said I was going to talk to Shauna? Well, I have. I've . . ."

She no longer heard him. She couldn't afford to listen, couldn't afford to let go the thought that had just that second, completely unbidden . . .

"Mark, I'm in a meeting, OK? I'll call you tomorrow."

"Liz, please, I . . ."

Ignoring his protests, she rang off.

Mackay grinned. "Who was that?"

But Liz was already standing. "Wait here," she said. "I want to look at that list on the laptop. I'll be back in a sec."

Leaving Mackay's room, she crossed the corridor to Temeraire. Switching on her laptop, and tapping in her password, she called up her incoming e-mail list. It took her less than a minute to find what she wanted.

"You were right," she told Mackay, back in Victory. "There is a Jean D'Alvéydre."

"Er, OK."

She consulted a handwritten list. "And a Jean Boissevin, and a Jean Béhar, and a Jean Fauvet and a Jean D'Aubigny and a Jean Soustelle."

"Right."

"And I bet you anything you like that one of them isn't a Jean, rhyming with *con,* but a *Jean,* rhyming with *teen."*

Mackay frowned. "Who's been put with the French men because she's got a French-sounding surname, you mean?"

"Exactly."

"My God," he murmured. "You could be right. You could be damn well *right."* He took the list of names from her. "That one would be my guess."

"I agree," said Liz. "That was my choice too."

She reached briskly for her bag. "Wait here. Give me five minutes."

If the phone box on the sea front had been unprepossessing in the day, it was worse at night. It was ice cold, the cement floor was covered with cigarette ends and the receiver stank of the last user's beery breath.

"Jude . . ." Liz began.

"I'm afraid the answer's no so far," said Judith Spratt. "About sixty per cent of the French names are in, and they're all negative."

"Jean D'Aubigny," said Liz quietly. "Second page, with the French men."

There was a pause. "Oh my *Lord.* Yes. I see what you mean. That could easily be an old English name. I'll—"

"Call me back," said Liz.

She and Mackay had time to finish the wine and drink a cup of coffee each. When Judith Spratt finally called back, Liz knew from her tone that she'd been right. In the phone box her back ended up pressed hard against Mackay's chest but she couldn't have cared less.

"Jean D'Aubigny, twenty-four," said Spratt. "Nationality, British, current address, *deuxième étage à gauche,* 17 Passage de l'Ouled Naïl, Corentin-Cariou, Paris. Registered as a fee-paying student at the Dauphine department of the Sorbonne, reading Urdu literature. Congratulations!"

"Thanks," said Liz, twisting round to nod at Mackay, who gave her a wide grin and a clenched fist salute. Got you, she thought. *Got you!*

"Parents are separated and live in Newcastle under Lyme; neither was expecting Jean for Christmas as she had told them she was staying in Paris with friends from the university. We've just finished speaking to her tutor at Dauphine, a Dr. Hussein. He told us that he has not seen Jean since the end of the term before last and assumed that she had withdrawn from the course."

"Can the parents get us pictures?"

"We're on to all that, and we'll e-mail them to you as soon as we get anything. Apparently Jean hasn't lived with either of her parents for several years now, but we've got a couple of people on their way up there anyway. We're also going to suggest that the French take a quiet look at the flat in Corentin-Cariou."

"We're going to need everything," said Liz. "Friends, contacts, people she was at school with . . . Her whole life."

"I know that," said Judith. "And we'll get it. Just keep checking your e-mail. Are you going to go on staying up there in Norfolk?"

"I am. She's in this area somewhere, I'm sure of it."

"Talk later, then."

Liz cut the connection, and hesitated, finger poised over the dial. Steve Goss first, she decided, and then Whitten. *Yes!*

40

What people saw in the Strand bungalows, mused Elsie Hogan, was more than she could fathom. They were poky, they were cold, you had to drive all the way to Dersthorpe if you wanted so much as a box of tea bags, and there wasn't a telly or a phone in any of them! Still, Diane Munday had to know what she was doing. She wouldn't hang on to them if they weren't turning her a profit.

Elsie "did" for the Mundays on the days that she wasn't "doing" for the Lakebys. She wasn't particularly fond of Diane Munday, who was rather liable to run an accusing finger along a dusty skirting board, and to argue the point when it came to totting up the hours. But cash was cash, and she couldn't survive on what the Lakebys paid her alone. If Cherisse fell pregnant . . . Well, it didn't bear thinking about.

Sunday was Elsie's morning for the bungalows. She didn't sweep them all out every weekend, especially if they were unoccupied, but she kept an eye on them, and as she lurched slowly up the uneven track in her ten-year-old Ford Fiesta, windscreen-wipers thonking back and forth against the steady rain, she could just see the front of the black car belonging to the woman staying in Number One. Student, Mrs. M had said. Well, she was welcome to her studies, especially on a morning like this.

From the front seat of the Astra, Jean D'Aubigny watched the Fiesta's slow approach through her binoculars. She had driven up to within a couple of feet of the track to give herself a clear field of vision in either direction, and for the last hour's watch had been listening to the local BBC station on the car radio, hoping for news of the Gunter murder. Nothing had come through, though, and she had been left peering through the sweeping curtains of rain and attempting to subdue her mounting agitation. The last time-check, a couple of minutes ago, had been 10:20 a.m.

When were they going to go against the target? she wondered for the hundredth time. What was the delay? The C4 was volatile, as Faraj knew, and couldn't be stored for long. But he was imperturbable. "We go when it is time," he had said, and she knew better than to ask again.

She blinked, and returned her eyes to the binoculars propped on the Astra's half-open window. Slowly, like a mirage, the other car crept towards her. It was old, Jean could now see, and almost certainly too clapped-out to be carrying plain clothes policemen or any other servants of the state. On the other hand, they might deliberately be using a cheap old car to get close to her. To be on the safe side she drew the Malyah, and laid it in her lap.

The Fiesta was almost on her now, and Jean could see the driver—a solid-looking middle-aged woman. Switching on the engine and putting the car into gear, she accelerated and let out the Astra's clutch, intending to reverse towards the house, well out of the other car's way. But the car was not in reverse. Somehow she had put it into first or second, and as the gears engaged the car leapt hard forwards and hammered into the wing of the oncoming Fiesta. There was a crunch, a lurching cough as the Astra stalled, and a cascade of headlight glass. Swinging counter-clockwise across the wet surface, the Fiesta came to an unsteady halt.

Shit, thought Jean. *Shit!* Shoving the Malyah into the waistband of her jeans, she jumped from the car, heart thumping. The Astra's bumper was dented and it had lost a headlight. The Fiesta's entire passenger-side wing, however, was a write-off and the car's driver was sitting motion-less, staring in front of her.

"Are you all right?" shouted Jean through the Fiesta's closed win-dow. Rain sluiced down, drumming at the car roof and drenching her hair.

The window opened a couple of inches, but the middle-aged driver continued to face ahead of her. She had switched the engine off and held the keys in her hand, which was shaking badly. "I've hurt my neck," she whimpered plaintively. "Whiplash."

Like hell you have, thought Jean savagely, crouching beside the win-dow with the rain running icily down her back. "Look, we really didn't hit each other very hard," she pleaded. "Why don't . . ."

"I didn't hit anyone," said the woman, her voice a little stronger now. "You hit me."

"OK, fine. I hit you. I'm sorry. Why don't I just give you a hundred and fifty pounds right now—cash, right—and we can . . ."

But to her horror, Jean saw that a phone had appeared in the woman's hand, and that the two-inch gap in the window was closing. She grabbed at the Fiesta's door but the rust-streaked handle locked solid as she reached it, and through the rain-blurred glass she saw the woman pulling away from her, her fingers stabbing with tremulous sus-picion at her phone.

No time to think. Wrenching the Malyah from her waistband and thumbing down the safety catch, Jean screamed, *"No! Drop the phone!"*

The two plinks at the windscreen were barely louder than the beat-ing of the rain, and the woman seemed to sink in her seat belt and fold forwards. For a moment Jean thought that she had somehow fired the Malyah without knowing, and then Faraj ran forwards with the PSS, shouldered her out of the way, and put two more aimed rounds through the driver's-side window. The woman's body jerked a little with each new impact, and sagged further forwards.

Reaching down to the ground for a large stone, Faraj heaved it through the bullet-crazed side window, reached inside, unlocked and opened the door, and rummaged beneath the woman's body. His arm came out bloodied to the elbow, and wiping the phone on the woman's blouse he glanced at the display and cut the connection.

"Load the car," he said quietly, rainwater streaming from the pale planes of his face. "Go."

Hurrying to the water's edge, he hurled Elsie Hogan's phone and the four brass-bright 7.62 shell cases out to sea. Inside the bungalow, desperately trying to ignore the shrieking panic that was expanding within her, Jean made up two bin-liners of clothes and bundled them into her rucksack with the Malyah ammunition, the map book, the compass, the clasp knife, the Nokia phone, the two washbags, and the velcro-sealing wallet containing the money. Keep doing things, she told herself unsteadily. Don't stop. Don't think. Faraj, meanwhile, carefully took the C4 device from the fridge, placed it in an open-topped biscuit tin that he had packed with a hand towel, and took it out to the car.

Everything else that might assist a forensic investigation—their used clothes, the sheets and blankets, the spare food—was bundled into the centre of the sitting room and sprinkled with petrol from the five-litre container Jean had filled at the Hawfield garage. Further fuel-soaked combustibles were packed around Elsie Hogan's body in the Ford Fiesta.

"Ready?" asked Faraj, surveying the bungalow's disordered front room. The air stank of petrol. The time was 10:26. It was just five minutes since the killing. They were wearing jeans, hiking boots and dark green waterproof mountain jackets.

"Ready," said Jean, flicking a plastic briquet lighter at the fuel-soaked sleeve of one of the shirts she had bought Faraj in King's Lynn.

They left the house at a run, heads down into the rain. As she leaned through the Fiesta window with the lighter, he swung the rucksacks into the back seat of the Astra.

Then she drove. They had planned for a fast exit, thanks be to God. She knew exactly where she was going.

41

It took Diane Munday several minutes to come to a decision. She hadn't picked up Elsie Hogan's call, she'd let the answering machine do the work, as she always did. That way she didn't have to relay tedious messages backwards and forwards between Ralph and his golfing chums—crashing bores to a man, in Diane's opinion.

When the call had come in—"Mrs. M? *Mrs. M* . . ."—something had stayed her hand. "It's Elsie, Mrs. M," the voice had shakily continued. "I'm at the bungalows, and I've—"

Then a shout of some kind. Not Elsie's voice, but stifled and indistinct. Two plinks, like a teaspoon on bone china, and a long gasping groan. The plinking sound repeated, a thump, and silence.

Elsie was on Diane's speed-dial list, and Diane tried calling her back, but got the engaged tone. Then, mystified, she rewound and played back the message. It made no more sense than it had before, but Diane knew that she ought to react in some way. Drive over there, perhaps. But she decided against this. Her fear was that some sort of tiresome medical episode had occurred. If this was the case, driving up to the bungalows could well entail driving Elsie to hospital, hanging around in King's Lynn, signing things and otherwise having her Sunday morning well and truly ruined, rather than merely spoilt.

She looked around her with mounting irritation. She had just dusted her cappuccino with slimline chocolate powder, the *Mail on Sunday* and *Hello!* were waiting on the kitchen table, and Russell Watson was singing on Classic FM.

Really, she thought. I'm not the woman's keeper; the whole cleaning arrangement had always been strictly cash in hand. If Elsie Hogan had had a dizzy turn down at the bungalows, then she should have rung that fat lump of a daughter of hers. The pub didn't open till 11:30 and Cherisse would almost certainly be at home, painting her nails or watching TV or doing whatever people did on Sunday mornings in council flats. Unless of course she hadn't *come* home, which was equally within the realm of possibility.

In the normal run of things Diane would have been tempted to ring the emergency services and leave the worrying and the problem-solving to them. On this occasion, however, she hesitated. She didn't want the police turning up at the bungalow and discovering that the girl was a cash-paying customer. She wasn't quite sure how the police and the tax people and the health and safety people connected up, but she was pretty sure that if they started talking to each other about her it could lead to problems. So she waited and she sipped at her coffee, telling herself that she should sit tight in case Elsie rang back.

After five minutes, during which the phone remained resolutely silent, Diane reluctantly punched out Elsie's number again. The mobile phone that she had called, an electronic voice informed her, was out of service. She glanced out of the French windows. It was still pouring with rain. From somewhere beyond Dersthorpe, a slender column of smoke was winding into the steel-grey sky.

Staff, Diane mused irritably, wondering where she'd left the keys to the four-wheel drive. One couldn't survive without them, but my *God* they could take it out of you.

On the way out she glanced at the kitchen clock. It was 10:30.

42

They let the first car pass. It was a Fiat Uno covered in unpainted patches of filler, and didn't look as if it had much life left in it. Parking the Astra at the side of the road between Dersthorpe and Marsh Creake—in the same layby, as it happened, in which Brian Mudie and Wendy Clissold had spent twenty happy minutes the night before—had been a calculated risk. If a police car had passed, that would probably have been the end of it.

But no police car came. The Fiat was followed by a Nissan, in equally poor shape, and as it disappeared a silent mushroom of flame-red smoke leapt into the sky beyond Dersthorpe. The Fiesta's petrol tank, thought Jean, as the fuel-enriched smoke joined the thickening grey coil from the house. The fire service would almost certainly be on their way already—someone would have seen the bungalow go up—but they probably had to come from Fakenham. With a bit of luck it would be a good five minutes or so before the police were on the case, and at least ten before any roadblocks were set up.

Rain streamed down her face, but strangely, Jean wasn't cold. Desperation, and the real possibility of capture, had taken her beyond fear to something like calm. She was steady now, and could feel the modest, comforting weight of the Malyah in the pocket of her mountain jacket.

A silver car—she didn't have time to identify it, but it looked newish and sporty—swung into view, and she heard the thump of a powerful bass speaker. She stepped into the road, arms waving and hair flying, forcing the driver to make an emergency stop.

He was in his late twenties, with an earring and a greasy centre-parting. Techno-trance music poured from the car. "Want to get yourself bloody killed?" he shouted angrily, half opening the door. "What's your problem?"

Wrenching the Malyah from her jeans, she pointed it at his face. "Get out," she ordered. "*Now!* Or I'll shoot you."

He hesitated, slack-jawed, and dropping her aim for a second she put a 9mm round into the seat between his tracksuited legs. The wind whipped away the sharp percussive crack.

"*Out!*"

He half fell, half climbed out of the car, bug-eyed with shock, leaving the key in the ignition and the engine and the CD player running.

"Into the passenger seat, now. *Move!*"

He scrambled unsteadily inside and she reached in and snapped off the music. In the sudden silence, she was aware of the loud beat of the rain on the car roof.

"Seat belt. Hands on your knees."

He nodded mutely, and she kept him covered as Faraj exited the Astra, loaded the rucksacks into the boot of the silver car, and took his place in the back seat with the map book and the biscuit tin on his lap. He was wearing the Yankees baseball cap beneath the hood of his waterproof jacket, and his face was all but invisible. For perhaps thirty seconds Jean familiarised herself with the gearing and dashboard controls. The car was some sort of Toyota.

"OK," she said, reversing sharply into the layby and swinging the nose back towards Marsh Creake. "Like I said, you just sit there, understand? Try anything—anything at all—and he'll shoot you in the head."

From his pocket Faraj drew the blunt-nosed PSS, reloaded with SP-4 rounds, and slapped back the magazine, which engaged with a businesslike click. The man, very pale, gave the ghost of a nod. Jean let out the clutch. As she drove off, they passed Diane Munday's metallic-green Cherokee speeding in the opposite direction.

"Navigate for me," she said to Faraj in Urdu.

43

The call was logged at 10:39. It was taken by Wendy Clissold, and Liz saw the police constable's face freeze at the significance of what she was hearing. Clapping her hand over the mouthpiece she turned and shouted across the village hall. "*Guv'nor!* House and vehicle alight at Dersthorpe Strand. Unidentified dead female in the vehicle."

Clissold's voice steadied as Whitten grabbed the landline phone in front of him. "I'm putting you straight through to Detective Superintendent Whitten, madam," she continued. "Can you give me your name and number in case we have to call you back?"

Whitten listened intently as Clissold took the details. "Mrs. Munday," he cut in smoothly. "Tell me."

Within a couple of minutes an investigative team had been dispatched to Dersthorpe Strand. Forensic officers were making their way from Norwich, and the local fire crew, it turned out, had just left the Burnham Market station. The burning car had been identified as Elsie Hogan's by a near-hysterical Diane Munday, and Diane had been pretty certain that its occupant was Elsie too.

Liz watched the activity around her, weighing up the ramifications of Diane Munday's report. There was a chance, she supposed— although instinct told her that it was unlikely—that this was the work of some deranged local arsonist rather than Mansoor and D'Aubigny. But *Elsie Hogan,* of all people? What had that poor, self-effacing woman ever done to upset anyone?

At 10:45 a call came through from one of the investigative team to say that, while en route to the Strand bungalows, they had discovered a black Vauxhall Astra matching the description of the vehicle sought in connection with the Gunter murder. The Astra was standing at Dead Man's Hole layby outside Dersthorpe, and an officer had been left to secure it. Despite the rain, its engine was still warm.

Diane Munday, the caller continued, had arrived before the fire had destroyed the safety glass in the Fiesta's windows, and had reported seeing what looked like bullet holes in the windscreen. No one, on this occasion, was inclined to doubt her.

As Whitten reported the situation to the Chief Constable in Norwich, Liz called Wetherby at his desk. Like her, he had been at work for several hours. Investigations had kept him informed about the identification of Faraj Mansoor and Jean D'Aubigny, and he was receiving regular reports concerning the questioning of the D'Aubigny parents.

Wetherby listened to Liz in silence as she summarised the events on Dersthorpe Strand. "I'm calling a COBRA meeting," he said quietly when she had finished. "Can I give them any clue as to a probable target for our terrorists?"

"Guesswork at this stage," replied Liz, "but one of the USAF bases would have to be most probable. Bruno Mackay's over at Mildenhall now, liaising with the station chief."

"OK, I'll go with that. Keep me up to speed."

"I will."

There was a faint pause. "And Liz?"

"Yes?"

"Be careful, please."

Smiling faintly, she replaced the phone. When things got rough, as they showed every promise of doing now, Wetherby seemed to be assailed by a curiously old-fashioned chivalry. He would never have told a male officer to be careful—of that she was certain. In anyone else she might have objected to this note of concern, but Wetherby was not anyone else.

She glanced over at Whitten. If a COBRA meeting was being convened, it was almost certainly only a question of time before the case was taken off his hands. The acronym referred to the Cabinet Office Briefing Room in Whitehall. The meeting would probably be chaired by a representative of the Home Office, with liaison officers from the Ministry of Defence, the police, and the SAS in attendance. Geoffrey Fane would be there too, she guessed, poised crane-like over the discussion. If the situation was considered acute enough, the case would then be nudged up to ministerial level.

Liz had sat up for most of the night in the village hall with Whitten, Goss and Mackay, monitoring the incoming information about Jean D'Aubigny, of which there had been quite a volume, and about Faraj Mansoor, of which there had been almost nothing, beyond the information from Pakistan liaison that someone of that name had attended one of the more radical *madrassahs* in the northern town of Mardan a couple of years earlier. It had been hard going—they were all heavy-eyed with exhaustion by the end—but it had had to be done. Around 5 a.m. Liz had returned to the Trafalgar and tried to sleep. But she'd drunk too much Norfolk Constabulary coffee and her mind was flying. She had lain there, the pub's pink nylon sheets pulled to her chin, watching a grey and unwilling dawn slowly illuminate the gap between the curtains. In the end she had drifted off, only to be dragged back to consciousness almost immediately by a call from Judith Spratt's deputy to alert her to an incoming message.

Blearily, Liz had switched on her laptop, and scanned and decoded the report. After several hours of questioning during the night, it seemed, the D'Aubigny parents had decided against giving any further information about their missing daughter. To begin with, under the impression that her involvement with Islamic fundamentalism had placed her in danger, they had been anxious to help. As the realisation had dawned on them that she was less a potential victim of terrorism than a wanted suspect, however, their answers had become more circumspect. Finally, claiming that their human rights were being infringed, and that they were being subjected to psychological torture in the form of sleep-deprivation—tell me about it, thought Liz wryly—they had refused to cooperate any further, and enlisted the services of Julian Ledward, a well-known radical lawyer.

Urgently repeat urgently need D'Aubigny's connection w E Anglia, if any, Liz typed in return. *Job? Holiday? Boyfriend? Schoolfriend? (Was D'Aubigny @ boarding school or UK university?) Tell parents they're risking daughter's life by not talking.*

She had encrypted and sent the reply, and hoped for the best. After a shower and a silent breakfast with Mackay in the Trafalgar dining room, she had been back in the village hall by 7:30. Mackay, as planned, had driven off to Mildenhall USAF base, armed with a sheaf of printout portraits of Faraj Mansoor and Jean D'Aubigny.

In the village hall, which she couldn't quite bring herself to call "the incident room," she had discovered Don Whitten, alone. The brimming ashtray at his elbow suggested that he hadn't gone home since she had taken her leave at 5 a.m. They had sat and stared together at a big A3 printout of Jean D'Aubigny. Taken four years earlier, it was an interior shot, and showed a surly-looking young woman in a black sweater standing in front of an out-of-focus Christmas tree. Short, unfashionably cut brown hair framed a pale oval face with intense, wide-set eyes.

"I've got one that age," said Whitten.

"What's she do?" asked Liz.

"Lives at home and gives us a shed-load of grief. Nothing like this, though. Jesus."

Liz nodded. "It'd be good to get her alive."

"You think we won't?"

She met Jean D'Aubigny's twenty-year-old gaze. "I don't think she'll come out with her hands up, put it like that. I think she'll want to be a martyr."

Whitten pursed his lips. The steel-grey of his moustache, Liz noticed, was yellowed with nicotine. He looked exhausted.

Now, three hours later, she watched as, with measured grimness, he stuck an arc of pins into a 1:10,000 Ordnance Survey map. Each pin, and there were twelve of them, marked a roadblock. Whitten had calculated that their targets couldn't have driven more than a dozen miles from Dersthorpe since abandoning their old car and—presumably—commandeering a new one. He had set his traps accordingly.

"I've also requested helicopters and a Tactical Firearms Unit," he told her. "We're getting them, I'm happy to say—the TFU are going to be on standby within the hour—but we're getting Deputy Chief Constable Jim Dunstan too. I've been bumped to second-in-command."

"What's he like?" asked Liz sympathetically.

"Good enough bloke, I suppose," said Whitten. "Not over-keen on your lot, though, from what I've heard."

"OK, thanks for the warning." Earlier she had looked at Jean D'Aubigny's portrait with a certain detached sympathy, sensing the maladjustment in that over-intense gaze. Now she just viewed their quarry as the enemy—two people who were prepared to murder a harmless creature like Elsie Hogan just because, for whatever reason, she had found herself in the wrong place at the wrong time.

They had to be stopped. Stopped before they destroyed more lives, and caused more desperate and needless grief.

44

Jean had been driving for twenty minutes when they saw the road-block. They were travelling at a careful twenty-five miles an hour along a rutted single-lane track, enclosed by high hedges of bramble and elder. According to the map the lane would soon connect with another, which after various bifurcations would lead them southwards between the villages of Denton and Birdhoe. The route had been planned on the basis that they were still driving the Astra, and as the one on which they were least likely to encounter a police car. Given their changed circumstances, there had been an argument in favour of heading for the fastest road out of the area, and attempting to outrun any roadblock, but on balance, thought Jean, they had probably made the right decision by sticking to the original route. Farm roads were slow, but they were discreet.

Beside her, the young man whose car she was driving had subsided into a silent, sulking torpor. His immediate fear of their weapons had subsided, to be replaced by a dull fury at his helplessness and at the liberties taken with his precious Toyota.

Jean saw the blue light at the same moment that he did. They were passing a gap in the hedge, a gap through which the junction with the Birdhoe road, half a mile ahead, was momentarily visible. The blue light had flickered just once—a mistake, Jean guessed. Praise be to God, she thought, for the flatness of this countryside, and then the fear kicked in, hard and painful.

"Police," the greasy-haired young man murmured fearfully. It was the first word that he had spoken.

"*Shut up!*" Jean ordered him tersely. Her heart was pounding. Had they been seen? There was a good chance that they hadn't, given the distance and the height of the hedges.

"Reverse," ordered Faraj.

Jean hesitated. To drive back past the gap would give the waiting police a second chance to see them.

"*Reverse,*" repeated Faraj angrily.

She came to a decision. A short way in front of them, to their right, was a narrow track leading to a motley collection of barns and farm outbuildings. No actual dwelling was visible.

Pulling the wheel over, ignoring Faraj's protests, she swung quietly up the track. As far as the roadblock was concerned, they were invisible. They just had to hope that there were no farm workers about. Thirty yards up the track the ground opened out into a walled yard in which stood a rusted tractor and harrow and a silage heap covered by a plastic sheet and old tyres.

Driving round the far side of the silage heap so that the car was hidden by the road, she came to a sharp stop. She turned to Faraj and he nodded, seeing belatedly that the idea was a good one.

"Out," Jean said to the youth, into whose fearful eyes a faint spark of hope had crept. "Get into the boot."

He nodded, and did so, tucking himself deep and fearful into the carpeted space. The rain lanced down, cold against Jean's face after the warmth of the car. For a moment his eyes met hers, frankly imploring, and then she felt Faraj press the butt of the PSS into her hand and knew that the moment had come. Around her, ghostly and transparent, crowded her fellow trainees from Takht-i-Suleiman, silently yelling and waving their weapons. "To kill an enemy of Islam is to be reborn," whispered the instructor. "You will know the moment when it comes."

She blinked and they vanished. Behind her back the PSS was heavy in her hand. She smiled at the young man. His knees were drawn up to his face, covering his chest. A head shot, then. The moment was unreal. "Could you just shut your eyes a moment?" she asked him.

The discharge was soundless and the recoil negligible. The youth twitched once, and was dead. It was the simplest thing in the world. The boot closed with a faint hydraulic whisper, and when she turned to Faraj to return the weapon, she knew that nothing now stood between them.

Wading through the thick brown midden they grabbed a corner each of the plastic sheet and dragged it off the silage heap and over the car. A half-dozen tyres came rolling with it, and they heaved three of these on top of the sheet. The rain poured down on the midden and the silage heap and the rusted tractor. It was the sort of scene you drove straight past.

She was leading Faraj now, across the yard and down to the narrow drainage cut. Their rucksacks were on their backs and their waterproofs zipped to the chin. The biscuit tin containing the moulded and wax-sealed C4 explosive was at the top of Faraj's pack.

The water in the cut was agonisingly cold as it crept up past her crotch to her waist, but Jean's heart was still racing with the relief that killing, when all was said and done, had proved to be such a simple thing. She hadn't given the corpse more than a flicker of a glance; the impact of the shot had told her all that she needed to know and she heard it again now, like the sound of a boot stamping on a rotten marrow.

Reborn, remade.

After a hundred yards they stopped, and peered through the dead foliage bordering the cut. Faraj passed her the binoculars. A flatbed truck was standing at the roadblock, and a policeman was clambering over its load of blue fertiliser sacks. Search on, thought Jean. The Malyah was zipped into her hood now.

"This *nullah* takes us close to them," murmured Faraj, scanning the open fields before them. "But the hedges are dead and we will be seen if we try to go across country. We have to assume they have good optical equipment."

"They're local police, not soldiers," said Jean, glancing at her watch. "My guess'd be that we've got another twenty minutes to half an hour. After that it'll be helicopters, dogs, the Army, everything."

"*Go,* then."

They pressed forward through the waist-deep water, rain slashing at their faces and marsh gas erupting around them with each step. It was hard going. The mud sucked at their feet, and in places the rotting vegetation fringing the cut thinned so that they had to proceed at an agonising crouch. The lower half of Jean's body was completely numb now, and at intervals the scene in the boot of the car replayed itself in her mind. Tiny details began to emerge: the curious sensation of the PSS's damped internal detonation, and the tiny whipcrack as the armour-piercing round met adult bone. That quarter-second glance had been enough. The image was imprinted on her memory as if on high-speed film.

Ten minutes later—ten freezing, dogged minutes that felt more like an hour—they were at the closest point of the cut to the checkpoint. The watercourse was less than three feet wide in places, and the banks were slick with the muddy run-off from the fields. Jean's back and hamstrings, meanwhile, were screaming with the dead weight of the rucksack and the stress and tension of their crouching progress. Carefully, as Faraj waited motionless beside her, she scanned the police post with the binoculars. She had kept well behind the bankside reeds so that no lens flash would betray her, and blurred images of this foliage and grey curtains of rain hung between her and the checkpoint. Indistinctly, she watched two officers in fluorescent yellow waterproofs checking a car. Several other vehicles were waiting in line, and the officers were moving in the constricted, hunch-shouldered way of men who were not enjoying their job. Three others, more shadowy figures, were waiting in a white Range Rover with police markings. There were no blue lights in evidence but Jean could hear a faint radio crackle on the wind.

She saw the helicopter before she heard it. It was a couple of miles to the east of them, moving in irregular patterns above the fields and coppices. At intervals, a thin white spotlight beam cut the rain-grey sky.

Soon, her forehead pressed into the mudslicked bank of the cut amongst the rotting bullrushes and flag-iris leaves and beneath the skeleton of an alder bush, Jean could hear the tiny flicker of rotor blades. Beside her, his face inches from hers, Faraj was similarly frozen. The helicopter drew nearer, its pencil beam nosing pensively at a patch of woodland half a mile away.

And then suddenly it was overhead, the heavy pulse of its rotors washing menacingly over the sodden fields. The beam played briefly over the farmyard that they had left ten minutes earlier, and Jean almost wept with relief that they had covered the car with the plastic sheet. It had been desperately close, and the reaction of the police in getting the helicopters up—she was under no illusion that there would only be one of them—had been very fast indeed. And this was just the beginning. There would be tracker dogs soon, and soldiers with rifles. They had to move on, or die.

But the helicopter pilot showed no inclination to depart, and Jean began to shake with the cold and the tension, and her teeth to chatter.

Extending an arm around her waist, Faraj pressed her upper body against his chest in an attempt to warm her. The gesture, she could feel, was purely utilitarian; there was no affection in it.

"Be strong, Asimat," he murmured into the streaming hood of her waterproof. "Remember who you are."

"I'm not afraid," she replied, "I'm just . . ."

Her words vanished in the clatter of the overhead helicopter. Prop-wash shivered the surface of the cut as the spotlight beam moved inexorably towards them. Closing her eyes tightly, willing herself into immobility, Jean began to pray. Over her head, as the hard white light pressed down on them, forcing its way between her eyelids, she could feel the shudder of the stunted alder bush. Were they using thermal imaging? she wondered. Because if so . . .

And then suddenly the helicopter was gone, banking away westwards as if bored with the whole process.

"Now move," said Faraj urgently, backing off her. "That won't be the last of them, and this rain won't last for ever."

Relief flooded through her. At the roadblock, she heard several cars drive through in close succession. The policemen, she guessed, had been watching the helicopter. They moved forwards, bodies bent against the sheeting rain and the drag of the muddy water, and soon found themselves a couple of hundred yards beyond the roadblock.

"Another mile, and we'll hit the village," said Jean breathlessly, crouching down against the bank. "Trouble is, if anyone who's just been through the roadblock sees us climbing up on to the road, they'll just go straight back to the police and report us. They'll have descriptions by now, and probably pictures."

Faraj considered for a moment, took the binoculars from her, and narrowing his eyes scanned the surrounding countryside.

"Right," he said eventually. "This is what we do."

45

The repair hangar at the Swanley Heath Army Air Corps base was impressively vast, and considering its size, impressively warm. At 11 a.m. the Chief Constable of Norfolk had ordered that his deputy, Jim Dunstan, should take over what was now officially an anti-terrorist operation. Dunstan's first act had been to request that the Swanley Heath base act as host to the inter-service operational team.

It was a good decision, thought Liz. Swanley Heath was halfway between Brancaster to the north and the Marwell, Mildenhall and Laken-heath USAF bases to the south. The operational team was now, hope-fully, at the centre of the area through which their quarry was moving. The base was secure, and able to accommodate with ease both the two-dozen-odd personnel involved in the running of the operation and the considerable array of their technical and communications equipment.

By midday, after a scramble of activity and a lot of hard driving with sirens blaring and lights flashing, this was almost all set up. The fifteen-strong police team, headed by Dunstan, and with Don Whitten and Steve Goss in attendance, occupied an area dominated by a nine-metre-square electronic map of the region, borrowed from their Army hosts, showing the deployment of roadblocks, helicopters and search teams. In front of each member of the team was an assortment of laptop computers, landlines and mobiles, most of them in use. In the case of Don Whitten there was also an ashtray.

Beyond them, parked in a ready-to-go line, were the three unmarked Range Rovers of the Norfolk Constabulary's SO19 Tactical Firearms Unit. Its nine members, all men, lounged on benches in their dark blue overalls and boots, passing round a copy of the *Sun*, rechecking their Glock 17 pistols and MP5 carbines, and staring blankly up at the distant roof of the hangar. From outside, at intervals, came the distant beat of rotors as Army Air Corps Gazelle and Lynx helicopters lifted away from the tarmac.

The official estimate, by default, was that the target of the two terrorists was either one of the USAF bases or the royal residence at Sandringham, where the Queen was now staying—as she did every Christmas. No one could quite envisage how the security net surrounding these establishments was supposed to be penetrated, but the worst had been assumed concerning the weaponry that the two were carrying. Neither chemical nor biological weapons had been ruled out. Nor, indeed, had a so-called "dirty" bomb, although the remains of the bungalow had shown no signs of radioactive material.

In his keenness to get the county's two Squirrel helicopters launched and over the search area, Whitten had explained to Dunstan, he had sent them up without their thermal imaging activated. The helicopters had been scrambled from Norwich, but of the supposedly available system operators one was on compassionate leave and the other had broken his ankle in the course of a motivational weekend. So the Squirrels had gone up two-handed, with a pilot and a Night-Sun searchlight operator each. Visibility had been atrocious due to the rain, but the search area had been thoroughly covered with the help of the spotlights, and Whitten was confident that D'Aubigny and Mansoor were still confined to the seventy-mile square whose northern boundary was Brancaster Bay and whose western boundary was the Wash.

Liz was not so sure. Apart from their predilection for murder, the two hadn't done too badly so far when it came to concealing themselves and moving across hostile terrain. The D'Aubigny woman clearly knew the lie of the land.

What was her connection with the area? Liz asked herself for the hundredth time. Why had she been chosen? Was it just because she was British, or did she have some specialised local knowledge? Investigations were checking every one of her known contacts, but the parents' silence was desperately unhelpful. Couldn't they see that there was only one chance of saving their daughter, and that was to catch her before it came to the final reckoning? Before it came to the killing time?

From the other side of the room she saw Don Whitten pointing in her direction. A neatly dressed young man in a green Barbour coat was walking towards the trestle table on which she had her own laptop set up. "Excuse me," he said. "I'm told you can help me find Bruno Mackay."

"And you are?"

He held out his hand. "Jamie Kersley, Captain, 22 SAS."

She shook the proffered hand. "He's due any time."

"Are you from the Firm too?"

"I'm afraid not."

He grinned warily. "Box, then?"

Short for Box 500, one of the Service's former postal addresses, this was one of MI5's many sobriquets. Traditionally, as Liz was keenly aware, the Army had always had a rather warmer relationship with MI6. As politely as she could, she ignored the question.

"Why don't you take a seat, Captain Kersley? When Bruno Mackay shows up I'll steer him in your direction."

"Er . . . thanks. I've got two four-man teams unloading a Puma out-side. Let me get them squared away and I'll be back."

She watched as he marched briskly away, and then turned to her laptop.

SAS here mob-handed, she typed out. *But ITS target still unknown. Unusual, surely. Something I shd know???*

Signing off with her identifying number, and encoding the message with a couple of swift key-strokes, she dispatched it to Wetherby.

The reply came back less than a minute later. Highlighting the text, she watched as the random-looking letters and numbers disappeared, to be replaced with legible text.

Agree unusual. Regiment present at request of G Fane. Essential ready deploy at short notice he told COBRA. Yr guess good as mine.

As she watched, the eight SAS soldiers passed the entrance to the hangar. Despite the rain, or perhaps because of it, they walked bare-headed and with studied casualness. They were dressed in black fire-proof battledress and carrying a wide assortment of weapons including carbines and snipers' rifles.

Altogether, a hellish volume of firepower was being brought to bear. Against what exactly? Liz wondered.

46

The pub in Birdhoe was called the Plough, and the sign showed the seven stars of that constellation. By 12:30 the car park was almost full; Sunday lunch at the Plough was a popular fixture, and there wasn't another pub for three or four miles in either direction.

Exiting the ladies' toilet in the corner of the car park, where she had been waiting until the coast was clear, Jean D'Aubigny looked about her. Luckily, it was still raining. No one was hanging around in the car park to chat. The car she had identified as the easiest to steal, if not necessarily the most suitable, was an old racing-green MGB. It was probably a quarter of a century old, but without being a collector's piece looked reasonably well cared for. Its great advantage was that due to its age it had no steering lock that had to be disabled. Jean was capable of breaking a steering lock—a length of piping braced beneath one of the struts of the wheel and forced downwards usually did the trick—but it was a hard operation to perform unobtrusively.

Arriving at a decision, she walked purposefully to the MGB, deftly slashed the wet vinyl top with her clasp knife, dipped in her hand, slipped the lock, and climbed into the driver's seat. Next to her, in the passenger seat, was a man's sheepskin jacket, which she laid over her sodden knees. Drawing back her booted foot, she smashed her right heel into the covering beneath the steering wheel. It was plastic, but old plastic, and half of it cracked away, revealing the white metal ignition barrel beneath.

Glancing quickly around her to make sure that she was still unobserved, she wrenched the four wires out of the bottom of the barrel, and stripped them back with the knife. Taking the red wire—the main ignition lead—she quickly touched it to the others in turn. With the third, a green wire, there was a brief lurch as the starter turned over. Isolating the green wire, she quickly connected the other two to the red one. The dashboard was now live. Depressing the clutch, she ran through the gears a couple of times before slipping the MGB back into neutral.

OK, she told herself. Here we go—*Inshallah!*

Carefully, avoiding the thumping electric shocks she'd suffered the first couple of times she'd tried it, outside a housing project in southeast Paris, she touched the green starter wire to the other three and depressed the accelerator an inch or two. The MGB howled, terrifyingly loud, and Jean jumped. But the weather must have dampened the noise, because no furious owner, beer glass in hand, appeared out of the pub. Instead, rainwater poured into Jean's lap from the knife slash in the vinyl top.

With the engine turning over, she switched on the heater and windscreen-wipers, put the MGB into reverse, let off the handbrake, and backed out of the parking space. Even the gentlest manoeuvre seemed to engender an outraged snarl from the old sports car, and Jean's heart was thumping painfully in her chest as she shifted to first gear, nosed towards the car park exit, and turned sharply southwards.

On the open road she felt no less self-conscious. This, surely, was a vehicle that local people would know and recognise. But the area seemed deserted. People were either at the pub, she guessed, or behind their locked front doors, watching TV sport or the Sunday soaps.

A mile beyond the village she came to the spot they had located on the map, where the cut they had walked along disappeared into a culvert under the road. She pulled up just beyond it, ensuring that the engine stayed running. Within moments, Faraj's head and torso appeared, and he was hauling himself up through the sodden dead brambles. Jean leaned over to open the door and Faraj handed in the black rucksack, which she placed alongside her own in front of the passenger seat. Dripping copiously, he climbed into the seat, arranged the rucksacks beneath his knees, and pulled the door closed.

"*Shabash!*" murmured Faraj. "Congratulations!"

"It's not perfect," she admitted, as the windscreen-wipers thumped noisily back and forth, "but it was the easiest to steal."

She pulled back on to the road. The petrol gauge read a quarter full, and her brief elation faded as she realised that they weren't going to be able to refill the tank, which almost certainly only ran on leaded fuel. Right now, though, she couldn't face explaining this. Her senses felt simultaneously taut-wired and dulled to a kind of slow motion. She was running on empty herself. It was too complicated.

"Let's get out of here," she said.

47

But why *this* man?" asked Liz. "Why send this particular man? He's never been here, he's got no family here . . . As far as we know he's got no connection to Britain whatsoever."

"I can't answer that question," said Mackay. "I genuinely have no idea. He certainly never came to our attention in Pakistan. If he was a player out there, it was at much too low a level to show up on our radar. But then I'm afraid that's how things were. There was a very high noise-to-signal ratio."

"Meaning?"

"Meaning that while there were any number of overexcited guys on street corners who were happy to scream and shout and burn the Stars and Stripes—especially if there was a CNN crew around—there were rather fewer who translated their resentment into direct action. If Pakistani agents were clocking every garage hand that al Safa so much as looked at, then they were doing what every agent has done since time immemorial—padding their reports to make it look like they were worth their salaries."

"But they were right about Mansoor. Right to have him on file, at least."

"So it turns out. But I'd guess that that's more coincidence than inside knowledge."

They were driving in Mackay's BMW to the Marwell USAF base. The MI6 man had returned from Mildenhall to Swanley Heath shortly after midday, and after swapping phone numbers with Jamie Kersley, the SAS captain (who, it turned out, was also an old Harrovian), and sitting down for a ten-minute sandwich lunch with Liz and the police team, had prepared to leave for the last, and nearest, of the three USAF bases. Mackay had asked Liz if she felt like coming too, and with both terrorists positively identified but with no other positive leads it had seemed as constructive a course of action as any other. Thanks in part to the atrocious weather, the search for D'Aubigny and Mansoor had stalled, despite the arrival of teams from the regular and Territorial Army.

By 1:45, finally, the weather was showing signs of letting up. The rain had almost stopped and the hard battleship grey of the sky had softened to a paler blur.

"They'll make a mistake," said Mackay confidently. "They almost always do. Someone up there will spot them."

"You think they're still contained in the search area?"

"I think they've got to be. I'd back Mansoor to make it through alone, but not the two of them."

"Don't underestimate D'Aubigny," said Liz, obscurely irritated. "This is not some thrill-seeking teenage bimbo, but a fully trained graduate of the North West Frontier camps. If either of the two has made mistakes so far, it's Mansoor. He got himself jumped by Ray

Gunter and ended up leaving us vital ballistic evidence, and I'll bet you anything you like it was him who killed Elsie Hogan this morning, too."

"Do I detect a note of empathy there? Admiration, even?"

"No, not an ounce. I think that she's a killer too, almost certainly."

"What tells you that?"

"I'm beginning to get a sense of who she is and how she operates. What I want is for her to start feeling twenty-four-hour pressure—the sense that she can't afford to rest, can't afford to stop, can't even afford to think. I want it on top of the pressure that's already there, the sense of being torn between two utterly opposing worlds."

"She doesn't seem very torn to me."

"Outside, maybe not. Inside, believe me, she's being pulled apart, and that's what makes her so dangerous. The need to prove to herself, through violent action, that she's committed to this . . . to this militant path."

He permitted himself an oblique smile. "So would you rather the rest of us just withdrew, and left the two of you to get on with it?"

"Funny guy. In any campaign, the first stronghold that you have to occupy is your enemy's consciousness."

"That sounds like a quote."

"It is a quote. Feliks Dzerzhinsky."

"Founder of the KGB. A suitable mentor."

"I like to think so."

Mackay put his foot down to pass a green MGB. They had just passed through the village of Narborough. "I had a car a bit like that once," he said. "An old '74 MG Midget. Bought it for five hundred quid and restored it myself. God, but that was a beautiful car. Teal blue, tan interior, chrome bumpers . . ."

"And a real babe magnet, I'm sure," said Liz. "All those Moneypennys."

"Well, it didn't put them off, that's for sure." He looked pensive for a moment. "The guy we're going to see, just to put you in the picture, is a man named Delves. He's a Brit, because Marwell is nominally an RAF station, but obviously he's being kept fully in the picture about the progress of the hunt for Mansoor and D'Aubigny. The American commander is a USAF colonel called Greeley."

"So is this more than just a courtesy call?"

"Not just. We have to assume our terrorists have done a very thorough recce of their target, whatever it is. Or possibly that someone else has done the recce on their behalf. Either way, we have to look at the station and the security setup through terrorist eyes. Put ourselves in their place. Decide what the weak spots are. Decide what we'd go for."

"Did you come to any conclusions from the other two stations?"

"Only that the security was damn near impassable. My first thought was that I'd go for a SAM—a surface-to-air missile attack. As you know, there are still quite a lot of Stinger systems in ITS hands. But I found I wouldn't be able to get anything like close enough to any of the runways. I wondered about concealing a bomb in the car of someone who lived off-base and then detonating it remotely when it had been driven into camp, but I discovered that all off-base personnel are given a strict car search routine—a proper, detailed ten-minute job, not just a quick flash with a mirror on a stick—and they stick to it. None of this stuff is abstract to these guys, believe you me. Those bases, from what I've seen, are sewn up tighter than a rat's proverbial."

"All security can be beaten," said Liz.

"Agreed. And the people we're after wouldn't be in play if there wasn't a weak spot somewhere. All I'm saying is that I haven't found it."

"Why have they sent Mansoor, that's what I want to know," said Liz. "What's his skill? What's his speciality? Do you think the fact that he worked in a garage has got anything to do with it?"

"If he was a player when he was working at that place—and they're not garages in the sense we know them, so much as truck stops—it would have been more to do with keeping a lookout, seeing who came and went, that sort of thing. Off the top of my head I'd guess that the Sher Babar people probably sold a few fifth-hand jeeps and reconditioned engines, but that their real business was running people and weapons over the border into Afghanistan. They may well have had a hand in the heroin business, too. You can't separate all that stuff out over there. What Mansoor wasn't, and I can pretty much guarantee you this, was a qualified repair guy with a framed certificate from Ford or Toyota."

"So could he be a suicide volunteer, do you think?"

"I guess we have to assume so, with the D'Aubigny girl here to steer him on to his target."

"If that's the case, why was there an arrangement made to ship him out again after the job? Remember what Mitchell said? That the special was to be taken back to Germany in a month's time? And why's he carrying a sophisticated weapon like a PSS? What's he waiting for?"

"To take your questions in order, maybe the return voyage is to get the girl out. The PSS suggests that he's going to be hitting a target that's got security on it, and probably at night. And maybe he was waiting in Dersthorpe—which sadly I never had the privilege of visiting—to take delivery of some sort of device."

"Don't know, don't know and don't know, then," replied Liz testily.

Mackay smiled his breezy smile and stretched. "That's about the shape and size of it!"

48

A quarter of an hour later, at a road bridge over the river Wissey, they were being flagged down by three uniformed policemen, one of them conspicuously carrying a Heckler and Koch carbine, another holding a dog. A Range Rover containing other uniformed men was parked at an angle at the roadside. The Marwell base was over a mile away, and not yet even visible.

Liz and Mackay showed their passes, and stood outside the BMW while a radio clearance was made. The officer with the dog, meanwhile, carefully searched the car.

"I see what you mean," said Liz. "You'd be hard pushed to get a Stinger system past that lot."

"Or even a lump of C4," said Mackay, as the senior officer returned them their passes.

Two minutes later the outer perimeter of Marwell airfield came into view. Mackay halted the car, and they surveyed the flat, nondescript landscape before them, with its steel gates, its distant guardhouse, mess halls and administrative buildings, and its endless expanses of grass and concrete. No planes were visible at all.

"Smile!" said Mackay, as a CCTV camera mounted above the razor-wire fence nosed suspiciously towards them.

Soon they were sitting in a large, well-heated office. The furniture was worn but comfortable. A portrait of the Queen shared the walls with squadron insignia and photographs of men and aircraft taken in Diego Garcia, Saudi Arabia and Afghanistan.

Wing-Commander Colin Delves, a pink-faced man in RAF blue battledress trousers and pullover, was the British station commander, while Colonel Clyde Greeley, solid and tanned in civilian golfing clothes, was his USAF opposite number. Liz, Mackay and Greeley were all drinking coffee, while Delves, as if in deference to the Special Relationship, had a can of Diet Coke at his elbow.

"We're damned pleased to see you guys," Greeley was saying, fanning out the prints of D'Aubigny and Mansoor. "And we appreciate the lengths you've gone to, but it's hard to know what more we can do."

"I'd defy the pair of them to get within a mile of our perimeter," said Delves. "Really, not a blade of grass moves without our registering it."

"Do you think you're a probable terrorist target, Colonel?" asked Mackay.

"Hell, yes!" said Greeley. "I have no doubts in my mind that we are *the* terrorist target."

Unease flickered across Delves's face, but Greeley spread his arms expansively. "The facts are on the record if you know where to look, and I assume that our terrorist friends know exactly where to look. Of the three East Anglian bases—the 48th Fighter Wing at Lakenheath, the

100th Air Refuelling Wing at Mildenhall, and us—we're the only one to have deployed in the Central Asian theatre."

"Where exactly?" asked Liz.

"Well now, until a couple of months ago we had a squadron of A-10 Thunderbolts stationed at Uzgen in Kyrgyzstan, three AC-130 gunships at Bagram, and rather less publicly, a couple more AC-130s supporting Special Operations out of Fergana, Uzbekistan. Police work, you might say."

"Did you deploy in Pakistan?" asked Liz.

"We deployed on the Afghan border," said Greeley, with the ghost of a smile.

"So did you make any new enemies out there?" asked Liz mildly. "If that's not a naive question?"

"Do you know," said Greeley after a moment's thought, "I wouldn't have said so. And it's certainly not a naive question. But I can honestly say that with the possible exception of certain diehard bad boys whom we tickled out of their caves with our Sidewinder and Maverick missiles, we made only new friends."

"So why would this particular man have crossed the world from Pakistan to attack this particular airfield?" she persisted.

"I guess we're a symbolic target," said Greeley. "We're American military and we're on British soil, symbolising the alliance that overthrew the Taliban."

"But nothing . . . *specific*?" asked Liz.

"With respect, who the hell knows? There were people who were mightily pissed at our presence there and there were people—rather more people—who were mightily glad to have us." He gestured at the portraits of D'Aubigny and Mansoor. "Concerning this trigger-happy duo and their grievance, I have to say that I have every confidence in our base security measures."

Colin Delves half rose in his chair. The gesture was an uncertain one, and Liz had to remind herself that the RAF man was officially in charge, rather than Greeley.

"Clyde, might I propose that, if they've got time, we show our guests round? Give them the big picture?"

"How about it?" grinned Greeley.

"I'd like to," said Liz, before Mackay could answer. In the last forty-eight hours, she guessed, he'd probably seen enough USAF runways and stationary aircraft to last him a lifetime.

They followed Delves and Greeley out into a scrupulously clean passageway where service personnel, most but not all of them in uniform, examined noticeboards holding neatly pinned order sheets, duty schedules and invitations to church services and socials. All looked up and smiled as Liz and Mackay passed. Their faces seemed to shine like the vinyl flooring. They're so *young,* thought Liz.

Near the exit, which was hung with paperchains and children's Christmas cards, they waited for the vehicle which would show them round. On the walls, computer-generated posters gave notice of the base tree-lighting ceremony and a Dorm-Dwellers' Cookie Drive. Santa Claus suits, Liz read, could be rented from the community centre—the ensemble to include wig, beard, glasses, hat, gloves and boots.

The vehicle proved to be an open-topped jeep, the driver a young woman with a blonde bob. Clyde Greeley handed them each a USAF baseball cap reading "Go Warthogs!," and they set off at a fast zip across the rain-darkened tarmac.

"Can you tell us about the USAF personnel who live off-base?" asked Mackay, bending the peak of his cap into a suitably cool, movie-hero curve. "Surely they're vulnerable to attack? Everyone must know where they live."

Delves fielded the question. "If you were an outsider round here," he said, smiling pinkly, "you'd find it pretty damn hard to get information like that. We have a very close relationship with the local community, and anyone asking questions of that sort would very quickly find themselves face to face with a military policeman."

"But your people have to let their hair down from time to time, surely?" persisted Mackay.

"Sure they do," said Greeley, his rangy smile belying the grimness of his tone. "But things have changed since 9/11. The days of our young men and women belonging to the local darts teams, stuff like that, that's way in the past."

"Do they get specific training in security and counter-surveillance?" asked Liz. "I mean, supposing I decided to follow a couple of them back from the pub or the local cinema to wherever they lived . . ."

"You'd last about five minutes, I'd guess, before encountering a hostile response involving security vehicles, and quite possibly helicopters. Put it this way, if you tried that, and we didn't know who you were, you certainly wouldn't try twice. We always tell our people not to go to bars that are too local. If they want to have a few beers, they go somewhere that's at least seven or eight miles away, so that they've got plenty of time to spot any vehicle that might be following them home."

"And what about yourself, Colonel?" asked Liz.

"I live on base."

"Wing-Commander?"

Colin Delves frowned. "I live with my family more than a dozen miles away, in one of the villages. I never leave this establishment in uniform, and I doubt there are half a dozen people in the village who have the first idea what I do. The house I live in, in fact, is a Grade II listed property, owned by the MOD. I'm very lucky—it's the last place you'd expect to find a serving RAF officer."

"And is it under police surveillance?"

"Broadly speaking, yes. But not in such a way that would draw attention to the place."

He fell silent as they approached a long line of jet fighters. Still in their matte green and brown desert livery, they seemed to crouch back on their tailplanes, rear-weighted by the massive twin engines above their fuselages. Ground-staff members worked at half a dozen of the aircraft, and several of the cockpit canopies were back-tilted open. From each nose a seven-barrelled cannon pointed skywards. Beneath the wings hung empty missile carriages.

"Here we are," said Greeley, unable to keep a quaver of pride from his voice. "The Hog-Pen!"

"These are A-10s?" asked Mackay.

"A-10 Thunderbolt attack jets," confirmed Greeley, "known to one and all as Warthogs. They're attack and close support aircraft, and they featured heavily in the combat operations against Al-Qaeda and the Taliban. The amazing thing about them, apart from the missile systems that they mount, is just how much punishment they can survive. Our pilots were taking armour-piercing rounds, rocket-propelled grenade strikes . . . you name it, they were throwing it at us."

Liz nodded, but as he began to use phrases like "loiter capability," "emphasised payloads," and "redundant primary structures," she found herself drifting into a semi-hypnotic trance. With an effort, she pulled herself back from the edge.

"At night?" she said. "Really?"

"Absolutely," said Greeley. "The pilots have to wear light-intensifying goggles but otherwise these aircraft are operational twenty-four hours out of twenty-four. And with the Gatling in the nose and the missile pay-load beneath the wings . . ."

"Uzgen must have been weird," said Mackay. "It's a long way from home."

Greeley shrugged. "Marwell's a long way from home. But sure, Uzgen was what we call an austere base."

"Did you come under attack?" asked Liz.

"Not there. Over Afghanistan, like I said, we encountered small groups with RPGs and armour-piercing rounds, and we had a couple of Stinger alarms, but nothing that put any of our aircraft at serious risk."

"And how far are we from the perimeter road here?" asked Mackay, gazing at the matt fuselage of the nearest of the A-10s.

"A mile, perhaps. I'll show you the fatboys."

The driver performed a sharp turn, and they drove for a further five minutes. Southeast, Liz told herself, struggling to keep her bearings in the flat grass-and-tarmac landscape.

The half-dozen AC-130s were huge, even from a distance. Great lumbering, deep-bellied things with down-pointing armaments like undersea feelers. Essentially, Delves told them, they were Hercules transport planes. With the addition of heavy cannons and fire-control systems, however, they became ground-attack aircraft capable of pulverising an enemy position.

"That's assuming that your enemy has no aerial capability, presumably," volunteered Mackay. "These things must make pretty easy targets for fighter planes and surface-to-air missiles."

The colonel grinned. "The USAF is not interested in what you Brits call a level playing field. If the enemy's still got an air force, the fatboys stay in the hangar."

He hesitated, and the smile faded. "These two terrorists. The man and the girl."

"Yes," said Liz.

"We can protect our people and we can protect our aircraft. I took three hundred and seventy-six people and twenty-four aircraft out to the Central Asian theatre, we worked our tour, and I brought them all back. Every person, every aircraft. I'm proud of that record and I'm not going to see it tarnished by a pair of psychos who like shooting up old women. Trust us, OK?" He indicated Delves, who nodded confidently. "We're on top of this thing."

49

Twenty minutes later Liz and Mackay were driving back towards Swanley Heath in the BMW. They were sitting in silence. Mackay had started to play a CD of Bach's Goldberg Variations but Liz had asked him to turn it off again. Something was worrying at her subconscious.

"That man Greeley," she said eventually.

"Go on."

"What did he mean when he was talking about Mansoor and D'Aubigny's 'grievance'?"

"How do you mean?"

"He said something about 'this trigger-happy duo and their grievance.' Why did he say that? What grievance?"

"I'm assuming he meant the same grievance that's led the ITS to bomb, shoot and incinerate innocent civilians all over the world."

"No, I don't buy that. You wouldn't use that word about members of a professional terror cell. They didn't kill Ray Gunter and Elsie Hogan out of a sense of grievance. Why did he use that word, Bruno?"

"Grievance *schmievance,* Liz, how do I know? I never met the guy before in my life."

"I didn't say you had."

He braked. The BMW came to an untroubled halt. He turned to her, solicitous. "Liz, you have to cool it. You've done brilliantly, and I'm genuinely in awe of the way you've moved this thing forwards, but *you have to cool it.* You can't carry the entire case on your shoulders or it will break you, OK? I'm sure you think me the worst kind of cowboy operator, but please—*I am not the enemy here.*"

She blinked. The sky was steel-grey over the long, level horizon. The temporary energy burst provided by Greeley and Delves's coffee had worn off. "I'm sorry," she said. "You're right. I'm letting it all get to me."

But he might well have met Greeley, she thought. Central Asia, when all was said and done, was not such a large theatre. *We deployed on the Afghan border . . .* Why did she feel as if she was in free-fall? Exhaustion? Lack of sleep? What didn't she know? *What didn't she know?*

They proceeded in silence towards Swanley Heath, and were five minutes away from the Army Air Corps base when a squawk from her mobile alerted Liz to a text message. It read *CALL JUDE.* They pulled up at a roadside telephone box, Mackay tipped his seat into the recline position, and Liz climbed out on to the wet verge and rang Investigations. Distantly, several fields away, she could see a police search team in fluorescent yellow jackets moving through the scrubland. The light was fading fast.

"OK," began Judith Spratt, "here's where we are. We've got from the parents that from the age of thirteen Jean D'Aubigny attended a boarding school near Tregaron in Wales named Garth House. Small co-ed establishment, progressive in character, run by a former Jesuit priest named Anthony Price-Lascelles. School has a reputation for accommodating troubled children and those unresponsive to conventional discipline. Classroom attendance optional, no organised sport, pupils encouraged to undertake free-form artistic projects, et cetera, et cetera, et cetera. We've had people visit the school but the place is locked up for the Christmas holidays and Price-Lascelles is in Morocco, at a place called Azemmour, where he has a flat. Six have sent a man round to the flat this morning but learned from the house-boy that Price-Lascelles has gone into Casablanca for the day, destination and time of return unknown. So they've got a bloke sitting outside the flat waiting for him."

"Isn't there anyone else we can ask about the school? Find out who was there with her, and so on?"

"Well, the trouble is the place is really very small. It has a website of sorts but there's no real information on it. We've done the usual online searches and talked to everyone we can find who went there, but no one remembers anything significant about Jean D'Aubigny beyond the fact that she was there about ten years ago, had longish dark hair and kept herself to herself."

"No ex-teachers you can talk to?"

"We haven't been able to track down any that remember anything significant about her. The impression we're getting is that there were fairly severe money problems and staff came and went pretty fast. A lot of the teachers and domestic staff were from overseas, and almost certainly paid on a cash-in-hand basis."

"Can't the police just unlock the place and go through the records? The Prevention of Terrorism Act makes that possible, surely?"

"It does, and that's in hand right now. As soon as we've got anything I'll let you know."

"And locally? Around Newcastle under Lyme? Who did she hang out with there, during the school holidays?"

"The parents aren't saying. The police have asked around and turned up a Pakistani family who knew her from the local Islamic centre, but that's about it."

"Anything from the Paris end?"

"Again, nothing significant. One fellow student named Hamidullah Souad knew her quite well. They studied for exams together and so on and apparently went to the cinema once or twice, but they stopped seeing each other when she told him that she disapproved of his lifestyle. Apparently she supported herself by giving English classes to business people through a language school, but the arrangement came to an end after complaints that she had expressed 'extreme attitudes' in front of clients."

"So we've still got no connection with East Anglia?"

"None at all. Does she need to have one?"

"No, she could just be Mansoor's cover, in which case all she has to be is English. But the pair of them are running now, and if she's ever been here before it might just point us to where she's gone to ground, or even what the target is. So don't let up, Jude, please."

"We won't."

Ten minutes later she and Mackay were back in the Swanley Heath hangar, sitting opposite Deputy Chief Constable Jim Dunstan. A large, bluff man with thinning sandy hair, he retained the bullish, blustering air of the prop forward who, three decades earlier, had led the Joint Services team to victory over the Barbarians at Twickenham.

"Bugger all," he told them morosely. "Not an effing sausage. We've had helicopters up all afternoon, both ours and the Army's, we've got dog-handlers and TA search teams beating the woodland from here to the coast, traffic backed up practically the same distance . . ."

"It was always going to be difficult, surely?" said Mackay diplomatically.

"Course it bloody was. That's what I've told the Home Office. I explained that just for once it's not a question of resources, and that the point comes when you've got to hold back or risk unmanageable levels of confusion and wire-crossing. In my view our best hope is for a sighting by a member of the general public, and to that end we've been pushing the local media angle. It would be a damn sight easier if it wasn't a Sunday, of course, but what can you do?" He looked from one to the other of them. "Have any of your people come up with anything?"

"Nothing that points to a specific target," said Liz with deep frustration. "And nothing that puts D'Aubigny in East Anglia at any time in the past. The parents have got some heavy-duty human rights lawyer telling them to keep their mouths shut, so . . . ."

"So they'd rather see her head blown off by those headbangers from Hereford. I know. Brilliant." He looked without enthusiasm at the activity around them and jutted his chin forward belligerently. "What we actually need is a break. A bloody great slice of luck. Right now, that's the best we can hope for."

Liz and Mackay nodded. There wasn't much else to say. The silence was broken by Liz's mobile. Another text message, this time a letter code announcing an e-mail. Retiring to an empty stretch of trestle table, she switched on her laptop.

50

O ut!" said Faraj urgently. "Put the bags under the tree and then help me with the car."

With care, Jean arranged the rucksacks at the base of the willow. It had begun to rain again, the light was fading, and the place was deserted. In summer there might have been a few people around: an angler, perhaps, after a chub or a perch, or a couple of picnickers. Late on a wet December afternoon, though, there was little to draw the passerby down the rutted lane and through the stand of trees to this bleak intersection of the Lesser Ouse and the Methwold Fen Relief Drain.

Jean D'Aubigny knew the place, knew that the water was deep there and that visitors were few. Remembered in a rush of memory almost painful in its intensity what it was like to be sixteen years old, to smell the green, muddy aroma of the river and feel the dizzying rush of vodka and cigarettes on an empty stomach.

It had taken them a fair amount of time to find the place, and they had been further slowed by the need to take minor roads and farm tracks across country, but they were now a clear twenty-five miles south of the village from where they had stolen the MGB, and since the road-block they had not encountered any police. They had heard a distant siren as they crossed the King's Lynn road, and ten minutes later they had seen a helicopter far to the north of them whose camouflage identified it as military, but that was all. Given that they had to assume that the theft of the MGB had been swiftly reported, they were grateful.

Faraj wound down the MGB's windows, and pulled back the vinyl top. The car stood beside the old bridge across the river. In front of it a flight of cracked concrete steps led down to a narrow towpath. From the far side of the river the narrower drainage channel led off northwards. The river was deep here, but slow, which was why, for all the place's bleakness, it had always been so good for swimming. Not that you would want to swim in it now. The level was much higher than Jean remembered it, and the water was a dense, swirling coffee-brown. A scum of foliage, cigarette ends and fast-food containers circled at the foot of the steps.

Turning, she looked around her. Nothing. Then Faraj caught her wrist hard and she froze, backing away from the bridge. There was movement in the relief drain. Something was silently displacing the bull-rushes and reeds. An animal? she wondered. A police dog? A police diver, even? Nothing was visible, just that slow, terrifying bending of the reeds.

They were well back from the bank now, crouching behind the car. Both were holding their weapons; both released their safety catches as a stray gust of wind caused rain to cascade from the wet branches over-hanging the river.

The reeds in the relief drain parted, and the pointed grey-green nose of a kayak moved silently into view. Sitting inside it was an unmoving figure in hooded olive waterproofs. Jean's first, paralysing assumption was that this was a Special Forces soldier, and when the figure slowly raised a pair of binoculars to its face this seemed to be confirmed.

But the figure was scanning the bankside vegetation, and completely ignoring the MGB standing by the bridge. There was another shower of raindrops from the trees, and a small, nondescript bird flew from under the bridge and alighted on the broken stem of a bullrush. Smoothly and unhurriedly the binoculars swivelled to focus on the bird, and now a smile was visible on the face of the hooded figure in the kayak. It was a young man, probably a teenager, and his lips seemed to be moving in soundless appreciation of the bird.

Her heart thumping with the sick, dragging ebb of tension, Jean thumbed on the Malyah's safety and glanced sideways to see if Faraj had registered that the young man was not a threat. The bird must have caught her slight movement, because it swung quickly away from its perch and darted back beneath the bridge. The young man looked after it for a moment, lowered his binoculars, paddled himself forwards into the bridge pool, reversed his kayak, and disappeared the way he had come.

They watched his progress, or at least the movements of the reeds, until nothing could be seen. For ten agonisingly extended minutes they waited by the car in case he should return, but the fenland landscape out of which he had so unexpectedly appeared had reclaimed him.

"We've got to get rid of the car," Jean said eventually. "Those were military helicopters we saw earlier, and it'll show up through the trees on their thermal imaging cameras."

Faraj nodded. "Let's do it."

Leaning into the car, he checked that it was in neutral and released the handbrake. They pushed from the rear. The old MGB was heavier than it looked, with a very low centre of gravity, and took several seconds to budge in the rain-slick mud. Then it nosed as if unwillingly to the top of the steps, lurched over the first of them, and with a loud grating noise stuck fast. "Axle's caught," muttered Faraj. "Bastard thing. We have to keep pushing."

They pushed, their shoulders to the MGB's chrome back-bumper, the cleated soles of their boots digging deep.

At first nothing happened, and then everything happened. The cement facing of the brickwork steps cracked, the rear of the MGB swung upwards, flipping Jean off balance so that Faraj had to grab her to prevent her skidding into the river, and the car commenced a slow-motion descent of the steps. At the bottom, with something close to stateliness, it somersaulted on to its roof with a crashing displacement of water and began to sink, coming to rest upside down with a single rear wheel exposed.

"Bastard thing," repeated Faraj, releasing Jean and wiping river water from his face. Moving down the cracked wet steps he sat himself on the bottom one and, reaching out with his feet, braced them hard against the exposed nearside wheel. Straightening his legs, jamming his back against the steps, he pressed with all his strength. The car rocked a little, but otherwise refused to budge.

"Wait," Jean ordered him. Pulling back her wet hair, she climbed down beside him, put an arm around him and grabbed a fistful of his jacket to brace herself. Hesitating for a moment, he did the same. She felt the heavy pressure of his arm against her. "On three," she said. *"Now!"*

They pushed until they were trembling and the steps at Jean's back were cutting agonisingly into her spine. At her shoulders, she could feel Faraj's arm quivering with strain. Against her heel, the faint give of the tyre.

"Almost," muttered Faraj, panting. "Once more, and this time don't stop."

She dragged new air into her lungs. Once again the cracked cement-covered brick drew agonising stripes across her back. Her body was shaking with the strain, her ears were roaring and her head was dizzy. "Don't stop!" gasped Faraj. *"Don't stop!"*

Slowly, almost thoughtfully, the inverted car moved from its obstruction, seemed to drift for a moment, and sank on the current into the deep water below the bridge. Gasping for breath, her chest heaving, Jean watched as the chrome of the bumpers faded, became invisible.

Slowly they climbed the steps again, and Faraj checked the biscuit tin containing the C4 charge.

"OK?"

Faraj shrugged. "It's still there. And we're still here."

Jean took stock. She was cold, filthy, hungry and soaked to the skin, and had been so for several hours. On top of this the day's terrors—the repeated jolt and ebb of adrenalin—had shocked her into an almost hallucinatory exhaustion. She sensed, as she had for some days now, an implacable pursuing figure. A figure that dragged at her like a shadow, that matched her pace for pace, whispering hell and confusion in her ear. Perhaps, she thought, it was her former self, trying to reclaim her soul. At that moment, and in that place, she would have believed anything.

Faraj, by contrast, appeared untouched. He gave the impression that his physical state had at some point been unharnessed from his will, so that neither pain nor fear nor tiredness played any part in his reckoning. There was just the mission, and the strategy required for its execution.

Jean watched him, and insofar as she was capable of a response at that moment, the austerity of his self-control impressed her. It also profoundly frightened her. There had been times, particularly at Takht-i-Suleiman, when she had been certain that faith and determination had empowered her in the same way. Now, she was sure of nothing. She had been reborn, certainly, but into a place of utter pitilessness. Faraj, she realised, had occupied that place for a long time.

Distantly, perhaps five miles away, the pulse of a helicopter. For a moment neither of them moved.

"*Quick!*" said Jean. "Under the bridge."

Leaving the rucksacks beneath the tree, they scrambled down the steps to the narrow towpath, and hurled themselves at the sodden canopy of brambles. Thorns tore at Jean's face and hands and then they were through, crouching in near darkness beneath the arch. There, but for the echoing drip of water, all was silence. She could feel blood on her face.

After about a minute the sound of the helicopter returned, louder this time, perhaps three or four miles away, and even though she knew herself invisible and far from the range of their viewing equipment she shrank against the bridge's curving brick wall. The pulse was steady for a few seconds, and then the sound fell away.

As Faraj looked into the shadowed dimness of the river, Jean peered through the arch of the bridge and the dark hatching of foliage at the sky. The light was going fast. Close to tears of exhaustion, shaking with cold, she began picking the thorns from her cheek and the back of her hand. "I think we should get the bags down and lie up here for the night," she said tonelessly. "They'll keep the helicopters up, but their infrared cameras can't read a heat signature through brick and concrete."

He glanced at her suspiciously, detecting the defeat in her voice.

"If we're caught in the open," she pleaded, "we're dead. *Dead,* Faraj. Here, at least we're invisible."

He was silent, considering. Eventually he nodded.

51

Liz was about to go online and decode her e-mail when, from the corner of her eye, she saw Don Whitten fold forward and bury his head in his hands. He held the position for perhaps a second before, his face contorted and his fists clenched, silently swearing at the distant roof of the hangar.

There were now eighteen men and three women in the hangar. Six of the men were Army officers, and all of these except Kersley, the SAS captain, were in combat dress. Of the three women one was a Royal Logistics Corps officer, one was local CID, and the other was PC Wendy Clissold. As one, they all fell silent and stared at Whitten.

"Tell us," said Dunstan, levelly.

"Young man named Martindale, James Martindale, has just reported a twenty-five-year-old racing-green MGB stolen from outside the Plough pub in the village of Birdhoe. Could have happened any time after twelve fifteen this lunchtime when he arrived at the pub."

There was a collective exhalation—a sound of extreme frustration. It was too much to hope for that the theft of the car was unrelated to D'Aubigny and Mansoor. Whitten reached glumly for his cigarettes.

"Birdhoe, as most of you know, is half a mile the wrong side of the roadblock. They must have outrun us across country while we were setting things up. And now they've got four hours' bloody start on us. They could be anywhere."

The Army officers looked at each other, tight-lipped. Two battalions of regular and TA soldiers and half a dozen Lynx and Gazelle helicopters were still in deployment in the northwestern sector.

"This man Martindale," said Steve Goss. "He's been in the pub all afternoon?"

"He and his fiancée went to the Plough for lunch, he says, and ended up stopping there to watch the rugby on TV."

"Wait," said Mackay, craning his head to where Liz was sitting, her fingers poised over her laptop. "A racing-green MGB? We *passed* one! I told you I used to—"

"Teal blue? The Moneypenny-magnet?"

"Yeah, that's the one—where were we? Let's look at that screen. We'd driven southwest from here, been going what, fifteen minutes? Must have been somewhere near Castle Acre or Narborough. So if our appointment at Marwell was for two p.m., and that was the right car we saw—and there aren't many of that vintage and colour on the roads these days—then it puts our two terrorists near Narborough at approximately one forty-five. Two and a quarter hours ago. You're right," he addressed Whitten, "they could be in London or Birmingham by now."

"But why steal such a recognisable car?" asked Liz.

The police looked at each other. "Because they're easy to hot-wire, love," said Whitten. "Most cars less than twenty years old have an automatic steering lock. You can break the lock by jemmying the wheel around, but it takes a bit of strength. Which points to the girl doing the taking away, I'd say."

"OK. Point taken. Surely, though, that makes it a bit of a last resort? A desperate dash to get the hell away from the roadblock. They couldn't have known the owner was going to sit in the pub all afternoon; they had to proceed on the assumption that he might come out looking for his car at any moment, find it gone, and dial 999 straight away. They certainly wouldn't have risked driving into a major city in an immediately recognisable car that, for all they knew, every policeman in the UK was looking for."

Dunstan nodded. "I agree. They'd allow themselves an hour's drive at most, sticking to minor roads, then they'd ditch the vehicle."

"An hour's drive on minor roads takes them to RAF Marwell," said Mackay quietly.

No one replied. The woman police officer manning the display computer generated a red line on the map. It moved southwards from Dersthorpe Strand, crossed the blue line representing the roadblock, and passed through Birdhoe and Narborough to Marwell. The line was vertical, and almost dead straight.

"Let's suppose that Marwell is their target," said Dunstan, looking around him. "It's a fair guess that (a) they're not going to drive too close to a secure government establishment in a stolen car, and (b) they ditched the car within an hour of passing through Narborough. That puts them right now either to the east of a five-mile circle surrounding Marwell, or to the west of it. Lying up out of sight, I should think—they've had a pretty stressful day. Either that or preparing to walk up to the target—they're certainly not going to risk stealing another car at this juncture."

Whitten crushed out his cigarette. "So what do you suggest?"

"That we draw two rings around Marwell. Establish an inner circle, radius five miles, which we saturate with police, Army and TA personnel right now. Give them night-vision goggles, searchlights, whatever they need . . . Basically, no one gets past."

A balding man in the crown and star insignia of a lieutenant colonel made a swift calculation with a pencil. "That's about eighty square miles in total. If we pull in all the search parties from the northwest sector, bring up another battalion . . ."

"And outside that," Dunstan continued, "a further ring, five miles wide—that's a two hundred square mile area—which we and our Army Air Corps friends overfly all night using thermal-imaging . . ." He looked around him for approval. "Anyone got a better idea?"

There was silence.

"How does that sound to you, gentlemen? Ma'am?" he asked the Army officers.

They nodded. "Good enough," said the lieutenant colonel. He turned to his fellow officers with a pale smile. "Let it not be said that we failed to protect our brave US allies from an unbalanced language student and a Pakistani garage mechanic."

The Army personnel smiled, if only faintly. The police didn't smile at all. "DS Goss," Dunstan continued, "I'd like you to get yourself over to Marwell and act as our liaison with Colonel Greeley. I'm going to call him right now and put him in the picture."

Goss nodded and left the hangar at a run, raising a farewell hand to Liz as he passed her. Kersley and the senior PO19 officer followed him out and made for the huts, in order to bring their respective teams up to date with developments.

Liz stared after them for a moment, and listened to the agitated crescendo as the Gazelle bearing Steve Goss lifted from the ground. In some way that she couldn't quite define, events seemed to be spinning out of control. There were too many people involved, and too many services represented. On top of this, instinct told her that a miscalculation had been made. Mansoor and D'Aubigny may have been prepared to lose their lives in the course of carrying out their operation, but there was nothing suicidal in their actions so far. The idea of them hurling themselves unavailingly at a USAF base and being cut to pieces for their pains was way off beam, she was certain of that. They had another plan.

With a start, she realised that she had not yet read her message, and without further ado flipped up the screen of her laptop and logged on.

The message, when she had decoded it, was a long one. Especially by Wetherby's standards.

Liz—attached report is for urgent attention yourself, Mackay, Dunstan. Source secret and reliable.

Liz smiled at the familiar cryptic style, and opened the attachment.

TOP SECRET—BEARER EYES ONLY
RE: MANSOOR, FARAJ

At midnight on Dec. 17, 2002, following reports of ITS activity on Pak–Afghan border near Chaman, an AC-130 transporter gunship departed a USAF base in Uzbekistan (believed to be Fergana), on a search and destroy mission. On board was the AC-130's crew plus 12 Special Operations personnel . . .

"Cup of tea? They've got Earl Grey, apparently, presumably in deference to our metropolitan palates. There's also a rumour of shortbread fingers . . ."

Liz looked up from the report. "Thanks, Bruno. I'd love a cup of something. And I'm pretty starving, too, so if you can see your way to . . ."

"Consider it done. Anything interesting come in from the Death Star?"

"Not sure . . . Let you know when you come back with those shortbread fingers and that black tea with two sugars."

"Two sugars! Do I detect a sweet tooth?"

"No." She frowned absently, one eye on her screen. "I'm in love with my dentist."

He sauntered off, shaking his head, his laptop swinging in its case beneath his right arm. En route to the folding plastic table designated as the canteen area, he encountered PC Wendy Clissold, who was mas-

saging her temples and watching an Alka-Seltzer dissolve in a Styrofoam cup.

"You haven't got anything for a pain in the arse, have you?" he
asked her, loud enough for Liz to hear.

Liz smiled, and turned her full attention to Wetherby's message. As
she read, however, her smile died. The activity around her seemed to fall
away, and the ambient buzz of the hangar to fade to silence. When
Mackay returned she was staring straight in front of her, her hands
folded, expressionless.

52

"How much do you think they know?" asked Faraj.

"I think we have to assume that they know who we are," said Jean after a moment's thought. They were both speaking Urdu now. "The weak links in the chain are the driver of the truck, who saw you, and the other migrants."

"The other migrants know nothing about me. Everything I told them was false."

"They would recognise you. Just as the woman who rented me the house would recognise me. They know who we are, take it from me. These are the British we're dealing with, and they are a vengeful people. They are quite happy to see their elderly starve to death on council estates or die of neglect in filthy hospital corridors, but harm the least of them—the fisherman, the old woman—and they will pursue you to the ends of the earth. They will never, ever give up. The people who are directing this operation against us will be the best that they have."

"Well, we shall see. Let them send their best man. They won't stop us."

Jean frowned. "They've sent their best man. Their best man is a woman."

Faraj shifted on the narrow flagstoned towpath beneath the bridge. An hour earlier they had changed out of their wet clothes into the dry ones that Jean had stuffed into the rucksacks that morning. Out of an instinctive sense of decorum they had turned their backs on each other for the purposes of this operation, but when all but naked Jean had unbalanced in the near darkness beneath the low brickwork. Flailing with her arms she had made sudden contact with Faraj, and only by grabbing her had he prevented her from falling into the river. He had held her for a moment, and then silently released her. Neither had said anything, but the incident lay between them, unresolved.

"What do you mean, a woman?"

"They've sent a woman. I can feel her shadow."

"You're crazy!" He lifted himself angrily on to one elbow. "What kind of stupid talk is that?"

She shrugged, although she knew that the gesture was invisible. "It doesn't matter," she said.

She heard his faint, irritated outbreath. They were lying head to head, wrapped in the thin blankets that Diane Munday had provided for her tenants. Now that Jean was dry, the cold didn't seem quite so agonising. She had known worse in the camp. And harder ground.

"We killed two people today," she said, the boy's head cracking open once again before her half-closed eyes.

"It was necessary. It was not a matter for consideration."

"I'm not the person that I was when I woke up this morning."

"You are a stronger person."

Perhaps. Was this strength? she wondered. This waking sleep? This frozen distance from events? Perhaps it was.

"Paradise waits for us," said Faraj. "But not yet."

Did he believe that? she wondered. Something in his voice—an oblique, faintly ironic note—made her unsure.

"Who waits for you in this world?" she asked. He had spoken of parents and a sister. Was there a wife?

"No one waits."

"So you never married?"

He was silent. Through the darkness, she sensed a sinewy resistance to her questions.

"Tomorrow we may be dead," she said. "Tonight, surely, we can talk?"

"I never married," he said, but she knew from his tone that there had been someone.

"She died," he added eventually.

"I'm sorry."

"She was twenty years old. Her name was Farzana, and she was a seamstress. My parents had wanted someone well educated for me, and a Tajik, and she was neither of these things, but they . . . they liked her very much. She was a good person." He fell silent.

"Was she beautiful?" asked Jean, conscious even as she spoke of the question's gaucheness.

He ignored her and Jean, helpless, stared at the ragged crescent of night sky. Never had the distance between them felt so great. Because of the swiftness with which he had adapted to his surroundings, it had been easy to forget that he had come from a world which was about as different from this one as it could possibly have been.

"Tell me about her," she prompted, sensing that at some level, and despite his protestations, he wanted to talk.

He shifted in his blanket, and for almost a minute said nothing.

"You want to know? Really?"

"I want to know," she said.

For several long moments she listened to his breathing.

"I was at Mardan," he began. "At the *madrassah*. I was older than most of the other students—I was already twenty-three or twenty-four when I went there—and in religious terms I was very much less extreme. In fact I think that, at times, they despaired of my untroubled attitude. But I was able to make myself useful around the place, helping with the administration, supervising the building work they were having done, and ensuring that the two old Fiat taxis that they owned remained in running order. I had been there for almost two years when a letter came from Daranj in Afghanistan saying that my sister Laila was about to become betrothed. The man was a Tajik, like ourselves, and like us he had hoped to try and resettle in Pakistan. Now, though, he had given up hope of establishing himself there legally and had resolved to return to Dushanbe, and my parents had decided to accompany them. First, though, there was to be a celebration to mark the betrothal.

"As Laila's elder brother I was naturally an important guest, but my father was concerned that if I crossed the frontier into Afghanistan I might not be able to re-enter Pakistan. I decided to take the chance, partly because I wanted to attend the betrothal and partly because I intended to get married myself. For some time I had had an understanding with Farzana, the daughter of a Pathan family who lived near to us in Daranj. Letters and gifts had been exchanged, and it was agreed that we were . . . we were destined for each other.

"Anyway, I made the crossing back across the border, and travelled to Daranj in the back of a truck headed for Kandahar. I arrived on the day of the betrothal, I met Khalid, whom my sister was to marry, and that night the celebrations began. There was the usual feasting, which lasted late into the night, and the usual high spirits. You have to remember that there was precious little opportunity for joy in these people's lives, and so the chance to dance and sing and let off *fatakars*—homemade fireworks—was not to be missed.

"I was the first to see the American plane. These were not such an uncommon sight in the area—there were regular operations around Kandahar and on the border—and they were generally ignored. The people of Daranj hated the Taliban for the most part, but they had no love for the Americans either, and gave no assistance to the intelligence-gathering teams who blundered through the village at intervals.

"What was unusual was that the plane was so low. It was a huge thing—an AC-130 transporter gunship I discovered later. The betrothal ceremony had taken place at a small encampment outside the town, and I had wandered away from the celebrations to a nearby hill to gather my thoughts. I was happier than I had ever been in my life. I had proposed marriage to Farzana, she had accepted me, and her parents had given their permission. Below me the celebrations surrounding Laila and Khalid, her betrothed, were in full swing, with fireworks exploding, music playing and rifles being fired in the air.

"When the searchlights came on—one at each end of the plane—I thought, stupidly, that they were sending some sort of signal. Responding to the fireworks and the musical instruments with some sort of friendly display of their own. The war against the Taliban, after all, was over. There were Americans and British security forces stationed in Kabul, whole regiments of them, and there was a new government. So I stood there, staring, as the gunship opened fire on the encampment.

"Within seconds, of course, I understood what was happening. I ran towards the encampment waving my arms, yelling at the plane—as if anyone up there could hear me—that the people were just letting off fireworks. And all the while the plane was moving in these slow, methodical circles, drilling every inch of the place with cannon-fire. The dead and dying were everywhere, with the wounded writhing on the ground and rolling in the embers of fires, screaming. I ran through the firing as if it was rain, untouched, but I couldn't find my parents or my sister or anyone I knew. And I couldn't find Farzana. I screamed her name until I had no voice left, and then I felt myself lifted off my feet and thrown face-down on the rock. I had been hit.

"The next thing I knew was that Khalid, my future brother-in-law, had dragged me to my feet and was yelling at me to run. Somehow he got me out of the killing zone and back to the hill I had been standing on earlier. I had been hit in the side with shrapnel and was losing blood fast, but I managed to drag myself beneath a fold of the rock. After that, I passed out.

"When I came to, I was in Mir Wais hospital in Kandahar. Khalid had loaded eight of us into a truck and driven us there during the night. My sister Laila was alive, but had lost an arm, and my mother had suffered severe burns. She died a week later. My father, Farzana and a dozen others had been killed in the attack."

Jean said nothing. She tried to synchronise her breathing with his, but he was too calm and she was too distressed. We are right in what we do, she told herself. And one day, long after we and thousands like us have given our lives for the struggle, we will prevail. *We will prevail.*

"That night the television carried a CNN report of a 'firefight' near Daranj. Elements loyal to Al Qaeda, the reporter said, had attempted to bring down a US transport aircraft with a surface-to-air missile. The attempt had failed, and the terrorists had been engaged and several of their number killed. Twenty-four hours later Al Jazeera ran a counter-story, in which Khalid was interviewed as an eyewitness. A US aircraft, they said, appeared to have launched an unprovoked attack on a betrothal party in an Afghan village, in the course of which fourteen Afghan civilians had been killed and eight critically wounded. Of the dead, six were women and three were children. None of those involved had any connection to any terrorist organisation.

"After refusing to comment on the incident for almost a week, a USAF spokesman conceded that it had taken place more or less as reported by Al Jazeera, and described the loss of life as 'tragic.' In mitigation, he said, the aircrew maintained that they had come under sustained small-arms fire, and the pilot stated that a surface-to-air missile had been fired at them. Pictures were published of the unit's commander, Colonel Greeley, pointing to what he claimed was bullet damage to the fuselage of an AC-130 transporter gunship. In the course of the subsequent military inquiry, which totally exonerated the gunship's crew, it was reported that two AK-47 assault rifles had been discovered in the area of the encampment, along with a number of expended 7.62 cartridge cases."

"Did you give evidence at the inquiry?"

"What would have been the purpose of that, other than to draw attention to myself? Like everyone else, I knew what its conclusion would be. No, as soon as my wounds were healed I returned to Mardan."

"That was two years ago?"

"That was almost exactly two years ago. Inside myself, now, I was a dead man. All that remained was the necessity of vengeance. The matter of *izzat*—honour. At the *madrassah* they were sympathetic—more than sympathetic. They sent me to one of the North West Frontier camps for a few months, and then sent me back across the border into Afghanistan. I took up work at a truck stop which operated as a cover for one of the *jihadi* organisations, and there, a few months later, I was introduced to a man named al Safa."

"Dawood al Safa?"

"The same. Al Safa was interested by my story. For some time he had been considering revenge against those responsible for the Daranj massacre. Not a general action, but a specific, targeted reprisal. Just as they had come to our country to bomb, burn and kill, so we would do the same. The Americans and their allies would be left in no doubt of the length of our reach, or of the inexorability of our purpose. Al Safa had just visited a camp in Takht-i-Suleiman, he said, where Fate had delivered to him a pearl beyond price. A brave fighter, a young Englishwoman, who had dared to take the name of Asimat—bride of Salah-ud-din—and the sword of jihad. An Englishwoman, moreover, with highly specialised knowledge. Knowledge that would enable us to take a revenge of such exquisite appropriateness . . ."

"I didn't know any of this," she said. "Why wasn't I told?"

"For your own safety, and that of our mission."

"Do I know everything now?"

"Not yet. When the time comes, trust me, you will know everything."

"It's tomorrow, isn't it?"

"Trust me, Asimat."

She stared out into the darkness. At that moment, the rain-dripping chamber beneath the bridge was the whole world. If this was to be her last night on earth, then so be it. She reached out her hand, and found the roughness of his cheek. "I am not Farzana," she said quietly, "but I am yours."

Silence, and from beyond the stillness surrounding them, the long sigh of the fenland wind.

"Come here then," he said.

53

"Well, at least we now know for certain what the target is," said Jim Dunstan. From behind him came a hydraulic hum followed by a muted shudder as the main entrance to the hangar closed.

"I'm afraid there was never much doubt that it was going to be one of those USAF bases," said Bruno Mackay, unwrapping an Army Air Corps–issue Mars Bar. All the phones in the place, for once, were silent.

"It's certain that the AC-130 involved in the Daranj incident was one of the ones based at Marwell, then?" asked Whitten.

"No doubt at all, according to the report," said Liz.

"What's the provenance of the report?" asked Mackay, a little testily. "Can you tell us that?"

"Everything in it except the involvement of Faraj Mansoor is public domain," said Liz evasively. "The story slipped beneath the radar here at the time—the Northern Ireland Assembly had just been suspended, and Saddam Hussein had just submitted his arms declaration—but the Arabic-language press went to town on it in a big way." She turned to Mackay. "I'm surprised the reports didn't cross your desk."

"They did," said Mackay. "And as far as I remember the Islamabad *Stars and Stripes* burners made quite a meal of the incident. I was just curious as to the Mansoor link. That's not mentioned in any file we've ever received from Pakistan liaison or any of our people in the field."

"I'm assured that the source is reliable," said Liz, conscious that Don Whitten was watching Mackay's discomfiture with undisguised pleasure.

"And tomorrow's the anniversary," said Jim Dunstan. "Do we think they'll try to stick to that?"

"Symbolism and anniversaries are hugely important to the ITS," said Mackay, recovering his authority. "September the eleventh was the anniversary of the British mandate in Palestine and of George Bush Senior's proclamation of 'New World Order.' October the twelfth, when the Bali nightclub bombing and the attack on the USS *Cole* took place, was the anniversary of the opening of the Camp David peace talks between Egypt and Israel. This is more local and perhaps more personal, but I think we can count on them moving heaven and earth to stick to it."

"Do we discount all possibility of a dirty bomb?" asked the balding lieutenant colonel. "They wouldn't have to be very near to their target if they meant to detonate one of those. A few miles upwind would do it."

"We've not found any trace of radioactive material near the Dersthorpe bungalow or in the Vauxhall Astra they were using," said Whitten. "We made a point of checking that."

"I'd put money on them using C4," said Mackay. "It's the ITS's signature explosive and, as you gentlemen will be aware, you can buy most of the ingredients in the average high street. The question is: how are they planning to deliver it? A field mouse couldn't get through the security surrounding that base."

"Jean D'Aubigny," said Liz. "She's the key."

"Go on," said Jim Dunstan.

"I just can't believe that Mansoor's controllers would waste an asset like her on a pointless assault on a high-security installation. I stand by what I said before: she must have privileged information of some kind."

But even as she said it, Liz was unsure that this was the case. Wasting operatives on hopeless suicide missions was an ITS speciality.

"Have your people got through the door of that Welsh school yet?" asked Mackay pointedly.

"Yes, they have. They're e-mailing me a list of D'Aubigny's contemporaries as soon as they can."

"Right . . . They've rather taken their time about it, haven't they?"

"It takes time," replied Liz acidly.

As you'd know if you'd any real experience of such things, she might have added. Her colleagues had had to get a warrant signed, inform the local uniform, transport an Investigations team to mid-Wales, disarm the school's BT Redline alarm system, and pick the locks of the front door and a filing cabinet—and that was before they came face to face with Price-Lascelles' chaotic filing system.

"Frankly," said Jim Dunstan, "I can't see how the hell an investigation of this young woman's school career is going to move things forwards. It seems to me that we've gathered all the intelligence we need. We know who we're after and we know what they look like. We have a target, we have a motive, and we have a date. We have a counter-strategy and we have people in place to implement it. All we have to do now is wait, so why don't you get some sleep, young lady?"

Not over-keen on your lot, Whitten had said about Jim Dunstan, and to begin with she had thought him mistaken in that respect. But the chain-smoking, baggy-eyed DS had been right. The old resentment lingered. Senior policemen, with their public face and their accountability, had long distrusted the state's secret servants, and the fact that she was a woman probably further prejudiced the Deputy Chief Constable against her. It didn't help either that the only other woman currently in the room, PC Wendy Clissold, was at that moment obediently carrying Don Whitten a cup of tea—white, one sugar.

Liz looked around her. The faces were friendly enough but the message from each of them was the same. This was the endgame, the point at which theory was translated into action. The cerebral stuff— the intelligence-gathering and analysis—was over. She had nothing further to contribute.

And she sensed something else. A muted but definite anticipation. The Army people, in particular, were like sharks. Twitchy with adrenalin. Smelling blood on the current. They wanted Mansoor and D'Aubigny to try and hit Marwell, she realised. They wanted the pair to dash themselves against its impenetrable wall of armed manpower. They wanted them dead.

A text message announced incoming mail from Judith Spratt.

Have school list for D'Aubigny's leaving year. Checking now.

54

Denzil Parrish arrived back in West Ford knowing that an unpromising evening lay ahead. His mother had warned him well in advance that her new in-laws were not the easiest-going people she'd ever met—"uptight suburban control freaks," in fact, was the expression she'd used—but she had also warned him that he was expected to put in some "serious quality time" with them, "and not go bunking off to the pub every night."

So Denzil had agreed to put a brave face on it and do his best. The fact that his stepfather's parents were digging in for a whole week had only been sprung on him once he himself had agreed to come down from Tyneside as soon as term was ended, and the subterfuge still rankled. His absence today until well after sunset had been part of the punishment he had chosen to inflict. Deep down, however, he understood his mother's predicament, and was forced to admit that since her remarriage she'd been happier than he could remember her, and since Jessica had been born she'd been almost . . . well, *girlish,* he supposed, although it had to be said that this was by no means a desirable attribute in a forty-year-old parent. Whatever, she was smiling again, and for that Denzil was grateful.

Braking the Accord a short distance beyond the gate, he backed into the driveway. Halfway down the incline he braked again, and got out of the car to unlock the garage and remove the kayak from the roof-rack. It had been, in its way, a fantastic day. He'd never thought of himself as the lone operator type, but there was something about Norfolk in winter—the uncompromising solitude, the vast rain-charged skies—which accorded with his mood. On the Methwold Fen Relief Drain he'd seen a marsh harrier, a very rare bird indeed these days. He'd heard the call first—the shrill *kwee, kwee* damped by the wet wind. A moment later he'd seen the hawk itself, hanging almost casually on a wing before plummeting into the reeds and rising an instant later with a screaming moorhen between its talons. Nature red in tooth and claw. The sort of moment you remembered for ever.

A moment not at odds, in a weird sort of way, with the helicopters that, at intervals, he'd seen hovering and whispering in the northern distance. What had that been about? Some sort of exercise? One of the helicopters had come close enough for him to see its military markings.

Rolling up the garage door, he hauled the kayak inside and shoved it up into the rafters. Then, parking the car and closing the garage door behind him, he returned up the ramp and climbed the balustraded stone steps to the front door. If nothing else, his mother's remarriage had certainly given the family a leg-up in the world, property-wise. Having pulled off his wet waterproofs and hung them to drip in the front hall, he found his mother in the kitchen, pausing from the preparation of a leg of lamb and the boiling of a kettle to open a jar of prune-based sludge for the baby's dessert. Jessica herself, meanwhile, temporarily at peace with the world, was lying on her back on a rug on the floor, sucking her toes. With his mother and half-sister stood a uniformed police officer.

The officer was smiling, and Denzil recognised him as Jack Hobhouse. A solid middle-aged man holding a peaked cap bearing the insignia of the Norfolk Constabulary, he had been to the house several times before when Denzil had been at home—most recently to advise on a new alarm system.

"Denzil, love, Sergeant Hobhouse has been warning us about something. Apparently there are a couple of terrorist-type people on the loose. Not near here, but they're armed, and they've apparently . . ." Reaching down in response to a sudden sharp cry from Jessica, she gathered up the child, arranged her over her left shoulder, and started patting her back.

"Apparently . . . ?" prompted Denzil.

"They've killed a couple of people up on the north coast," she said as Jessica, burping, released a milky posset down the back of her mother's expensive black cardigan. "There was that whole thing about the man who was found shot in that car park."

"Fakenham," said Denzil, regarding his mother's back with fastidious horror. "I saw something about it in the local paper. They're looking for a British woman and a Pakistani man, aren't they?"

"That's what they think," said Hobhouse. "Now as your mum said, there's no reason to suppose they're anywhere near here, but . . ."

He was interrupted by the ringing of the wall-mounted phone. Denzil made a move for it but his mother snatched it up, listened for a moment, and then replaced the receiver. At the same moment the baby started to cry.

"Traffic backed up for a mile because of roadblocks," she announced despairingly over the baby's wails. "Thinks he's going to be at least an hour late back. And I've got his bloody parents arriving at any minute. Which reminds me, we're going to need some wine and some more tonic water . . . My *God*, Denzil, is that them?"

"I'll, er . . . I'll leave these," murmured Hobhouse, handing Denzil two photocopied A4 sheets and replacing his cap, "and be on my way. Any worries, don't hesitate. And obviously, if you spot anyone . . ."

Denzil took the sheets, gave the officer a distracted thumbs-up, and glanced out of the window. Judging by the five-year-old Jaguar and the intolerant bearing of the couple stepping out of it, it was indeed "them."

"Mum, you've got sick on your back." He took a deep breath, thought briefly but longingly of the serenity that the afternoon had held, and made the supreme sacrifice. "Give me Jessica. Go upstairs and change. I'll hold the fort."

55

Faraj watched dispassionately as Jean, kneeling naked to the waist on the flagstoned towpath beneath the bridge, bent forward to rinse her hair in the river. Beyond the arches of the bridge lay a grey, baleful dawn. It was 9 a.m., and very cold. Jean's fingers scrabbled methodically at her scalp, a thin soapy cloud drifted downstream, and finally she raised her head and wrung out the dark rope of her hair. Still crouched over the water, she took a plastic comb from the unzipped washbag, and dragged it repeatedly forwards from the nape of her neck until her hair was no longer dripping. Then she shook it out, and pulled her dirty T-shirt back on. Her hands were shaking now after their immersion in the river, her head ached with the cold, and hunger was knotting her guts. It was essential, though, that she be presentable.

It was the day.

Pressing her flattened hands into her armpits to warm them for a moment, she searched in the washbag, found a pair of steel hairdressing scissors, and handed these and the comb to Faraj. Events had taken on a strange clarity. "My turn for a haircut," she said, a little self-consciously.

He nodded. Frowned as he took the scissors. Flickered them experimentally.

"It's simple," she said. "You work from the back to the front, cutting so that every strand"—she held up her index finger—"is this long."

The frown still in place, Faraj seated himself behind her. Taking the comb and scissors he began to cut, carefully dropping the severed locks into the river as he went. Fifteen minutes later he laid down the scissors. "Done."

"How does it look?" she asked. "Do I look different?"

A word of tenderness. A single word would do.

"You look different," he said brusquely. "Are you ready?"

"I just want to take a last look at the map," she said, glancing sideways at him. He was not yet thirty, but the stubble on his chin was silver. His face was blank. Reaching for the book, squinting in the dim light, she re-examined the topography of the area. As the crow flew, they were just three miles from the target.

"I'm still worried about the helicopters," she confessed. "If we go across country and they spot us, we're finished."

"It's less risky than taking another car," he said. "And if they're as clever as you say they are, they won't be searching round here anyway. They'll be concentrating on the approaches to the US bases."

"We're probably fifteen miles from Marwell here," she admitted. "Maybe sixteen."

But fifteen or sixteen miles still didn't seem very far. It was the infrared cameras that she really feared. *Their heat signatures on a screen, two pulsing dots of light growing larger and larger as the beating of the rotors grew louder and louder, roaring now, blotting out all sound and thought . . .*

"I think we should walk to West Ford along the towpath," she said, levelling her voice with a conscious effort. "That way, if we hear any helicopters, we've . . . we've got a chance of hiding under the next bridge."

He looked expressionlessly down at her hands, which had begun to shake again. "All right," he said. "The path, then. Pack the bags."

56

In the Swanley Heath mess hall, Liz sat in front of an untouched slice of buttered toast and a cup of black coffee. So far, Investigations had turned up nothing of interest concerning any of the names on the Garth House school list. Several of the pupils lived in Norfolk or Suffolk, or had done so at some point in the past, but while most remembered Jean D'Aubigny, none had any significant connection with her. A loner, had been the universal judgement. Someone who was happiest by herself.

And at a school like Garth House, where most of the children would have had problems of one sort or another, the desire for solitude was something you respected, Liz guessed. Children knew when to leave each other alone in a way that adults often didn't. Mark had rung her the night before but she had left her voice mail to field the call. She would not be returning it.

Investigations had also informed her that the D'Aubigny parents were still refusing to talk, or indeed to assist the police in any way. Reading between the lines, Liz suspected that this was the lawyer's doing, and that if any pressure was put on the parents—if they were charged with the wilful obstruction of justice, for example—Julian Ledward would use the case as an opportunity for civil rights grand-standing.

And despite an extensive search operation involving several units of the Moroccan police, MI6 had still not located Price-Lascelles. The latest theory, based on the fact that the Garth House headmaster had loaded several spare containers of diesel into his jeep before leaving Azemmour, was that he had not gone to Casablanca, as reported by the house-boy, but had driven up to the Atlas mountains. The search area, Judith Spratt had reported glumly, had expanded to approximately a thousand square miles.

Liz looked around the room. The police and firearms officers were in one group, the Army officers in another, the SAS team in a third. Bruno Mackay, she saw, was standing with the SAS team, and at that moment laughing uproariously at something that Jamie Kersley had just said.

Liz had taken a seat next to PC Wendy Clissold, who had spent much of the meal giggling on her phone. At the table's far end, a tactful distance away, sat half a dozen excruciatingly polite young Army Air Corps helicopter pilots.

"They reckon today's the day, then," said Clissold, "that they're going to have a bash at that Yank base."

"That's what they reckon," said Liz.

"It's not what I reckon," said a familiar voice at her shoulder.

Liz looked round. It was Don Whitten, and he had clearly had a bad night. His eyes were bloodshot and the bags beneath them purplish-grey. The tips of his moustache, by contrast, were yellowed with nicotine.

"Remind me never to join the Army, Clissold. The beds don't suit me. You're not allowed to smoke in them, for a kick-off."

"Isn't that a violation of your civil rights, Guv'nor?"

"You'd have thought so, wouldn't you?" said Whitten mournfully. He turned to Liz. "How did you do? Accommodation satisfactory?"

"Quite satisfactory, thanks. Our hut was very comfortable. Are you going to have some breakfast?"

Whitten patted his pockets for his cigarettes and peered at the serving counter. "I'm not sure whether all this fried food is appropriate for a fitness guru like myself. I may confine myself to a Filter King and a cup of tea."

"Go on, Guv'nor. It's free."

"True, Clissold. Very true. Have you heard from Brian Mudie this morning?"

"What d'you mean, Guv?"

He looked at her wearily. "When he rings you, tell him I want that inventory on the forensic from the bungalow fire ASAP. Everything. Every button, every razor blade, every Kentucky fried chicken bone. And packaging. I particularly want to know about packaging."

Clissold looked uneasily at her fingers. "As it happens, I have just been speaking to Sergeant Mudie. They're still making up the inventory . . ."

"Go on."

"There was one thing he said . . ."

"Tell me."

"When you were a kid, Guv, did they have that stuff called Silly Putty? That bouncy stuff you squeeze and . . ."

Whitten seemed to sag in his chair. Beneath the strip lighting, his skin was the colour of a corpse's. "Tell me," he repeated.

"More than a dozen melted containers, Guv. All empty."

His eyes met Liz's. "How much would that make?" he demanded tonelessly.

"Depends on the size of the containers. Enough to flatten this building, though."

Wendy looked from one to the other of them, mystified.

"C4 explosive," explained Liz. "Putty's one of the principal ingredients. The toy shop sort is best."

"So what's the target?" Whitten demanded.

"RAF Marwell seems to be the popular favourite right now."

"You don't think that, though?"

"I haven't got a better suggestion," said Liz. "And we've rather run out of time."

Whitten shook his head. "That lot over there"—he nodded at the Army officers—"think that Mansoor and D'Aubigny are just going to walk slap-bang into one of our search teams. They're crediting them with no intelligence whatsoever." He shrugged. "Perhaps they're right. Perhaps we're overcomplicating things. Perhaps the two of them are just going to find the largest concentration of people that they can, and . . ." He made a starburst with his hands. From the Army officers' table, there was more laughter.

"I told Jim Dunstan," said Whitten. "I said we wouldn't be here now if it wasn't for you."

Liz shook her head. "Wouldn't be where? Inside a razor-wired enclosure trying to pretend we know what we're doing? Waiting for a couple of trigger-happy maniacs who could be anywhere in East Anglia to do us the favour of showing themselves?"

Whitten regarded her in silence. Liz, angry at herself, took an exploratory bite of her toast, but she seemed to have lost all sense of taste. More than anything she wanted to walk out to her car, and leave. Draw a line under the case. Leave it to the police and the Army. She had done all that she could do.

Except that she knew she hadn't, quite. There was still a single thread, tenuous but nevertheless logical, to be followed. If the D'Aubigny parents thought that their daughter had no connection of any kind with East Anglia, and had never been there, then they would unquestionably have said so. Julian Ledward could huff and puff as loud as he liked, but the fact was that the D'Aubigny parents' silence had to mean that they knew of a connection. And if this was the case, given that they didn't have much clue about the path their daughter's life had taken after she left home, the chances were that it was a connection established *before* she left home. Which took her—and Liz—back to school, and Garth House.

Go for it, Jude. Find the key. Unlock the door.

"It's like a bullfight," said Wendy Clissold.

Liz and Whitten turned to her.

"I went to one once, in Barcelona," explained Clissold hesitantly. "The bull comes in, and the matador comes in, and everyone knows that . . . that there's going to be a death. You dress up, put perfume on, and buy a ticket to watch a death. Then you go home."

Whitten tapped a cigarette on the plastic tabletop. His eyes were the colour of old beeswax. "Key difference, love. At a bullfight, you're pretty sure who's going to be doing the dying."

57

From the confluence of the Lesser Ouse and the Methwold Fen Relief Drain to West Ford was about three miles as the crow flew, but the towpath distance was closer to four. The going was not uninterruptedly easy, either. There were broken-down stiles to negotiate, stretches hundreds of yards long where the towpath became impassable cattle-trodden marshland, and places where farmers had interrupted the right of way by running barbed-wire fences to the water's edge. All of these obstacles had to be surmounted or bypassed, and by 10 a.m., despite the cold of the riverbank and the gusty wind, Jean was sweating freely.

They saw several helicopters, but these were far away, swarming like gnats over the dim eastern horizon behind them. None came within five miles of them; above their heads there were only the clouds, racing thinly on the wind. And with every step she and Faraj lengthened the distance between themselves and the search's epicentre at Marwell.

They passed several people on the riverbank. There were walkers hunched into jackets and coats, there was a pair of elderly fishermen with thermos flasks, keeping a chilly vigil beneath their umbrellas, and there was a blowsy woman in a turquoise windcheater chivvying an elderly Labrador along the towpath. None of them paid Faraj or Jean any attention, preferring to remain enclosed in their private worlds.

Finally, at about quarter to eleven, the edge of the village came into view. The first dozen or so houses passed by the towpath were red-roofed boxes with pseudo-Georgian detailing, part of a late-twentieth-century speculative development. Beyond these, the river narrowed and passed between, on the north side, a stand of mature yews marking the boundary of the churchyard, and on the south side a coppice of rough evergreen woodland bisected by a public footpath.

Jean and Faraj were on the south bank of the Lesser Ouse, and a flight of shallow stone steps led them into this patch of woodland. When Jean thought of it, it was as it had been that summer ten years ago—a place of slanting green light and curling hash smoke. In December, however, there was little magic about it. The path was boggy and littered with bottles and fast-food wrappers, and the trees had a dank, sodden look about them.

But they provided cover, which was all that was necessary at that moment. Beyond the wet trees stood the village cricket ground. By following the path through the woodland it was possible to approach the back of the cricket pavilion, a crumbling 1930s structure resembling a miniature mock-Tudor villa.

There was a rear door through which the pavilion could be entered, secured by a simple lock. It quickly yielded to Jean's Banque Nationale de Paris credit card, and scrambling into the dimness with the rucksacks, they pulled the door closed behind them. Exhausted by the release of tension, they slumped down on to a wooden bench that ran the length of the back room. Having weighed up the risks, they had agreed that as long as they kept completely silent and showed no lights, they were probably safe in there. If there was a danger, it was that other people might try to break into the place. Kids, perhaps, looking for somewhere to do drugs or have sex. Beyond that, neither of them could think of a reason why anyone would want to go into a cricket pavilion in midwinter.

Jean looked around her. They were in some sort of changing area, lit by two small, high, cobwebbed windows. A line of hooks ran along the wall above the wooden bench, a couple of them still holding limp cricket shirts, and a heavy stoneware sink stood in one corner. Beside the sink a door led into a toilet stall. There was a faint residual smell of damp and linseed oil.

Cautiously, she opened the door to the forward part of the pavilion. This was an open area, wooden-floored, fronted by a locked door and two sets of green-painted shutters covering windows through which players could watch the game. As in the back room two high side windows admitted a thin light to the interior, showing stacked deckchairs and wicker laundry baskets holding pads, bats and batting gloves. On the long wall hung a pair of umpires' coats and several dusty team photos.

"Play up, play up and play the game!" murmured Faraj.

"I'm sorry?"

"Just a poem I learned in school."

Jean stared at him blankly for a moment. "We need to make a lookout position. Maybe cut a hole in these shutters or something."

He shook his head. "Too risky. And we haven't got the tools to do it with." Climbing on to the pile of deckchairs, he peered through the small side window. "Try this."

He climbed down and she took his place. Through the small opening, barely a foot square, she could see right across the northwest quadrant of the cricket ground. Beyond the post-and-rail fence at its boundary, several hundred yards away, the perimeter road was visible, and on its far side the rain-darkened sweep of the Terrace and the George and Dragon.

Disappearing into the back room, Faraj returned with the binoculars and passed them up to her. Outside Number One, the Terrace, stood a dark red Jaguar. On the ground floor, through the tall windows, she could see a tall, unmoving figure. Was that him? she wondered. The man who, on the other side of the world, had been selected to die. To die with his family around him, as so many innocent citizens of Iraq, Afghanistan and other states had died. Blown to pieces without warning. Casually—jokingly, even—and by strangers, as if they were no more than a cluster of pixels in a computer game. And then dismissed as "collateral damage."

She shook her head. These people were about to learn about damage. About to learn the difference between the real and the remote.

The tall figure moved away from the window, and Jean was about to lower the binoculars when a figure in the road caught her eye. A man in a pale raincoat had just exited a black car in order to stretch his arms and legs.

"There's security there," she whispered urgently. "A man in a car, and . . . yes, another inside the car."

Faraj nodded. "It was to be expected. We'll have to approach the house from the back."

"There's a back alley running between two of the houses. When it's dark I'll find my way in there. The garden's probably alarmed or spotlit, but I should be able to lower the device over the wall. It'll go off near to the side door of the house."

"They're well built, these old houses, no? Solid?"

"Pretty well built."

"We might not kill them all."

"It's the only option we've got, Faraj."

"Let me think about it. And get changed, you have to buy us some food."

She nodded, and went into the back room. There, making sure to keep her head below the level of the windows, she washed her hands, using a cracked rind of Lifebuoy soap that she found in a saucer by the sink, and dried them on one of the cricket shirts. Then, locating her washbag, she took out her small stock of make-up, and went through the half-forgotten ritual. A faint skim of foundation, a touch of shadow on the eyelids, and a pale dab of lipstick. She wanted to look like someone who had woken up in a comfortable middle-class home and had muesli and fresh orange juice for breakfast, not like a terrorist who had slept filthy and hungry beneath a fenland bridge. From her rucksack she took one of the knotted bin-liners of clothes. There was a soft lilac cashmere sweater, grey combat pants and a fitted denim jacket with a quilted lining, all bought in a mid-range Parisian department store. As she had hoped, the hiking boots looked more or less OK with this outfit, in a studenty sort of way. And the ensemble teamed up well with its final component—a small grey mono-strap backpack.

When she was ready, she looked at herself in the changing room mirror. The transformation was startling. Her hair, instead of falling flat and lank to her shoulders, now neatly framed her face. He had made a surprisingly sensitive job of it. And the make-up, of course, made all the difference. There was nothing remotely threatening about the bland and conventionally feminised creature that looked back at her. Hesitantly, she went through and showed herself to Faraj. He nodded, and said nothing, but some unreadable emotion touched his gaze.

"I should go shopping," she said, patting her trouser pockets to check that she had the velcro wallet.

"I'll wire up the weapon," he answered. "Don't be seen on the way out."

"When I knock six times, let me in. Any other number of knocks, it's not me, or they've taken me."

"I understand. Go."

58

A quick look through one of the high changing-room windows established that the coast was clear, and Jean let herself out. She walked
back into the wood and then took the northeasterly path, coming out at
the side of the road bordering the cricket ground. The shops—a panel-
beating and exhaust repairs yard, a newsagent's, and a village stores
incorporating a sub-post office, were at the near end of The Terrace, and
as she crossed the road she saw a fair-haired young man saunter down
the steps of Number One. Like her, he seemed to be heading for the
shops. This must be the man's son, she thought with a crawl of fore-
boding.

She steadied herself. In the long term, the action that she was taking

today would save lives. It would make the West think twice before raining bombs and bullets on those they considered faceless and of no consequence. The cascading triple detonation in which the British family
would die would serve as the scream of those countless others across the
world who had died without a voice. The young man would have to
give up his life with the rest.

The two of them reached the village stores at the same time, and he
stood aside politely as she pushed the door open. Inside, as she crammed
a basket with bread, mineral water, fruit, cheese, chocolate, and for
good measure a couple of Christmas cards and a packet of green tinsel,
she felt the young man's eyes on her. Covertly glancing between the
aisles, she saw a tall figure in jeans, a T-shirt, and a motorcycle jacket.
He was unshaven, and his hair stuck up on one side of his head as if he
had slept on it that way. Catching her eye, he grinned amiably at her,
and she looked away. She was prepared to kill him, but she couldn't
bring herself to smile at him. And why—*why*—did she think that she
recognised him?

Near the counter, and with a heart-thumping shock, she saw a
photograph of herself on the front of the *Daily Telegraph*. It was a particularly unsympathetic portrait that her mother had taken at Christmas
three or four years ago. *WOMAN, 23, SOUGHT* . . . Taking a copy,
forcing herself not to read further, she refolded it so that the images
were on the inside.

"Rain's stopped, anyway!" It was the young man—a boy he was,
really; he couldn't have been more than eighteen—by now in front of
her in the queue.

"That's true," she said flatly. "How long for, though?"

The question, as she had intended, was unanswerable, and he did
not reply, just shuffled good-humouredly from leg to leg. When the till
girl had scanned his Cheerios and his six-pack of Newcastle Brown Ale
cans, he asked for the total to be put on account.

"Which account would that be?"

"Mrs. Delves'—I'm her son."

The girl leaned comfortably back in her chair. "That'd be your little sister, then—that Jessica. I had a big smile off her yesterday. She's *gorgeous*!"

"Well, she's certainly got a strong pair of lungs on her."

"Bless! Give her a smacker from me, won't you?"

"OK. Er . . . who shall I tell her it's from?"

The girl spread her fingers and glanced downwards. She was wearing an engagement ring with a pale blue stone. "Beverley," she said.

"OK, I will. See you."

As intended, he had seen and taken note of the ring. The faint but unmistakable note of disappointment in his voice, however, had given Jean an idea. It was not going to be easy, but she knew what she was going to have to do. Dumping her basket on the inclined ramp of the counter and letting the girl take the items out and scan and bag them, she reached out and touched the boy's arm as he made for the exit. He looked round at her, surprised.

"Can I just ask you something?" she whispered. "Outside?"

"Er, sure," he murmured.

Turning, Jean pulled two ten-pound notes from the velcro wallet. Engrossed in the business of the till, Beverley had not registered the exchange.

Outside the shop Jean assumed her friendliest expression. It was not easy. Smiling was almost painful.

"Sorry to sort of . . . grab you like this," she said. "But I was wondering, do you know of any good pubs round here? I'm staying nearby . . ." she nodded vaguely westwards, "and I don't know the area, so . . ."

He scratched his head cheerfully, further disordering the straw-coloured hair. "Well, let's see . . . there's the George," he jerked a thumb left-handed, "but it's a bit Ye Olde, if you know what I mean. A bit mums 'n' dads. I usually go to the Green Man, which is a mile or so up the Downham Road."

"That's good, is it?"

"It's the best round here, I'd say."

"Right," said Jean, meeting his anxious, self-conscious gaze with a warm smile. "That's . . . Can you tell me exactly how to get there on foot? Because I'm not a hundred per cent sure that I'm going to be able to borrow my parents' car."

She was amazed at herself. She had thought that it would be next to impossible, this close-up deception, but it was so easy. As killing, when it had come to it, had been so easy.

"Well, you want to cross the cricket ground, and . . ." He looked down at his feet and took a deep breath before once again meeting her wide-eyed, enquiring gaze. "Look, I can . . . I can take you if you want. I was going up there myself tonight, so if you, er . . ." He shrugged.

She touched his forearm. "That sounds *really* great. What sort of time?"

"Oh, er . . . eightish?" He looked at her with a kind of dazed disbelief. "Say eight thirty? Here? How would that be?"

"That would be lovely!" She gave his arm a quick squeeze. "It's a date, then. Eight thirty here."

"Er, OK. Great. Where was it that you said you were staying?"

But she was already walking away.

59

On the tarmac outside the hangar, the SAS were taking on the PO19 Tactical Firearms Unit at football, and losing. Without doubt, the players were having a considerably better time than their immediate superiors, who were sitting inside waiting for news. Phones rang at intervals, and were snatched up, but no news of any importance had come in. Helicopters and regular and Territorial Army teams were maintaining their patrol.

The area was not a densely populated one, and the locals were somewhat bemused by this activity, and by the huge resources of camouflaged manpower that had been mobilised. The county had been intensively leafleted over the course of the morning, and everyone now knew that those suspected of the murders of Ray Gunter and Elsie Hogan were an Asian man and an Englishwoman.

This time when her phone went off Liz did not dive to reach it. All morning, as the negative results came in from each sector, she had had an increasing sense of her own uselessness, and only a terrible fascination with the endgame process prevented her from slipping away and driving back to London. Leaving was what Wetherby would certainly have counselled under the circumstances; there was no advantage to the Service or to anyone else in her staying around.

But Wetherby's advice had not been sought, and until all the intelligence had come in from Garth House, Liz was going to stay put.

At 3:30 p.m. one of the Army officers voiced the thought that no one else had dared put into words: that perhaps they were searching the wrong area. Was it possible, he ventured, that they had been sold a dummy? Led by a false process of deduction to guard the wrong institution? Could Lakenheath or Mildenhall be the real target?

The question was greeted with silence, and all present turned to Jim Dunstan, who stared expressionlessly in front of him for perhaps a full quarter of a minute. "We continue as we are," he said eventually. "Mr. Mackay assures me that the Islamic regard for anniversaries is absolute, and we have several hours until midnight. My suspicion is that Mansoor and D'Aubigny are lying up waiting to run the cordon under cover of darkness, and darkness will be with us within the hour. We continue."

Shortly after 4 p.m. the rain came, wavering grey sheets of it, lashing the hangar roof and dimming the outlines of the waiting Gazelle helicopters. The air smelt dangerously electric and the Army Air Corps pilots glanced anxiously at each other, mindful of their airborne colleagues.

"All we bloody well need," winced Don Whitten, forcing his hands frustratedly into his jacket pockets. "They say rain's the policeman's friend, but it's our enemy now, and no mistake."

Liz was about to answer when her phone bleeped. The text message indicated a waiting e-mail from Investigations.

Price-Lascelles still n/a in Morocco but have identified and contacted one Maureen Cahill, formerly matron at Garth Hse. MC claims D'Aubigny's closest friend Megan Davies, expelled from GH at age 16 after various drug-related incidents. MC says she treated D'Aubigny & MD in school infirmary after psilocybin (magic mushroom) overdose. According to school records Davies family (parents John and Dawn) lived near Gedney Hill, Lincs, but house has had several changes of occupants since, and no current record of Davies family whereabouts. Do we follow up?

Liz stared at the screen for a moment, and then printed out the message. That final sentence suggested that she was clutching at straws, but in truth it was all she had to go on. If there was any chance, however slim, of saving lives by ordering an investigation into the whereabouts of the Davies family, then she had to take it. That this investigation would be manpower-intensive did not have to be spelled out. Davies was a very common name indeed.

Go for it, Liz typed out. *Use everything. Find them.*

She looked outside. The rain was pounding remorselessly down. Dark was falling.

60

A gain," said Faraj.
     "When we get to the pub I ask to leave my coat in the car. I leave
the bag, too—under the coat—in case they're running bag checks on the
pub door. I persuade him to stay at the pub for as long as possible, preferably till closing time, and then take me back to the house. When it's
time to leave the pub, I set the timer to one hour, turning the red button
all the way to the right. In the car I drop some coins, and squeeze round
to the back seat to retrieve them. While I'm down there, I stuff the backpack under the passenger seat. When we get back to his house, I stay for
ten minutes maximum, perhaps arranging to meet him tomorrow, and
then I leave. I walk back around the cricket ground by the road, and

knock six times on the door to this pavilion. We then have an estimated thirty-five minutes to get away."

"Good. Remember that he must not take the car out of the garage once he has returned there. That's why I want you to return as late as possible. If there seems to be any possibility of him or any other member of the family taking the car out again, you must prevent him. Either steal his car keys or disable the car. If you cannot do these things, then take the backpack into the house with you and hide the bomb somewhere there."

"Got it."

"Good. Put the backpack on."

They had prepared this earlier, when there was still light. He had wired up the C4 device—a fairly straightforward job, necessitating a single small screwdriver and pliers—and together with its digital timer and electronic detonator this was now enclosed in an aluminium casing. At one end of the casing was the red timer-activator button, and protruding from the other a stubby inch-long aerial. If necessary, the timer could be over-ridden and the device remotely detonated by a matchbox-sized transmitter which was zipped into the inside breast pocket of Faraj's mountain jacket. The maximum range for remote detonation was four hundred yards, however, and it went without saying that if either of them was that close when the device went off, things would have gone badly wrong.

Rolling up the casing in the muddy jeans she had taken off that morning, Jean had tucked it at the bottom of the backpack. It had been decided that there was no point in trying to disguise the device. It was light, less than two pounds in weight, but the volume of explosive was too great to fit inside a camera or radio or anything else that she was likely to be carrying. Besides, there was no reason to suppose that she was going to be searched. She had stuffed a dirty T-shirt and her make-up bag on top of the jeans, and zipped up. Now she folded her waterproof jacket through the backpack's strap, so that it hung in front of her.

He squinted at her shadowy form. "Are you ready to do this thing, Asimat?"

"I'm ready," she said calmly.

He took her hand. "We will succeed, and we will escape. At the hour of vengeance we will be miles away."

She smiled. An impossible calm seemed to have settled over her. "I know that," she said.

"And I know that what you are doing is not easy. That talking to this young man will not be easy. You must be strong."

"I am strong, Faraj."

He nodded, holding on to her hand in the darkness. Outside, the wind scoured the pavilion and the dark, wet trees.

"It's time," he said.

61

Denzil Parrish had no desire to conform to the unhygienic science student stereotype, and had prepared himself carefully. After a half-hour session in which he had exhaustively bathed, shampooed and shaved himself, he had dressed from head to foot in clean clothing. Encounters like today's were once-in-a-lifetime opportunities, and he was determined not to squander this one. The woman had appeared as if from outer space—cool, chic and confident. He didn't know her name, he didn't know where she was staying . . . He knew nothing about her.

Was she attractive? Yes, there was a self-possession about her which was definitely attractive. She had one of those faces that you couldn't immediately summon up. Wide-set eyes and cheekbones, and an oblique-set mouth. A strange sense of urgency about her, as if her thoughts were elsewhere.

"You look very smart, all of a sudden," said his stepfather, carrying an early-evening beer from the kitchen into the sitting room. For security reasons Colin Delves changed into and out of his RAF uniform at Marwell, and now he was wearing jeans, loafers and the tan leather jacket he habitually wore to drive to and from the base. Despite his casual clothes, however, a palpable air of tension surrounded him.

"And you look a bit knackered," said Denzil. "Are the Yanks pushing you too hard?"

"It's been a long day," said Delves, settling into an armchair opposite the television. "There's been another big security alert. This time they think terrorists might have targeted the base because of the Fighter Wing's involvement in Afghanistan. So Clyde Greeley and I decided all off-base personnel should clear off home, me included, and let the security people lock the place down."

"Is that for my ears only?" asked Denzil.

His stepfather shrugged. "Hard to keep it completely quiet, given that they've erected roadblocks around the base and moved three battalions of troops into the area."

"So what'll happen to them? The terrorists, I mean."

"Well, they won't get anywhere near the base, put it like that. What are you up to this p.m.?"

"Pub," said Denzil, lowering himself on to the chintz-covered sofa. "Green Man."

"Right. Shut those curtains, would you?"

The curtains, a worn yellow damask, hung in front of the tall front windows. Standing there, Denzil looked out for a moment at the dark expanse of the cricket field, the distant form of the pavilion against the trees, and the scattered, rain-blurred lights of the houses beyond. It was a good house, he thought, but it just happened to find itself in the middle of the deadest, most desolate patch of countryside in Britain. The security people were parked out there somewhere, he guessed, keeping a weather eye on the place.

Colin Delves' parents came into the room, and looked about them with the bright, enquiring air of people requiring substantial alcoholic drinks. Buoyed with the secret knowledge of the evening ahead of him, Denzil took their orders himself, and in sympathy with his stepfather's exhausted state, made a point of pouring them at least quintuple measures.

"Lord!" said Charlotte Delves a minute later, touching her pearls in surprise. "There's enough gin in here to tranquillise a horse."

"Enjoy," said Denzil. "Chill out."

"Aren't you going to have one?" Royston Delves, who had made his money in commodities, was a pinker, fleshier version of his RAF officer son.

"I'm driving," said Denzil piously.

"Yes, straight to the pub," said Colin.

They were still laughing when Denzil's mother came in with Jessica. The baby had been bathed, fed her bottle, and dressed in a clean white babygro. Now, sleepy-eyed and talcum-scented, she was ready to be shown off before being tucked up for the night.

It was the moment Denzil had been waiting for. Amidst the cooing and clucking, he slipped away. The woman was waiting outside the shop, as she had said she would be. Denzil didn't see her at first, but then she stepped quickly towards the Honda and climbed in.

"Sorry," he said, as she buckled herself in. "It's a bit of a tip. Try and pretend it's a Porsche."

"I'm not sure I like Porsches very much," she said. "A bit flash, don't you think?"

He turned to look at her. She was dressed as she had been earlier, and was carrying a dark green waterproof jacket. "Well, I'm glad you see it that way," he grinned. "Have you had an OK day?"

"A quiet day. How about you? I'm Lucy, by the way."

"I'm Denzil. So what do you do, Lucy?"

"Very boring, I'm afraid. I work for a company which produces economic reports."

"Wow, that . . . that really *does* sound quite boring!"

"I have dreams," she said.

"What dreams?"

"I'd like to travel. Asia, the Far East . . . Hot places."

"There's a tandoori place in Downham Market. That can get quite hot."

She smiled at the windscreen. "Well, perhaps that's as far as I'll get this Christmas. How about you?"

"I'm studying geology at Newcastle."

"Interesting?"

"I wouldn't go that far. But it can take you to some interesting places. There's a Greenland trip next year."

"Cool."

"Yeah—icy, even. But I'm a cold places person, if you know what I mean. Like you're obviously a hot places person."

"That's too bad."

"Well, perhaps we could meet in the middle. In some temperate zone. Like the pub."

Denzil pulled in to a car park.

"This is it. The Green Man. *L'Homme Vert. El hombre* . . ."

"It looks nice," she murmured. "Do you mind if I leave my jacket and bag in the boot?"

62

"Yes, Minister," said the Deputy Chief Constable. "I believe absolutely that they will go tonight, whatever it costs them. We now think it's not just a question of jihad, but of familial honour. In this context, neither is negotiable . . . No. Thank *you*, Minister. Goodbye."

He replaced the receiver. "Home Office," he explained for the benefit of the dozen or so individuals watching and listening. "And those two jokers damn well better bomb something tonight, or . . ."

A dozen or so pairs of eyes stared at him. The SAS captain sniggered. The moment was saved by the ringing of Mackay's landline. The MI6 man snatched up the receiver. "Hello? Vince? Where are you, mate? Right. And you've got . . . *Brilliant!* Good man. Hang on, I'll . . ."

He covered the receiver and beckoned to Liz. "Price-Lascelles. That headmaster from Wales. Our bloke's found him. Bad line."

Liz's eyes widened. "OK. Don't transfer it."

She walked over to his desk. The headmaster's voice was very faint, and sounded as if it had been strained through several thicknesses of blanket. ". . . do you do. I understand you . . . speak to me."

"I need to know about one of your ex-pupils. Jean D'Aubigny . . . Yes, Jean D'Aubigny!"

". . . remember her very well. What can I . . . ?"

"Did she have any particular friends? People she might have stayed with in the holidays? People she might have stayed in touch with?"

"Have *lunch* with?"

"WHO WERE JEAN D'AUBIGNY'S BEST FRIENDS?"

". . . difficult young woman, who didn't make friends easily. Her closest, as I recall, was a rather troubled . . . named Megan Davies. Her people . . . up in Lincoln, I think. Her father was in the forces. RAF."

"You're sure about that?"

". . . what they told me. Nice couple. John and Dawn, I think their . . . pillar to post . . . Megan very wild in consequence. In the end it turned out that we . . . permit pupils to bring drugs on to the premises."

"Did Jean D'Aubigny go and stay with the Davies family?"

". . . to my knowledge. She may have done so after Megan left Garth House."

"Where did the Davies family go after Gedney Hill?"

"Sorry, can't help you there. They . . . at the time of Megan's departure."

"Do you know where Megan went on to? Which school? Mr. Price-Lascelles? *Hello?*" But the line was dead. Everyone in the room was staring at her. Mackay and Dunstan wore particularly indulgent smiles.

Was she way off beam here? Was this complete whimsy?

Replacing the receiver, meeting none of the eyes which followed her, Liz returned to her desk. Pulling down the contacts file on her laptop, she rang the Ministry of Defence. Identifying herself to the duty officer, she had herself put through to Files.

"I'm actually just shutting up shop," a pleasant-voiced young man told her. "It'll have to be quick."

"It'll take as long as it takes," said Liz levelly. "This is a matter of national security, so if you don't wish to find yourself outside a job centre this time next week, I suggest that you remain exactly where you are until we are finished, is that clear?"

"I hear you," said the young man petulantly.

"RAF records," said Liz. "John Davies, D-A-V-I-E-S, senior officer of some kind, probably admin, wife's name is Dawn, daughter's name is Megan."

"Hang about, I'm just . . ." There was the sound of keyboard strokes. "John Davies, you say . . . Yes, here we are. Married to Dawn, née Letherby. He's over at Strategic Air Command."

"Did he ever have a posting in Lincolnshire?"

"Yes. He spent, let's see, two and a half years running RAF Gedney Hill."

"Is that still operative? I've never heard of it."

"It was sold off in the cuts about ten years ago. It was where they used to do the escape and evasion courses for aircrews. And I think the Special Forces Flight did some Chinook training there too."

"So where did Davies go after that?" asked Liz.

"Let's see . . . Six months' attachment in Cyprus, and then he was given command of RAF Marwell in East Anglia. It's one of the American—"

Liz felt her hand tighten on the receiver. Forced her voice to remain level.

"I know where it is," she said. "Where did he and his family live when he was there?"

"In a place called West Ford. Do you want the address?"

"In a minute. First I want you to look up a man called Delves, Colin Delves, D-E-L-V-E-S, who holds that post at Marwell today. Find out if he lives at the same address."

Another muted flurry of keyboard strokes. A brief silence. "Same address. Number One, The Terrace, West Ford."

"Thank you," said Liz.

Replacing the phone, she looked around her. "We're guarding the wrong target," she said.

A frozen silence, utterly hostile.

"Jean D'Aubigny's dowry. The reason she was fast-tracked to operational status. She knew classified information vital to the ITS—namely, where the RAF Marwell CO was billeted. She stayed there with a friend from her school. She probably knows every secret inch of the place. They're going to take out Colin Delves' family."

Jim Dunstan's eyelids fluttered. The blood drained from his face. He looked blankly from Mackay to Don Whitten.

The SAS captain was the first to move, punching out an internal number. "Sabre teams scramble for immediate action, please. Repeat—*Sabre teams scramble to go.*"

"West Ford," said Liz. "The village is called West Ford."

A dozen voices at the level edge of urgency. Running feet, the slash of rotors, and the spotlit hangar falling away beneath them.

63

The Green Man was large and plain and beery, with a long oak bar and an impressive array of pumps. There was no jukebox or fruit machine, but the clientele was young and boisterous and noise levels were high. A cloud of cigarette smoke hovered a little above head height. After a brief search, Jean and Denzil found a table against the wall, and Denzil went to buy the first round. At the bar, as he waited, Jean saw him surreptitiously counting his money.

He returned with a pint of Suffolk bitter for each of them. As a Muslim, Jean hadn't drunk alcohol for some years, but Faraj had suggested that she have at least one drink to show willing. The beer had a sour, soapy texture but was not altogether unpleasant. It gave her something to do with her hands and, equally important, something to look at as they talked. Early in the evening she had made the mistake of looking Denzil in the eye—of meeting his open, inquisitive gaze—and it had been almost unbearable.

Talking to him was harder than she would have believed possible. He was awkward and shy, but he was also sensitive and self-deprecating and kind. He was almost painfully concerned that she should enjoy her evening with him, and she sensed him casting around for subjects of conversation which might engage her interest.

Don't look at him, look *through* him, she told herself, but it didn't do any good. She was sharing a small and intimate space with a young man whom she found herself liking very much. And planning to kill him.

When it was her turn to buy the drinks, she returned with a pint in each hand and gave them both to him. Her first pint was still only half drunk.

"To save time," she explained. "It's a bit jam-packed up there."

"It gets a lot more crowded when the Americans are here," he told her. "Not to mention making things a lot harder with the girls for us local boyos."

"So why aren't the Americans here tonight?"

"Grounded, probably. Apparently there's been a terrorist scare. There've been a couple of murders up towards Brancaster and they think it might be something to do with Marwell."

"What's Marwell?"

"One of those RAF bases that the US Air Force use. You know, like Lakenheath . . . Mildenhall . . ."

"So what have they got to do with Brancaster? I thought that's where people went sailing."

"To be honest, I haven't followed the whole thing very closely. My stepfather told me. He's . . ."

She waited.

Denzil frowned awkwardly at his pint. "He's, um . . . he's a bit more clued up than me, localwise. They reckon the people who committed the murders on the coast might be about to launch some sort of attack on Marwell."

"Why?"

"Honestly, I haven't really followed the whole thing. I've been out for most of the last few days."

"Is it near here?"

"Marwell? About thirteen miles." He raised his glass as if to check the steadiness of his hand. "And given that there are three battalions of troops between us and it, I'd say we're probably pretty . . ."

She turned to him. She could feel the faint, dizzying effects of the alcohol hitting her system. "Suppose we weren't? Suppose it all ended tonight? Would you feel you'd lived . . . enough?"

"Wow! That's a bit of a heavy . . ."

"Would you, though? Would you be ready to go?"

He narrowed his eyes and smiled. "Are you serious?"

She shrugged. "Yeah."

"Well, OK. If I had to, like, *die,* this would probably be as good a moment as any. My mum got remarried a couple of years ago and is happy for the first time that I can remember, and I've now got a baby sister—seventeen years younger than me, can you imagine it, *seventeen years younger than me*—who hasn't really had the chance to get to know me, and so wouldn't be hurt by my death, but who my mum would still have. And I haven't really begun doing anything with my life, careerwise, so in a sense there wouldn't be anything wasted, so . . . Yeah, if I had to go, now would be as good a time as any."

"What about your father? Your real father?"

"Well . . . He walked out on us years ago, when I was a boy, so he can't ever have really cared for us . . ." He rubbed his eyes. "Lucy, I really like you, but why are we having this conversation?"

She shook her head, her eyes unfocused. Then, draining her pint glass, she nudged it towards him. "Could you . . . ?"

"Yeah, sure."

There was a distant roaring in her head, as if she had her ear to a giant sea shell. Yesterday morning she had killed a boy, much the same age as this one, with a silenced Russian pistol. She had smiled at him and squeezed the trigger, felt the gasp of the damped recoil, and seen the boy's head empty itself into the corner of the car boot. Now she was reborn, a Child of Heaven, and at last she understood what the instructor at Takht-i-Suleiman had always found so funny—so funny that it regularly reduced him to shaking incoherence.

She had been reborn dead. The moment had, as promised, changed everything. It had thrown a switch inside her, jamming the circuitry and paralysing the networks. She had feared that she would feel too much; instead, infinitely worse, she felt nothing. Last night, for example. She and Faraj had been like reanimated corpses. Twitching in each other's arms like electrified frogs in a school laboratory.

And Jessica. She had put aside the question of the baby. Lifting her forearm, she bit it until the teeth met, and when she released herself there were two purplish crescents in the skin, oozing blood. It wasn't that it didn't hurt, it just didn't matter. For a moment, a split second, she felt the dark presence of her pursuer.

". . . Another pint for *Mademoiselle* Lucy. You're not married by any chance, are you?"

"Not by any chance, no." She drank.

"So tell me, unmarried Lucy, just where exactly are you staying round here, and just why are you inviting yourself to pubs with strangers?"

Familiarity, she saw, had emboldened and calmed him. Her head sank slowly forward until her forehead touched her glass. "That's a good question," she said. "But a very hard one to answer."

He leaned forward. "Try."

She was silent. Took a deep swallow of the beer. And another.

"Or not, of course," he murmured, straightening up and looking away.

The alcohol raced round her system. In the old days, with Megan, it had never taken much. A couple of glasses and she was flying. "If I told you that the conversation we've just had was the most important of your life . . ."

"I'd . . ." He shrugged. "I'd guess that's possible."

In his eyes she could see the dawning of the knowledge that the evening was not going to end magically. That she was just one more flaky, difficult woman who was not for him.

She took his hand. It was large, warm, and damp from his beer glass. Holding it by the fingers, she examined his palm, and as she did so, something—in fact, everything—became blindingly obvious. She laughed out loud. "See," she said. "Long life!"

"We're a long-living family," he said warily.

She smiled at him, and releasing his hand, drained her glass. "Lend me your car keys," she said. "I need to get something."

Outside, at the car, she put on the backpack and zipped up her coat over it. When she returned, wearing her waterproof, Denzil looked at her resignedly. "You're going to disappear, aren't you? And I'm never going to know anything about you."

"Let's see," she said. And touching her hand to his cheek for a moment, she walked out.

Outside, the rain blew gently across her face. She couldn't feel her feet on the ground; instead, she seemed to be floating, buoyed by a lightness of spirit that she had never known. It wasn't a question of rationalisation—she simply wasn't going to do it. She had been cut loose from the need to obey anyone, or any creed, ever again. They couldn't kill her; neither Faraj and his people, nor her pursuer and her people. She was already dead.

How long she walked, she didn't know. Not more than fifteen minutes, probably. The beer had filled her bladder, and as she crouched at the side of the road with her combat trousers round her ankles—memories of Takht-i-Suleiman—she saw Denzil sweep past in the Honda Accord. She walked on. It was as if she stood still and the road unrolled beneath her feet. She was smiling, and the tears were coursing down her cheeks with the rain.

The noise of the helicopters was small at first, and then it became a snarling, slashing fury all around her. Before her was the cricket ground, spotlit from the sky—a scene of unearthly theatricality and beauty. At its centre, hissing faintly and rocking on its struts, a British Army Puma from which the black-clad chorus ran to take their positions. Heckler and Koch MP5s, she noted approvingly. The SAS. And on the road beyond them the sapphire winking of police vehicles against the Georgian frontage, more running figures, and the bouncing echo of a loud-hailer.

Jean D'Aubigny kept walking. She would have liked to stop weeping but the beauty of it all, and the attention to detail, was just too much. Faintly, at the edge of her consciousness, she heard the multiple snicker of rifle bolts drawn back and locked. Police snipers, she thought, but quickly forgot them, for there at the scene's centre, downlit by a police helicopter, was a slight, determined-looking figure whom she knew immediately. The woman's dark hair was slicked back from her face and her leather jacket was zipped to the chin.

Jean smiled. Everything was somehow so familiar. It was as if the scene had played itself out an infinity of times before. "I knew you'd be here," she called out, but the wind and the updraught from the helicopters plucked her words away.

In the pavilion, Faraj watched as the security forces flooded the area, and knew himself a dead man. He saw the soldiers leap from the Puma, the cricket field flooded with light, and the police marksmen pour down the ropes from the hovering Gazelles on to the surrounding roofs. Thanks to the binoculars, however, he knew one further thing for certain: that the boy had driven the Honda into the garage several minutes before. The bomb had to be in the car, and he kept the binoculars trained on the front door of the target house. Where the girl was he had no idea, presumably in the house with the boy, but he had to act before the police evacuated the place and the entire operation was in vain. From his jacket pocket he took the remote detonator, kissed it, bade farewell to the fighter Asimat, and spoke the name of his father and of Farzana, whom he had loved.

· · ·

As the woman walked uncertainly on to the illuminated cricket ground, Liz realised that she was looking at Jean D'Aubigny. The hair was wet and cropped short, and the face was much thinner and sharper than that of the puppy-fatted teenager in the posters, but it was recognisably her. She was wearing a waterproof jacket, unzipped. Beneath it a high-necked sweater was intersected by the grey, bandolier-style strap of a bag.

As their eyes met the woman smiled, as if in a kind of recognition, and the lips moved in the rain-blurred face. She looked younger than her twenty-four years, Liz thought. Almost childlike.

The connection between them held for an instant, and then the night shivered and tore apart. A tidal wave of darkness roared towards Liz—pure force, pure hate—lifting and pitching her through the air like an unstrung toy. The ground slammed up to meet her, and for a moment, as the reverberating undertow of the explosion rolled over her, dragging the breath from her lungs, she knew and understood nothing.

There was a silence—a long silence, it seemed—during which soil and clothing and body-tissue fragments rained down, and then, by inclining her head, which hurt atrociously, she saw people moving soundlessly around her, ghostlike beneath the wavering spotlights. To one side a policeman was kneeling on all fours with his uniform hanging from his body and bloody mucus issuing from his nose and mouth. To the other, the overcoated figure of Don Whitten was lying face-down, shuddering, and beyond him an Army officer was sitting blank-eyed on the ground, bleeding from both ears. In her own ears she could hear a high, thread-like scream. Not human, but some kind of an echo.

A police officer ran up to her and shouted, but she could hear nothing, and waved him away. More running feet, and then the helicopters and the lights swung away from them to rake the cricket pavilion and the woods at the far side of the cricket ground. They must have found Mansoor. *"Alive!"* she tried to shout, clambering to her knees with the rain in her face. *"Get him alive!"* But she couldn't hear her own voice.

She was running now, slipping on the wet grass, pushing away Wendy Clissold and another, vaguer figure. Running at an oblique angle to one of the SAS Sabre teams, who were working their way fast and purposefully around the perimeter towards the pavilion. Every step that she took was like a hammer-blow behind her eyes, and she could feel the warm, steely taste of blood in her mouth. She could still hear almost nothing beyond the thready scream in her ears and the slashing pulse of the helicopters, and so was unaware of Bruno Mackay until, launching himself at her from behind and wrapping his arms around the wet calves of her jeans, he brought her awkwardly to the ground and held her there.

She groaned, dazed. "Bruno, we . . . can't you see, we . . ."

"Don't move, Liz," he ordered her, pinning her down hard by the wrists. "Please. You're not thinking straight."

His voice was just a whisper. She bared blood-darkened teeth, and writhed.

"I said *don't move*! You'll get us shot."

She lay there, immobilised. Watched as the police helicopter's spotlight bleached the pavilion. Day for night. She wasn't even sure what she'd been trying to do.

"I'm fine," she murmured.

"You're *not* fine," he hissed. "You've got severe blast concussion. And we've *got* to get away from here. If there's a firefight we're likely to get our—"

"We need Mansoor alive."

"I know. But move back now, *please*. Let the SAS do their job."

The four soldiers moved towards the pavilion with their MP5 carbines raised to their shoulders, but as they did so, its front door slowly opened, and a wiry, aquiline figure stepped on to the spotlit players' terrace and narrowed his eyes against the glare. He was wearing jeans and a grey T-shirt. His hands were raised. He was not holding a weapon.

Liz stared at Faraj Mansoor, fascinated. Watched as the first spatters of rain darkened his T-shirt. Mackay, however, barely glanced at him, and in a sudden, terrible rush of comprehension Liz knew exactly what was going to happen, and why.

There was a moment's frozen stand-off, and then one of the SAS men yelled, *"Grenade!"*

Leaning forward into their weapons, and from a range of no more than half a dozen yards, the four men each fired a controlled burst of shots into Faraj Mansoor's chest. Speechless, Liz watched as his body kicked and bucked and twisted to the ground.

There was a brief silence, and then one of the soldiers stepped forward, and with an air of brisk formality fired two further shots into the back of the fallen man's neck.

Rain streamed from Liz's face as she stared at the spotlit tableau. She felt Mackay take her arms from behind, pinioning her, and wrenched herself free. She could feel the blood on her face congealing now, and the rain streaming through her hair and down her back. She was almost weeping with fury. "Do you realise—*do you fucking realise*—what you've done?"

Mackay's voice was patient.

"Liz," he said. "Get real."

64

Footsteps, which she disregarded. Someone else's problem. She began to drift away again, but heard—as if from a great distance—someone speak her name. Then the footsteps again.

Unwillingly, Liz opened her eyes. She couldn't remember where she was, but from the even bleed of the light through the thin cotton curtains she estimated that it was mid-morning. She blinked. The room was spacious and its walls sky-blue. Between her bed and the window stood a stainless-steel drip apparatus and an oxygen canister on a trolley. There was a breathing tube in her nostrils, her bed was banked with pillows, and the mattress had been tilted at a comfortable thirty or so degrees above horizontal. From outside, she could hear the distant grumble of jet engines.

Slowly, the sedative fog cleared. It was over, and Faraj Mansoor and Jean D'Aubigny were dead. But parts of the previous evening, Liz knew, were lost to her for ever. The bomb blast and her subsequent concussion had ensured that. Something that she remembered clearly, and which afforded her an obscure gratification, was that after witnessing Mansoor's death, she had refused Bruno Mackay's help in returning to the emergency services vehicles. She had walked half the way and then fallen to her knees, and an Army Air Corps paramedic crew had run to meet her with a stretcher. She remembered the sting of the needle in her arm, the soft kiss of the rain on her face, sirens, and blue lights. Then there had been the helicopter's skywards surge, its engine's narcotic thrum, and the faint crackle of radio communications. Then nothing.

She pulled the breathing tube from her nostrils. Her head ached and there was a thick, stale taste in her mouth. The temperature was ambient, neither hot nor cold. She was wearing a white hospital gown which laced at the back.

The door opened. It was a young blonde woman in combat pants and a USAF T-shirt. "Hi there! How *are* you this morning?"

"Er . . . OK, I think." Liz blinked, struggling to an upright position. "Where am I?"

"Marwell. The Air Force base hospital. I'm Dr. Beth Wildor." She had a brisk manner and dazzling teeth.

Liz nodded. "Ah, OK. Um . . . Can I get up?"

"I'll just have a quick look at you?"

"Fine."

For the next ten minutes Dr. Wildor peered into her eyes and ears, tested her hearing, took her blood pressure, and conducted other tests, noting the results on a clipboard.

"You have impressive powers of recovery, Miss Carlyle. You were not a well woman when they brought you in last night."

"I'm afraid I don't remember much about it."

"We call it blast trauma. There are elements of the experience you probably won't recover, but perhaps in this case that's not such a bad thing."

"Did anyone die?"

"Apart from the bombers, you mean? No. There were injuries, but no loss of life."

"Thank God."

"Absolutely. You're police, right?"

"Home Office. Can I get up now?"

"You know, Miss Carlyle, I think I'd rather you took it easy. Why don't you receive your visitor, and when I've done my round, we'll talk?"

"I have a visitor?"

"Indeed you do," she said with a conspiratorial flash of her teeth. "And he seems *most concerned* about you."

"If his name is Mackay, I have no wish to speak to him."

"I don't think that was the name he gave. It was . . ." she glanced at the clipboard, "a Mr. Wetherby."

"*Wetherby?*" She felt an inexplicable flutter of surprise. "He's here?"

"Right outside." She regarded Liz levelly. "I take it he's welcome?"

"He's very welcome," said Liz, attempting without success to wipe the smile from her face.

"Oh-*kay*! Perhaps you'd like a minute or two to freshen up?"

"Perhaps I would."

"I'll tell him five."

When Dr. Wildor had gone, Liz swung her legs over the edge of the bed and walked to the washbasin. She felt unsteady, and was shocked by the face that regarded her from the mirror. She looked pinched and tired, and there was a dark mask of bruising around her eyes from the blast. She did the best job she could with a vacuum-sealed washing pack that she found at her bedside, and feeling slightly absurd and fraudulent, rearranged herself decorously in the bed.

Wetherby came in carrying flowers. She would not have found it easy to imagine such a thing, but here he was waving a rather lurid spray of semi-tropical blooms.

"Can I put these somewhere?" he asked, looking around him with worried, unseeing eyes.

"In the sink, perhaps? They're lovely, thank you."

He busied himself for a moment with his back to her. "So . . . how do you feel?" he asked.

"Better than I look."

He sat himself a little awkwardly on the end of the bed. "You look . . . Well, I'm glad it's not worse."

It struck Liz that hospital visits were a grimly regular feature of Wetherby's life, and she felt a little ashamed to be lying there like a tragic heroine when, in truth, there didn't seem to be anything seriously wrong with her. "I gather there were no deaths on our side?"

"Detective Superintendent Whitten's in the room next door. He was hit by shrapnel—the bomb casing, they think—and lost a fair bit of blood. A couple of the Army people were also cut about quite badly, and there are half a dozen blast trauma cases like yours. But as you say, no deaths. For which, in large part, we have you to thank."

"There's been no shortage of corpses in all of this." She looked away. "You know about Faraj Mansoor, don't you? Who he really was?"

He looked at her quizzically. "Would you like some breakfast while we talk?"

"Very much."

He glanced at the door. "I'll ask them to bring something. What would you like?"

"I'd like to get dressed. Find a canteen or something. I hate eating in bed."

"Are you allowed out? I wouldn't want to get on the wrong side of that woman with the teeth."

"I'll risk it." Liz smiled, conscious of the faint awkwardness of protocol that prevented them from using each other's names. Buoyed by a sudden reckless effervescence, she stepped out of bed in her shapeless gown, and twirled around.

Wetherby stood, bowed with ironic chivalry, and made his way to the door.

She watched him go, and then remembering that her gown had no back to it, began to laugh. Perhaps she didn't feel completely normal.

Her clothes were nowhere to be found. In the locker by the bed, however, some thoughtful hand had placed brand-new underwear, training shoes, a GO WARTHOGS! T-shirt, and a zip-top grey track-suit. All fitted perfectly. Thus attired, she opened the door.

"Follow me," said Wetherby. "Fetching ensemble, by the way."

They stepped out on to the tarmac. It was bitingly cold. In the distance, glinting dully beneath a shelf of black cloud, was a phalanx of Thunderbolt attack jets, with their Gatling cannons pointed skywards.

" 'They make a wilderness, and call it peace.' "

"Who said that?" asked Liz.

"Tacitus. About the Roman Empire."

She turned to him. "I assume you were up all night, following everything as it happened?"

"I was in COBRA when your call came through saying that you were on your way to West Ford by helicopter. Five minutes later the police were reporting an explosion with at least a dozen feared injured or dead, and then another report came in almost immediately of some sort of SAS firefight. Downing Street was jumping up and down by this time, as you can imagine, but luckily by the time I got there I'd been able to extract some hard facts from Jim Dunstan—including the fact that one of my officers was down." He smiled drily. "The Prime Minister was naturally extremely concerned. He informed me that you were in his prayers."

"That must be what pulled me through. But tell me; I only saw scraps of what happened. Was there time to evacuate the Delves family? One of the police officers in my helicopter was trying to ring them to tell them to get the hell out, but their phone was engaged and she couldn't get through."

Wetherby nodded. "Evacuating the area was Dunstan's main worry, especially as most of the local force was deployed a dozen miles away guarding this place here. In the event he managed to get a warning to Delves' security people, and they evacuated the pub and got the family clear."

"Where did everyone go?"

"Church hall at the other end of the village, I gather."

"And meanwhile we all land on the cricket pitch. Enter Jean D'Aubigny. I can remember her walking towards me. What happened? Why was she walking away from the target?"

"We don't know. It looks as though she must have changed her mind. She was carrying the bomb and Mansoor had a transmitter. We think he must have detonated it. Explosion followed by total chaos, as I understand it. There was a big helicopter search for Mansoor, somebody reported heat traces around the pavilion, and one of the SAS teams moved up to investigate." He smiled wryly. "A process of which, I'm informed, you were quite a close observer."

"I'll have plenty to say about that in my report," murmured Liz. "Never fear."

"I look forward to it."

The cookhouse was huge—a shining ocean of vending machines and wipe-clean tabletops, thousands of square metres in area. Mid-morning, the place had little traffic—a dozen individuals, perhaps, mostly dressed for sport—and the two of them were the only customers at the long tray-counter. Liz secured herself coffee, orange juice and toast. Wetherby contented himself with coffee.

"You asked me if I knew who Faraj Mansoor really was," he said, stirring pensively.

"That's right."

"The answer is yes. Geoffrey Fane told me early this morning. I came up here on a helicopter with him."

"So where's Fane now?"

"Debriefing Mackay on the flight home, I'd imagine."

Liz stared out disbelievingly over the vast, empty canteen. "Bastards. *Bastards!* They deliberately kept us in the dark. Watched us struggle. Watched people die."

"It does rather look that way," said Wetherby. "How did you find out?"

"Mackay's behaviour last night. When Mansoor came out of the cricket pavilion with his hands up—and we'd been hunting the man night and day for a week, remember—Mackay barely glanced at him. In fact he kept his head turned away as if he didn't want to be recognised."

"Go on."

"They knew each other. It was the only possible explanation."

Wetherby peered incuriously at a Coca-Cola machine. "Faraj Mansoor was MI6's man, as his father had been before him. By all accounts he was a first-class agent. Very brave and steady."

"And Mackay ran him?"

"He inherited him. Mackay arrived in Islamabad at about the time of the US intervention in Afghanistan, and reading between the lines, he pushed Mansoor a bit too hard. For whatever reason, Mansoor asked Mackay to back off. Said that he was being watched very closely, and insisted that for the time being they cease all contact."

"So Mackay backed off?"

"He didn't have much choice. Mansoor was Six's best asset in theatre. He had to be kept happy."

"And then the USAF shot up his family."

"That's right. A tragic accident or lethal incompetence, depending on your reading of the facts, but Mansoor reads it as revenge. As punishment for breaking off contact with Mackay. So—unsurprisingly, perhaps—he turns, and throws in his lot with the *jihadis*. His father and fiancée are dead, and some kind of retaliatory gesture is expected of him. It's a matter of honour, as much as anything else."

"An eye for an eye."

"All that, yes."

"Enter D'Aubigny."

"Enter D'Aubigny. Somewhere in Paris, at much the same time, she's telling her controllers that she has privileged information: she knows where the Marwell commander's private residence is. Messages cross the world and the ITS planners realise that several symbolic birds can be killed with one stone. It's just too good a chance to miss."

Liz shook her head. "From the way Mansoor behaved at the end, I'd say that, for him, it was almost entirely personal. When he saw that the task of eliminating Delves' family was no longer possible, he simply gave up. He was armed, and could easily have taken out at least one of those SAS guys, but by that stage . . ." She shrugged. "I'd say he saw no purpose in causing further loss of life. He probably didn't even particularly hate the West."

Wetherby shrugged. "You may well be right."

Liz frowned. "Tell me something. If our information about Pakistan was coming to us via Six, and they were suppressing information about Mansoor, how did you find out that it was his family who were killed by the USAF?"

Wetherby regarded her with an oblique smile. "Six's principal liaison in Pakistan, as you know, is with Inter-Services Intelligence, who answer to the Defence Ministry. Six spend rather less time talking to the Intelligence Bureau, who answer to the Interior Ministry, and whose regard for ISI is, shall we say, a little jaundiced."

"And you've got chums in the IB?" asked Liz.

"I maintain one or two friendships, yes. People to whom I can make a direct approach, if need be. I fed them the name Faraj Mansoor and their data bank threw up a suspected terrorist whose father and fiancée had been killed at Daranj. What they didn't know, and I didn't mention, was that Mansoor had been a British agent."

"So why—*why*—didn't Fane and Mackay tell us all this? I mean . . . we would have understood, wouldn't we? We would have kept quiet?"

"It's an information-sharing issue," said Wetherby. "As Fane sees it, they have to tell everyone—the Americans included—or nobody. And they very quickly decide it has to be nobody."

"Why?"

"Imagine if Mansoor succeeds. Succeeds in blowing up a London nightclub, say, or doing serious damage to some major defence or business establishment, and perhaps killing a lot of people, and then the world discovers that he's a former MI6 agent. The damage would be incalculable."

"And if the establishment and the dead happened to be American . . ."

"Exactly. It would be off the scale. Much better to keep stumm, get us to find him, and then have him eliminated before he has a chance to speak."

Liz shook her head. "I'm sorry. I take the political point but I still consider what happened last night indefensible. It was murder, plain and simple. There was no grenade. The man was standing there with his hands in the air."

"Liz, I'm afraid that's academic. Mansoor and D'Aubigny killed several innocent people, and now they're dead themselves. Vis-à-vis the SAS action, there will be an inquiry, but you can guess the conclusion."

She shook her head again. Beyond the long windows and the even blankness of the cookhouse the sky was a bruised, angry grey. A party of young servicemen and -women wandered in, glanced incuriously around them, and left.

Liz regarded her empty coffee mug for a moment. "We lost, didn't we?"

Wetherby reached across the table and took her hands in his. "We won, Liz. You saved that family's life. No one could have done more."

"We were always a step behind. I tried to out-think D'Aubigny, but I couldn't do it. I just couldn't get inside her head."

"You got as close as anyone could have done."

"At the moment her life ended we were face to face. I think she was even speaking to me. But I couldn't hear what she was saying."

Wetherby said nothing. He didn't release her hands, nor did she attempt to take them away.

"What are we going to do?" Liz asked eventually.

"I thought we might get someone to take us over to Swanley Heath and pick up your car. Then I thought I might drive you back to London."

"OK," said Liz.

Acknowledgements

I have dreamed for years of writing a thriller and have had the main character, Liz, in my mind all that time. She has changed and developed as the years have gone by and as I have changed. She is obviously in large part autobiographical but she also draws on a number of other female intelligence officers I have met during my professional career. The other main characters in the book are entirely imaginary, as is the story. They first emerged in a conversation over dinner at the Winstub Gilg in Mittelbergheim Alsace in June 2001. I have to thank John Rimington, who was sharing the dinner, as well as the Gilg Tokay Pinot Gris, which stoked the conversation and the imagination. The art of novelist and that of intelligence officer are very different, whatever some people may think, and had it not been for the perseverance and encouragement of Sue Freestone, my publisher at Hutchinson, I would not have been able to turn myself from one into the other. Huge thanks are also due to Luke Jennings whose help with the research and the writing made it all happen.

Stella Rimington

A NOTE ABOUT THE AUTHOR

Stella Rimington joined MI5 in 1969 and during her nearly thirty-year career she worked in all the main fields of the Service's responsibilities—counter-subversion, counter-espionage, and counter-terrorism—and became successively director of all three branches. Appointed director general of MI5 in 1992, she was the first woman to hold the post and the first director general whose name was publicly announced on appointment. Following her retirement from MI5 in 1996, she became a non-executive director of Marks and Spencer and published her autobiography, *Open Secret,* in the UK. She is currently busy at work on her second novel.

A NOTE ON THE TYPE

The text of this book was set in Sabon, a typeface designed by Jan Tschi-chold (1902–1974), the well-known German typographer. Based loosely on the original designs by Claude Garamond (c. 1480–1561), Sabon is unique in that it was explicitly designed for hotmetal composition on both the Monotype and Linotype machines as well as for filmsetting. Designed in 1966 in Frankfurt, Sabon was named for the famous Lyons punch cutter Jacques Sabon, who is thought to have brought some of Garamond's matrices to Frankfurt.

Composed by Creative Graphics, Inc.
Allentown, Pennsylvania

Printed and bound by Berryville Graphics
Berryville, Virginia

Designed by Soonyoung Kwon